The Corruption of

Alston House

The Corruption of Alston House

by

John Quick

PART ONE

RENOVATIONS AND REVELATIONS

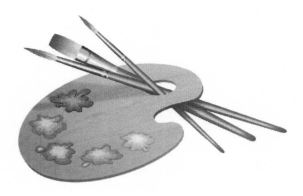

CHAPTER ONE

As she rounded the final curve in the long, winding driveway and saw Alston House for the first time, Katherine thought it must be the classic house on a hill you heard about in stories, poems, and songs. The dense trees and foliage gave way to a wide expanse of lawn that—while in need of a good trimming—would be quite the scenic view during the springtime when everything was blooming, fresh and new. Even now, as fall settled in, the world felt as though it was bracing itself for the winter to come, the few remaining leaves on the multitude of trees that gave the town of Poplar Bend its name caught the final rays of the gently setting sun and dotted the surrounding countryside with bright yellow and gold highlights. It might well be the most idyllic thing she had ever seen.

The three-story Victorian was backlit by the same picturesque sunset, giving it what some would consider an ominous appearance, but when combined with the natural beauty surrounding it, the entire image appeared as if it belonged on a postcard. To Katherine, it was a picturesque scene that should define autumn in the south, so perfect was the panorama before her.

Beyond the initial thrill of beauty came the harsh lens of reality. This was hers now. The enormity of such a concept threatened to overwhelm her. She knew the house was still in need of a considerable amount of work despite the extensive renovations completed in the last couple of years. She had seen the paperwork that proved they had brought the electrical and plumbing up to meet current codes, but it said nothing for the structural work still needed. If the mental image she had in her mind was even close to accurate, she would forget all about this gorgeous view the moment she opened the door and stepped inside for the first time.

She would just have to make herself remember, then. Perhaps it would be her first new painting in over a year, a fitting reemergence onto the path she began nearly two decades ago. Not that she would ever attempt to sell this one. It would hang over the mantle once she completed all the repairs, an honorarium and a reminder of what made her choose this house. Just the act of completing such a painting would be enough reward. Breaking her long period of creative silence and beginning to heal would be worth more than any price the finished product might bring her.

There was always the possibility the repairs needed would be too much, either in the quantity of work required, or the cost incurred in accomplishing such a task. The pictures she saw didn't seem to indicate that, but they could have taken them from such an angle as to hide the worst of the damage. It was a definite possibility. The realtor she had spoken with on the phone seemed surprised she would even consider buying this place based solely on the pictures posted online, which guaranteed to show the best views of the house. The woman had been forthright about the needed work, and had been willing to send additional, less flattering shots if Katherine wanted her to. Why go to all that trouble just to hide something the most casual of inspections would catch?

And if she was wrong, her father could tell her "I told you so" instead of just complaining she wasn't acting rationally. He was right about her recklessness, but there was a purpose to the spontaneity, a reasoning she could not explain. If she ever hoped to find herself again, to regain her center, she had to stop doing what her mind told her was right and start trusting her heart again. She saw the house online and fell in love with it immediately. The price was unbelievably right, and she had the money, so she leaped in with both feet. To her, it was better to find out the water was too deep or there were rocks just beneath the surface this way than by being overly cautious. She'd done that for nine miserable years and look where it got her. No, it was better to go with her gut instinct.

Despite what Daddy thought, she *had* done her research. Once she saw the price for both the house and the property well below what the comps were going for, she called the realtor and asked what the catch was. The woman was honest with her, and told her the person who owned it before and began the remodeling died suddenly, leaving large chunks of the work incomplete. On the plus side, the remaining repairs wouldn't involve alterations to the core framework that would create undue safety hazards, so the place was inhabitable, if a little run-down at the moment. Katherine already had a contractor scheduled to come out and give estimates at the end of the week, but she had a feeling much of what it needed was soap, water, and a few gallons of paint. With nothing tying her down and enough money in the bank to sustain her for a while without a steady income, she would welcome the chance to get her hands dirty. It would make the place feel more like home, more like *her* house.

She parked next to the unattached garage and eyed it. The house itself might not be too bad, but there was no way she would chance putting her truck in that. Trying to open the massive double doors would probably be enough to send it crashing to the ground, possibly killing her. She made a mental note to ask the contractor how much it would cost to have the existing structure torn down and something a little more lasting erected in its place. If she could afford it, great. If not, no big loss. Her old place back in Charleston didn't have a garage, so she would do just fine without one here. Satisfied she was balancing practicality and free-spiritedness, she shut off the engine, hit the button on her key fob to open the Pathfinder's back gate, and got out, standing on the driveway to her new house for the first time.

The wind was strong and crisp as it cut through her thick sweater, raising chill bumps along her entire body and hardening her nipples to the point they hurt. It had been just under seventy degrees when she left South Carolina at four this morning, so she gave little thought to any potential temperature variance here in Tennessee. Now she wished she'd paid more attention to the weather. It was easily fifteen degrees colder, and from the feeling of the wind, it would only drop further as the evening progressed. She rubbed her hands over her arms rapidly as she moved to the back of the SUV and pulled out her larger suitcase. All of her winter clothes were in boxes that would not arrive until tomorrow, but she might have something warmer than the thin blouse she wore beneath her sweater she could change into. She paused, then grabbed her sleeping bag as well before shutting the rear door. The rest of the unloading could wait until the sun was back out tomorrow. That way, all she had to worry about was trying to get the house warmed up enough to not freeze to death while she slept.

Katherine mounted the steps to the long, covered porch and smiled as she pictured a pair of old wooden rocking chairs with a small table between them. She could see herself sitting there in the spring and summer, sipping a glass of wine or maybe some tropical mixed drink as she watched the stars. Her smile slipped a bit when she remembered she only needed one chair nowadays, not two. She shook the thought away, refusing to allow herself to slide back into the deep depression that threatened to consume her this last year.

This place was a new start, a clean slate. As her best friend kept telling her: treasure the past but stop dwelling on it, and above all, live your life.

She set the suitcase and sleeping bag down and studied the front doors while she dug in the back pocket of her jeans for the little envelope the realtor had mailed her containing the keys. The paint was peeling, but there didn't seem to be any cracks in the wood, and it was flush with the frame. She ran one palm along the seams, trying to feel any hint of air from inside escaping and found nothing. Not conclusive by any means, but it was a good sign.

At first, the key didn't want to go into the lock, but then she realized she had it upside down. The tumblers were on the top instead of the bottom like the door of her old house. She smiled and shook her head, inserted it properly, and turned it. The key moved easily in the cylinder, without even the hint of a catch. She heard the lock release with a satisfying *ka-chink*, turned the knob, and pushed the door open before grabbing her things and heading inside.

There was just enough light trickling in from outside to tell she was in the foyer, but not enough for her to find the light switches on the wall. She put her bags to the side and felt around blindly, then stared at the wall, hands on her hips, and wondered where the switch could be. After a moment, she shook her head, remembering her phone had a flashlight app that would come in handy right about now.

When she entered her passcode to unlock the screen, she noticed a circle with a line through it replaced the little series of bars denoting her signal strength, the universal symbol for "you're shit out of luck." She hadn't used a landline in years, but it looked as if living out here in the middle of nowhere would feel as though she had stepped into a time machine. This place was so remote, it probably didn't even have cable television. Not that she watched much TV, but the fast internet would be something she would miss.

The light on her phone showed her the switch, a full foot below where she had been feeling for it. Either they designed the house for people shorter than her or she was more tired than she thought. Shaking her head, she flipped the light on and turned around.

To her immediate right was a massive and ornate staircase leading to the upper floors. Beyond it, she could see an open room with badly chipped and pitted hardwood floors, dulled from age and abuse. Remembering the floor plan in her head, she knew ahead of her, on the right, would be a hallway leading to the side porch, and beyond would be the living room at the back of the house. Opposite the living room would be the dining room, and the little archway she could see just ahead of her on the left would be the kitchen. There would be a full-sized pantry on the other side of the wall next to her that also provided access to the circular tower at the house's corner. There were four total bedrooms upstairs. The master bathroom featured not only a tub and a shower, but also a walk-in closet and dressing area.

The wind gusted in behind her, sending icy tendrils up the back of her sweater and inching down the waistband of her pants—a goosing from Mother Nature to remind her not to leave the door open. She turned and closed it, mentally thanking the former owner for installing updated plumbing before he died. First order of business was getting the furnace or whatever provided heat to the house running. Barring that, she would hopefully find enough wood out back to get a fire going in the living room fireplace. Immediately after, she would take a long, hot bath. Her muscles were screaming from being crammed into the car for nearly twelve hours—thanks to the delays of heavy traffic—and being exposed to the cold while walking from the car to the house had seeped into her bones.

But for now, she paused, her eyes roaming over the yellowing wallpaper and pitted floors. To most people, it would look bad. She was not most people. She was an artist, a painter, and she could see the potential this place held in her mind's eye. A little work, and it would be a sight to behold.

"Welcome home," she told herself, her voice echoing though the empty hallway. "Now get to it."

She left her bags where they were and went in search of a thermostat.

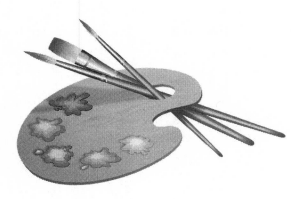

CHAPTER TWO

It only took a cursory glance into the basement for Katherine to discover the combination boiler and hot water tank that fed the radiators scattered throughout the house and the faucets. It sat against the wall just to the side of the basement stairs. From the looks of things, they updated it from the original gas burners to an electric one relatively recently. Not that she was any real judge of age on the thing. All she knew was the wiring looked new. She was in luck—she had already turned on the electric and water to the house. If natural gas fed this, she would have been in trouble.

Katherine went back upstairs and found the main thermostat on the wall across from the master staircase. She flipped it on and set the temperature to what she hoped would be a comfortable seventy-two degrees. She smiled when she heard the click and felt a slight thump against her feet as the boiler engaged. She had no way to know whether the radiators were working in every room, so she would explore a bit. Right after she got a few more things out of the truck. As much as she would prefer to let it wait until morning, there were things she would have to get tonight, primarily her coffee pot and the little plastic can of French roast. She did not want to go out in the cold for it in the morning, when she wasn't completely awake.

In just the short time she had been inside, the sun had completed its downward journey behind the trees, leaving the sky streaked with purplish-orange hues deepening into full twilight. The wind had picked up, whipping her hair across her face as she rushed to her truck and unlocked it. She pulled out the box with her "kitchen essentials" and hurried back to the house. She got the door open without dropping the box or having to dislocate her wrist and sighed as the door closed behind her again.

She could already feel the difference, minuscule as it might be. Those old radiators would take a good long while before they had the house up to a temperature resembling what she would consider tolerable, but at least the ones on this floor seemed to work. One less thing to add to her list of immediate repairs. She would have to remember to check into having a modern central heat and air unit installed, if the other repairs didn't end up being too expensive. She could heat the place through the winter, but the thought of relying on open windows and box fans to survive the southern summer ahead was not a pleasant one. As much as she wanted to believe herself capable of surviving anywhere, she had lived in the city with modern conveniences too long to give them up easily.

The thought of a hot bath tugged at her, but she forced herself to wait. Until the house warmed up, getting naked and crawling into and back out of a tub of water would be a little more brutal than relaxing. That would be her reward at the end of the night, her way to unwind before trying to get some sleep.

Since the box in her hands contained kitchen implements, that would be her first stop. The room was impressively large, easily twice the size of the galley kitchen in her old townhouse back in Charleston. She flipped on the light and moved deeper into the room, smiling at the sight of the island in the center. The countertops were a faded green tile, functional but not visually appealing. The cabinets themselves weren't bad; sand them down, stain them, and they would be as good as new, but those countertops had to go. The appliances desperately needed updating. No dishwasher, but there was the perfect spot for one not too far away from the double sink, so that would go on the list for sure. Otherwise, the room looked perfect. Maybe get two bar stools set up next to the island, and it could double for her usual eating area.

She retrieved a pad of paper and a pen from her purse, scribbled down her notes for the kitchen, then moved into the dining area. This room looked to be in good shape overall. The walls needed some cleaning and maybe a fresh coat of paint, but otherwise it was perfect. She didn't know when she would ever use such a large formal dining room—not anymore, at least—but maybe it could double as a home office or a storage area for any paintings she completed.

She moved across the hall, making sure the seals on the back doors were as secure as those on the front, then continued on to the living room. When she flipped on the light, she saw a massive fireplace on the far wall dominated the room, apparently the first place the previous owner had renovated. There was no wallpaper here. Instead, they had painted the walls a rich cream color that matched the original tone of the hardwood floors perfectly. Even the fireplace appeared refinished, the stonework around it practically shining compared to the rest of the house. She decided if she could find some wood, she would sleep in here until the movers arrived and she had her bed assembled upstairs.

The front den almost matched the living room in terms of progress made on it. She recognized the common three-prong electrical outlets and what looked like an antenna hook-up for a television set. She felt some tension ease from her shoulders. The three biggest rooms on this level of the house, and aside from the floors, they only needed minor amounts of work to be perfectly livable. She could budget for any repairs the house might need, but she wasn't wealthy by any stretch of the imagination. Anything that helped make her budget stretch further was a good thing in her book.

She considered going back through the kitchen and checking out the walk-in pantry, but she held back for now. Based on the floor plan and the pictures she had seen, the tower connected to the pantry had stairs leading to the top floor. She would save that for last, maybe imagine she was a princess in a castle tower descending to meet the brave knight who had come seeking her hand in marriage.

The thought brought back memories of Dave, and the incessant screaming and arguing that had taken over the last year of their lives before culminating in a bitter divorce less than four months ago. For the six years of their marriage, and the two years of dating before, she had believed he was her prince come to sweep her off her feet. He had proven how wrong that childish fantasy was though. He corrupted the dream so thoroughly, she wasn't sure if she could ever recover from it.

But she didn't want to think about Dave. She had moved so far away and into such a secluded house in part to forget about what an asshole he had become. She wanted to start her life over again, not dwell on his selfishness. She shook her head, forcing the thoughts away, and started up the stairs.

The second floor contained the four bedrooms and a pair of mirrored bathrooms at either end of the house. Strangely, the access to the tower from this floor had been closed off at some point. Judging from the peeling wallpaper, it had been long before the previous owner began his renovations. Tapping on the wall produced a hollow sound, so she thought the opening from the ground floor to the top was still there. She did not understand why it was closed, but she would have to ask about the potential of reopening it when she spoke to the contractor.

Here, the damage was more pronounced. Some walls had cracks running along them, and the stains on the floors were almost black from years of neglect. She had been hoping the updates in the kitchen would be her biggest expense, but it looked like so far, that would be this entire floor. She could wait to do it. It wasn't like she had any real use for the spare rooms, but it would be better to get it all done at once and have it finished.

If the second floor had been a disappointment, the third floor renewed her excitement about the house. The insanely large master suite dominated this floor on one end and another large room lined floor to ceiling with shelves on the other. This must have been a library or study for the original owners. Katherine shook her head as she surveyed all the space on the walls. She liked to read, even if she didn't get the chance much anymore, and while she owned several books, she didn't think putting them in here would even make a dent in the space. It would be like building a house from scratch using only three bricks a day. You would get there eventually, but you would probably die of old age by the time all was said and done.

Still, there was a second fireplace here, so she looked forward to the challenge of filling this room. She could see herself sitting in a comfortable chair facing a cozy fire, a glass of wine beside her and a book open on her lap before her, content after a long and productive day in front of her canvas.

When she turned on the light and saw the master bedroom for the first time, her breath caught in her throat. The pictures had not done the room justice. This one suite was as large as her first apartment with room to spare.

A pair of glass double doors opened onto a covered balcony that spanned the entire back of the house. Full-length windows flanked the doors, casting the room in the pale light from the rising moon. During the day, the natural light came in through those windows would prevent the need for lights at all. On nights like tonight, when the moon was rising full in the sky, it would be the same way. Even barren and empty, the room was incredible.

Of all the rooms in the house, this one was the best maintained. The floors shone, the same cream paint from the living room making them look lighter than the really were. The smell of dust was there, just as in the rest of the house, but it was faint, almost undetectable. This room alone was worth what she paid for the house and land. To her, the rest was just a bonus.

Stricken by its opulence, she crossed through the room and entered the master bathroom. The master bath split into two rooms: the one she now stood in contained a large two-person vanity sink and a partitioned stall with a toilet. The one directly to her right was, for lack of a better term, the actual bathing chamber itself. A huge garden tub sat in one corner, a walk-in shower in the other. Convenience and comfort all in one space. She wasn't too sure about the continuation of the tall windows that flanked the corner, but since there were no neighbors to speak of who might see her naked as she climbed in and out of the tub, she could live with it. She smiled, thinking how it would feel to stand unclothed and see nature practically all around her.

She went back through the other part of the bathroom and crossed into what the floor plan called a dressing area. It was, as far as she could see, just another small room attached to the substantial closet. Impressive, but less so than the bedroom and master bath had been. She went through to the door on the right, the one that led into the top level of the tower. This was what she had been waiting for, the deciding factor in buying the house to start with. She took a deep breath and opened the door.

It felt like she was walking into a room made entirely of glass. Windows dominated the walls, giving her a panoramic view of the surrounding property. When you added in the house's elevation, her vantage allowed her to see over the tops of the trees lining the driveway almost all the way to the main road. Looking the opposite direction, she could see the gentle slope of the hill as it descended to a creek some distance behind the house. She had a feeling that even in broad daylight she wouldn't see anything resembling other houses or people back there, giving the illusion she truly was alone out here. The thought was both wonderfully freeing and terrifyingly isolating.

Smiling, she descended the steps to the lower levels of the tower, the smile fading when she noticed that not only was the second floor access closed off, they removed the flooring too, leaving the tower as only the bottom and third floors. It was a strange concept, and while she was sure there had been a perfectly rational reason for them to have done this, she didn't know what it could have been.

The first floor had three doors. One opened out into the back of the house, one opened onto the front porch, and one led into the pantry. She smiled. She could go straight up to what would be her studio on the top floor without having to even see anything else in the house. Likewise, if she needed to go somewhere, she could clean up, get dressed, and go out this way without having to cross back through the bedroom, down the main stairs, and then out the door. Convenient, so long as she made sure the doors were secure before she went to bed each night.

After making sure she locked the doors, she checked the seals on them, nodded with satisfaction that they would not let heat escape easily, and entered the pantry.

Or rather, the rooms that had once been a pantry. At some point, probably during the last owner's renovations, he erected an additional wall here. She now stood in a much smaller pantry, the shelves empty, waiting for canned goods or whatever else she might store here. Through this was another small room that contained hookups for a washer and dryer. This, unlike the modifications to the tower, made sense. It was the modern age, and driving into town to do laundry would be impractical. She did not own a washer and dryer, but it was just the thing she needed to put on her list.

She reemerged in the kitchen and dropped her notepad onto the counter. At least it looked like all the radiators were working, the exterior walls all sealed up. That would help with the utility bills. She might have the contractor double-check just so there would be no surprises come the dead of winter, but it looked like she could focus her expenses elsewhere.

She frowned as she thought about the second floor and how dilapidated it appeared, not to mention how it compared to the rest of the house. The previous owner had ignored that floor it seemed. That was where most of her money would go, so hopefully it wouldn't be as bad as it looked. Perhaps they could repair the cracks without having to replace entire walls or anything extreme.

A thump against her feet followed by a clicking sound from the other room made her jump until she realized it had been the boiler shutting off. She cocked her head, finally noticing she had not been shivering for a little while now. The radiators had done their trick. The house was relatively warm. Not where she would have liked it to be, but she had been guessing when she set it to the temperature she had, anyway. That was an easy fix.

She went to the suitcase she brought in, opened it, and hoped she remembered to pack a towel in this one. She smiled when she saw she had. She grabbed it, her flannel robe, a nightgown, and fresh underwear, then pulled the toiletry bag from the outside pocket. She stopped by the thermostat, bumped it up another five degrees, and then headed upstairs. By the time her bath was ready, the temperature in the place should be about perfect. For now, though, she wanted to try out that garden tub. She only hoped the water didn't make her so drowsy she wound up drowning in it her first day here.

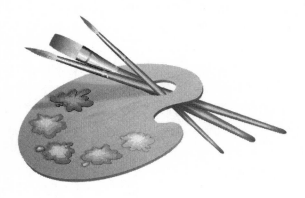

CHAPTER THREE

He was being especially quiet. Maybe it was more noticeable because of the tantrum he had just thrown in the store, but the unexpected silence was so welcomed that she appreciated it while it lasted rather than allow herself to become concerned over it. She could understand why Dave begged off watching him while she went to the store. If their roles had been reversed, she might have accepted her sullen look as just payment for an afternoon of peace, too.

After she put the last of the bags in the cargo compartment, she closed the back gate and turned around to tell him to go get in the truck. He wasn't there. When she started loading the groceries into the Pathfinder, he was standing next to the cart, but now he was missing. She frowned as she surveyed the parking lot, the people bustling to and from their vehicles in the hazy fall afternoon, but she couldn't find him anywhere.

Maybe he was more upset with her than she thought. He got like that sometimes after he didn't get his way. Her refusal to buy the overpriced Halloween costume he would have lost part of or torn up before they even made it home only added to his irritation. Five years old and already thinking he didn't need his mommy and daddy for anything, that their only purpose in life was to deny him the things he wanted. She dreaded how things would be in his teenage years, still a ways off by the calendar but feeling like they were just around the corner in her mind.

She moved up to the driver's side rear door and opened it, fully prepared to let him sulk but not willing to forsake his safety by not securing him in the booster seat before they headed home. When she discovered the seat was empty, her heart suddenly beat faster in her chest, and she could feel her stomach clenching into knots. If he was not by the cart and he was not already in the truck, then where had he gone?

She returned to the back of the truck, forcing herself to remain calm. It was entirely possible he was so angry he had hidden from her. This was a relatively new weapon in his retaliatory arsenal, and one he had not used in public before, but if his mood truly was as foul as it appeared to be, he may have elevated his methods. The toddler version of going nuclear. If that was the case, he was about to see what the parental version of nuclear discipline looked like, too.

Making sure to not stray too far from the truck in case he wandered back and found her missing, she looked behind the other nearby vehicles. After searching six in either direction and even crossing into other rows for good measure, her desire to find him and punish him quickly gave way to the need to find him, hold him, and never let go. She breathed deeply, trying to keep herself from flying into a blind panic. That wouldn't solve anything. She needed to stay rational if she stood any hope at all of finding him.

Then the reality of her situation set in, that her child had gone missing in this familiar grocery store parking lot in broad daylight, and she began to scream.

Katherine's eyes flew open, and, for a moment, she was so disoriented by the fact she was sleeping on the floor that panic threatened to overtake her again. Then she remembered: this was her new house, she only had a sleeping bag since the moving truck with all her furniture would not arrive until the next day, and she had slept in the living room in front of the fireplace. She blinked rapidly, her breath still ragged, and told herself over and over it was only a dream. That it was in reality more of a memory come to the surface than a dream did little to help calm her down. She could only remind herself she was not in that moment anymore, it was over a year in the past.

She reached up with a shaking hand and found tears drying on her cheeks. This was the first time she had cried in her sleep in months. Occasionally, the memories would strike while awake, but being assaulted by them through her subconscious? She thought she was past that. She supposed she never could *fully* be past it, though, nor was she certain she wanted to be.

She unzipped the sleeping bag and sat up, rubbing her hands over her face. The air in the room felt chilly, even though she could hear the furnace running in the basement. When she stood up, she realized her nightgown was clinging to her body, glued to her with sweat. It might just be from her body heat being trapped inside the nylon sleeping bag, or it could be from the terror the nightmare brought on. Possibly even a combination of the two. Either way, she felt disgusting. She got to her feet, peeled the sodden garment over her head, and dropped it to the floor next to her.

The cool air felt good against her naked skin and helped to bring her body temperature back down to something resembling normal again. She held her arms out to the side, away from her body, and allowed the air to drift over her, helping to bring her back fully to the wakeful world and away from the sadistic replay her mind had forced upon her during the night. She concentrated on her breathing—the only thing she felt had been beneficial out of all the therapy sessions she had gone to since things went so badly—and felt the stress ease from her muscles. It did not leave her completely, it never did, but it was back to manageable levels.

She considered just lying back down and trying to get to sleep, but if she didn't hear the movers knocking in the morning and they came around to the back of the house, it would mortify her to think their first view would be of her helpless and sound asleep wearing nothing but a pair of skimpy threadbare panties. She did not have any other nightgowns in the suitcase she brought in last night, but there were some t-shirts there. She would take one of those to sleep in. Images of horny moving boys firmly in mind, she also decided to grab a pair of pants to keep handy, just in case.

Her phone was where she left it next to the head of the sleeping bag, so she kneeled and hit the button to turn the screen back on. It was just after four in the morning. She sighed. Even if she got back to sleep, she would have to be up in less than three hours, dressed and caffeinated by the time the movers arrived at seven—if the contractor didn't beat them here. She could always take a nap this afternoon once she had dealt with all of that. Better to get on with the day.

She padded into the kitchen, wincing at how cold the hardwood floors were beneath her bare feet. The rest of the room was tolerable, if a little cooler than she preferred, but those floors were downright brutal. She would need to pick up some rugs before winter set in. That, or resort to slippers like her mother and grandmother. She always vowed she would never do it, since to her it was the epitome of being an old woman, but here she was thinking about it. Only twenty-seven and already turning into her mother. She could hear the woman's laughter as if she were standing next to her.

At least she could be content her mother would rather die than be caught standing topless in the kitchen, with most of her ass hanging out. She smiled as the laughing face in her mind adopted a scandalized expression instead.

She hooked up the coffeepot, filled the chamber, loaded it up with what she considered the "immediate wake-up" amount of grounds, and set it brewing. While she waited, she put on some pants and a shirt. Amusement factor aside, this house was still too new for her to feel comfortable walking around in it for very long while undressed. Not that she had anyone around to either impress or annoy by it. Still, her newfound rebelliousness only went so far.

Once she dressed, she closed up the suitcase. May as well get it up to the bedroom and out of the main hallway. Almost as an afterthought, she grabbed the sleeping bag and her nightgown and started hauling it all upstairs.

As her eyes broke the floor level of the second floor, she stopped. For a moment it looked like something had just darted across the hallway from one bedroom to another. She waited, holding her breath without even realizing it, her eyes locked on the spot at the far end of the hall where she thought the movement had been. She also focused her ears to search for the sound of footsteps or anything else that might alert her to an intruder. There was nothing. No repeated sounds or movement. The house was old and set back in the woods. There was every possibility she had a mouse problem to deal with, too.

It was one more thing for her to worry over. She would have to remember to put "call exterminator" on her to-do list downstairs.

Combined with her nightmare, the potential of infestation had her on the verge of full-scale paranoia. She laughed at the foolishness of it and continued on up to the master suite. She set the suitcase just inside the door, making sure she tucked the nightgown underneath the unrolled sleeping bag. She shook her head, knowing even as she did it how ridiculous it was. Just another holdover from her mother's way of thinking: the things a woman slept in at night were just as intimate as the things she used to cover her most private areas. Sometimes Katherine wondered how her father ever talked her mother into having kids at all.

When she returned to the kitchen, the coffee was ready and waiting for her. She pulled out her large mug emblazoned with the slogan "The more people I meet, the more I love my dog" and chuckled as she poured in sugar from a plastic container. She wanted the mug the moment she saw it. Dave thought it was the stupidest thing he had ever heard. They didn't even own a dog, he insisted. Why would she want that mug? She could never seem to get him to understand that to her, not having a dog made the slogan even more funny and cutting. He would just shake his head and say she had a strange sense of humor. He was right, but that was beside the point.

Looking back, it was not so much her sense of humor was strange as Dave was just a judgmental asshole, but that was neither here nor there either.

She poured in the coffee and added a healthy dollop of powdered creamer before stirring the mixture together and taking her first sip of the day. It nearly burned her tongue, but it was worth it. Something about the first cup of coffee in the morning was magical—from the taste to the warmth to the way the steam rose just above the rim of the mug before dissipating. It was even better when there was nothing but natural sunlight in the room, but since that was still at least an hour away she would have to be content with this diminished version instead. It was her first cup of coffee on her first morning in her new house. The trade off with natural light was worth it, at least for today.

There was nowhere to sit and enjoy the coffee, though. She had been so focused on getting it made, she completely forgot about the fact all of her furniture—what little there was, anyway—was in the back of a truck. She did not have any chairs, nor did she have a table to put the coffee on. She shook her head and decided if it had been good enough to sleep on, the living room floor would also be good enough to sit on, for now. She grabbed her notepad and pen before taking her coffee to the other room.

She settled against the wall near the fireplace and wished she had some wood to burn in it. She had been hoping for it last night, but once she finished her bath and dressed for bed, she had been too tired to even bother looking outside for scraps she could use. She sat the cup down beside her and flipped to a fresh page in the notepad so she could continue the list of things she needed to purchase.

She listed "firewood" and "bar stools" but hesitated before putting down the next entry. "Groceries" was a little too vague, and she didn't feel like starting a new list just yet. Remembering the dream also left her feeling uneasy about the whole process of grocery shopping. She skipped it for now and wrote "throw rugs" instead.

When she finally heard a knock on the door and looked up, the sun was well on its way to cresting in the sky and her mug was empty. She stood up, wincing at the tightness in her back and legs from sitting in such an awkward position for so long, and went to answer the door. She saw the massive white panel truck before she even had the door all the way open and smiled at the movers who waited on her porch.

Now the real work could begin.

CHAPTER FOUR

The movers were just beginning to unload the truck and stage everything for transport into the house when a beat-up black pickup rounded the bend in the driveway and stopped alongside the moving van. A tall man in a flannel shirt got out, a clipboard held in one hand, a tool belt strapped around his waist—her contractor had arrived. She gave him her list of things she noticed that needed attention and sent him off to check it out, then remained behind to direct the movers where to unload her belongings. She would take care of them later.

The entire process took a depressingly short time, cementing the fact that, since she now owned such a large house, she would need to spend a considerable amount on additional furniture unless she wanted most of the rooms upstairs to remain bare and empty. However, the contractor confirmed the entire second floor would need extensive renovation before it would be close to the condition of the rest of the house. This meant there was no need to be in a rush.

After paying the movers and going over the estimate—which was not as pricey as she had feared—with the contractor, it was time for lunch. She still had yet to make a grocery list, and the only food she brought with her from Charleston were two boxes of cereal, so she decided it was time to head into town and do some exploring. The piles of boxes and pieces of furniture still covered by the plastic sheeting the movers used to protect it were more than a little intimidating. Funny she should become depressed by how little was being brought inside, but now that she had to unpack and arrange everything, it seemed like too much. Perception truly was the center point of truth.

At least she would have some options for clothes to wear. She headed upstairs to the bedroom and opened up the box that held the bulk of her clothing. She pulled out a fresh pair of jeans and a sweatshirt and draped them over the top of her dresser. She considered having a quick shower, but the rumbling in her stomach told her food was more imperative than freshening up. She raised one arm, tilted her head, and sniffed. She did not stink, and what little odor there was, deodorant would easily take care of it. The shower could wait. She changed quickly and headed out, locking the door behind her. Just because she was out in the middle of nowhere, in a place with an open-door feel, did not mean she was foolish enough to tempt fate.

She hoped to enjoy the scenery today, as she headed into town, now that she got a good night's sleep. Yesterday, she missed most of it after being exhausted from such a long day of driving and now regretted not taking it in as she arrived. It would have been the perfect introduction to the town.

The trees came right up to the side of the road, making the entire series of turns onto the main street feel like she was still on her own driveway. She could see the occasional mailbox and a packed gravel path cutting into the woods, so she knew other people lived out this way. It looked like her closest neighbor was easily a mile from her house. Her concerns about being spied on while she bathed were for naught. With the seclusion she had, she could wander around in the *yard* naked and not worry about being seen.

She smiled at the mental image, a sixties free-love version of herself traipsing through the tall grass behind her house, dancing and spinning, maybe even with a haze of purplish marijuana smoke around her head. She would have to hold on to that, maybe paint it at some point. She could even stand a mirror next to her canvas, use herself as the model, too. As long as she altered the body and face, no one would ever know it was her. The thought of people admiring her naked form without even realizing it warmed her cheeks and settled into her as a slightly naughty temptation. She even had a title for the painting, something to reflect how personal it would be to her: *Newfound Freedom.*

Finally, she came to the T-intersection at the end of her road. Here, the trees gave way to wide expanses of farmland; fields dotted with aging corn stalks and tall grass they would soon cut and bale to feed whatever livestock the people owned through the winter months. She turned left and headed toward town, smiling at the old, classic-style farmhouses resting back off the road. As a little girl, she had dreamed of living in houses like that, always loving their character and hominess. The attraction was still there now that she was an adult, only it had expanded. The Victorian she now lived in was not substantially different from those farmhouses, and the added character more than made up for the extra opulence.

She turned right at the next intersection, onto the main drag though town, such as it was. What she assumed was the business section only contained a handful of buildings, none of them especially large. The post office, city hall, and the town marshal's office sat in a row on one side of the street opposite a gas station and a decently sized grocery store. For a moment, she thought about continuing on to the state highway and making the half-hour drive west to Murfreesboro, but her stomach was cramping, as it was. Any longer without food and she would be downright nauseated. The argument decided, she turned into the grocery store lot and parked near the entrance.

The interior was a surprising contrast to the expectations set by the exterior. She was imagining a few rows with just enough staples to get her through the day yet still requiring a trip to a larger store by tomorrow, but what little space the building had was being used to maximum effect. The staples were all there: milk, bread, canned goods, and a long floor cooler with packaged meat, cold cuts, and cheese. Unexpectedly, she also saw a fairly well-stocked section for fresh produce, a "home-grown local" section, and even a magazine rack near the front of the store. She could think of some larger chains that did not even have those anymore.

A grizzled old man with a face like a gnarled tree root sat behind the lone register at the front of the store, his distrustful eyes never wandering from her as she looked around the store. His expression was not hostile—not yet, at any rate—but was nowhere near welcoming or friendly, either. He had immediately sized her up and slapped the "outsider" label on her. It was true enough, she supposed. Although, she now called this town home. She wondered how long it would take before the old-timers, like him, accepted her, if they ever would.

She offered him a warm smile regardless and took one of the wire buggies he had lined up next to the door. She may as well stock up on what she could here. It would save her the trip to Murfreesboro and get her back to the house sooner. She at least wanted to get her bed set up so she didn't have to spend another night sleeping on the hard floor. Maybe that was the reason for her nightmare, or maybe it was something else, but she could get up tomorrow without additional aches and pains for her trouble.

Besides, if she did the bulk of her grocery shopping here, it might go a long way to earn her some welcome points with the locals, show she was being a part of the town and not just someone who slept here and cared less about it.

She took her time browsing the shelves, mentally wincing on some items but realizing the owner probably did not get as much of a discount from the wholesaler as the big chains did. The only way he could make any money was to charge more than they did. Sad, and the reason so many of these mom-and-pop places were closing down, but it was the unfortunate reality of living in the modern era.

The produce was considerably more reasonable than the chain stores, though, giving her the distinct impression they grew locally. The "local" section helped confirm this, with shelves of honey, apple cider, and assorted fruit jams, jellies, and preserves all with exceptionally reasonable prices. She stocked up on things she would normally eat from here, reasoning that if she didn't like it, she could always just buy replacements when she was at a Walmart or Kroger or Publix or something.

When she wheeled the cart up to the register, she realized even after all the time she spent shopping, she was still the only customer in the store. Admittedly, it was around one in the afternoon on a random Tuesday, but she would have thought at least one other person would come in. She supposed it was just one of those things about living in a small town.

The man at the register didn't bother getting up from his seat, only continued watching her as she began unloading the groceries onto the conveyer belt that would bring them close enough for him to scan each item. Instead of showing some pleasure at the amount she was purchasing, though, his scowl only deepened as her stack grew larger. When he finally stubbed out the cigarette he had been smoking and began typing numbers into the keypad before him, she understood the annoyance. Unlike the chain stores, he had to enter all the prices manually. There was no laser scanner to expedite the process here. She mentally kicked herself. Her attempt to make a good impression with the man had backfired.

"Having a good day, so far?" she asked, hoping friendly conversation might distract him from her blunder.

The man grunted, looked back at her briefly, and then returned his attention to tallying up her purchases. Since he showed no sign of doing it himself, she moved to the end of the belt and began bagging up her purchases. Paper bags only, she noted, no plastic. Combined with the low-tech register system, she was feeling as though she had somehow gone back in time.

"Ain't seen you 'round before," the man said, not looking at her.

She waited for him to ask a question, but he seemed done with only that simple statement.

"Just moved here," she said, answering anyway. "Got in last night and realized I didn't have any food in the house."

"They don't norm'ly come fully stocked when you buy 'em," he said. While she could have taken the statement as a joke, from the disdain clear in his voice, he meant it as anything but. "Didn't know there was no houses for sale 'round here."

She was not sure if the additional comment was progress or not. "It's out on Forest Road."

He paused and looked up at her again, his eyes wary. "You bought that place on Dead Hollow Road?"

"No," she said, confused. "Like I said, it's on Forest Road."

He shook his head, snorted, and went back to ringing up her purchases. "Used t'be Dead Hollow. Damned aldermen decided the name was too morbid back 'bout ten years ago and changed it. Don't change what it was, though. Buncha worthless kowtowing political idjits."

"Why did they change it, then?" she asked. "Dead Hollow has a strange but nice ring to it."

He snorted again. "You'll learn all you need soon enough."

And with that, he clammed up. She tried a couple more times to engage him, but whatever conversational ability he possessed seemed spent by those few snarky comments. The only other thing he said was to give her the total on her purchases. She didn't even bother looking for a credit card machine. Katherine paid in cash and felt by doing so she had escaped another harsh remark from the man. After silently collecting her change, she stacked her bags neatly back into her cart and left the store.

She was down to the last couple of bags left to load into the back of the truck, when one broke in her hands and sent canned goods rolling across the parking lot. Katherine swore under her breath, thinking this the perfect cap to an overall horrible experience with the locals. She dropped to her knees and started trying to catch as many of the cans as she could before they ended up rolling out into the street. She reached for some coffee that was picking up speed, and stopped when a black-booted foot caught the can on its toe and flipped it up neatly into a waiting hand.

Katherine looked up to find a man in brown pants and matching shirt smiling down at her, the coffee balanced on his palm. He was middle-aged, perhaps in his late thirties or early forties, with just the beginning hints of gray starting to come in with the dark hair along his temples. Her eyes dropped to the gun belt around his waist and then back up to the silver badge pinned to the breast pocket of his shirt.

"Looks like you had some escapees," the man said, his voice jovial. It was a pleasant contrast to the crotchety store owner. "I think I caught the ringleader for you, though."

She stood and returned his smile while she collected the can. "Looks like you did at that. Good work... officer?"

"Marshal, actually," he corrected. He waited for her to put the coffee in the back of the truck and then extended his hand. "Frank Bradshaw."

She shook hands with him. "Katherine We... Ransom. Call me Kat."

His eyes flicked briefly to her hands and then back to her face. "Recently divorced, am I right?"

She felt the smile freeze on her lips. "How did you know that?"

"Only two reasons I can think of for a lady to stumble over her own last name," he said. "Well, three, but since you don't look like a criminal on the run or anything, that brings it back to two. Either you're freshly married, or freshly divorced. No ring, so it has to be the latter."

She could not help but relax and allow her smile to widen. "Not bad at all, Marshal Bradshaw. You're a good detective it seems."

He nodded. "All part of the job. And if you're Kat, I'm Frank. Fair enough?"

"Fair enough," she agreed. "And I have to say it's nice to find someone friendly in town."

Frank laughed and nodded to the store. "Don't mind old Clay in there. He was just as ornery when I was a kid as he is now. Tell the truth, he may have mellowed some in his old age. It's just his way, he don't mean nothin' by it. Just don't go thinking he's an accurate representation of the rest of the town, though. Got about two hundred or so folks living here, bound to be a few unfriendly ones in the bunch."

She laughed. "I'll try to keep it in mind."

"You do that," he said. "So, you must be the one moved into Alston House."

"You're two for two today, Frank," she said. "Maybe we should go to Vegas."

He smiled. "I'm sure my wife'd be thrilled at that. No secret there, though. Your realtor let me know somebody'd be moving in this week so I wouldn't think nobody broke in there or nothing. If you don't mind me saying, though, that's an awful lot of house for just one person. You got kids, too?"

She caught herself hesitating before she answered. "No," she said. *Not anymore, anyway.*

If Frank noticed it, he didn't comment on it. "Well, hopefully you don't get yourself lost in there. You get a job around here or something?"

"Not really," she said, glad he had moved past family. "I'm an artist, a painter, or at least I used to be. I'm hoping being out in the woods in a place with that much history will inspire me again."

"Don't think I ever met a professional artist before," Frank said. "Decent money in that? If it's none of my business, just say so."

"No, it's fine," she replied. "And it depends. Art's pretty subjective. A painting's only worth what somebody wants to pay for it. Sometimes you only get a few bucks, sometimes you get lucky. I never got rich, but I managed to get by. I stopped for a while, now I want to get back into it again."

"Fresh start all the way around," Frank said, nodding. "Say, you do commissions?"

She looked at him askance. "Depends on what it is."

"My twentieth anniversary's coming up," he said. "If I gave you a picture of me and the wife, you think you could turn it into a painting?"

"Should be easy enough," she said. "I haven't tried copying a picture since I was just getting started, but it shouldn't be a problem."

"How much you charge me?"

She shrugged. "I can't put a price tag on my work. How about if you want it done, I do it, and you pay me what you think it's worth after you see it?"

He nodded. "Seems like a strange way to do business, but like I said, I've never dealt with an artist before. I'll give you a few days to settle in, then I'll run that picture out to you."

"Sounds like a plan to me," she said. Something else the man told her was gnawing at her as being a little strange. "You said the realtor called to tell you I was moving in. Why would she need to do that?"

"No real secret," he said, shrugging. "Not around these parts, anyway. Alston House is on my normal patrol route. Sometimes kids would break in, try and scare themselves silly. Maybe a boy'd take his girl out there hoping he could literally scare the pants off her. That sort of thing."

"The realtor never mentioned it," Katherine said. "Seems like the kind of thing you might want to tell a prospective buyer."

"Ethically, sure," Frank agreed. "But not if you wanted to keep that buyer on the hook. Anyways, how do you tell somebody all the kids in town think the house you're trying to buy may be haunted?"

She blinked, not entirely sure she heard him correctly. "Did you say the house was haunted?"

"No," he said, chuckling. "I said the kids around here think it is. Never said I believed it."

"Why would they think it?"

He shrugged. "Old house, back in the woods, abandoned for years. Makes perfect sense. I'm willing to bet every little town's got a house like that, and in every one of those towns, the kids all think the place is haunted. Seems like at that age all they want to do is scare each other, so they need a good place to do it. In Poplar Bend, that's Alston House."

Rather than being upset at hearing her new house was a local legend, Katherine found the revelation endearing. She smiled. "Does that mean they're going to think I'm a witch or something?"

Frank laughed. "Who's to say? Might be fun around Halloween to play it up. I'm sure most of the adults'd get a kick out of it, anyway."

She rolled her eyes in mock-disappointment. "Why did I have to wait until November to move?"

The two laughed together, and for the first time since she arrived, Katherine felt like she might make it here.

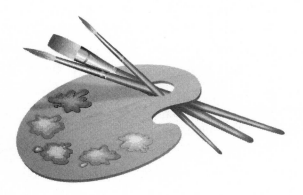

CHAPTER FIVE

She couldn't stop thinking about it on the drive back home, how she somehow ended up living in the local haunted house. The concept in no way frightened her. In fact, she thought it might help with her artwork. She could alter the picture she had in mind slightly for that first impression, the color palate shifting just a twinge toward the darker end of the spectrum, and the entire work would come out with a different tone from what she initially intended. She could even expand on the idea and do two different paintings of the same scene; one, the bright, new beginning she saw it as and the other, the darker, eerie version the town saw it as. If she was feeling especially brave, she could do a split scene in a landscape format with one on the left and the other on the right.

It was something she would have to give serious thought to. She wanted the image to be bright, like her memory, but darker imagery was all the rage now, with shows about zombies and vampires and other ghoulish creatures dominating the television. Even some of the bestselling books in the last several years were in the same vein, from *Twilight* with its teenybopper shimmering vampire love story to something as mundane as *Harry Potter* with child wizards being confronted by a creature of pure evil that terrified adults.

Changing the tone would mean compromising her artistic integrity, though. Some of her old friends who she lost touch with during her married life would turn their noses up. Katherine was more of a pragmatist, though. The vision would still be hers, and if she altered it without giving up the purity of the vision itself, so be it. It would not be the first time she had painted solely for the concept of getting a paycheck. Artistic integrity was fine, but there comes a point where you have to consider the desire to eat and pay your bills, too.

And had she not just agreed to do what amounted to piecemeal work on commission just to earn a few bucks? It was all a part of the same. Sure, she had *some* money now, but with the way the expenses of moving in and getting her new house renovated were piling up on her, it would not last very long. She figured she had until around the first of the year before she started to worry. Her alimony would keep the mortgage paid, but not much more. If she managed to get a tax return, it would help, but without the ability to file as part of a family anymore, it would be severely limited. It might be enough to buy her another month at most. That meant three months, the length of a season until she was scrabbling for whatever money she could get her hands on. The entire purpose of this move, this new start, was to be free so she could pursue her dream of being an artist who got paid for their work. If she had to end up getting some menial job somewhere to pay her bills, it would be one more dream she could consider lost and pointless.

The house scene would have to wait then, while she decided within herself about the direction it should take. In the past, she bemoaned the forced delay or abandonment of an inspiration, but this time was different. She had another project in mind she could work on: *Newfound Freedom.*

As if making the choice to paint gave the mental image permission, it returned as strong as it had been when she conceived it. No one would need to know it was born of a self-depreciating joke. It would be as the title implied, a verification she had made the right decision in pulling up stakes and moving here.

There were still things to do before she could start on it. There were groceries to put away, a too-long delayed lunch to prepare, and the assembly of her bed so she would have a place to sleep tonight being the front-runners. It would be a reward then. She would finish her tasks and then set up her easel and reward herself with a few hours lost in the blissful waking dream that was the creation of art. The perfect way for her to unwind before bed, and a chance to exhaust her mind enough to hold any further nightmares at bay for at least one more night.

It was a trick she discovered back before she was even in her teens. She believed, whenever she had nightmares, they directly resulted from her mind being overfilled by her imagination. When she painted, it allowed some of that vividness to transfer from her subconscious onto whatever medium she was working in. Sketching and drawing on pads helped, but nothing cleared the synapses like putting a brush to canvas and getting down to the real crafting. Whenever she was working on something new, her sleep was practically dreamless. If she was between projects, or at a full stop like she had been for the last few years, the dreams were more active. Add stress, and it almost guaranteed her to have nightmares. Some, especially after those horrible few days a year ago, had been so intensely detailed they crossed into the realm of night terrors rather than simple nightmares. Many people thought there wasn't any difference between those two. Katherine knew from experience how distinct they were.

She busied herself with putting away the groceries, folding each bag neatly before placing the entire stack on top of the fridge. Silly, but it was also another habit she got from her mother that she could not seem to get rid of. The logic was relatively sound: you simply never knew when you might need a bag, so it was better to have some on hand, just in case.

Once everything was away, she cobbled together a simple peanut butter and jelly sandwich to hold her over for a few hours until dinnertime. After the first bite, she had to admit there was something to say for using fresh, local ingredients instead of the mass-produced, processed stuff. The jelly actually still had bits of strawberry in it and tasted like it was picked and prepared the day before. For all she knew, it was.

Her arguing stomach pacified for the time being, she went upstairs, changed into a pair of shorts and a tank top, and began putting her bed together. For the first time since she had met him, she found herself thankful Dave had been so lax with doing housework. It had forced her to learn how to do some basic home repairs, a skill easily transferrable to assembling the wooden bed frame, attaching the steel runners, and placing the slats. The box spring was fairly light and easy to set in place, but the mattress was another matter altogether. It was heavy and bulky and awkward, and by the time she finally shoved it the rest of the way onto the box springs with a massive grunt of effort, she was practically dripping with sweat and could feel the muscles in her arms and shoulders twitching from the exertion.

She headed to the bathroom, stripping her clothes off as she went before finally tossing them into a pile against the wall opposite the vanity. If she kept going through clothes like this, she would need to invest in a washer and dryer sooner rather than later. She was already planning an all-day trip tomorrow to finish getting the things she would need, including home phone service and a trip to Walmart, so she would just have to add appliance shopping to the list. The contractor would handle the ones for the kitchen when he replaced the countertops and stained the cabinets, but they had not discussed the laundry room, so she may as well take care of that herself.

The bathtub looked tempting, but if she indulged in a long soak again, she was apt to lose her focus on painting for the night. Besides, if it went the way her previous sessions did, she would end up with paint spattered over nearly every inch of exposed skin. Considering the subject she had in mind and her intention of using herself as a model, it might be better to just hold off altogether. She gave the tub and shower one last longing look and then left the room, electing to let herself air-dry while she set up her new studio.

It didn't take long to bring in the little cabinet where she would store her paints and set up the easel facing the backyard. Unpacking the boxes with her art supplies took considerably longer, and by the time she finished the sweat had not only dried, but she was feeling a bit of a chill from wandering around the upper floor naked for the last hour. She checked her cell phone in the bedroom and saw it was going on five. She was already losing the light, but if the moon was still as bright and full as it had been the night before, she should be able to manage it, for a little while. That meant, of course, she could not get started until the moon rose. She grabbed her robe and pulled it on as she left the room to figure out something for dinner.

She kept it relatively light, opting for another sandwich rather than unpacking her cookware to make something more substantial. That could go on the list for tomorrow, once she got back from all her errands. She went for another basic, ham and cheese this time, just so she could say she switched up the proteins in her diet. She chuckled at trying to subsist on nothing but sandwiches for a while until she remembered the potential time crunch she would be under if she couldn't make this artist thing work. Suddenly the idea seemed less like a joke and more like a distinct possibility.

Poring over the mental version of her intended painting helped keep her occupied as she ate, and kept her thoughts from trailing down such dark and depressing paths. She finished the sandwich, washed it down with a handful of water from the tap, and then headed back upstairs to get to work.

Her hands started to tremble as she set up her full-length mirror next to the easel. It had been a long time since she had so much as picked up a paintbrush intending to do any work, and her excitement at the prospect was becoming more and more tangible by the second. Once she positioned the mirror the way she wanted it, she turned and began picking out the paint colors she thought she would need. She chose a few shades of green to cover the grass, some reds and golds for the leaves still on the trees, brown and gray for the tree trunks and branches, and finally some pinks and off-whites to blend into a skin tone she felt would be appropriate. To further distance the painting-girl from herself, she went with yellows and light browns. Since she was a brunette, her subject would be blonde. A few additional alterations to the facial features and she should be well disguised.

She paused before she started mixing the colors on the wooden palate. To get the perspective right, she would need to do the trees and sky first, then the girl, and finally the grass. She could change clothes again, risk ruining her robe with the oil-based paints, or go ahead and take it off, and paint in the nude. She was alone in the house. There would be no one to walk in on her and ask her what the hell she thought she was doing. The only danger would be if someone were to pull into the driveway, look up, and catch sight of her naked ass in the tower window.

The solution was simple, and she felt foolish it had not come to her immediately. She returned to the bedroom, opened a box filled with sheet sets, and pulled a black one from the stack. She went back into the little studio and got it tacked into place over the front window with relative ease. She stepped back and smiled at her ingenuity. It wasn't perfect, and she had no intention of leaving it in place permanently, but it would work until she could pick up an old-time draw shade while she was out tomorrow.

Satisfied she thwarted any potential peeping toms, Katherine removed the robe, folded it neatly on the end of the table furthest from her work area, and mixed her colors. Once they were the shade she felt represented her subject, she picked up a medium-width brush and took a deep breath. This was the moment of truth, the moment she would either step up to meet the challenge of making her dream happen, or fail and abandon it forever.

She had endured much over the last year. This would be like preschool in comparison. She dipped the brush in the paint, touched it to the canvas, and began transferring the image from her head.

CHAPTER SIX

The first thing Katherine noticed when she awoke was that she was cold. Not just as though she caught a little chill, either, but involuntarily shivering even while she was asleep *cold*. The other thing she noticed was that while her mind was awake, if a little foggy, her left arm was asleep. She forced her eyes open, blinking rapidly to focus her vision, and discovered a third thing she had not expected: sunlight was streaming through her bedroom windows. She glanced to her nightstand. Surprised at not seeing her digital clock staring back, she then remembered she had not yet unpacked it.

She rolled onto her back and immediately discovered the reason for both the coldness and the numb arm. She was lying on her bed crossways, her feet dangling off the side, her arm beneath her. She was also naked. She wanted to chastise herself for not bothering to put on clothes before coming to bed, but she could not even remember leaving the studio at all last night, much less cleaning up. She must have worked well into the night, lost in her creative flow, and then wandered into the bedroom and collapsed. It was not something she had ever done before, but she remembered being so lost in creation that hours would pass without notice. It had been a long time since she painted anything. Maybe this was just an extension of that.

At least there had been no dreams last night, as she hoped.

After a few minutes of rubbing her arm, it began to tingle as the blood started flowing again. A minute later and she could wiggle her fingers easily. One problem solved, now to take care of the other.

She got up and started toward her suitcase, idly glancing down at herself as she walked. Paint streaked her chest and belly and made crazy patterns on her hands and forearms. She stopped walking and frowned, raising one arm to study the streaks staining it. Even lost in the throes of imagination, she had never neglected to clean up after a painting session before. She didn't know how long she worked on her painting last night, but it had to have been until she was already on the brink of collapse before she ever gave up for the night.

Almost as an afterthought, she went back to her bed and looked down. She had not put sheets on, which was good, but there were smudges of dried paint on the fabric covering the mattress which was not. It was possible she could get those stains out, but the act of scrubbing at them with acetone was liable to damage the mattress as much as it cleaned it. She sighed. At least the spots were small. She should consider herself lucky she didn't wake up stuck to the mattress where the paint transferred from her skin.

She grabbed a towel and headed into the bathroom, no longer interested in soaking as she was last night, just wanting to get clean and warmed up. She was growing more and more curious about the painting that had consumed her last night and wanted to get the business of washing herself done so she could look at it.

It took a good deal of time, and no small bit of pain, but she finally washed the paint from her body. It left her skin red and slightly tender to the touch because of the amount of not-so-gentle scrubbing the endeavor required, but she managed it. She shut the water off just as the temperature began to drop, saving the warmth she had built up. She dried thoroughly, not wanting the ambient temperature of the house to mix with any residual moisture and make her cold again, then wrapped the towel around her body and went back to the bedroom to get dressed.

When she walked into the tower studio, she held her breath, anticipation building like a kid on Christmas morning. After she turned and took her first look at the painting from the night before her excitement tempered with confusion. She stepped closer, her eyes examining every inch of the canvas, trying to remember what had been going through her mind while she painted it, and did not come up with anything.

Except for some minor detail work, such as going over outlines in black with a thin-tipped brush, the painting was complete. Of all the things she was seeing, this was perhaps the most remarkable discovery. Even when she was painting daily the fastest she had completed anything was two days, and that was stopping only to eat, go to the bathroom, and sleep for a few hours to recharge. She did not know what time she had gone to bed last night, but figuring if she crashed just before the sun came up, she had finished this one in around eight hours. An astonishing feat for a master, much less someone like her who was merely competent at what she was doing.

The image had transformed considerably from how she first conceived it in her mind's eye. The woods surrounding the field seemed darker somehow, more menacing. There were streaks of deep red and purple hues in the sky, lending it a slightly disturbing tone. It was a sky on the verge of a terrible storm. Had the topic been fantasy, she would say that sky was the harbinger of a coming apocalypse.

Even with the scenery changes, the most striking alterations were to the girl, the metaphorical representation of Katherine herself. She was no longer facing the viewer, arms spread wide as she danced naked through the field with unbridled joy. Now her back was turned and her arms posed as if they were helping propel her away from something. The hands were not open, but were clenched into fists. Katherine leaned closer and confirmed that yes, she had even added some paleness to the knuckles to represent the force the girl was exerting. If her palms were open, Katherine was sure she would see little red crescents where the nails had bitten into the skin. The girl was looking back over her shoulder, and even without the final shading in place, her expression was not one of pleasure, but of abject terror. She was running away from something, trying to escape some terrible thing chasing her.

Considering what she knew about the things not seen in the painting, to Katherine it looked like the girl was trying to escape this house.

She had meant the piece to reflect joyous freedom. Instead, it reflected self-doubt and fear. It had come out the polar opposite from her intention, and that she had painted it with no real recollection of doing so, had made such a massive change in tone without consciously considering it, was most unsettling of all.

Katherine turned on her heel and walked out of the room. Something about the painting, the way the girl in it was staring at her, naked and terrified specifically, was making her skin crawl. The thought she had been the one to create such a thing made her feel slightly nauseated. She knew art should have an emotional component—if you felt nothing when you looked at a painting, then the artist had failed in their attempt—but the feeling she got from this one was so opposed to her initial intent she could not bear to see it another second.

Thankful she had plans that would take her out of the house today, she went downstairs, grabbed her shopping list, her purse, and her keys and left. If Dave were here, he would accuse her of running from the painting the way the subject was running from her unseen boogeyman, but he was still in South Carolina, probably doing his best to ruin someone else's life instead of hers. That his assessment would have been correct was beside the point. She would argue she just had things to do today.

After she turned out of her driveway, she started to believe that.

Once she left Murfreesboro and began the long drive back home, Katherine realized how foolish she had been that morning. She was sure she would find a rational explanation for the painting, at least to why the tone had changed after she started working on it. Her art extended from her subconscious—that was why she could sleep without vivid dreams after working on a new painting. She experienced some dark things in the time leading up to her painting session. From the lingering effects of the nightmare to the old man at the grocery store—Clay, the marshal called him—to learning of the rumor around town that she lived in a haunted house. She had even been considering how works with darker tone were more in demand than pleasant ones. All of that combined, and the result had been what she saw on the easel this morning.

None of it explained how she finished such a complex piece so quickly, but she supposed it was possible her creative juices had been building up over time and once they had a license to run free, they had come out in a torrent. It made sense and definitely made the accomplishment that much more impressive.

What was the alternative? That some demonic force possessed her and controlled her actions? She didn't believe in such nonsense. It was right up there with the lunatics who killed someone and then claimed the Devil made them do it and actually believed it. Utterly ridiculous, superstitious bullshit.

And if the painting disturbed her, what of it? If it disturbed her, the one who created it, then she guaranteed it would disturb a potential buyer. She had originally intended to keep it, but under the circumstances it wasn't for her. That was why you had a showing— to find the person who was a perfect fit for the painting. She would finish up the detail work on it tonight, then set it to the side and start on something else tomorrow. There was no rush. She would not even have internet or phone service at the house until Monday, so she could just wait until then before she took a picture of the painting and posted it online for sale. She would need a new title though, since the old one no longer fit. She liked the concept and thought she could change the original idea just enough to fit with the finished product. Maybe instead of *Newfound Freedom*, she could call it *Freedom?*, bringing in the unknown factor. Had the subject escaped from whatever was chasing her, or was she still in danger? What exactly was chasing her to start with? It would all be up to the viewer to decide for themselves.

Katherine elected not to bother trying to answer those questions. She was too close to the work to think objectively.

The only problem now was she didn't know what to try working on next. She had already done something dark related to the house, so she really didn't want to try the arrival scene yet. Too much of that and she might start believing the rumors about her house being cursed and tainting her thoughts with its evil. A silly notion maybe, but she was sure there was some kind of psychological underpinning at work. Better not to take the chance of pushing it deeper into her subconscious. Her father already thought she was nuts for buying the place. Why feed the notion?

It was better not to think of anything in particular. She already saw what good that did. Her original concept came out almost unrecognizable and freaked her out enough her initial reaction was to run away from it. No, she would not try to force anything this time. She would just put herself in front of the canvas with brush in hand and paints at the ready, and allow her subconscious to take over, painting whatever it wanted. That was how good art supposedly worked, anyway.

Satisfied she had made a good start on the road to fulfilling her dreams, she allowed her attention to return to fixing up and decorating her new house instead. She had arranged for the delivery of a washer and dryer on Monday, the same day she scheduled the tech from the phone company to show up and get her wired for a landline and internet. It would not be as fast as cable, but it would get her back in touch with the rest of the world. If things worked out right, the contractor should return on Monday as well to begin the work on the kitchen. The long process of completing the renovations would begin.

Between now and then, she had rooms to unpack and arrange, and plans for what to do with the second floor to worry about. As much as she wanted it to be at the forefront of her mind, painting would have to remain in the background for now, only coming out at night once she completed everything else. She hoped this time she would actually be able to stay awake long enough to clean everything—including herself—up before falling asleep. Maybe she could even make it underneath the covers this time.

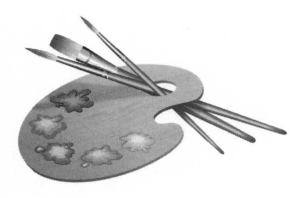

CHAPTER SEVEN

Try as she might, Katherine just could not make any sense out of what she was seeing. She stood in her studio, staring at the new painting that appeared last night. She wasn't even really sure if "appeared" was the right word to use, but she certainly couldn't say it was the new painting she'd done since she had no memory of doing it at all. She remembered coming into the studio the night before, putting the old painting to the side to allow the previous night's detail work to finish drying, and setting a fresh canvas in its place, but beyond that, the night was a blank. She awoke in her bed this morning, and until she walked back in here and saw the result, believed she had failed to create anything new.

Obviously, she was wrong, even if she couldn't remember doing it.

It was also clear she was not over her phase of doing darker works.

This one was also a portrait, like the previous painting. It was indoors instead of out in the backyard, and judging from the deep shadows that threatened to obscure the subject, late at night. The scene was down a hallway and showed a young girl dressed in a ratty once-white nightgown staring back at the viewer. Shadows hid her face, making it impossible to guess her actual age, but from her build and the way she held herself, Katherine thought she might only be twelve or thirteen. Her arms and legs were long and slightly gangly, a condition she remembered well from her own pre-teen years when her body seemed trapped between the girl she had been and the woman she was to become. The girl's hair was dark and loose, hanging straight down her back and across her shoulders. Her arms were at her sides, her head cocked slightly to one side.

The only description Katherine could come up with to fit that pose was "dejected" or maybe "resigned". But what caused the dejection or the resignation, she did not know. There was not even enough detail in the background for her to tell where this might be, other than down a long hallway.

And there *was* detail there. That was another of the strange things about this particular painting. Whenever Katherine worked, she always built up the colors and the rough version of the painting first, then went back and added the fine detail strokes later. It was a characteristic of her personal style and a hallmark of her process. Here, the detail was already *in* the painting. The outline strokes appeared blurred and hazy, but they were definitely there. She had done them the same way whenever she wanted the finished product to have an indistinct and almost dreamlike quality. The style on display was definitely hers. She just could not remember doing it.

As with the other painting, something about the emotion this one evoked made her want to run away, to stop looking at it. She forced herself to stay where she was instead, determined to figure this out.

On the one hand, it thrilled her that she had completed two new paintings in less than a week's time. It was a personal record for her, even when she had been so inspired, she could not bring herself to leave the canvas to eat or sleep or use the bathroom. She was lucky to get a painting a week done in those times, two if she worked every day. Now she had done two in three days with no recollection of anything more than the first stroke. She could not even identify the source of inspiration for this newest one, and that was something that had never happened before.

She wanted to believe it was something about this place, about the mindset she had been in since she arrived. She made up her mind to give her art the dedication it deserved, and she had definitely done that. Maybe the trick was simply to get her mind in the right place to create with such rapid output. It made sense, and more than that, it explained what was happening. For the most part, anyway.

What it did not explain was the blackouts associated with the act of creation. Putting aside how disturbing the images were, they were *good*. Her critical eye could see nuances she never would have thought to add had she given it conscious thought. Not only did it feel as though she were channeling some strange art spirit, but she didn't get the thrill of feeling the emotion flowing from her center to the canvas, did not get to experience the exposure of her hidden heart.

Which, from the looks of things, was much darker than she would have ever thought it to be.

She supposed it was possible a mixture of stress and exhaustion caused the blackouts. She was in a new place, still dealing with things in her past she knew would not fade anytime soon. In addition, she was trying to coordinate the renovation of this house, and had the concern of how limited her funds were really were. Combine all that with the fact she had been going almost nonstop since she pulled into the driveway a few days ago and it was bound to play havoc with her mental state.

But that still didn't explain her creative output as of late. One or the other, it seemed, but never both. Even trying to pick parts of both explanations to try to make sense of everything did nothing to help. In many ways, one explanation cancelled out the other. That meant there had to be a third, but she could not fathom what it could be.

Katherine sighed, ran a hand across her face, and left the room. She could stare at that painting all day, but she found no answers within it, only more questions. They would come to hook up her phone in a couple of days. Once they did, she could try calling Leslie back in Charleston. She had been Katherine's best friend since middle school, and often knew her better than she knew herself. If anyone could help her figure out what was going on, it would be her.

Katherine glanced at the clock she finally remembered to set up on her nightstand which showed it was going on eight. The contractor and his crew would arrive at ten, so she had just over an hour to get dressed and eat before they showed up. Today's project would be the kitchen, and she had a lot of moving to finish before the day was over. She hadn't bothered unpacking much since she knew this would be the first room they would tackle, but there were still some things she needed to find a temporary home for until the process was over.

After she got dressed, she went back into the studio for one more look at that painting. She tried not to focus on the girl—a task made much more difficult since she was front and center in the image—but rather studied the background itself, the texture of the walls, the areas where the shadows condensed and where they lightened. There was something vaguely familiar about it, like it was somewhere she had been in her past, but she could not pinpoint it. She shook her head and started to leave the room, but paused, went to the easel and removed the painting. She leaned it against the wall under the window, with the back facing out. It might smudge the paint at the top if it was not dry yet, but such an imperfection was more likely to give a painting of that type more distinctiveness than to detract from it.

She had just finished moving the last of the stuff from the kitchen to the dining room, leaving only the contents of the fridge in place, and was pouring her second cup of coffee when she heard a knock at the front door. As expected, it was the contractor and his crew. She let them in and spent the next couple of hours doing her best to stay out of their way as they went about sanding down the kitchen cabinets and began moving out the old appliances. They waited patiently while she transferred the perishables from the old fridge to the new one before hauling the old one away, and then she started working on cleaning up the den so she could get all her furniture arranged in there and mark one more room off her list.

It was just after one and she was giving serious consideration to digging up something for lunch when she heard a loud, persistent hum coming from the direction of the kitchen. The lights flickered and finally went out as the hum became a loud popping sound, immediately replaced by frantic voices from the construction crew.

Confused, she rushed back into the room and found several of the workers crowded around her contractor, who was kneeling on the floor next to a man who was trembling all over and appeared to actually be smoldering. Her eyes went wide as the early afternoon sunlight streaming through the windows illuminated the pair of black streaks on his hands and the raw red line across his face.

"What happened?" she asked, her voice shocked and terrified.

Her contractor looked up, his face concerned. "Phone," he said, ignoring her questions. "Do you have one hooked up yet?"

"No, not yet," she replied. "And there's not much for cell service out here."

The contractor checked his phone and then looked to one of the older men on his crew. "Get him loaded up and get him to town fast as you can. Take my truck. I'll drop the other guys off and meet you at the hospital. Just text me where you're going so I know."

The older man nodded and got a couple of the other guys rounded up to take their injured partner outside. The contractor stood and walked over to her, shaking his head.

"Is he going to be okay?" she asked.

"I don't know," the man said. "I think so, but until he gets looked at, your guess is as good as mine."

"What happened?" she repeated.

"Damnedest thing," the man replied. "He was running the wire for your dishwasher, we heard him grunt, and when I looked over, he was holding onto that wire like his life depended on it. One of the other guys tackled him, and that wire popped loose and smacked him square across the face. Looks like he got electrocuted, but that's not possible."

"Why not? You just said he was running the wire for the dishwasher."

"Yeah, he was. Only, the way we do it, we go from here to the breaker box, not the other way around. It's safer to run it, label it, then kill the power and hook everything up at once. That wire wasn't hooked up to the power yet. So yeah, it looks like he got electrocuted, but I'll be damned if I can figure out how it happened."

She frowned. "Are you sure he didn't have it hooked up yet?"

The contractor looked at her like she was an idiot for asking such a thing, then started back into the kitchen. "Come here and look at this."

She followed, stopping beside him and looking down at the bundle of white electric cable he was pointing at.

"You see the loose end there?" he asked. She glanced around on the floor and finally spotted it, bare strands of copper sticking out the end of the white insulated shielding. "That's the end that was being fed down to the breaker box in the basement. The other end is inside that coil of cabling there. When he got tackled, he pulled that out of the hole it was being run through. So yeah, I'm sure it wasn't hooked up to anything."

"Could it have hit another wire?" she asked. "Maybe one that wasn't connected right, like from the stove or something? That could have done it, right?"

"Maybe," the man replied. He did not sound convinced. "But that's not how electricity works. It might have shorted out the power to the breaker, but that's about it. It shouldn't have traveled back up an unconnected, ungrounded wire with enough current to do that to him. Besides, I checked the wiring in this house. It looks like it all got replaced sometime in the last few years. The odds of there being a piece so frayed it could cause a short at all are pretty damned slim."

He shook his head and looked back to her. "Hate to say it, but I think that's gonna be it for appliance installs for the day. We'll check the breakers, get your power back on, but we're gonna have to finish it up tomorrow. I'll send a couple guys back to finish sanding and re-staining those cabinets, but I need to get to the hospital and make sure my guy's okay."

"Of course," she said, holding up her hands. "I can understand that. I'm in no rush. Tomorrow's fine."

He nodded and followed the rest of his crew outside. Katherine found her eyes settling back on the coil of disconnected wire. What the contractor said made sense, but there had to be some explanation why his worker got electrocuted. She knew nothing about it other than you turned on a switch, and something started up. If that didn't work, check to see if the breaker had a red line on it. If so, reset it. If not, call an electrician. Beyond that, she was clueless. If the man said her suggestion was unlikely, she had to accept he was probably correct. Still, something had to have done it, and if not that, then what?

The day was almost over, finally. The workers had got the first coat of stain on the cabinets before the sun started going down. They told her to make sure not to touch them the rest of the night and promised they would be back tomorrow for the second coat. A spray of clear coat after that, and they would be ready to install the new countertops. Provided there were no other unforeseen delays, they would finish her kitchen by dinnertime Tuesday. One more room down, one more thing marked off her list.

As she rounded the corner of the landing onto the second floor, her eyes fell across the dark hallway that led between the bedrooms. She paused, frowning, her mind making unconscious comparisons faster than she could comprehend them. Finally, her eyes opened wider as familiarity sank in. She rushed upstairs to her studio and grabbed the painting from the easel. Something about that seemed wrong, but her excitement was too great to bother trying to figure out what it was just now.

She stopped on the second-floor landing again and held up the painting so she could see both it and the hallway beyond. The details matched, down to the way the shadows pooled across the walls and floor. The girl in her painting was standing in this very hallway. It must have crept into her subconscious without her even being aware of it, and when the time came to put her subject in a location, her mind chose this one. It definitely matched the foreboding tone of the painting. It still didn't answer everything, but at least it helped to explain and identify it.

Strange she hadn't thought of it before, but perhaps she had been so busy dwelling on the mysterious way the painting had come to exist in the first place that she had overlooked the obvious. It happened and was what spawned the old saying about not seeing the forest for the trees. She allowed her focus to narrow so sharply on the little things that she had simply not seen the bigger picture right in front of her.

She took the painting back into the studio and started to put it back on the easel when something on the wall caught her attention. She looked at the line of smeared paint there, then turned to look at the top of the painting in her hands. Her stomach dropped as she noticed the smear along the top edge matched the length and width of the one on the wall exactly. She dimly remembered leaning the painting there this morning before she went downstairs, but yet she had found it back on the easel when she went to get it so she could compare the location in the picture with the view of her second-floor hallway. She had not been back upstairs all day until now, and none of the workers had gone upstairs, so who had moved it?

Her hands began to tremble, and she had to fight to keep her breathing steady as she put the painting back on the easel. She did not want it there, no longer even wanted to *look* at it, but the idea it might move on its own again was too much for her to bear. It was all she could do to not run screaming from the house. She would not stop until she either dropped from exhaustion or that town marshal arrested her and shipped her off to the loony bin. If it happened again, she would probably drop to the floor dead from fright.

For the first time since she heard them, Katherine began to wonder if the rumors were true and the house was haunted. Instead of finding the concept endearing as she had before, now it sent a cold wave of dread coursing through her. She didn't believe in ghosts. Nothing in her life had ever given her any indication such things existed. On the heels of this reminder came the old adage her grandmother used to describe atheism: *they may not believe in God, but He most definitely believes in them.*

It was not a comforting thought.

CHAPTER EIGHT

She never realized how isolated she felt until the technician handed her the piece of paper with her new home phone number on it and told her everything was hooked up and ready to go. Katherine could remember back when she was a teenager and her dad finally relented and had an extension hooked up in her bedroom. The feeling now was almost identical. It was like being a part of the larger world, of being in touch with anyone and everyone. In fitting with her entire reason for coming here, it felt like freedom.

It was silly, in a way. She had a cell phone in her purse. Since there was no cell service out here in the middle of the woods, that had done her as much good as a kid's toy phone would have. Any time she wanted to make a call, she had to drive into town or—especially if the weather was bad—down the main highway toward Murfreesboro. While it hadn't been an issue so far—if you didn't count the man getting electrocuted the day before—it was like tempting fate. Katherine was more than willing to take risks, but the thought of lying on the floor dying from some unknowable condition and being unable to call for an ambulance was beyond what she could chance.

She dug through the box of things she had purchased at Walmart and then stored in the living room area until the renovations were complete. The item she looked for was at the very bottom, naturally, and took a few minutes to dig out. Once she had it in hand, she smiled. It was a moderately high-tech three-part cordless phone set consisting of a base station with handset and two additional satellite handsets for placement elsewhere in the house. The range was fairly extensive. She took a handset outside and made it almost all the way to the tree line on either side of the house before losing the signal.

The only downside was it would take time for the handsets to charge. Had she been thinking the day she bought the set, she would have plugged them all in so they would be ready to go once the line went live. She had other things on her mind, though, so now she would have to wait. Only six hours, but still a wait. Then again, after being unable to communicate with the outside world for nearly a week, six hours would be like a drop in the bucket. She hooked everything up where it would stay—the base station just inside the den, one handset in the master bedroom, and one set aside to go in whatever room she eventually chose as her office—and found herself at a loss for what to do until they were ready.

She checked in on the workers in the kitchen, but they were still deeply involved in trying to get the room finished up. The man who got electrocuted two days before was not among them—not that she expected him to be—but his replacement was taking no chances about potentially having a repeat of the incident. He wore gloves so thick Kathrine thought they might well insulate him against live current from one of the poles along the side of the road.

The contractor told her when he arrived this morning that the man who'd been electrocuted would be fine after a couple days resting and putting ointment on his hands. His heart was fine, and his injuries hadn't been as bad as they first seemed. The smack across his face ended up being the least of them.

He also told her he would like to bring some people in the following day, to try to get them back on schedule to have the job finished. He insisted it would only be for a half-day, to make up for the exact amount of time lost, and she agreed.

There was nothing she could do to help out downstairs, nor would she really have any idea how to do whatever task they might have given her, despite her desire to have this finished as fast as possible, so she wandered back upstairs to her studio. The easel sat empty since she had purposefully not attempted anything the night before for fear she would lose track of time again or paint another disturbing portrait that revealed a darkness inside herself she was not yet willing to confront. Now, however, she wasn't the least bit tired and found she wanted to try something minor and low-key. The sound of the workers downstairs was faint but still audible, which further distanced her from her normal routine when painting. It was worth a shot. The worst that could happen was she would lose time again and end up with a finished result that made her want to pee her pants.

She picked up a fresh canvas from her dwindling stack and thought idly that if she was going to keep going at this pace, she would need to make a stop at Hobby Lobby to pick up a few more of them before the weekend was out. She set it on the easel, grabbed her paints and palate, picked a broad-tipped brush, and began working on the image of the house when she first saw it as she came up the driveway a few days ago. Not the dark version she had imagined later, but the original one, filled with hope and freshness.

When she finally took a step back and twisted to stretch out the kinks in her back, she let out a sigh of relief. The painting, while still not complete, was coming out almost exactly as she envisioned it in her mind. Any darkness resulted from the setting sun portrayed in the scene, and not from some undefinable terror she hadn't even been aware of. Either she had finally worked the darkness out of her subconscious, or the subject matter was not an appropriate enough vehicle to draw it from her. Whatever the reason, the painting looked like it would come out bright and normal, and after the last ones she finished, that was a good thing.

She glanced at the clock and saw that while she hadn't killed the entire six hours, she made a serious dent in it. She had begun working on the painting just before one, and it was now close to five-thirty. Her timing was perfect. The workers downstairs would be getting things ready so they could leave for the day, and she could talk to the contractor and come up with a game plan for the next couple of work days.

To her surprise, the renovations had progressed further than she expected, especially after the contractor's assertion they needed to work tomorrow. They had installed the countertops, the cabinets had their second coat of stain on them, and all the new appliances were in place. Even the dishwasher that caused so much trouble the other day was sitting snug beneath the counter next to the sink. According to the contractor, the only thing left was for them to do a clear coat on the cabinets then install the backsplash she picked out and the kitchen would be finished. That was all on the agenda for tomorrow so they could start the final cleanup on the first floor Wednesday. Barring any further accidents or other delays, they should finish the entire renovation in another three weeks. She questioned whether that was moving too fast, but the man assured her his time frame included a buffer in case they needed to spend extra attention on things up on the second floor where the majority of the work would be. It also figured in a break for Thanksgiving, which had completely slipped her mind.

She was overjoyed at the prospect. She had resigned herself to not having the house finished until sometime after the first of the year, but now it was looking like she would have it ready just in time for Christmas. For a moment, she gave thought to maybe going out and picking up a tree to celebrate, then she remembered what brought her here in the first place and the urge faded. Next year she might be in a better frame of mind to celebrate the holidays. This year, however, everything was still too raw. Any decorating would simply be going through the motions and would not be based on any actual Christmas cheer she felt in her heart. She saw no sense in decorating for herself when she didn't feel like celebrating at all.

And just like that, her good mood was gone, replaced by a melancholy that somehow seemed to hurt her heart more than the deep depression she had battled for so long. She wished it was a shock, but this was how it had been for the better part of the last year. There would be days where she thought everything was going well, where she truly believed she was beginning to heal and move past all that had happened, and then something would come out of nowhere and drag her back down to where she started. It was always random, never anything she could prepare for, and it always hit hard.

She sighed and closed the door before turning around and letting her eyes settle on the phone sitting in its new stand just inside the den. The little light on top was still blinking yellow, indicating it was charging. Dave's voice spoke up in her head, chastising her that if she didn't let it charge all the way, the battery would be trained to think its capacity was considerably lower than it really was. She snatched the handset from its cradle with an irritated shake of her head and started for the kitchen. So the phone only held a charge of four hours and not the recommended six; what of it? The odds she would ever leave it off the charging cradle long enough for it to matter were slim to none, anyway. She had waited long enough to reach out from the comfort of her new home. It was time to break the silence.

After a moment's debate, she turned on the phone and verified there was a dial tone before punching in the area code for Charleston and then pausing while her mind scrambled to come up with the rest of the number. She never realized how much she had come to rely on her cell phone to keep track of things as mundane as phone numbers for her friends. She recalled having to remember them on her own as a kid. This was just one more thing to prove aging was more of a process of forgetting things than learning them. Finally, it came to her, and she punched in the last seven digits, hoping she had them in the right order. If not, she could laugh at the first call she ever made in her new home being a wrong number.

Someone picked up just before it switched over to voicemail.

"Hello?" a woman asked, her voice a mixture of genuine curiosity and irritation. Katherine smiled.

"That you, Leslie?"

"Kat?" came the reply. "Holy shit, you didn't just drop off the face of the earth, even if it seemed like you did. 'Bout damn time you called."

Katherine laughed. "I'm still around. Just been trapped out in the sticks where there's no cell service."

"I'd die," Leslie said. "Forget CPR, just bring on the worms."

It was harder to laugh at that considering the direction her thoughts had gone just before she made this call. Had Leslie known, it may or may not have made a difference. She had been Katherine's best friend since elementary school, and in all those years she had only shown the barest understanding of the word "tact," let alone any desire to actually practice its meaning. Normally, Katherine found this amusing. At the moment, it was annoying, if still a bit comforting.

"Yeah," she said, letting the remark pass without comment. "It's ten minutes to town, but that's no guarantee I'd have the service to make a call."

"Christ, girl," Leslie said. "You weren't kidding about getting away from it all, were you? So how are things out there in the boonies?"

"Not bad," Katherine replied. "Very quiet. Well, the nights are quiet. Days I've got people in here finishing up some renovations on the house so it's pretty loud. Still, all I have to do is go outside. I swear, I can't even hear any other cars from where I am. It's weird."

"I bet. Getting any painting done?"

Katherine hesitated. "Some."

As she should have expected, Leslie caught the slight hesitation. "What's wrong? Seems like you're leaving out a lot more than you're telling. Spill it."

"It's too freaky."

"That makes it even better. Come on, out with it. Don't make me bring up shit from high school to prove why you can't keep things from me."

Katherine winced, not entirely sure which particular incident Leslie might be referring to and not really wanting clarification. There were several things she could choose from, none of which were particularly flattering.

She told Leslie about the inspiration she'd experienced since arriving, and how the work she finished came out much darker than she wanted. She mentioned not understanding where the one of the girl on the second floor had come from, and how she didn't remember painting it at all.

When she was done, Leslie snorted. "And you really don't understand where it's coming from?"

"No," Katherine replied. "I don't. Normally I have some idea, even if it wasn't anything specific other than a feeling I wanted to explore on the canvas. That girl was disturbing on more levels than I care to consider."

"Makes sense to me," Leslie replied. "Think about it. You pull stakes and move hours away from home, partly to escape the asshole you'd tethered yourself to for the better part of the last decade. You're in a new place, with people you don't know, unable to reach out to your friends and family back home. Can you honestly tell me you were all berries and roses over that?"

"Not exactly," Katherine replied, starting to see where she was going with it. "But I wasn't in a dark place. Your reasoning isn't really that good."

"You weren't in a dark place at all," Leslie replied. "You were just in a *new* place, stressed out, and more scared of the future than you're willing to admit to. Makes sense to me your paintings would reflect that, even if you aren't willing to own up to it."

Katherine shook her head, even though she knew Leslie couldn't see it. "You just don't understand. That girl in the hallway? There was something about her, something in the eyes maybe. Something that said she knew she was about to die or something."

"First," Leslie said. Katherine could almost see her raising fingers as she ticked off her points. "You said the eyes were shadowed, so how the hell could you even imagine what kind of expression was in them? And second, not to be indelicate, but is it really that surprising your subconscious would spit up an image of a kid that was either dead or dying? Sorry to be so harsh, but you know better."

Her heart lurched in her chest, but as much as Katherine wanted to be offended or angered by her friend's remark, she could only acknowledge there might be a bit of truth in it despite the sting it carried. That was always how Leslie was, though, and one reason

Katherine valued their friendship so much. It didn't matter if you wanted to face something or not, if it needed to be dealt with, Leslie would beat you over the head with it and *make* you deal with it. Anyone could tell you what you wanted to hear. It took a real friend to tell you what you *needed* to hear.

"Maybe you're right," she said at last. "I did have a nightmare the other morning. About... about that day."

"See," Leslie replied. Her tone softened considerably. It was another of her better traits. She might hit you a little harder than you wanted her to, but she always had an ice pack ready to soothe you afterward. "Painting always used to be how you dealt with shit. You haven't done it in a while so it built up. Now that you're facing it head-on, it's coming out quick and dirty. Just stick with it. Once you work it all out of your system, you'll be able to do the fluffy bunny bullshit again, if that's what you want to waste your talents on."

Katherine rolled her eyes. "It's not 'fluffy bunny bullshit.' I just like doing things that make people feel good, not stuff that terrifies them."

"Yeah, but I bet the scary shit sells better," Leslie said, echoing Katherine's own thoughts from a couple of days ago. "And you didn't exactly set yourself up with a backup plan here. You need to get shit selling on a semi-regular basis or you're going to find yourself on the broke-ass bitch diet, and that's no fun for anybody."

"I don't know. I could stand to lose a few pounds."

"And I could stand to grow a dick out of my forehead," Leslie replied. "Doesn't mean it's something I actually want or need to do."

Katherine smiled. "I don't know, I bet Marie wouldn't mind that at all."

"Yeah, right," Leslie said, chuckling. "She's got more of an aversion to penis than I do. Maybe if I grew a second tongue instead..."

"Okay, ew," Katherine said, wrinkling her nose. "Now we're slipping into 'TMI' territory."

"You started it."

"Actually, you did, but that's beside the point."

"Look," Leslie said after a long pause. The humor dropped out of her voice, replaced with a supportive tone that was so pure it nearly brought tears to Katherine's eyes. "I get why you moved out there, I really do. And I've got your back. Just... don't push yourself too far. If you start feeling lonely, give me a call. It's not like I do anything for the holidays, anyway. I'd be more than happy to come spend a couple weeks with you keeping you company."

"I might take you up on that," Katherine said. "But not right now. Let me get settled in on my own first. Then maybe I'll have you out here."

"Fair enough. Just know all you have to do is ask and I'll come on the next flight."

"I know that. And thanks."

"You take care of yourself," Leslie said. "Maybe see if you can't get one of those construction guys you hired to do a little renovation alone in your bedroom with you, too. Tell him you got some cobwebs need to be cleaned out or something. Knock the dust off it, that kind of thing."

"You're disgusting," Katherine said, laughing. "I don't know why I keep talking to you."

"Cause let's face it," Leslie said. "When you get right down to it, we're the only ones willing to put up with each other's shit."

Katherine hung up, still laughing. That was how most of her conversations with Leslie went when she was upset. It was like lancing an infected wound: Leslie would puncture it and squeeze all the infection out, and while it hurt like hell at first, once it was all over there was a sense of relief and the knowledge that particular wound could finally heal.

She made herself a sandwich for dinner, thankful this would be the last night she was forced to endure a cold meal, and then went back upstairs. She had a million things she needed to do, but right now, all she wanted was to finish up that painting she began earlier. She had a feeling it was going to be better than she originally hoped, and not just because it would be a ray of sunlight in what had otherwise been a dark and turbulent creative landscape. Even partially done, she could see a level of nuance and detail she had only accomplished a handful of times in her work. The other two felt like warm-ups by comparison, good as they were from a technical aspect. She would finish it, then take a trip to Murfreesboro next week to have it framed so she could hang it over the fireplace. She even had a title for it now: *Home at Last*.

With a little luck, soon she would feel all that title implied herself.

CHAPTER NINE

Any time a woman screams in an otherwise quiet parking lot during daylight hours, people come running. It was human nature at its finest, the desire to protect and defend, or maybe just an urge to figure out what was wrong so the piercing noise would stop. She did not know where they all came from. She hadn't noticed them while conducting her search earlier. Of course, that would have required a level of attention she was incapable of giving at the time, lost in a single-minded focus to find him at all costs, ignoring everything else in favor of that lone imperative.

They surrounded her, asked her questions, but she was too lost in her terror and worry to answer them coherently. After some indeterminate time, she looked up and saw the blue uniform, the flash of shined nickel at the breast. Some primitive part of her mind registered what this meant, and relief attempted to flood through her before being slammed back out by the realization the officer was alone, and her son was still missing.

She spoke, and the officer listened. The officer asked questions, and she tried to answer clearly. At the officer's request, she dug through her purse and found a relatively recent picture to show him.

The officer nodded and spoke into the radio handset attached to his shoulder through some means that might as well have been magical for all she could discern of it. The officer listened to whatever response came back and then led her to the front of her truck and told her to sit down, please, before she fell down.

He spoke words of encouragement meant to calm and soothe her, but they couldn't penetrate the screen of panic that closed over her mind. She was trembling by then, a combination of adrenaline and shock enhancing every emotion, despite her desire to just go numb. She was usually good in a crisis, but whenever her child was involved, her normal strength left her. She wished this were not so. Nevertheless, it was as it was.

She barely noticed as the patrol car pulled up behind her truck and parked, disgorging another pair of officers, one male and one female this time. She saw the female officer approach and kneel before her like a lover—a strange thought at this horrible time, but her mind was wandering beyond what she could control—and heard the mummer of her voice even if she could not understand the words being said. Finally, something cut through the fog that enveloped her, not from the female officer but over her radio. An announcement to any officers in the area to be on the lookout for a missing child, named Thomas Weaver, age five, who disappeared around fifteen minutes ago.

Hearing it aloud from another source brought her out of her stupor and forced her to accept the fact once more that he was missing. She did not scream this time—she didn't have the strength left in her to do so—but her head sank to her knees and she began to sob.

She didn't awake with a start, or jerk herself awake, or any of those stereotypes for how someone woke up after a nightmare. Instead, one moment she was asleep and dreaming that terrible dream and the next her eyes were open wide and staring at the ceiling through the haze of tears that formed while she slept. She wiped them away and wished she were surprised it happened, but she was not. She hadn't expected it, either, though considering the topics of conversation earlier in the day she probably should have. Part of her wanted to blame Leslie and her direct approach to healing, but that wasn't fair. She had been thinking of it before she even spoke to Leslie. If there was blame to place, it belonged with the man responsible for causing this memory in the first place and no one else.

She rolled over and looked at the clock: just after five in the morning. Close enough to the time she would get up that trying to sleep more would be pointless, yet early enough she didn't feel like she got all the sleep she needed. She really wished if these nightmares would come and be potent enough to wake her, they would do it earlier in her sleep rather than nearly at the end. Better yet, they could stop altogether. She would have no complaints about that.

Katherine sighed and got up. The longer she laid there and wished she could go back to sleep, the more irritated she would become that she was awakened early. Might as well get on with the day. She pulled her robe around herself and headed downstairs to the kitchen to start some coffee. While it brewed, she went back and checked on her painting from last night. It was not quite finished, but she had made a little more progress on it before going to bed.

Her concern was that she had done more without realizing she had, like with the others.

Everything was as she remembered it, complete except for the sky and the fine detail work that would make everything stand out. There was a slight smudge on one of the upstairs windows, apparently the one on the second floor of the tower, but that was easily fixed. She would not do it now, though. She had learned that occasionally those things she thought minor mistakes ended up being the little something extra that made the painting work better than it would have without it.

She left the room, showered, dressed, and then returned to the kitchen for her coffee. She timed it perfectly. The sun was just starting to peek over the treetops as she poured. A smile crept onto her face. She had loved the sunrise since she was a kid. She never woke early enough to see it anymore, which only added to the magical quality it held in her memory. It was a painting she would never attempt, fearful she could not do justice to the concept of a new day being born from the mists of night. Poetry come to life, art on a universal scale. The epitome of beauty.

On a whim, she went out onto the porch and sat on the steps, sipping her coffee as she watched the sky lighten before her. The temperature, which had been hovering in the low to mid-fifties since she arrived, seemed like it would go higher today. She had a lot of work to do inside, but it could wait for a colder day. This seemed like the perfect opportunity to explore her property, something she had not yet done. If nothing else, it would be a good excuse to get out of the four walls of the house that were starting to feel constricting. She did not know how bad the winters would get here, but if they in any way made those barely-traveled roads slick, she would spend more than enough time trapped inside. She may as well get out and explore while she could.

Her mind made up, she went back inside and refilled her coffee before busying herself with little things while she waited for the construction crew to arrive and finish her kitchen. They finished up in much less time than she would have expected, coming to her just before lunchtime to let her know they were done. After a brief suggestion that she allow the clear coat a couple of hours to dry completely and a further advisory that she should not get the backsplash wet for at least twenty-four hours so the adhesive could set, they departed, leaving her alone again.

She looked over her completed kitchen and smiled. It was not the massive gourmet affair she envisioned as her dream kitchen once upon a time, but it had a homey feel that more than made up for what it lacked in size or technical upgrades. The stove was gas, and a respectable four burners with a built-in grill section in the middle. She would have liked a double oven, but with only her to worry about except for potential holiday hosting down the line, the single built-in would be plenty. The fridge was a side-by-side with an ice maker that provided either cubes or crushed at the press of a button. The dishwasher was basic, but for one person it should be absolutely perfect for the job.

She glanced into the dining area and considered moving everything back in here, but she didn't want to risk marring the cabinets the very same day they had refinished them. Besides, what she really wanted to do was go exploring like she planned first thing this morning. By the time she got back, everything would be dry and she could put her kitchen back together and leave it that way.

Katherine locked the front door, grabbed a light jacket from the box labeled for storage in the hall closet, and headed out onto her back deck.

It was strange seeing the yard from this angle. Until now, she had only really looked at it from the window in her studio, two floors up. From here, the grass did not look nearly as high. It had not yet succumbed to the cool temperatures and begun to brown as she was certain it would when fall gave way to winter, so it provided a lush carpet that invited her to come and see what secrets it might hold. She accepted the offer, stepping off the deck and making her way up the gentle rise that hid whatever might lie beyond.

She smiled and raised her face to the sky, savoring the feel of the sun on her skin. She favored the outdoors as a child, her tastes changing as she progressed into her teenage years and holed up in her bedroom with a sketchpad and pencil and later canvas and brushes. Art was a portable creative outlet, yet she had never taken advantage of that fact. She trapped herself inside as she focused on it, ignoring the obvious fact that the outside world would provide much more inspiration than the small rooms she limited herself to. Perhaps she would take advantage of it now, as she neared her thirties. She could almost picture herself setting an easel atop that hill, relishing the natural scenery around her while she crafted something new and wondrous.

When she got to the top, she paused. If she had figured it correctly, she was standing in the exact spot she imagined she would be when she came up here to paint. She looked behind her first, holding the surprise of what lay beyond for the last minute to build her excitement. She chuckled to herself at how sad it probably was such things would be a thrill for her now, but she couldn't help it. Maybe she just matured quicker than most other people of her generation. Then again, after everything she had been through, was that not to be expected?

The house was further away than she thought it would be, and from here she had a clear view of the downward slope beyond it. She had thought it the house on the hill when she first arrived, but that was not exactly accurate. It was the house on the middle of the hill it seemed. What she originally thought was the top was only a slight plateau before it began sloping upward again. From the front, it was barely noticeable; from back here at the true hilltop: decidedly obvious. The view was completely different, and not just because it was from the back. The tower was barely visible over the top of the roof, the angle just enough for her to see the window that led into her studio. The view was more impressive, but less picturesque than it had been from the front.

Her vantage point also allowed her to see how the woods curved on either side of the house, creating a circular clearing with the house in the direct center of it. Again, it was something she hadn't noticed during her initial drive in. She could not tell for sure if the trees had been cleared this way before the house was built, or if they had grown that way on their own. Strangely, it seemed like the latter, as if the trees were pointedly trying to avoid the house. Yet another curiosity for a house that was starting to become a wellspring for them.

She turned around, more curious than ever what lay beyond the crest of the hill behind her house. Unsurprisingly, there were more trees at the base of the hill, but that was not what caught her interest. A small section near those trees surrounded by what looked to be a black iron fence lay nearly at the end of the property and slightly off to one side. Without getting closer she couldn't be sure, but Katherine thought the design was that of an old family cemetery plot. Not overly large—definitely not where generation upon generation of people might be buried—but large enough it would hold several graves. Considering the apparent age of the house itself, the stones might prove to be an interesting journey back through time to when this was all newly constructed.

Getting to it would be a bit of a walk, but she didn't have anywhere in particular she needed to be anytime soon, so she may as well go ahead while the weather was nice and she was motivated. She started off, noticing immediately the descent on this side was considerably steeper than her trip thus far had been. Heading down was not an issue. The return trip back up wasn't something she was looking forward to.

It took much less time than she expected to reach that wrought-iron fence, probably because the steepness of the hill itself allowed gravity to do a lot of the work. She could already see her guess was correct: it was indeed a graveyard, and she understood why it was located here, down that steep embankment. Whoever put it here had obviously been unable to guess how large it would grow. If it had become an ancestral thing, there could end up being dozens of family members buried here over the years. It needed space to expand, should there be reason for it to, and that meant locating it near the end of the property. Since the front was all trees, the back made the most sense. And coming down that hill with a coffin in tow would be much easier than even carrying it over level ground. The real trick would be keeping the added weight from making you lose your balance and becoming the next permanent resident down here.

The fence looked to have come later. It didn't look as old as the stones inside the barrier. Again, this made perfect sense. They wouldn't have bothered fencing it in all the way until they knew for sure how many people would end up here. That seemed to indicate the family either died off relatively soon after the graveyard was begun, or they had all moved away to parts unknown, never again to return. Both were sad to consider. The house was majestic, despite the repairs it needed, and this lonely resting place was so far off the beaten path it was unlikely anyone would just stumble upon it by accident. There were no well-worn walkways down that hill to it—though at one time there may well have been—which meant no one had visited here in a very long time.

She found a gate around on one side of the fence. It was unlocked, the latch nearly rusted open. She pushed against it and winced at the squeal of worn metal grinding against itself. She didn't bother opening it the entire way, only creating enough of a gap for her to get through. Respect dictated she would close it again on her way back out, but the less she had to hear of that squealing noise, the better. She squeezed her way through, taking care not to get her jacket snagged on any of the rough and worn metal, and took her first look at the stones inside.

There were perhaps an even dozen of them, give or take a few, and they were unlike any stones she had seen before. Most were relatively small in size, lined up neatly before a trio of larger monuments at the back that appeared to hold two graves each—husbands and wives perhaps. A curved name in simple block script adorned the top of the central monument: Alston. If she had to guess, it would be the ones the house was named after. She decided to save that one for last and began looking over the smaller stones surrounding it.

The inscriptions were not at all what she had been expecting, either. Instead of a first name and surname—probably Alston as well, with a few others to reflect marrying into other families—and a pair of dates, most of these bore only a single name and a line indicating what she thought was the person's age at the time they died. There was a mix of both males and females represented, and many of them had a question mark carved into the stone after their age, indicating it was only a guess. The only commonality was that none of them were older than their mid-teens when they died. The oldest she found was named Mary, and had died at sixteen. Right beside that one was the youngest, called simply Baby Boy, who the stone said died "near birth."

Katherine felt a shudder run down her back as she made her way to the larger monuments. She looked at the one in the center, the largest with the surname carved atop it, and saw she was correct about it being husbands and wives buried together. This one was for

Edward Thatcher Alston who was born in 1798 and died in 1872 and his wife Theresa Montague Alston, born 1820 and died 1868. Considering the age of the house, it was safe to assume this was the original owner and his wife. It also had the distinction of being the oldest date she had ever seen on a gravestone by a long shot. That the elder Mister Alston had lived so long in the era he had was also fairly incredible considering the lack of proper health care in those days.

To the right of this one was a second monument, this one for Matthew Henry Alston, 1835 to 1891 and his wife Louisa Farmington Alston, 1842 to 1899. Apparently this was one of Edward's children and his wife, though it was a bit shocking to see he had not been born until his father was nearly forty years old. Equally interesting to Katherine was the fact Matthew's mother was only fifteen when she had him. Evidently, this was their first child. From what she had learned through her admittedly condensed studies of history, people of that time generally married young and began having children of their own equally young so they would have help with chores around the house or in whatever business the father was in. That Edward waited so long was strange. That he was by modern accounts a cradle-robber was simply disturbing.

She immediately felt bad for prejudging the situation. The house and the land it sat on would have been worth a considerable amount of money back then, proportionately more than now, in fact. Perhaps this had been an arranged marriage, or one of convenience. As foreign as the concept seemed, it was a different time she was having to think about. The situation may have been quite common in those days.

Shaking her head to force away any potential thoughts of impropriety on the part of a man she never met, she moved to look at the monument to the left of the largest one. This one was for someone even closer to the current year: Henry Alston, born in 1860, and his wife Grace, born in 1868. Henry died not long after the turn of the century, in 1908. Strangely, his wife died the same year. Katherine leaned closer and tried to make out more of the dates etched into the stone, but they had been worn away through exposure to the elements making it difficult to read. Still, she could make out enough to think they had not only died in the same year, but on the same day.

There was something else engraved below the dates, something obscured by years of built-up grime and rotted foliage. She looked around and found a sturdy looking stick, which she used to scrape away as much of it as she could. Once it was as clean as she could get it, she leaned back and frowned as she read what was inscribed there.

"Died outside the grace of our Lord and condemned to the fires of Hell."

She had never in her life seen anything like it on someone's gravestone. This was supposed to be an eternal memory of the departed loved one. She could not imagine why anyone would want to remember someone they cared about this way. Then again, she had never seen gravestones that bore only a first name and an approximate age, either. The combination of the two things gave the place a much more macabre feel than it had at first. Old graveyards and cemeteries never bothered her. She often found some of the architecture made for good inspiration for her own artwork. This one on the other hand was disturbing in a way she could not begin to identify.

Suddenly, the urge to be anywhere but here began to consume her. She rose quickly and tripped over her own feet as she tried to turn and leave. She fell backward, landing hard against the monument stone for Henry and Grace Alston. She tried to push against it to get back to her feet, but the top of the stone gave way with a loud crack and sent her sprawling to the ground again. She finally rolled over and got on her feet again, then turned and looked in horror at the gravestone.

The corner had broken off, the jagged edge neatly bisecting Henry's name and removing the first two letters. She rushed around to the back of the monument, intending to replace the part that had fallen off, madly hoping it might somehow repair itself if she only gave it a head start, then saw the damage was much too severe for such things. The broken corner had landed against the stone outcropping at the base of the monument and shattered, leaving shards of old stone and dust covering the back side of the grave. There was no repairing it, and without knowing who in the Alston family was still alive to speak with, it would feel weird replacing it.

It had been an accident, but the results did not change based on intent. It was broken, and she blamed herself for it. Based on the lack of evidence supporting visitors to this graveyard, unlikely to matter in the long run. After all, stone grew old and brittle along with everything else. Still, she felt bad it had happened at all.

"I'm sorry," she said to the broken stone, as though by speaking to it, the ones who rested beneath it would hear and understand her. She immediately felt foolish, but done was done—in more ways than one, this time.

She left quickly, barely noticing the awful noise this time as she pushed the gate closed behind her. As she made her way back up that steep hill, she realized just how rattled her nerves were, how deeply that strange graveyard affected her. The sun was still up, and she had no other plans, so she thought a trip a Murfreesboro in order. She would stop at Hobby Lobby for more canvases, then hit up a liquor store on her way back for a couple bottles of wine. She neglected to get any on her last trip despite normally keeping some around the house for the times she felt like enjoying a glass with or after dinner. If ever there was a night she needed a drink, it was tonight.

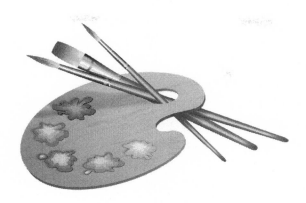

CHAPTER TEN

It started shortly after she laid down for bed, her head swimming pleasantly from the three glasses of wine she drank before heading upstairs. At first she didn't know what it was, just a soft pattering sound somewhere below her, then her mind finally translated the noise to what could only be footsteps. They were slow and purposeful, as though whoever made them was determined to get where they were going but was in no real rush to get there. That she heard them at all was disturbing enough; the gait added a hint of menace into the mix.

She sat up in bed and listened closely. There was a pattern to the footsteps, the sound coming closer before stopping for a few seconds and then moving away again. She could imagine someone walking from the stairs down the hallway and then returning to the staircase again. There was only one place she could think of that would allow those footsteps to reverberate to the degree they were: the empty second floor.

Her first instinct was to reach for the phone on her nightstand and call the police, but once she actually touched the handset, she realized how silly such a thing would make her seem. She had just walked up those stairs and had only been up here long enough to change into pajamas and brush her teeth before lying down in bed and hearing the footsteps begin. The front, back, and side doors were all locked. If an intruder broke in, she would have heard it, not to mention the speed in which he would have had to get upstairs. It was possible, of course, but also highly unlikely.

The more reasonable explanation was that she truly had an infestation of some kind. She was slightly drunk and managed to scare herself pretty succinctly with the trip to the graveyard earlier in the day. The two things were combining in her mind to inflate the sound of a mouse traversing that empty hallway into a full-sized person. The explanation was plausible, and the logic was sound.

Not that it did anything to calm her racing heartbeat. There was only one thing that would accomplish that feat: going downstairs and checking it out for herself.

She got out of bed and went to the row of boxes still stacked neatly against the wall, patiently waiting for her to stop procrastinating and unpack them. She browsed through the stack until she finally came to the one containing assorted knick-knacks that had been in and on her nightstand back in Charleston. She opened it up and pulled out a flashlight, then dug a little deeper and retrieved a pack of fresh batteries. She changed them out and then hit the little thumb switch to turn on the light. To make sure it worked, she turned the beam toward her face, stupidly looking directly into the bright white light and sending a tendril of pain through her optic nerves.

"Smart, girl," she said, closing her eyes tightly as she chuckled to herself. "Real good. Have another drink, I think you need it."

It took several fast blinks to make the spots fade from her vision. Once she could somewhat see straight again, she left the room and crept downstairs.

As she expected, the hallway was empty. She made her way down it slowly, moving the flashlight's beam from side to side, paying close attention to the baseboards. The last thing she wanted was to alert someone—if there was indeed an intruder in the house—and wind up being beaten. Or worse. It confused her when she reached the end of the hall seeing no telltale signs of urine scattered along what she was sure must have been a regular old freeway for the mice that had invaded her house. She made her way back to the stairs just as slowly, not moving the beam other than to guide her down the hall, keeping it trained on the baseboards the entire time. She repeated the process in the other direction with the other side, but still came up with nothing.

She stood at the end of the hallway looking back toward the stairs, her hands on her hips as she tried to work out the solution to this particular puzzle. She cocked her head to the side and listened closely, but the footsteps were not repeated. She knew mice usually hid whenever a person came looking for them; hence the old adage that if you saw one mouse, there was no telling how many had taken up residence. That had to be it, then. She had come downstairs, the little bastards freaked out and were now hiding somewhere inside the walls until the big bad human went away so they could resume their nocturnal explorations.

Calling an exterminator had been on her to-do list, anyway. This just meant she needed to assign a little more priority to it than she had originally. First thing tomorrow morning, she would make that phone call. The last thing she needed was for a mouse and his newlywed bride to start their family in here over the winter. Had they remained out in the woods, she would have wished them well so long as they stayed away from her. Now that they were squatting in her house, it left her with no alternative other than to have someone come in with traps and snap their diseased little necks.

"Should've honeymooned somewhere else," she told the walls. "You'd better clear out fast, or it's gonna be the Wild West up in here."

She giggled at her pathetic, drunken joke and started back toward the stairs, fully intending to go back to her bedroom and turn the radio on low so she could drown out their fuzzy little feet and get some sleep. She had barely taken a few steps when she heard another sound coming from behind the closed door to the bedroom on the far right of the hall. She turned around and listened closely. It was a steady squeaking sound, not like the mice she would have expected, but more like door hinges in dire need of oil being opened and closed repeatedly. She turned and went to the door where she gently leaned her ear against it. There were other sounds there, softer ones, beneath that squeak. One sounded almost like a grunt, the other bore a striking resemblance to a muted whimper. Her curiosity getting the better of her, she opened the door and froze at the sight before her.

All the rooms on this floor were empty. She knew this without any shadow of a doubt. Katherine had looked into them her first day here and had not even used them for storage due to the significant amount of work needed on them. Come to think of it, she had even seen them a second time, when she did the walkthrough with her contractor to get his estimate on how much fixing everything up would cost. It was just a fact, one she could not dispute no matter how drunk she was. Yet her eyes now proved that fact to be anything but truth.

The room was fully furnished now, albeit shabbily, strange as that seemed. A single long chest of drawers sat against the far wall underneath the window, its finish cracked and peeling in the gentle moonlight. To the right was a set of bunk beds, equally run-down and encased in a deep veil of shadow that kept her from being able to see if anyone was in them. The single twin bed opposite them, however, was most assuredly not empty, and was in fact the source of the squeaking sound.

It was not door hinges making that noise, but bedsprings being compressed and released through the act of copulation. A man was there, his bare bottom shining in the moonlight as it thrust down and back up in a steady rhythm. He was not especially big, though obviously full-grown, his face obscured from view, preventing her from being able to even guess his actual age. She likewise could not make out many details about his companion since he was large enough to obscure her almost completely. At least Katherine assumed it was a woman beneath him. What little swath of bare leg she could see appeared smooth and much too lithe to belong to a man.

She wanted to look away, but found she could not. Despite what she was seeing, it simply could not possibly be there. It could not be happening. There was just no way.

When she stepped back to turn and retreat—to where, she did not know—her foot caused one of the floorboards beneath it to emit a creaking noise audible even over the bed and the exaltations of its occupants. The man's hips stopped in mid-thrust, and he turned to see what had disturbed him.

Katherine choked back a scream when she saw nothing but empty, black pits where his eyes should have been. That absence, combined with the harsh scowl he wore, created an effect as polarizing as it was horrific. His movement also exposed his partner, not a woman as she originally thought—not exactly, anyway—but more a girl who could be no older than fifteen. Her eye sockets were vacant, her expression one of resigned misery.

"Unless you want to be next," the eyeless man said, his voice rasping like barbed wire drug through dead, fallen leaves. "Get the fuck out."

Reason left her along with conscious thought, and Katherine found herself downstairs with her hand on the front doorknob before she was even fully aware she had moved. She caught herself before she threw it open, her breathing coming at a near pant, her heart hammering away in her chest like one of those speed metal drummers Dave used to have such an affection for. Sweat dripped into her eye, burning with its salty sting, and she reached up to wipe it away with a trembling hand.

Nothing she had just seen made any sense. There was no way those people could have been in that room, much less been in there having sex on a nonexistent bed. Still, she had seen it with her own two eyes. Three glasses of wine was nowhere near enough to make her hallucinate. Even had she been drinking Absinthe, which once had hallucinogenic qualities, it wouldn't have happened since the stuff you bought nowadays had all the trippy stuff removed from it.

And if it *was* happening, then that meant...

She did not own much in the way of home protection. Dave had shown her how to shoot a gun, but she had never went out and bought one for herself since she figured if the need arose, she could always use his. Even after they separated, she never thought about it. What she *did* have, however, was a wooden baseball bat she kept right next to the front door in case of emergencies. It might not be enough against a determined intruder, but it would give her something she could use to fight back with.

She reached for it now, her nerves calming marginally at the feel of the polished ash in her hand. Possible or not, she had every reason to believe there was a man upstairs sexually assaulting—no, call it what it was: he was *raping*—a young, defenseless girl. Katherine was not brave by nature, but this was something that set her blood boiling. If she could put a stop to it, she would. She had to try. It might end up with her seriously injured if not dead, but at least she could heal or go to whatever life lay beyond this one with the knowledge she had done *something* other than stand idly by and allow such a travesty to happen—and under her own roof, no less.

With every step she took back up the stairs, her mind screamed at her to slow down, or better yet to stop and go the other way. Call the cops, let them deal with it. Anything but what she was planning. She ignored that nagging voice and forced herself to rush up the stairs and get back to the room as quickly as she could. If she caught the bastard by surprise, maybe she would stand a better chance of success than if she allowed him time to get himself collected and pull his pants back up.

She practically ran down the hallway. The door was still open, so she would not have that to impede her. She could just turn the corner, barrel into the room, and crack the bat across the bastard's skull before he even had a chance to look around.

This thought in mind, she raised the bat in both hands and cocked it behind her shoulder as she entered the room, screaming incoherently with rage. She nearly overbalanced when she caught herself mid-swing, her war cry changing to a strange, gurgling sound of shock as she stopped fast enough to drive a splinter from the floor deep into the ball of her bare foot.

The room was as she remembered it. That is to say, it was empty, the shadows deep and barely touched by the moonlight streaming in through the curtain-less window. The chest of drawers was gone, the bunk beds were gone, and more importantly the twin bed with its rutting occupants was gone as well. She spun in a slow circle, confused, looking for some clue as to exactly what the hell was going on here, but nothing changed. The room remained empty. The former occupants did not materialize from thin air.

She spotted the flashlight on the floor where she dropped it during her earlier flight downstairs. She picked it up, not setting the bat down in case something should leap out at her from those shadows before she could make sure they were empty. She shined the light across the room, but there was nothing there, nor was there any indication anyone had been there in a very long time.

A series of pale streaks on the floor where the twin bed had been caught her eye. She approached them warily and knelt to look at them more closely. They were deep, scraped grooves in the wooden floor that not only marred the finish but actually dug into the wood itself. If she didn't know better, she would almost swear they had been left by the legs of a bed being scraped across the floor over a long period of time. Maybe by a forceful sexual encounter. Maybe even by one like she had just witnessed.

Whatever they were and however they had been caused, there was nothing here now. She checked the other rooms on the floor, but they were as empty as she remembered them from the first two times she had seen them. She did not see other scrapes like the one from the room at the end of the hall, but then she had seen nothing in these to make her more aware or sensitive to the possibility such a thing would be there in the first place. She vowed to check them again more thoroughly tomorrow when the sun was out and banished those encroaching shadows for another day.

She limped back to her master bathroom and tended to her wounded foot, wincing as she saw how long that splinter actually was: easily two inches, with stains from her blood covering two-thirds the length of it. She dropped it into the wastebasket and stuck her foot over the bathtub before pouring peroxide over it. She hissed softly as the liquid worked its way into the wound and sent pinpricks of pain through her entire leg, but the sensation faded relatively fast once the initial cleansing was over. She spread on a generous dollop of antibacterial cream and covered it with a large adhesive bandage. She stood and took a test step, gauging the pain. It was not so bad if she tried to walk on her heel, so she thought she could live with it the couple of days it would take before the pain faded completely.

She came back out into her bedroom and looked over to her rumpled bed. She did not feel the least bit tired, her adventure had also burned away her soothing buzz. There was another bottle downstairs, but she had no intention of going back onto that second-floor tonight, especially not in the dark. She was too wired to try painting, so the only option left was to lie back down and try to get some sleep. She sighed as she propped the bat against her nightstand and began straightening the covers some before crawling back underneath them. Almost as an afterthought, she moved the bat to the floor next to her. The last thing she needed now was to have it fall over in the middle of the night, once she had finally fallen asleep, and scare the living shit out of her all over again.

As she lay there staring at the ceiling in the dark, wondering how long it would take for sleep to claim her, she realized the girl she saw downstairs had been familiar, like she had seen her before. It came to her just before her mind allowed her to drift away why the girl *should* look familiar.

Katherine painted a picture of her just a couple of days ago.

CHAPTER ELEVEN

The last time Frank Bradshaw could remember coming out to the old Alston House was back when his own father had been the town marshal nearly thirty years ago. There had been no particular reason for the trip, just a random check to make sure everything was in order and no one had disturbed anything. This would have been not that long after the previous owner met his early demise, on the front porch if he believed the rumors. Frank remembered as a kid looking carefully at the wooden planks there, hoping to see remnants of the bloodstains that were supposed to have been there. He had seen nothing, though whether it was because there had not been as much blood as the rumors said or because the cleanup crew had done an especially good job he did not know, then or now. His bet was on the former. Rumors had a way of running away with themselves and growing to proportions beyond simply unbelievable and closing in on pure fantasyland storytelling.

What he remembered was hearing about what supposedly happened and asking his father why the man had done it. The few times he had seen Paul Blackmore in town, he had seemed like a nice enough, if slightly lonely man who always had a kind word for

Frank. To think such a person could then turn around and take his own life with no apparent cause or provocation was unsettling. Frank's father had told him no one could really know what went on in a person's head, no matter how they acted to the rest of the world. He said people were different behind closed doors, and Alston House should be a perfect reminder. In the years that followed, when Frank finally learned more about the night Blackmore died than he ever wanted to, the strange warning from his father always stayed with him.

His father also said something that made little sense to young Frank, something that stuck with him throughout the years: he said Alston House was not a good place, and if there was something hidden deep inside a person's soul, it would come out to be judged in the light of day once you spent any amount of time in that place.

Frank didn't know if he believed that any more than he believed the current rumors about the place being haunted. It was a house, no more and no less. Bad things had happened there over the years—some of which he knew, some of which he did not—but that did not mean the house itself retained any taint or whatever from those events. It was wood and brick and mortar and stone, not alive, now or before. People dictated what happened to themselves or others, not an inanimate structure. It was just how the world worked, despite what people seemed to think.

Of course, thinking this way did not stop him from worrying about the young woman who had just moved in there. She seemed nice enough when he met her outside Clay's store that day, and the fact she hadn't been around town since then meant nothing. The way he understood it, she was from somewhere out east, some bigger city, so she probably did most of her shopping or what have you over in Murfreesboro which would be closer to what she was used to than Poplar Bend had to offer. Besides, she had construction crews out there most every day of the week for the last couple trying to fix the place up. To finish what Mister Blackmore started all those years ago. It was unlikely she had much time to do anything.

He tried to convince himself the only reason he was going out there now was to see if she was still willing to do that painting of him and Elizabeth for their anniversary, but if he looked deep and admitted to himself what he normally would not, he wanted to make sure nothing... untoward... had happened to her because of living in that house. It was silly, and not very becoming thoughts for a man of the law like himself, but there you go.

"Any particular reason we're bothering this woman, boss?"

Frank turned and raised an eyebrow at Bradley Morgan, his deputy who was riding shotgun with him on patrol today. Sometimes Frank was sure Bradley could read his mind. It was one reason the two of them worked well together. It was also one thing Frank found most infuriating about the younger man. He found it damned hard to keep a secret when you had someone as perceptive as Bradley working alongside you.

"We're not botherin' nobody," Frank replied, looking back to the road and getting ready to turn into the driveway that led to Alston House. "Lady offered to do something for me, and I promised to wait 'til she was a little more settled in to talk brass tacks with her. I figure it's about that time."

"Uh-huh," Bradley said. "If you say so."

Frank scowled at him, but the man was not even looking his direction, just staring out the passenger window with the hint of a smile on his face. Damn him.

"You got anything better to do today?" he asked.

"Not a thing," Bradley said. "Just passing the time, boss. Don't take offense."

"Maybe I'm playin' matchmaker," Frank said. He had to fight back a smile of his own when he saw Bradley's amused expression slip at the suggestion. "After all, you and Susan been done and over since last Halloween. Maybe I think more'n a year's long enough to be mopin' around."

"I'm not still hung up on Susan," Bradley replied, more to himself than to Frank. "I just haven't found anybody worth moving on with yet. It'll happen. Besides, I'm enjoying the single life right now."

"Sure you are," Frank said, on a roll now. "You're thirty something years old and haven't been on so much as a date since your last girl pulled stakes on you. Sounds like being hung up on somebody to me, but what do I know, right?"

"What makes you think I haven't been on a date since then?" Bradley asked, turning to look at him with a scowl on his own face now. "You following me or something?"

"Nope. Don't got to. Every time there's an extra thing where we're needed, you volunteer. You work every school game night, and half the time I gotta run you out of the office."

"That doesn't prove anything," Bradley replied. "I just like my job, that's all."

"Whatever helps you sleep at night," Frank said. "But this ain't my first rodeo, buddy."

Bradley had no reply. Frank was sure he would have argued the point further, but the man had enough sense to know when he was caught. He would probably spend the rest of the patrol sulking about it. That was okay, too. At least it gave Frank some peace and quiet.

He rounded the final corner in the driveway and Alston House came into view, looming over the yard that was somehow still lush and green despite the turn for the cold the weather had taken this last week. Frank felt an involuntary shiver run down his spine—a reaction that happened every time he saw this place, logic be damned. He never would have thought such a thing possible after all the years he had been coming out here, not only as a cop, but as a teenager out to have some fun at the local spook house.

Kat's Pathfinder sat parked in front of the remnants of what once had been a detached garage if Frank's memory served him right. It looked like the structure, which had been on its last legs, had either fallen over on its own or been torn down completely. Considering all the repairs the woman had going on, it did not surprise him she was taking care of the worst looking thing on the property as well. He parked next to the SUV and killed the engine.

"You coming or staying here?" he asked.

Bradley sighed. "I'll come along. May as well meet our newest resident. If I stay, you're just going to say it's because I'm still pining after Susan any damned way."

"You're not wrong," Frank agreed as he opened the door and got out.

He waited for the other man to join him before walking the short distance to the porch. He was not a hundred percent sure, but he thought maybe the wooden floor had been refinished. It seemed brighter somehow than the last time he had been out here on patrol. He started to knock and saw the faint orange glow of the newly installed doorbell set into the frame next to the door itself. It was becoming obvious why she had not been around town these last few days. He hit the button and waited, nodding to himself in admiration of the musical chimes that rang out inside the house.

After a brief wait, he heard the distinct sound of footsteps on hardwood coming closer. The curtain over the door glass twitched to the side briefly, and then the door opened. What he saw made him fight back a frown.

The woman he met in front of Clay's grocery store had been vibrant and full of life. The one before him now had dark circles under her heavily lidded eyes and a face that appeared drawn and tired.

"Miss Ransom?" he asked, forgetting for a moment she had already told him he could dispense with such formalities. Somehow the situation seemed to call for it. "Are you all right?"

She nodded and tried to force a smile. "I'm fine, Marshal. Just haven't been sleeping well the last couple of nights."

"You don't mind my sayin' so, you look pretty pale," he said. "Hope you're not comin' down with a cold or nothin'."

"I'm sure it's just stress," she replied. "Trying to get this place fixed isn't as easy as I thought it would be. So am I dangerous enough you needed backup?"

He blinked, confused, and then remembered he was not alone on this trip.

"Oh, sorry 'bout that," he said. "This here's my deputy, Bradley Morgan."

She held out her hand to Bradley. "Kat Ransom. Pleasure to meet you, Deputy."

"Please," Bradley said, shaking her hand. "Call me Bradley, or just Brad. Deputy makes me think I'm acting in a Western out in Hollywood or something."

"Sorry you didn't catch me at a better time," she said, retrieving her hand. Frank noticed she almost seemed to show a pang of regret at breaking the contact with Bradley. Maybe his joke about playing matchmaker had not been as far off the mark as he thought. "What brings you two esteemed law enforcement officials out my way?"

"We was just out on patrol," Frank said. "And I figured I could stop in and check on you, maybe see if you thought you might have the time to do that paintin' for me we talked about."

For a moment she looked confused, then her eyes lit up a bit as she remembered their earlier conversation. "The one for your anniversary! I am so sorry, with everything going on I totally forgot about it. Please come in so we can talk about it."

She stood to one side and motioned for them to come in. Frank went first, briefly glancing over at his deputy on the way past. Bradley was doing all he could to not be obvious about looking at Kat while she was not paying attention to him. Frank wanted to laugh out loud. Maybe this visit would kill two birds with one stone after all.

He paused by the staircase and glanced around while Bradley came in and Kat shut the door behind them. Even from here he could see the changes made to the inside of the house. The kitchen looked finished and inviting, and he thought he could detect the faint hint of a fire burning nearby. Maybe there was hope for this old place yet. If anyone had asked him back right after Paul Blackmore killed himself whether or not he thought Alston House would ever feel like a home, he would have said it probably wasn't possible. Now, he had to admit Kat had done a good job of pushing it strongly in that direction.

She led them into the living room and confirmed his suspicions about a fire burning. The furniture here looked new, creating a strange combination with the age of the house itself, but it was no less comfortable for it. If her eye for painting was as skilled as her eye for decorating, he was confident whatever she came up with for him would more than do the job. The room had the feeling of a parlor straight out of the early 1800s, only updated for the twenty-first century.

She sat down on the loveseat and motioned to the pair of armchairs across from it. Frank waited until Bradley was seated before pulling a photograph out of his shirt pocket and handing it over to Kat, then sat down himself. She studied it for a moment and then looked over at him.

"This what you want me to work from?" she asked.

"Yes'm, it is," he replied. "If it's not too small or nothin'."

She smiled and shook her head. "No, it's fine. How big are you wanting me to go with it?"

He laughed. "I have no idea when it comes to this. What would you suggest?"

She laughed back, and it pleased him to see how much more life it brought to her face. For a while there, he had been giving serious consideration to those rumors about Alston House. The only word he had been coming up with to describe how she looked was *haunted*.

"That all depends," she said. "Where are you thinking about displaying the finished piece?"

He shook his head, still smiling. "That'll be up to the missus, but I'm betting either over the mantle or on the wall side the stairs."

She nodded. "You go somewhere and have it done, they'll do it as an eleven by fourteen, so why don't we go with that? At least that way it'll be somewhat standard."

He nodded back. "That sounds perfect to me. So what'll I owe you?"

"I already told you," she replied, playfully scolding. "I do the work, then you make an offer. We can negotiate it from there."

He sighed. "Give me some idea. At least so I don't offend you by what I offer. How 'bout this: what'll the materials cost you, so all I'm trying to do is come up with a value for the work you put into it?"

She cocked her head to one side, considering. "That's fair, I guess. Canvas should be about twenty, the paints I'll use maybe another ten, fifteen at the most. That's what? Say, thirty-five?"

"Won't you need brushes, stuff like that?"

"Already have those," she said, still smiling. "No need to buy new ones. But if you like, you can figure in another five bucks for a bottle of cleaner."

He nodded, adding it all up in his head. "How long you think it'll take you?"

She bit her lip as she considered. "Maybe a week, week and a half? I don't have anything else I'm working on right now, so I'll be able to focus on it."

"That's sad," Bradley said. Frank and Kat both turned to look at him. His face went a little red when he noticed the attention he had gained. "That you're not working on anything else, I mean. Shouldn't an artist always be working on something? Sorry, I really don't know how this works, either."

Kat offered him a smile that Frank thought looked a little forced. "I'm just between things right now."

"Is the place helping?" Frank asked, trying to salvage some possibility of a chance for something between them. He had to remember to kick Bradley's ass once they got out of here for not knowing when to just shut the hell up. "I'm thinkin' you said you was hopin' it would."

The hesitation was brief, but it was there, along with a slight tightening of her eyes. Something about either painting, this place, or the combination of the two bothered her, but she would not tell them what, exactly.

"I've done a couple of pieces," she said, and Frank could not help but think what she didn't say spoke more about those pieces than anything she might say beyond that. "It's just not consistent yet."

He nodded. "And with all the stress of the renovations you got goin' on, I'm sure that ain't helpin' none, either. I wouldn't worry none. I'm sure once everything's said and done, you'll find a pattern for you that works out."

She smiled, forced again. "I'm sure you're right."

"Well," he said, getting to his feet. "I don't want to keep you longer'n need be. I'm sure you need some rest, so we'll get on out of your hair."

"It's no bother, really," she said, but he noticed she got to her feet. "Should I just bring it by your office when it's done, or call and leave you a message, or what?"

"Oh," he said, startled. He hadn't considered that part of the arrangement. "Best not do that. Elizabeth's my secretary slash dispatcher, so last thing I need's havin' the surprise blown on accident. You got something to write on? I'll give you my cell. Bradley's too, case you can't reach me."

He could feel the other man's embarrassed look, but he ignored it. If Kat noticed, she didn't comment on it either. A good sign, despite the man's earlier blunder.

"You actually get service out here?" she asked as she led them to the little phone table in the hallway. "I had to get a land line since I couldn't even get a single bar."

"It's the trees," Bradley said. "Plays hell with your signal. Not so bad in town, depending on who your carrier is."

"Guess I got the crappy one, then," she said, handing Frank a pen and a pad of paper. "I usually can't make a call on my cell 'til I'm halfway to Murfreesboro."

"Yeah, that happens," Bradley replied. "I went through three before I got one that worked myself."

Frank smiled as he wrote his and Bradley's numbers on the paper, making sure to put his deputy's first. She might notice, she might not. If not, maybe it would be a subconscious thing for her to try to call Bradley before calling him. Another little matchmaking trick he picked up over the years. Elizabeth said he just liked to meddle. He thought it part of his duty as a community servant. The truth was probably somewhere in the middle.

He handed her the paper back. She glanced at it, then looked back up at him with an eyebrow raised slightly. He felt a slight blush come to his cheeks. Maybe he was not as subtle as he thought.

"Give me about a week," she said, thankfully not commenting on the order he put the phone numbers in. "If you haven't heard from me by then, feel free to check in yourself. If nothing else, you can come by and check on the progress, see if it's going in the direction you're hoping for it to."

"Sounds like a plan," he said.

He was walking out the door when inspiration struck. He turned back to her and smiled. "If I'm out of place here, you just let me know, but Thanksgiving's in a week. Can I ask if you had anything planned?"

She smiled back, a little warily he thought. "I don't, actually. I'll probably just hang around here and try to get some more stuff unpacked."

"Look," he said. "You don't really know me, and you ain't met the wife at all, but why don't you come have some turkey and fixin's with us? I know the wife'd love to meet you, and I know she'd 'bout have a fit thinkin' you're sittin' out here all alone in this big 'ole house on Thanksgiving."

For a moment, he thought she was about to start crying. Her eyes moistened slightly as her smile became more genuine. "Are you sure it'd be okay?"

"We'd love to have you," he said. "The kids're all gone off to college now, and won't be back 'til Christmas. Tell the truth, house feels damned lonely without a passel underfoot no more."

"Thank you," she said, and this time he saw a tear slip from her eye. She wiped it away unconsciously. "You have no idea what that means to me."

"Small town," he said, shrugging. "That's just how we are. Just to show you how okay it is, I'll have Elizabeth call with the details. Fair enough?"

"More than," she said, using his pen to scribble her home number on the sheet where he had written his and Bradley's numbers. She tore the scrap off and handed it to him. "And I'll start on that painting tonight."

"Then I'll let you get to it," Frank said, putting his hat back on and tipping it at her like the Old West marshals he sometimes imagined himself to be. "Glad to see you're settlin' in."

She laughed. "Thanks for stopping by. Pleasure to meet you, too, dep... Bradley."

"Pleasure's mine," Bradley replied.

She offered them both a final smile and went back inside. Frank turned and started back to his Bronco, Bradley following close behind.

"You're about as subtle as a brick to the face," Bradley said once they were out of easy earshot.

"No idea what you're talkin' about," Frank replied.

"Really?" Bradley asked. "I notice you didn't tell her I'd be at your house on Thanksgiving, too."

"I didn't?" Frank said, opening his door. "Must'a slipped my mind. But now that you mention it, I notice you didn't bother offerin' up that little tidbit your own self, either."

Bradley said nothing, only went around to the other side of the vehicle and got in without another word. This time, Frank didn't bother holding in the laugh.

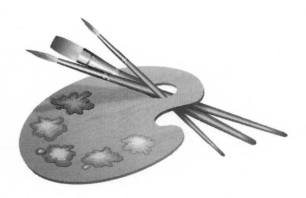

CHAPTER TWELVE

Something was coming. He could feel it in his old bones, as clear and sharp as the arthritis that set in several years back. Clayton Randolph Davison was not a betting man, but if he were, he would lay good money whatever it was, it came from that old house out on the Hollow, as those his age called it. He knew it had a name, but like his daddy before him, he refused to utter that name aloud. If he could help it, he did not even think it. Most of the younger folk would say it was nothing but superstitious nonsense, and maybe that was true, but Clay had done well in his life by paying attention to that "superstitious nonsense" and he was not about to stop now.

As he locked the door on the grocery store his late wife had burdened him with when she up and died on him, he once again gave serious consideration to selling it and moving on with his last few years. He knew he never would. It was one more reminder of Lilian, one of the few he had left, truth be told. As much as he tried to believe she abandoned him when she passed nearly ten years ago, deep down in the hardened chunk of coal that used to be his heart, he knew better. Just like he knew she was better off now, wherever she was, instead of here, fighting through another year of forgetting everything worth knowing. By the end, she was lucky if a day went by she didn't shit her pants. That was no way to live, nothing but a burden on those who cared about you. It was not something she would want, if she could state her wishes, and damn the doctors and the lawyers to the deepest pits of Hell for neglecting common sense and only focusing on what papers she signed while all her marbles were still in the bag. Goddamn Democrats wanted to give the whole country away to those who felt like staying home and spitting out one kid after another was a profession. The second somebody who actually needed the help asked for it, all you got was denial because you were not the one sick, and the one who was never asked for the help back before they knew they would end up needing it. Government logic, which meant utter and complete dumbassery to anyone with half a brain.

Clayton let out a sigh, the weariness of every single one of his eighty-three years clearly defined in that simple exhalation of breath. More and more, it seemed like there was nothing worth waking up in the mornings for. Some days he wondered if he ought to just grab that old Browning twelve gauge and suck on it like a damned cigarette while he got his big toe wedged into the trigger guard. Again, not something he would ever do. Questions of whether there was a God or a Heaven or Hell did not cause him to miss no sleep. Why take a chance and end up with the Devil poking your ass with that pitchfork of his 'cause the Catholics were right with their "suicide is a mortal sin" concept? The day would come soon enough when he would wake up and suddenly find he was in whatever passed for an afterlife, and he saw no real need to rush the process along. Still, it was tempting, especially when his mind went all maudlin like tonight.

Maybe that was just another product of age and becoming more and more jaded with each passing year. It was easier to lay the blame at the foot of that place and the dumb woman what bought it and was trying to fix it up.

She was nothing like that smartass Blackmore what tried fifteen, twenty years back or whatever it was. Clayton had him pegged straight away, despite what he had everybody else convinced of. That crazy bastard was planning to drop some money on getting that hell-hole up to something resembling standards and then dump it on the highest bidder. Clayton could appreciate that, even if the very concept would have sent half the damn town scurrying back to their houses out of the sheer indignity of such a thing. Everybody was so all-fired shocked when word spread he offed himself on the porch that night. Clayton and his buddies, all of who had been born in this town and were apt to wind up dying here, too, understood completely. That damned place being what it was, what else should folks have expected to happen?

Now that dumb little girl was out there trying the same thing, only she was doing something Blackmore had enough sense not to do: she was planning on staying, leastwise if the rumors Clayton had been hearing from the local construction boys out there working on it were true. Worse yet, locals were encouraging that happy horseshit, led by the idiot town marshal himself, it seemed. If there was anyone in town of a younger generation what ought to know better, Clayton would have thought it would be Frank Bradshaw. His pappy had been the one who had to go out and clean up the Blackmore mess and had been one who chummed around with Clayton's group on more than one occasion. Still, it looked like either Maxwell Bradshaw had done a piss-poor job of telling his boy the truth about the dangers of that stretch of land, or it had not taken root like it should have. Either way, it was a failing on Max's part and him being in the ground these last five years did nothing to absolve him of it.

The wind picked up as Clayton made his way to his old pickup, cutting through the heavy flannel shirt he wore and sinking in bone-deep as he always heard it said. Christ, but he hated being old. He could remember back when he was just a teenager, ignorant as shit and full of fire and fury. Back in those heady days before he joined the Army and won himself an all-expenses paid trip to Korea. Course, he spent the next couple years dodging bullets 'til his luck ran out and one planted itself alongside his kneecap. That injury may have slowed him down once he got out of the hospital in Tokyo and found himself back here in Poplar Bend, but it certainly had not dulled his desire to try to recapture those glory days. No, it had taken years and the ravages of time to do that. He could remember being outside in the snow in nothing but a short-sleeved shirt and a pair of thread-bare blue jeans. Now his blood was thin, his skin was damn near transparent, and his joints ached the second the thermometer read less than fifty degrees.

Of course, it wasn't lost on him the wind that currently made him think maybe he needed to go ahead and dig out his heavy coat for the season came from the northeast. Same direction as that damned house.

As if to reinforce his suspicion, the wind picked up, blowing hard enough to ruffle his white hair across his head and almost instantly make his fingers go numb from the chill. He looked up and faced it directly, and imagined he could see that old place staring back through the miles of trees and buildings between them.

"You keep your ass in Hell, you old bastard," he mumbled. Anyone who heard it would think he was talking to himself. Those who knew who he was addressing would understand the sentiment completely and might even add their own admonitions to his. "Burn a little longer, you evil cocksucker you."

The wind died down, causing Clayton to wonder again why some folks thought it garbage when there was just too much happening with that place to be some simple coincidence. He unlocked the truck and pulled himself in behind the driver's seat. He sat there for a minute, considering, then started it up and drove the block down the road to Poplar Bend's only bar. As he expected, he recognized the two other vehicles parked outside the ramshackle building. That was good. He wouldn't have to track either of them down.

Clay did not get out immediately, but sat tapping his gnarled fingers against the top of the steering wheel as he stared at the bar's entrance. He knew he had to speak with the others, but in many ways, it would be a waste of time. Their reactions were so predictable to him now, after all these years, he was positive he could tick off their daily routines as easily as they could. He also knew by the time this night was over, they wouldn't have determined shit about how to deal with the outsider girl or that damned house of hers out on the Hollow.

He let out a weary sigh and opened the door, wincing at both the scream of worn hinges and the twinge in his lower back at the way he twisted to step down from the cab. He was too damned old for this, and too damned tired to be as concerned as he knew he should be. If it was up to him, he would pay that ignorant girl a visit and let her know what kind of hell-hole she done moved into. Either she would get spooked enough to high-tail it out of there, or she would try to fight back somehow, finally break the cycle of misery.

Not that either of the old bastards he was about to talk to would agree with that.

Inside, it was barely bright enough to see by, the only real illumination coming from the assorted neon beer signs behind the pockmarked bar and a pair of fluorescent lights in dire need of having most of their bulbs replaced. It was enough. He saw the very men he had been hoping to find gathered along the far end of the bar, next to the wall where the old wood stove churned merrily along. He limped over and mounted a stool next to Wally Barton, who looked over and nodded. Horace Price, the owner and bartender, set a rocks glass with two fingers' worth of Jack Daniels in front of him. Clayton drank it down without even the hint of a wince, sighing as the warmth trailed its way down his throat and settled in his stomach.

"Long day, Clay?" Wally asked, motioning for Horace to refill Clayton's glass and his own.

"Got me a feelin' it's 'bout to get longer," Clayton replied. "That old place is startin' to wake up again."

"Damn you to Hell, Clayton Davison," Wally said, banging a fist on the bar. "I was tryin' to think that was just in my head. Now you go comin' in here and tellin' me it's not. Damn you all to Hell."

"It's that damn fool girl, ain't it?" Horace asked, pouring himself a shot of the bourbon and leaning on the bar near them. "She's done gone and stirred up some shit, ain't she?"

Clayton killed his second shot and shook his head. "Don't rightly know, but it sure seems that way. Guess the question is: what're we gonna do 'bout it now?"

"Way Blackmore got dealt with seemed to calm him down," Wally replied. "You plannin' something like that again?"

"Goddamn it," Clayton said, giving him a dirty look. "How many times I got to tell you I didn't do shit to that man? He done what he done of his own choice. I never got up the nerve to get out there. That problem solved itself. This one ain't doin' that, least not yet."

"You think she will, though," Horace said. It was not a question. "You just wonder if she'll do it in time."

Clayton met the man's eyes and held them. "Either she will, or she won't. I told ya'll before, she looked like somethin' was eatin' at her insides the first time I saw her. She was fightin' awful hard against it, but it was there all the same."

Horace sighed. "You didn't come over here to tell us nothin' at all, so out with it. If you don't want to speed her along, what then?"

"I just think we need to make ready," Clayton said. "Deal's a deal, after all, even if it's a deal with the Goddamned devil hisself. If that fool girl ain't takin' care of things on her own, the question we got to ask ourselves is what exactly are we willin' to do about it?"

As the others began to gather around, Clayton thought Wally was right. This was about to be a very long night indeed.

PART TWO

DEEPER AND DEEPER

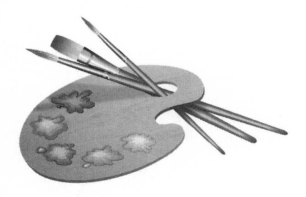

CHAPTER THIRTEEN

For the first time since she'd moved to Poplar Bend, Katherine felt as though she actually belonged. She'd experienced no more of the footsteps and sounds of copulation that had been nearly constant on the second floor since that night she first saw... *whatever* it was she saw. Then, Thanksgiving dinner had gone so well tonight, despite her nervousness about it, and relaxed her in a way she could never seem to manage over the last *year*, not to mention the last several days.

She dropped her keys onto the table just inside the front door and smiled at the memory of the marshal's awkward but heartfelt attempts to set her up with his deputy. It was cute and endearing, and she found she didn't mind in the slightest, although every time Leslie had attempted such a thing since Dave left, Katherine had been ready to strangle her before any first date could even get to the planning stages. It probably helped Bradley was a relatively good-looking man and did not seem interested in pushing more than she was willing to allow. Not that he seemed uninterested, just that he understood such things could not be forced, and that the two of them barely knew one another. Marshal Bradshaw—Frank, she reminded herself again—thought he was being subtle, but everyone else in attendance understood the opposite was happening. Bradley accepted it with good humor and his reaction caused Katherine to do the same.

Frank would probably be amazed he was succeeding, not because of his efforts, but in spite of them. At least there was a possibility for something. Bradley asked if she might be interested in dinner after the holiday madness died down, and—much to her own shock—Katherine agreed. Maybe it would go somewhere, maybe it would go nowhere, but she was willing to take the chance. It was more than she would have done two months ago.

She shivered as she took her shoes off and put her bare feet against the hardwood floor. The temperature had been dropping steadily over the last week, with today's high not even making it all the way to fifty degrees. Now that the sun was long since down, it was closer to thirty outside, and the weather said it would continue sliding downward the rest of the weekend. She hadn't adjusted the thermostat to compensate for the decline, and it was much colder in the house than she would have liked. She padded to the wall, trying to stay on her tiptoes to keep less of her exposed skin from touching that cold floor, and inched the dial up to nearly eighty. When she heard the thump from downstairs in the basement, she smiled. The heating in this house might be old, but at least it was functional and responsive. She still wanted to upgrade it to a more modern unit, but it would last a little while longer.

It was well past time to get out of the clothes she had worn to dinner, but she dreaded the thought of going all the way upstairs and changing before the temperature warmed up. For once, though, it looked like her habit of putting things off would work to her advantage. There was still a load of clothes in the dryer she had not yet bothered to put away. If memory served, her flannel pajamas were among them. She could grab those, then go get a fire started in the sitting room and change there where it would be warmer. Then maybe she could settle in on the new loveseat with a book and a glass of wine, give her mind a chance to unwind before bed. She glanced at the clock in the kitchen on her way past and laughed to herself. Not even nine o'clock yet and she was already thinking about bed. She really would turn into an old woman if she kept this up.

Her memory was spot on: not only were her flannel pajamas in the dryer, but there was a nice, thick pair of socks in there as well. She slipped those on, grabbed her night clothes, and headed to the sitting room. Despite never having to deal with a fireplace before moving here, she got the kindling lit on the first try, and saw the bigger logs catch relatively quickly. She was becoming an old pro at this, she thought.

As she warmed her hands and waited for the fire to grow big enough and warm enough for her to consider getting undressed in front of it, she found her gaze settling on the darkness outside her window. There was only the barest hint of a moon out tonight, but she could still see a ways into the yard. The night looked so peaceful, as it always did when the air was crisp and cold and the days grew shorter and shorter. She hadn't thought of the graveyard at the end of her property since the day she visited it, but she found her thoughts drifting there now. She wondered what it had been like in the days when the house's original owners were alive, what it had been like out here. She had a funny feeling that aside from the modernized appliances, wiring, and plumbing, it probably was not that much different. She could imagine the woman of the house preparing the table across the hall for their own Thanksgiving dinner, children and grandchildren running about underfoot, the entire first floor redolent with the scents of the season.

She smiled, and though bittersweet, it was not sad as it might have been not so long ago. Thanksgiving had never been big in her house while she and Dave were married. Occasionally, they would go to her parents or his for lunch, but then they always came back home where they would pore over the sales papers to prepare for Black Friday shopping. Other years they would do nothing, simply sit on the couch and watch television until it was time for bed. That made it easier, now, she was sure of it. Come Christmas, however, she knew it would be hard. Not as bad as last year—at least, she hoped not—but still a difficult time. For now, she could enjoy a holiday without the extreme heartbreak that had pervaded every one of them so far this year.

Maybe next year she would invite her brother and his family out for the holidays. While it was technically not too late for her to have children again, she had no real desire to. Still, it would be nice to have a house filled with family and childish laughter. Her nieces and nephew could fill that void for the time being. If something more happened in the future, so be it, but a temporary fix would still be fulfilling in its own way. Who knew, maybe Bradley would be here with her next year, and they could have Frank and Elizabeth over as repayment for this year and as thanks for bringing them together.

She laughed and rubbed her hands together in front of the fire, savoring its warmth. That was putting a little too many "ifs" in the basket. One good night did not a relationship make. Dave taught her that, if she needed any reminders of it from her failed attempts during high school and college.

The fire was good and warm now and had made her sweat a little from standing so close to it. She pulled her sweater over her head and dropped it onto the armchair nearby, then took off her shirt and bra and put them next to it. They would go to the laundry room before she went upstairs. The sweater could go upstairs for her to wear one more time before heading to the dry cleaners. She stepped out of her skirt and considered tossing it onto the same stack as the shirt and bra, but took the time to fold it and place it carefully atop the sweater. It was a soft velvety texture, and would need to go to the dry cleaners as well. It was one of the most expensive pieces of clothing she owned, and she saw no reason to chance damaging it by being careless.

She paused before putting on her pajamas, turning slowly in front of the fire to evenly warm herself on all sides, hoping she could trap some of that heat once she got dressed again. Content, she started for the love seat and made it two steps before she discovered she could not move any further. She frowned, confused, and tried to step backward, but she couldn't go that way either.

A slight chill trailed its way across her belly in a slow, steady line. She shivered, even though she was otherwise comfortable. She tried to reach up and rub a hand over the spot, but her arms remained frozen at her sides, as unable or unwilling to move as her legs. The sensation repeated the other direction, and then moved higher, drifting across her ribs and the undersides of her breasts.

As it occurred to her the sensation was not unlike the caress of a lover's hand, the scent of aftershave filled her nostrils, snapping everything into sharp focus. It was as though someone stood behind her, one arm held around her arms and lower belly, the other hand exploring her body with its fingertips. A pressure against her back confirmed this. She could almost feel the gentle nudge that signified this person had sprouted an erection.

Her first thought was a terror-filled realization that she was about to be raped, followed closely by the confused certainty she was alone in the house. She could move her eyes, and in the slight reflection provided by the darkened window, she could see she was standing by herself in the middle of the sitting room, the fire illuminating her like a backlight. She was leaned forward slightly as though fighting against bindings, but nothing was there to hold her, no one was there running their hands across her body despite what her nerve endings kept telling her.

She whimpered as the invisible hand passed across her breasts, the unseen fingers pinching and rolling her nipples between them. Her body responded despite her fear, her nipples hardening under the ministrations bestowed on them. She closed her eyes and bit her lower lip, wishing whatever this was would end, let her free so she could run away, find some place to hide until the morning sun burned away whatever had found her.

She felt the hand trail across her neck before working its way back down her body. Her sock feet slid apart on the polished wood floor, and her eyes snapped open. The hand continued down, caressing, leaving trails of ice across her skin, then finally probed against the elastic waistband of her underpants. She tried to shake her head, as if determination would make it stop. She knew what came next, and the anticipation alone nearly drove her mad. If that frozen, spectral hand touched her *there*, she would no more be able to hold on to her sanity than she could hold water in her splayed fingers.

The touch halted just above her pubic hair, tracing frozen spirals across the sensitive flesh there felt like they went all the way down to her toes. Her legs trembled from the effort to break away from whatever held her captive, and she felt as though her heart would break free of her ribcage.

Soon, a deep, resonant voice whispered in her ear. *You'll be mine soon. But I can wait. I want to savor you.*

Katherine fell forward as whatever mysterious force had been holding her let go. She barely had time to throw her hands up to break her fall, but her knees still slammed into the wood floor hard enough to make her teeth smack together painfully. She was sprawled half on the loveseat and half on the floor, her skin still tingling where that probing hand had touched her. She rolled over and slid the rest of the way onto the floor, breathing hard, wild eyes searching for whoever or whatever had been holding her, something that would help her make sense of what just happened.

The room was empty, the fire crackling away in the fireplace, the air considerably warmer than it had been when she first entered the room. She snatched her shirt from the loveseat as she scrambled to the switch for the overhead light, pulling the shirt on and fastening it even as one hand slapped at the wall. Finally, her fingers found the switch and the light came on, bathing the room in its gentle glow and proving again that there was no one there except for her.

"Leave me alone!" she screamed, unsure of who she was screaming at, yet feeling the need to do it all the same. "Why are you doing this to me?"

Something crashed into the window nearest her hard enough to send a spiderweb of cracks racing across it. She screamed and backed away, tripping over her own feet and landing on her ass in the middle of the hallway with her legs spread wide and her palm flat against the wall. Katherine forced herself back to her feet. She turned toward the front door, fully intending to run for it, grab the keys on the way past, get to the truck and get the hell out of there when her vision began to darken at the edges. In seconds, all she could see was a narrow strip directly in front of her. She knew she was about to faint, but before she could do anything to try to stop it her body was slamming against the floor again, her mind went blank.

She did not know how long she was out, but when she awoke, her head pounded and her muscles ached. She no longer wanted to run, but she did not want to be alone, either. She staggered to the phone and snatched the piece of paper next to it. She read and dialed the number without paying attention to what she was doing. She heard the other end picked up and heard a voice asking who it was.

"Kat Ransss… Ransom," she said, her tongue feeling thick and useless. "Need someone here. Come now. Pleasssss…"

Her hand seemed unable to hold onto the phone any longer, so she let it slide from her fingers, not caring when it hit the ground hard enough to pop the battery out of the handset. She stumbled back into the sitting room and grabbed hold of her pajama bottoms before she sat down hard on the loveseat and began to pass out, hoping help was on the way.

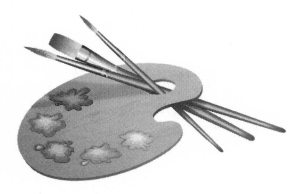

CHAPTER FOURTEEN

When Bradley showed up at Alston House and began pounding on the door just as hard and rapidly as his heart was in his chest, he wasn't sure what to expect. Kat sounded so strange when she called, as though she were speaking from far away, maybe even under water. It was enough to unnerve him as much as his patrols in Afghanistan had a few years ago. Back then, the reason was because of the sheer danger involved, never knowing if you were about to take a wrong step and discover much too late someone had put an improvised bomb in your path, or if you would open a door and be greeted by the loud blast of an AK-47 on full auto. Now, it was the concept that someone he knew and liked might be in trouble.

He had begun to think the situation was worse than he originally believed and was considering breaking the door down when he finally heard the lock turn. He took a step back so as not to startle her when she opened it and was shocked when the door opened to reveal her standing there wearing only a pajama shirt. If not for the dark circles under her eyes and the hectic patches of red across her cheeks, the sight would have been unexpectedly titillating. As it stood, it clearly defined how serious the problem must be.

"What's wrong?" he asked, not bothering with formalities. "What happened?"

She looked confused for a moment then glanced back into the house. He couldn't see what her eyes landed on, if anything specific at all, but whatever it was seemed to bring her back to herself a little more. When she turned back to him, her eyes were clearer—still not focusing well, but more aware than they were when the door first opened. She glanced down at herself and a slight blush rose to her cheeks as she realized her current state of near-undress. As much as he was enjoying the opportunity to look at her shapely legs, that was a good sign. Embarrassment meant awareness, and based on how out of it she sounded on the phone and how dazed she appeared when she first answered the door, she had barely known of anything at all before now.

"I..." Her forehead creased as she frowned, trying to clear her head. "I think I passed out."

"Do you need me to call the paramedics?" he asked, watching her closely for any sign that there had been more to it than just that. He was sure there was—there had to be a reason she passed out, after all—but he wanted to make sure it was not some severe physical trauma at the root of it she made worse by standing here. As a burst of wind cut through the light coat he wore, he realized standing here in this cold probably was not helping her any either. "Or do you maybe want to go get something else on, then have me come in so we can talk inside?"

She glanced down at herself again, and he saw the blush deepen. "Sorry. Come on in, just wait by the door a minute. I'll be right back."

He stepped inside and shut the door behind himself as she walked deeper into the house and disappeared around the corner into the living area where he and Frank sat and spoke with her when they came before. While she was gone, he looked around the room and found his eyes drawn to the shattered remains of the phone on the floor ahead of him, a scrap of paper not far away. He saw with no surprise it was the same paper Frank had written their cell numbers down on, with Bradley's first. That explained why she called him instead of Frank. The feathery tear at the bottom fluttered slightly as the gust that snuck in while the door was open dissipated across it.

He heard footsteps on the porch outside and turned to open the door before Frank even had the chance to knock. Bradley had called him as soon as the line went dead from talking to Kat, not knowing if he would need backup on this one or not, but unwilling to take the chance. It was deeply ingrained in him: always err on the side of caution. Better to have too many people on a scene than not enough.

Frank raised an eyebrow and stepped inside. "Figure out what's going on yet?"

Bradley shook his head. "All she's said is that she thinks she passed out. No idea what prompted it or anything else yet. She went to get dressed. She'll be right back."

"Was she not wearing anything?" Frank asked, confused. He kept his voice low so as not to broadcast the question to Kat if she was nearby.

"Shirt and socks," Bradley replied. "Looked like she was changing whenever it happened, whatever *it* was. Is it really that important?"

"No idea," Frank replied. "Until we know what happened, we have no clue what's important."

Kat chose that moment to reappear, now dressed in the matching pants for the pajama shirt. She did not even pause when she noticed Frank standing there next to Bradley, only offered a slight smile still tinged with residual embarrassment, now from the situation as opposed to how she was dressed.

"Hey, it's a party," she said. Her voice was still a little weak and wavering, but much stronger than it had been when Bradley first got here. Combined with her half-hearted attempt at a joke, it was another good sign.

"Seems like you're havin' something of an adventurous night," Frank said. "So what's been goin' on here that got you so rattled?"

"I don't remember everything," she said, choosing her words carefully. "I got home from your place, and it was cold in here. I started a fire and changed next to it. While I was changing, something hit the window in there and cracked it. I think I ran out here to call you guys and must have slipped or something, because the next thing I knew I was waking up to Bradley knocking on my door."

Bradley could tell there was something more, something she was holding back, but he restrained himself from asking about it. Frank had taken the lead here, and the old man knew what he was doing, so it was better to just let him handle it for now.

Frank nodded as Bradley pulled out a notepad and jotted down the basics of what she said. "Mind if we take a look around? See if we can't figure out what happened to the window at least?"

She waved a hand toward the sitting room. Frank led the way in there, with Bradley following and Kat bringing up the rear. As soon as they entered the room, Bradley saw what she was talking about. The large window was damn near shattered in the frame, one spot at the center of the concentric rings of cracks actually broken all the way through. Chips of glass scattered the floor nearby. Not a lot, but enough he could tell whatever hit that window had some force behind it. The rest of the room was undisturbed, the only thing out of place being the clothes Kat wore to dinner sitting on the chair beside the fireplace. He turned away when he glimpsed her bra strap beneath the skirt.

Frank was studying the window, his head cocking from side to side as he mentally compared the potential objects used to break it. Finally, he nodded and turned back to Kat.

"We're goin' to go take a look-see outside," he said. "See if we can't figure out what did this, then maybe start puttin' the pieces together on *who* might've done it."

She nodded and shot him another attempt at a smile that failed nearly as well as the one before had. It was blatantly obvious something about this whole thing had her spooked to her very core, something more than she was saying, but Bradley couldn't even begin to imagine what it could be. Maybe he and Frank would find something outside that would prompt her to open up more.

Bradley followed Frank out the back door and onto the deck, already pulling his flashlight out of his back pocket. He clicked it on and shined it toward the broken window, looking for some sign of where whoever did it must have been standing. Frank stepped off the deck and began feeling around in the grass under the window, starting close to the house and working his way backward, moving further and further away with each sweep.

"What's your thoughts on this?" Frank asked as he worked.

"Sounds pretty straightforward to me," Bradley said, shining his light across the pane of shattered glass. He kept his voice down so as not to scare Kat any more than she already had been tonight. "Some kid's out here skulking around, not knowing or caring that someone lives here now. He sees her getting changed inside and decides to get himself a free peek at something he's got no business peeking at. She sees him and starts yelling, he breaks the window, she slips on the floor and bangs her head, stays with it long enough to call us, then loses consciousness. I get the feeling there's something more, too, but I've got no idea what that missing piece could be."

Frank glanced up at him and even in the dim light provided by the moon and the light inside Bradley could make out the wry smile on the man's face. "That's your idea of straightforward? Sounds like a bunch of guesswork with nothin' backin' it up."

Bradley rolled his eyes and sighed. "How you figure?"

"I'm with you on the peeping Tom," Frank said. "It's after that you lose me. She never mentioned seein' anybody, so what really made our suspect break the window? And I agree she passed out after makin' the call, but she didn't hit her head on nothin'. Did you notice how the cushions on that loveseat was all dragged half off? She passed out in there, I think, not on the floor. I also happen to agree with you that she's holding something back. So the big question is *what* isn't she tellin' us and *why* isn't she tellin' us?"

"That's two questions," Bradley mumbled. He sometimes forgot there was a reason Frank had been elected town marshal for three terms now, and it was not because the man was good at campaigning. He was good at his job, and anyone who ever had cause to call him out for something knew it. "So what's your theory?"

"Like I said," Frank replied, turning back to his search through the grass. "I'm with you as far as the peeper. I think he liked what he saw and decided to try for more, only the window didn't break the first time around. She freaks out and runs for it, starts feeling woozy, makes the call, goes back to tell the asshole she called the cops and faints before she can, just out of plain 'ole fear. Also explains why she didn't tell us that part, since she was so ashamed it happened."

"That why you think she didn't mention the peeper, too?"

"Yup," Frank agreed. "And lookie what I found here."

He held up a large chunk of stone. Bradley shined the light on it and frowned. It was too even to be some random rock out of a field and there appeared to be something engraved on one side of it. "What the hell is that?"

"At a guess?" Frank said, looking it over. "Part of a grave marker. Maybe add desecrating a grave to peeping on women for our guy."

Bradley frowned. "That's an impressive list for somebody to have, especially when you tack on potential rapist. So here's the million dollar question: Who do you think in town's capable of all that?"

It was Frank's turn to sigh as he stood back up, the chunk of stone balanced in his palm. "That is the big one, ain't it? And honestly, I have no idea. I would say Bill Traynor, but he's still locked up over in county on drug charges. It almost seems like a kid done it, but this chunk-a rock's pretty damned heavy, so to throw it with enough force to cause that kinda damage would take some power. I just can't see none of the ones could do it as the type to try."

"Where you think that came from, anyway?" Bradley asked, motioning to the stone with his chin.

"Had 'ta guess, I'd say that old Alston plot on the other side of the hill back there," Frank replied. "I run more'n a couple kids out of there over the years, but none of 'em been down there in a long while. Don't know what's so special about tonight that they'd start up again. They didn't do it Halloween, why Thanksgiving?"

Bradley considered, then shook his head. "Hate to disagree with you, boss, but it still doesn't add up. Why wouldn't she mention a strange guy? Yeah, I get the shame bit about fainting and all, but to not tell us about the guy watching her through the window? That's a bit of a stretch, don't you think?"

Frank looked at the chunk of rock in his hand again, looked back toward the graveyard, then shook his head and sighed. "Yeah, I know that. But what else we got? There's no trampled grass around here, so I don't see where anybody been standing, so the only other option we got is to subscribe to the teenage rumors and say a damned ghost done it."

"I'll go talk to her again," Bradley said. "I don't think we're getting anything more out of her, but at least I can try. Maybe get something to go off of."

Frank shrugged. "Can't hurt. I'll poke around out here a little more, see if anything turns up. If not, this'll have to wait for another day."

Bradley nodded and headed back inside, relieved to be back in the warm air and out of the cold. Kat was where they left her, sitting on the loveseat in front of the fire, her face pinched with worry. He noticed she had moved her clothes, probably into the laundry room. He moved to the chair where they had been and sat down, leaning forward with his wrists on his knees and spun his flashlight idly in his hands.

"Was there anything else?" he asked. "Anything at all, no matter how minor it might be. Every little detail can only help us."

"You don't have any idea what happened, do you?" she asked, not looking at him. Her voice was not accusing in the slightest, was actually a bit resigned, but the words hit him like a slap to the face, regardless.

"No," he said, sighing and leaning back in the chair. "We don't. No footprints, no sign anyone was out there, just the hunk of gravestone they used to break the window."

Her head snapped up at that, her eyes going wide. "What did you say?"

He shrugged, frowning at her reaction. "Just that we found the chunk of gravestone they threw at the window to break it. Probably came from that old graveyard at the back of your property. You seen that yet?"

She nodded, her head dropping back to stare at the floor again. "I don't know anything else, I'm sorry."

"No need to apologize to me," he said. "I'm the one should be saying sorry to you since we're not coming up with much toward figuring this all out."

She looked up and smiled slightly. "You guys came out. Maybe that's enough."

Bradley snorted. "That's only part of the job. It's pretty hard to make sure you feel safe if we can't even figure out how your window got broken."

"There is a way you could make me feel safe," she said, her voice so low he could barely hear it. "But it's going to sound stupid."

"Try me," he said. "You spent some time with Frank tonight, you know I'm used to stupid."

That got a genuine laugh out of her, which made him relax a bit for the first time since answering her phone call earlier tonight.

"I really don't want to be alone tonight," she said, still not looking at him. "You think you could stick around until morning, when I can see what might be coming at me?"

"Not a problem at all," he replied, not bothering to think about it. He had been about to suggest she go and stay with Frank and Elizabeth tonight anyway, but this would be better. If she stayed here, it showed she was willing to fight for what was hers, and refused to be run off. It said a lot about her character and her inner strength. "I'll even set up a chair outside your bedroom door if you want me to."

"I don't plan on sleeping up there tonight," she said. "I'll just crash on the sofa in my front room. There's a recliner in there too, so you can at least be comfortable while you're humoring me. Hell, you can even watch television if you want. The noise won't bother me since I doubt I'll be falling asleep anytime soon, anyway."

"I think you might be surprised," he said. "And really, it won't be a problem. You try and get some sleep, I'll stand guard. Won't be the first time I've been up all night, and I can almost bet it won't be the last either."

When she smiled at him, her face lighting up with the depth of her thanks, he felt like he would do whatever she asked of him, no matter how ridiculous it sounded or was. The only problem he could foresee was how he would ever live this down once he told Frank the plan. The man would see it as proof positive of his matchmaking skills, and would probably try to give him the talk about keeping duty and fun separate. Bradley had no designs on the "fun" part of that, not tonight, and Frank knew him well enough to realize that. Not that it would stop the teasing, though.

Still, as he looked at her grateful expression, he had to admit a little teasing would be a small price to pay for making her feel safe and secure after such a traumatic night. Truth told, it was something Bradley could get used to. He was never much of a believer in love at first sight, but he did believe people could feel a connection to one another from their first meeting. Just because it had never happened to him before didn't mean it couldn't happen now. He would never in a million years try anything while he was here tonight, but he hoped in the days to come, as the events of tonight faded, something new might grow. He had been alone too long, and he thought he could see familiarity with that feeling in her eyes.

Only time would tell, and he was willing to wait as long as it took.

CHAPTER FIFTEEN

Too much time passed with nothing happening, and the helplessness that dominated her thoughts was taking its toll on her. To the average passerby, this scene probably looked like complete and utter chaos, even if it was organized chaos, but to her, sitting at what felt like the absolute center of it all, it appeared to be more of a show of strength than anything else. Police parked their cars everywhere, uniformed officers spoke into their radio handsets attached to the epaulets of their blue shirts, and plainclothes detectives wandered around checking in and basically asserting their control over the situation.

It was all a lie. There was no control to be had. If there were, her son would be on his way home with her, or at the very least getting checked out in the ambulance that sat to one side.

Desperate for something to do, she tried calling Dave again but as was the case the last dozen times she tried, his phone went straight to voicemail. She could understand the need for some alone time once in a while—though once this was all over, she had absolutely no intention of leaving her son alone anytime soon—but this was bordering on apathy. He was off work today, and he told her he planned to do nothing but sit around and watch television until she got back. Why did that require turning his phone off? He wasn't mad at her, as far as she knew, so it made no sense whatsoever.

She ended the call without bothering to leave another message and fought the urge to break into tears again. She had been crying steadily for the last half hour and was starting to wonder how it could be possible to still have tears left to shed after all that. The urge she understood. *It was the physical ability that baffled her. The officers who kept stopping by to check on her and update her on their lack of progress in finding her child tried to soothe her and almost seemed to encourage the tears, which was another thing she could not understand. Then again, she wasn't in the best position to judge. All she wanted right now was for this to end.*

A sudden flurry of motion drew her attention. Several of the uniformed officers rushed to their cars and tore off through the parking lot. Others went on foot, running at a dead sprint toward the side of the grocery store that was detached from the rest of the shops in the strip mall. She called out a couple of times, asking what was happening, but no one would answer her. It was obvious they found something, so she did the only thing that made any sense to her at all: she followed them. If they had found him, she wanted to be there so he could see her face and maybe not be so terrified by the crowd of strangers descending on him.

When she rounded the corner and followed the procession to the back of the store, what had first been a sense of impending relief turned to confusion. The officers were standing around in a semi-circle, talking softly amongst themselves and looking at something near the receiving door. She moved around them, trying to glimpse whatever it was, assuming it to be one or two of the officers speaking with her son, trying to calm him and figure out exactly what happened to him, but they effectively formed a human barricade that kept her locked out. It was a deterrent, but not much of one. She was small, she was agile, and more importantly, she was a mother desperate to see her child. A few people standing in her way would be no obstacle at all.

She managed to maneuver her way almost to the front of the group before one of the uniformed officers finally noticed she was not a cop or a paramedic. With no real surprise, she saw it was the same cop who first encountered her in the parking lot, while her hysteria was reaching its peak.

"Missus Weaver," he said, putting his hands on her shoulders and attempting to steer her in the other direction. "Don't go over there. Let's you and me go sit down so we can talk."

She saw a pair of plain-clothes detectives standing near one of the dumpsters talking with someone dressed in a paramedic's uniform. A stock boy from the grocery store sat against the wall beside the dumpster, his head between his knees as he hyperventilated. She saw them all, and noted them, but her attention remained drawn to the open door in the side of the dumpster and the swatch of cloth she could see inside it. It was blue and white striped, the same shade as the one her son had been wearing when the left the house this morning, but while similar, there were hints of something else that made it hard for her to tell if it was his shirt or not.

With some effort, she shrugged out of the policeman's grip and hurried away from him before he could grab her again. She was dimly aware of his footsteps on the pavement behind her, the low mummer of the crowd behind them, the panicked breathing of the stock boy, and the whispered conversation of the two detectives and the paramedic, but all of that was in her periphery. Her focus was on that small scrap of cloth and whatever seeing it there might mean.

As she moved closer, more of the cloth came into view. She had been right that it was a shirt, and from the shape of it, there was something inside of the shirt. Large splotches of dark red came into view spattered across it, practically soaking what would be the neck and chest if her perspective was right. Her heart was slamming against her ribs, she was struggling to catch her breath, and her stomach felt as though a lead weight had been planted directly in the middle of it. She did not want to see more—she had to see more. She had to know. One way or another, she had to know.

When she saw the ragged tear across that little neck, her vision went hazy. When she saw that familiar face above the slash, once so sweet and loving, now a mask of pain and terror, the world went dark, the echo of her agonized screech following her into the black.

He wasn't even aware he had fallen asleep until he awoke to the sound of her screaming. Bradley fought the near-overwhelming disorientation at going from sound asleep to wide awake in an unfamiliar place and came close to flipping the recliner he was stretched out on when he got to his feet. As it was, he banged his shin pretty good on the metal support for the extended footpad as he scrambled to the couch where he could see Kat thrashing in her sleep as her screams continued.

He knelt next to her and reached out to wake her from whatever nightmare she was having, then stopped when he caught sight of her face in the flickering light of the television screen. Her eyes were open, staring at nothing at all, her face a rictus of pain and fear. He knew this look, had probably worn it himself from time to time since returning from his stint in the Marines. This was no normal nightmare—this was a full-scale night terror. The emptiness in her eyes seemed familiar. He'd seen it before, in guys he'd served with. Those times, it was caused not by imagination, but by memories.

Anyone who had been in the military and served in a combat zone understood the reality of Post-Traumatic Stress Disorder. What he saw on Kat was quite possibly a full-scale example of what it could do to someone.

Knowing what it was and having dealt with it himself from time to time meant that he had some idea of how to handle it now. He gently but firmly took hold of her wrists, stopping her arms from flailing about wildly and running the risk of hurting either herself or him. He leaned close, not so much that she would panic when she came out of this, but enough that he could speak in a soft voice and she could hear him. He could smell her sweat, filled with fear, and a hint of something sharper, more pungent beneath it. He was not about to check, but he was fairly certain her bladder had let go at some point during this episode. It didn't matter. She would be embarrassed afterward, but that was a concern for then, not now. At this moment, he had to help her back to the real world, the here and now where whatever it was that caused such a reaction in her was gone and done.

"Kat," he said. "Katherine."

She did not respond, but he thought he could feel her arms settle in their struggle. He shifted his grip so both her wrists were clasped in one of his hands and brushed the matted hair away from her forehead. She was cool to the touch, her skin clammy beneath his fingers. She was in shock, closing in on catatonia. He needed to figure out a way to snap her out of it, fast.

"It's not happening anymore, Katherine," he said, adding just a hint of forcefulness to his voice to try to break through the barrier of her tortured mind. "You're not there anymore. You're safe, in your house, on your couch. You're not wherever you think you are. I couldn't be talking to you if that's where you were. So come on back, now. Come back to where you're supposed to be. Come back home."

Her body began to tremble all over, the gentle force making it feel like there was one of those old Magic Fingers devices hooked up to the couch. Unaware of how her episodes progressed, Bradley didn't know if this was a good or a bad sign. He elected to take it as the former and pressed on. He looked her in the eyes, though she was as yet incapable of meeting his gaze. Her eyes continued to dart from side to side, still seeing whatever her mind was forcing her to relive.

"Katherine," he continued, adding more authority into his voice. "You are not there. You're in your house in Poplar Bend, Tennessee. I'm Bradley, and I'm here with you in your living room. You're on your couch, the television is on, and I think I broke your recliner when I tried to come over here and help you out."

Her lips twitched at that as though she wanted to smile but couldn't remember exactly how to make her mouth do so. Definitely a good sign.

"Yesterday was Thanksgiving. We ate dinner together, then you came home. You had an incident here and asked me to keep watch over you tonight. I've got to say, it's hard doing that when you go running off somewhere else in your head, so why don't you come on back here and keep me company?"

The trembles began to ease and when he chanced letting go of her wrists, her arms remained where they were. Her eyes blinked once, twice, a third time, and then drifted closed. Her breathing was still ragged, but it was evening out, no longer the frantic panting it had been.

"That's good," he said. "You keep on coming back. Looks like you're almost here. Just keep coming."

She sucked in a deep breath and her eyes fluttered open again. This time, they locked onto his face, confused but aware. Then she seemed to remember what had possessed her and her face crumpled, tears already forming at the corners of her eyes. She sat up and wrapped her arms around him, sobbing uncontrollably into his shoulder. She was hurting, but the worst was over. She would need help to put herself back into something resembling normalcy again. That was fine. He could do that, too.

For now, he returned her embrace and ran a hand soothingly over her back, whispering what he knew were meaningless words of comfort but unable to stop himself. He held her as she cried and wondered what she had experienced that would leave such a mark on her.

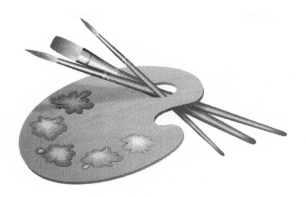

CHAPTER SIXTEEN

The sun was just breaking over the horizon as Katherine poured a cup of coffee for herself and another for Bradley. He held up a hand when she offered the small container of half-and-half, so she topped her mug off with it and took a test sip. It was just the right balance of creaminess and bitterness—perfect. She took a longer, more meaningful sip and then set the mug on the countertop while she began placing things back where they belonged.

She was stalling, knew it as sure as she knew she was breathing, but she was powerless to stop herself. Bradley deserved some answers. The way he calmed her down and helped her get out of that terrible memory earned him those answers, but she didn't know if she was ready to give them just yet. It had been over a year since that horrible Saturday afternoon at the grocery store, and in all that time she had not discussed the events with anyone, not even Dave. She had tried, but it only cemented his contempt of her when she needed his comfort the most. She had also tried once or twice to bring it up with Leslie, but the woman was dead set that she did not need to hear the details. Katherine needed her. That was enough for Leslie.

Still, maybe talking about it would allow her to both acknowledge the event in a way she could not so far, and might even help her find the closure she was sorely lacking. And Bradley was willing to listen; she could see it in his eyes, the way they followed her around the kitchen yet never intruded upon her moment of private reflection. He might not have seen her at her worst, but he hadn't commented or even seemed to care that she had pissed all over herself while she slept. In fact, he pulled her out of a nightmare so vivid it was more like reliving the worst day of her life. He also hadn't run away afterward. In fact, he insisted on sticking around and making sure she was okay.

A part of her was infuriated by this insult to her independence, but deep down she welcomed the sentiment behind it. Dave was months behind her now, and by all accounts he had wasted little time in moving on after her. It was about time she tried to do the same, even if it was a giant leap when it should be a tentative first step.

The kitchen had not been that badly in need of cleaning when she started, so it didn't take her long to run out of things to occupy herself, to keep her from facing him again. She turned back to him, but found she could not hold his eyes. The moment she saw that genuine caring in them, she found she had to look away.

She took another small drink of her coffee to buy herself the last few moments she could, then sighed.

"About last night," she said, and though the phrase would have been funny at another time, under different circumstances, she found even her juvenile sense of humor could not capitalize on the opportunity and pull her out of her despondency. "I suppose you're curious what that was all about."

"I am," he agreed. "But only if you want to tell me. I'm not going to ask, and you should feel free to tell me it's none of my business."

She offered him a small smile. "You've basically seen me pee. I think that reflects a level of intimacy you could argue makes it your business."

He smiled back and didn't point out the obvious: her uncontrolled bladder was not the thing that connected them more intimately than even sex could have. "Let's start with something easy, then. Has that ever happened before?"

"No," she said. "Not like that, anyway. The nightmares come from time to time. I've had those since I was a kid, actually. It was one of the reasons I started drawing and painting. If I had a creative outlet, it helped keep the bad dreams under control. But I've been painting, and they're still coming, so I guess that trick's not going to work anymore. And I've never had one that bad, where I couldn't wake up from it. I've woken myself up screaming more than once, but I've always woken up. This was... different."

"The nightmares when you were a kid," he said, considering. "Were they anything like this one?"

"No," she said again. "They were scary, but there never seemed to be any real reason for them. My mother took me to a doctor once after I complained about them enough. I was maybe seven or eight at that point and had gone through about three weeks of almost constant nightmares every time I laid down to sleep. I was exhausted, which made them worse, I think. Anyway, the doctor said he thought it was just how I was wired. Everyone's subconscious processes things differently when we dream, and it rarely makes any sense. That's why so many people think dreams need to be interpreted or analyzed to figure out why we had them in the first place, or what they're trying to tell us. The truth is—as he said, and as I later learned through my own research—dreams are simply our brain dumping information it no longer needs to process. It could be a collection of things from that day, or that week, or even from the entire year up to the point you have them, and it rarely organizes them into anything resembling normal order. That's why we have such strange dreams at times, or why we'll be with people in a place or time those people could not possibly have been. It's just the brain resetting itself. I guess a modern comparison would be filling the little recycle bin on your computer desktop over a long period, and then trying to read the files while they're being deleted. If you try to put them all together into one thing, it probably wouldn't make much sense."

"I'm with you so far," he said, taking a drink of his own coffee.

"The doctor thought my brain just processed all this information through a darker lens," she continued. "It wasn't the product of anything going on around me, it was just a part of my nature. This freaked my mother out, as you could guess, and it did me as well to tell the truth. But when I didn't grow up to be a psychopath or anything, she let up and I stopped worrying. Like I said, I ended up dumping some of that on my own through art, so it never got run through that dark filter. Since I grew up with them, I guess I kind of got used to them, too. Does that make sense?"

He nodded. "I was in the Marines, and some of those guys who had been in for a while and had seen a lot of combat action were a little scary. They had been around death and killing so much, it wasn't even something they noticed anymore. I suppose anyone can get used to anything if they're exposed to it enough. I take it the nightmares came back not long after you moved here?"

She thought about this, then shook her head. "They started long before that. They just seem to have reached their peak after I moved. But when they really started getting bad, that was just over a year ago."

"Did anything change then?" he asked. "Something that might have added fuel to the fire, so to speak?"

She nodded slowly, still unable to meet his eyes. "That was when I lost my son."

She sensed more than saw how his body tensed at that briefly before relaxing again. She wondered if he had to force his muscles to un-clench.

"I'm sorry," he said softly. "I never knew you had a child."

"His name was Tommy," she said, staring at the swirls of steam above her. "He was five when it…when he was murdered."

He drew in a hissing breath across his front teeth as though her words burned him. In a way, perhaps they had. They burned her heart to say them, so why would they not burn his ears to hear them? Tit for tat, as her grandmother would say.

"Could I ask what happened?" He raised a hand slightly. "If you're okay telling me, that is."

She sighed again. "I suppose I need to tell someone. My best friend back home didn't want to talk about it, I think because in some ways she saw him as part of her own family, too. And Dave, that's my ex-husband and Tommy's father, he heard all he needed to from the cops that night."

Her legs felt loose and wobbly, so she pulled a stool around to the side of the kitchen island and sat down before she collapsed. She had hoped she could remain on her feet to tell this, but it was still too raw, especially in light of last night's episode. She supposed she should consider it a minor miracle she had even said the words without falling down.

"It was right before Halloween," she said, finally looking at Bradley's face. His expression was one of compassion so pure it nearly brought tears to her eyes. She fought them down. There was a distinct probability she would break down before she finished this story, but if she could hold it until she was done, she could feel like she was making progress. "Tommy was in a bad mood because we hadn't been able to track down the costume he wanted for trick-ortreating. I needed to get some groceries, and Dave convinced me to take Tommy with me in case the grocery store had the costume. I argued it would be more of a letdown if they didn't, but Dave had this way of turning me around to his way of thinking with little real effort, so in the end I loaded Tommy up and away we went.

"The store didn't have the costume—some comic book movie character, Thor, I think—but they did have one he suddenly loved even more. Only he didn't want the cheap plastic mask one that was reasonably priced. He wanted the deluxe model that was almost two hundred dollars. There was no way I was about to spend that much on something he would wear once, so I said no. Naturally, that put him in an even worse mood than he had been in before the trip. He whined and complained the entire time we were shopping, and once we finished paying, I guess he realized his chance for that costume was gone, so he really got going.

"I was doing my best to ignore everything—Tommy's screaming, the people staring at me like I was the worst mother in the world because I couldn't get my kid to be quiet, all of it. I turned my back just long enough to put the groceries in the back of the truck, and when I turned around to get Tommy out of the cart, he was gone. I looked everywhere, but couldn't find him. So I started screaming his name over and over again.

"A cop must have been passing by and noticed how panicked I was, or someone told him what was happening, because he came over, got Tommy's name and description from me, and then called it in. Next thing you know, the parking lot is full of cops, all looking for Tommy, none of them finding him."

She closed her eyes and fought the urge to break down. She was trying to stay somewhat detached while she told Bradley the story, but she should have known how impossible that would be. There was no way she would make it to the end before she started crying.

She could already feel tears starting to run down her cheeks. She wiped them away with the back of her hand and continued.

"It was a stock boy from the store who found him when he went to take out the trash. He flagged down a cop who called for paramedics. This got everyone moving, me included. I worked my way through the crowd and looked inside that dumpster and..."

Her voice broke into a loud moan. She closed her eyes tighter and put a hand to her mouth to stop that awful noise, choking as she fought against the overwhelming heartbreak. This was worse than the dreams in a way. Those came without her invitation. The story she was telling was of her own volition. She was subjecting herself to the agony this time around, not her sleeping mind.

When a hand touched her shoulder, she flinched and opened her eyes. Bradley was there, his face expressionless, his eyes filled with sympathy. She doubted he had ever lost a child, but he was a cop, and said he had been a Marine. There was every possibility he had seen others in this situation before, only this time it was someone he actually knew, albeit not that well. It was enough for her, though. She leaned against him and sobbed into his chest while he held her for the second time in as many hours, attempting to soothe her despite her being well beyond such things.

After a while, she collected herself enough to pull away and offer him a grateful smile. She thought she could finish, but she sorely wished she had something stronger she could have put in this coffee first. Then again, she was glad she didn't. Becoming the stereotypical drunken artist who started into the bottle before it was even past breakfast time was not a path she was willing to allow herself to go down.

It felt easier to recite the facts without personalizing them, so that was exactly what she did.

"He was in there, thrown away like someone's old garbage. His throat was cut, and his pants were gone, and..."

"Don't," Bradley said. "I get the picture. Don't put yourself through any more of it than you already have."

"No, you don't," she said. Some of the anger she felt in the days following Tommy's murder bubbled to the surface and she grabbed onto it like a life raft across the sea of her despair. "I'm sorry, but there's no possible way for you to 'get the picture'. Unless you've seen your own son abused, killed, and tossed out with the trash, there's no way you could understand what I saw that day."

"You're right," he said, his voice still firm and calm. "And I won't pretend to. I just mean that I understand the situation was horrible, and probably beyond any words you could use to try and explain it. But there's no way I could fully comprehend what you were dealing with, then or now, so there's no point in tearing yourself up trying. I wasn't trying to insult you by saying I understood what you felt, only that I don't want you to make it worse *now*."

She closed her eyes again and took several deep breaths, calming herself. She already knew what he was trying to say before he explained it, but there was no way she could make him understand why she needed to be angry at someone, *anyone* in order to get through this.

"Did they ever get him?" he asked. "The bastard that did it. Did they ever catch him?"

His voice said he already knew the answer, but somewhere deep inside her mind she understood he was directing her anger onto the target that deserved it. She opened her mouth but found she could not speak the words, so she closed it and shook her head.

"That fucking monster's still out there, somewhere," she said. "Probably doesn't even remember Tommy at all, or what he did to him."

Bradley looked as though he wanted to comment, but remained silent and still to give her the chance to move on without his prompting. Considering the way she had bitten his head off already, it was probably the wisest choice he could make.

"Dave blamed me, of course," she said, remembering the look on her ex-husband's face after the police left their house that night. He had looked so lost, so broken, and so angry, and that anger had only grown whenever he turned his eyes on her. "He didn't say so, not at first, but he finally told me so. It was about two weeks after Tommy's funeral. We were sitting in the kitchen, eating some tasteless leftovers someone had given us when he looks up and says 'you should have just bought the costume, then none of this would have happened. You could have stopped it, but it was easier to let him die.' It was the first unprovoked thing he'd said to me since I left for the grocery store with Tommy, and I was too shocked to fully comprehend what he'd even said. I didn't say anything back, I just remember staring at him, shocked and hurt. He stood up and threw his plate into the sink so hard it shattered, then left the room. He moved out the next day."

"What an asshole," Bradley grumbled. "You needed him, and he needed you, too, even if he was too damned stupid to realize it."

She nodded. "True, but remember that they had no suspects, and it was looking more and more like they wouldn't catch the person responsible. He had to blame someone, and he chose me. I'm not defending him, and believe me, he did plenty enough during the divorce proceedings to make me hate him, but at least that first shot I could understand. Well, now I can. At the time, it hurt almost as much as losing Tommy, and I was more than happy to see him go.

"As the days and weeks passed with me alone in the house, seeing memories of both of them everywhere I turned, that hurt just got worse and worse. I actually thought about killing myself at one point, about four months later. Then I realized Tommy wouldn't want that, and if I did it, it meant that bastard who killed him won everything. He killed one little boy, but two people effectively died. I refused to let that happen. I decided no matter what, I would make my life mean something. I would live because my son no longer could. The next day, I got a check in the mail. I had signed Tommy up for a life insurance policy through my job. I'd forgotten all about it since Dave had done the same thing and that was the money we used to pay for…everything afterward, but here it was, staring me in the face. I felt like Tommy was telling me he *wanted* me to make a fresh start, *wanted* me to live for him. He always loved my painting, would sit quietly and watch me the rare times I tried after he was old enough to understand it. He even had his own little easel set up next to mine. Sad to say, but his got more use than mine did. I was so wrapped up in 'the real world' that I never found the time to go back to the art I loved so much.

"I didn't need much more prompting. I called that same day and quit my job, then went out and deposited the check and bought some paints and supplies. I tried for a couple of weeks, but nothing happened. Then I realized with so many memories of Dave in that place and all the negative connotations that now held for me, there was no way I could truly start over. I went looking around on the internet, found this house for such a cheap price, and thought if there was ever a place that would allow me to focus on painting again, it would be one like this. A house that was back out in the woods, secluded, close to civilization but far enough away I wouldn't have to worry about it intruding on me. So I bought it sight unseen and here I am."

Bradley was smiling when she finished, and Katherine was a little surprised to realize she was as well.

"Good for you," he said at last. "You were right, you know. If you gave up, the bastard won. You didn't, and you refused to let what happened to Tommy consume you. That's a good thing, Kat, whether you believe that right now or not."

"It's hard to," she admitted. "Considering the nightmares and what you saw last night."

She bit her lip as she looked at him, considering. He had not run away after hearing her story, and actually seemed more relaxed than she expected him to be. Most people who learned she had a son who was murdered either treated her with syrupy sweet sympathy or were too nervous to even form a coherent sentence around her. Bradley was different, though. He simply accepted it as a part of who she was, and by extension, accepted her. With everything that had been happening to her since she moved here, she needed someone she could talk to, someone she could trust. Bradley might actually be willing to help her through it, and he had a distinct advantage over Leslie: he was here, she was not.

"Can I ask you something?" she asked. "And you not think I've lost my mind?"

"I guess so," he replied, shrugging. "I'll give it a shot, anyway."

"What do you know about this house?" she asked, her eyes narrowing as she gauged his reactions. "It's history, I mean."

He shrugged. "Not a lot, really. I moved here with my parents my senior year, then left for the Corps after graduation. I just came back a couple years ago. Why?"

She sighed and decided to go for broke.

"Because I wasn't completely honest with you or Marshal Bradshaw last night," she said. "There was more to it than what I told you. In fact, there's been a lot of things I've seen and heard and experienced since I moved here that don't make a lot of sense, last night just being the most recent of them. I'm starting to think all the rumors about this house are right. I think it really might be haunted."

She expected him to laugh or scoff or arrest her for being crazy or something, but he did none of those things. Instead, he studied her eyes before leaning closer.

"I'm not saying you're right," he said, choosing his words carefully. "But I'm not saying you're wrong, either. I can't promise I'll believe you, but I'll hear you out. Tell me more."

It wasn't all she hoped for, but it was a start. She refilled their coffee, and in the end, she told him everything.

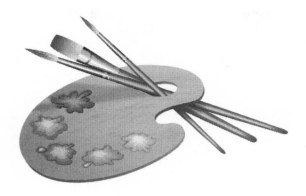

CHAPTER SEVENTEEN

Frank was a little surprised to see Bradley walk through the office door, more surprised even when he saw his deputy had gone home to change at some point. It was only ten in the morning, and if the man had stayed up all night watching over Kat, he should be ready to crash right about now. Yet, here he was, not in uniform but what he sometimes jokingly called his "undercover outfit" of a long-sleeved button-down blue shirt and khaki pants. He wore something similar on the rare occasions they had to go to court down in the county seat or when asked to attend meetings with the mayor and the town recorder.

He started to smile and give the younger man some gentle ribbing about spending the night with such a lovely young—and single—woman as Kat, but the expression on Bradley's face held him at bay. Obviously the man was thinking about something troubling, which made some sense under the circumstances but was still strange to see since the deputy was usually so composed.

"What's going on Bradley?" he asked, setting down his pen and turning his full attention to the man. "Don't tell me our peeping Tom showed back up last night."

"No," Bradley replied, shaking his head. "Nothing like that. Tell the truth, I don't think there was a peeping Tom in the first place. I think it was just someone trying to scare her, make her think the rumors about the house being haunted were true."

That caught Frank's attention for several reasons. The one that worried him the most was that he should have thought of it sooner, seeing how it was a likely scenario. The problem was any potential culprit in that case wouldn't be one of the local kids like Bradley thought, but someone considerably older. Someone with a reason the deputy wouldn't know about. Frank wished *he* didn't know about it.

"What makes you say that?"

Bradley appeared to consider the question, which to Frank meant he already had some conclusive evidence he just wasn't comfortable sharing. It was starting to look like his deputy was sweeter on that woman than Frank had given him credit for.

"Just some of the things she told me," Bradley said slowly, as though he were making sure he did not give away more than he wanted to in the words he chose. "She's had...well, let's just call it a rough year or so before moving here. She's pretty fragile, even if she doesn't act like it. If someone tried something like that, it wouldn't be a hard sell on her."

Frank sighed and shook his head. "Look, I get it. You don't want to tell me all her secrets, that's fine. But I can't do nothin' to help her if I don't know nothin' about what's goin' on. You got to give me somethin' here."

It was Bradley's turn to nod. "I know, you're right. I'm trying not to speak out of turn. She confided some things, but all that's relevant is that she's been seeing and hearing strange things since she moved in there, and last night was the worst of it so far. I don't think she had anybody spying on her last night, but I do think someone's trying to scare her out of there."

Bradley had given him something all right, but it was nothing Frank could work with. Still, he didn't want to push the deputy too hard. If the man truly was starting to feel for Kat, the last thing Frank wanted was to screw that up for either of them. He just had to trust if it was important enough, Bradley would tell him, and if he said nothing, it wouldn't be anything useable, anyway.

"Fair enough," Frank said at last. "Just answer me this, then. When she told you about the stuff she'd seen and heard, did you believe her? Tell the truth, now. You mightn't think it matters, but it does."

"Truthfully?" Bradley replied. "I don't know. Some of it was, I don't know, a little out there. But I believe *she* believes it, if that helps."

"It does," Frank said. "Not sure how just yet, but it feels like it does."

"She asked me if I knew anything about the place's history," Bradley said. "I told her I didn't, which is true enough since all I know are the rumors I've heard since I moved back here. You know anything about it?"

"I know the previous owner killed himself on the front porch," Frank said. "That's about it."

It was a lie, but one he didn't think Bradley would pick up on. Any other day, maybe, when he was fully rested and his mind wasn't on other things, but not today. He hated lying to his deputy, but beyond the instinctual nature of it, born the night his daddy told him the God-awful truth about that house, it was better to keep a man as pure and earnest as Bradley in the dark about certain things. Hear no evil, see no evil maybe.

Frank believed in evil. He believed in God, and if He existed, it only made sense the other side of the coin would exist as well. By extension he believed in the Devil. The Bible talked about people being possessed, so that was possible, too, even if it was something he didn't think had been seen since those long-ago days when Jesus walked the Earth. But he had seen nothing to make him believe that a place, a physical building made of brick and wood and stone could be where such evil things lived. After all, the Bible pretty much said the Devil was a fallen angel bent on corrupting and influencing mankind, of whom he was so jealous he questioned God Himself and got kicked out of Heaven. Nowhere in there did it indicate he was a real-estate mogul stockpiling getaway houses outside of Hell.

If the administrative efforts of running eternal Purgatory were anything like the ones involved in running a small town's police department, when would he have the time, anyway?

The way his Daddy talked, if there were a place where old Satan *would* set up shop on Earth, it was Alston House. Frank remembered that miserable night, the stink of antiseptic as Daddy lay on his deathbed and confessed those terrible secrets. Max Bradshaw had been a proud man, but the heart attack that reduced him to nothing and claimed his life not even a full day later had stripped away his pride. It left him with a burning need to make his son understand the what's and why's of things, even if they came along with his final breaths. In the ten years since then, Frank never had cause to feel any concern about the things his father told him.

Not until now, at any rate.

"What're you thinkin'?" he asked, more to distract himself than hoping to learn something useful.

"I don't know yet," Bradley said. "Maybe some local kids thought it'd be funny, then things got out of hand, something like that. They probably won't be back to try again, but it couldn't hurt to ask around some, put a little fear into them that they nearly got caught. Reinforce the idea it would be a bad idea to keep it up."

Frank fought the urge to narrow his eyes in suspicion at his deputy. Such a plan would accomplish exactly jack shit in the long run, and he was sure Bradley knew it. Kids would be kids, and the threat of getting busted would only make it that much more exciting for the kind that would try to scare a woman living on her own. The only reason Frank could think of for the man to even suggest such a thing was if he wanted the case to collect dust and never actually get solved. And the only reason he might want *that* would be if he believed more of what Kat told him than he would admit.

If that was how he wanted to play it, that was fine by Frank. If something else like this happened out there, it could always be revisited then. And truthfully, it was unlikely the case would get solved as it stood, anyway.

Frank had his own idea about who might be responsible, even if it wasn't anything he could prove or felt like discussing with Bradley. The man hadn't been born here, after all, and to many of the old-timers in town the deputy was still something of an outsider. What Frank was considering would fall under a local matter to that ilk. If he involved someone else, especially an "outsider", those old bastards would just clam up and ignore him altogether.

"Sounds good to me," he said. "You goin' to start on that, or you want me to do it?"

"It's nothing major," Bradley said. "I can handle it, unless you'd rather be the one…"

Frank held up a hand to stop him. "I have every faith in you to deal with it. I'm up to my ass in paperwork, anyway. For such a small town, the place goes absolutely batshit between Thanksgiving and Christmas with all the parties and decoratin' and such. Much as I'd like to trade with you, I'd rather not make you quit on me just yet."

Bradley smiled. "I bet. Who'd help you out with the high school home games once football starts back next year? But if you don't need me right now, I'm going to go get started on that, then take a nap. I promised Kat I'd stop by tonight to check on her."

"Ooo," Frank said, allowing himself the teasing he intended before. "Two dates in a row, sounds serious to me. Wait 'til Beth hears she was wrong."

Bradley laughed and chose not to respond, which told Frank he was close to the mark. Still, once Bradley left his good-natured smile faded as the realization of how irritated he was liable to become over this new development sank in. He supposed he could put it off, but it was better to go ahead and get it over with. If he didn't, there was a chance the ones responsible might end up trying something worse than just throwing rocks at the woman's windows next time.

If that was all this was. He didn't want to consider the other possibility. Not yet.

When he was sure Bradley was well on his way to wherever he was going, Frank stood and left his office, making sure to lock the door behind him. Normally he would leave it unlocked since Elizabeth would be inside answering phones or helping him with the paperwork or something along those lines, but she was off in Murfreesboro doing some Black Friday shopping for God-knew-what and would not be home until late tonight.

The weather was relatively nice today, cool without freezing him half to death, so he elected to walk the short distance and leave his truck in its reserved space outside the station door. Nothing in this town was far from anything else, except big city aggravations.

It didn't take long to find himself in the parking lot to Davison Grocery. It was deserted, as it usually was nowadays, other than Clayton Davison's beat-up old truck. Much as his wife had back when she had been in good enough health to run the place, the old man never took a day off other than Sunday when they were closed, and Christmas which he once said was only proper for the Lord's birthday. He had even been open for a few hours yesterday, wisely thinking if somebody needed some last-minute thing for

Thanksgiving dinner, they were not about to spend all that time driving into Murfreesboro to try to find a place that was open when he was right up the road from them. Frank thought it had more to do with the fact those same people would gladly pay inflated prices just to not go without that one key ingredient on the biggest cooking day of the year, but that was between Clayton and his customers.

The man was in his accustomed spot behind the single register, a lit cigarette dangling between two fingers and the daily paper spread out across the bagging area in front of him. He looked up at Frank but offered nothing in the way of greeting other than a surly grunt before going back to his paper.

"Morning, Clay," Frank said, walking over to stand across the counter from him. "How's business?"

"It's shit," the old man replied, not bothering to look up. "Just like t'always is. Goddamned chain stores runnin' us decent folk right into the poorhouse."

"Sorry to hear that," Frank said, and meant it. The only reason he didn't shop at Clayton's store more was because Elizabeth did all the shopping, not him. Still, he dropped in a couple of times a week to pick up something for lunch, or a drink. It wasn't much, but at least he felt like he was supporting a local institution.

"That'n a dollar'd buy me a cup a' bad coffee," Clay said, taking another long drag from his cigarette. "You need somthin', Marshal, or you just feel like wastin' both our time today?"

Frank sighed, suddenly remembering the other reason he didn't shop here more often. It was tough to want to return somewhere the owner made you feel more worthless than the manure out in the nearby pastures. "You seen Katherine Ransom lately? The one what bought the old Alston House?"

"Yep," Clay said, somehow turning the page on the paper without burning it with the cigarette still clenched in his fingers. "Came in two, three days back to restock on some a'them local preserves over yonder. Guess she reckons buyin' local made lets her fit in. Still an outsider, don't matter what she buys, but I don't 'spect no city folk to know better."

"Seems she had a speck of trouble out at her place last night," Frank said, nodding. "Somebody threw somethin' at her window, busted it up real good."

"Ain't that a cryin' shame?" Clay asked, deadpan. "There a point to this yarn?"

"Best me and Bradley can figure, it was a chuck of marker stone from that graveyard down behind her house used to do it," Frank continued. "Damnedest thing."

Clay looked like he was still reading the paper, but Frank could tell he was paying attention, even if he wasn't looking at him yet. He was sure that would change soon enough.

"My deputy stayed out there with her, got her talkin'," Frank said, watching Clay closely. "He seems to think somebody's tryin' to scare her off. Some kid tryin' to prove the place really is haunted or some such nonsense. You happen to hear anything like that?"

"Nope," the old man said, and was that a slight tremble in his voice? "Any idea which'n a'them Alston's it was had their marker broke?"

"Not yet," Frank said. "I was thinkin' about takin' a ride over this afternoon, maybe hike down there and take a look. I'm bettin' whoever it was may've left some clues down there, help me narrow down who to go after. Could be they got careless."

"May have," Clay said. "But that ain't why you's here, jawin' at me 'bout it. Come out with it, Marshal. Say your peace."

"No peace to say, really," he said. "Just got to thinkin' it don't sound like somethin' a kid would pull. They'd go for somethin' out of some scary movie, or knock on the door and run or somethin' minor like that. Actually bustin' a window? That's serious right there. That's the kind of thing might be done by somebody tryin' to make her up and leave, not some kid pullin' a prank. The kinda thing might be done by those what don't care none for change."

"Folk like me," Clay replied, looking up at him for the first time. "That what you're sayin', Marshal?"

"Not a'tall," Frank said, shaking his head. "I'm not about to go around accusin' nobody when I got nothin' to back it up. I'm just spitballin' is all."

"Well, lemme fill you in," Clay said, stubbing out the cigarette and getting up from his stool. "If'n I wanted to scare that woman off, all I gots to do is fill her in on that den of evil she done up and bought. She'd be packed and gone 'fore the sun was up the next mornin'. And you done lost your damn mind you think I'm up for dumbass hijinks like throwin' shit at winders at my age. 'Sides that, you know well as I do scarin' folk off from out the Hollow's the last thing needs doin'."

"Like I said," Frank said, not dropping his gaze from Clay's. "I'm just spitballin'. I know you and some'a your buddies don't care much for anybody moves into that old place. Figured if one of you wanted to pour some salt in the wound, that'd be a good way to do it."

"We don't like 'em on 'count no local ever gonna move in there," Clay replied. "Just damn outsiders, and we got enough sense to know it was outsiders started this damned mess in the first place. Which'n you'd have too, had your daddy told you proper 'bout the place."

"Well, I guess he didn't," Frank said. He was normally even-keeled when it came to his temper, but this old fart's thinly veiled insult to his daddy got his hackles up. Besides, Daddy made it clear he was to keep what he was told to himself. Frank was sure some of the other old coots around town knew, but he saw no real reason to confirm that fact to this arrogant son of a bitch. "Why don't you fill me in, seein' how you're so smart?"

Clay studied his face, then shook his head and sat back down before pulling another cigarette from the battered pack in his breast pocket and lighting up. "Time for that done passed, Marshal. Anything I told you, you'd just end up arguin' with me over it. You really wanted to know, you'd've asked your pappy 'fore he died. Educatin' you proper was his place, not mine. Dead or not, I ain't about to step on his toes. He pussy-footed around what he told you 'bout that old place down the Hollow, ain't no reason I should clear it up. You really think I done it, you go on and arrest me for it. Kinda want to see how far you think you'd get with that one, tell the truth. If not, we're done with this. I got a business to run, case you ain't noticed."

Frank should have expected the old man would shut down completely if he pushed too hard, but he had been too irritated with him to consider things that far ahead. It had risen up and bitten him on the ass, just like Daddy warned him it would if he lost his temper. Not that it really mattered. He had learned enough from Clay's body language to decide the old man had nothing to do with it, anyway. It didn't rule out some of the other old-timers Clay was buddied up with, but if one of them was responsible, Clay knew nothing about it, despite that strange tremor that had briefly come into his voice when Frank mentioned the thing used to break the window had been part of a grave marker.

"I reckon you do," Frank said, nodding. "You hear anything, you let me know."

He turned and walked away, but stopped at the door when Clay called out to him.

"Marshal."

Frank turned around and looked at him, barely managing to cover his shock at the unfamiliar look of what might have been compassion that had come over the man's face.

"I might not care for that woman none," Clay said, and for once his voice did not carry its normal harshness. "And I 'specially don't much care for nobody what thinks they can turn that shit house into somethin' somebody might consider a home, but that don't mean I wish no ill will on her. You keep a watch on her, you hear? You hear 'bout more strange goins on there, you pay close attention. Your Daddy wasn't no bad man. Little hard-headed, maybe, but all us who get on in years get like that. We just grew up in a different time's all. He had his reasons for not tellin' you all 'bout that place, and I got to respect that. All I'll say is that place is just flat *wrong*, and ain't no other way t' put it. You just mark me, Franklin Bradshaw. You watch that city girl and try not t'think she's off her nut she comes to you with some story sounds made up. You just might find it ain't, but you might find it too late to help her out."

He always suspected Clay and his Daddy never got along well, and hearing confirmation the old man believed Frank knew nothing about that place only reinforced that suspicion. Stranger, though, was that from the way he was talking it seemed like he was trying to make amends for what he said earlier. It was the nicest he had ever heard the old man talk to anyone, much less someone that was not part of his own generation. It meant something, but Frank was clueless as to what. Since asking the old man would be pointless, especially in light of what he said about respecting his Daddy's wishes, he simply nodded and left the store.

As he made the walk back to his office, Frank realized what that tremor in Clay's voice meant. It had taken the man's last expression and his parting words for it to click in his mind.

That tremor and the look in his eyes when Frank left had both been from fear.

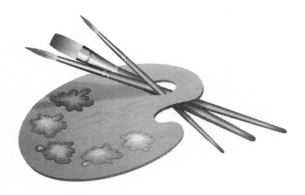

CHAPTER EIGHTEEN

The evening started out so well. Bradley stopped in for dinner and then stayed for a while afterward to have a glass of wine with her. Katherine even thought they would share their first kiss, but he had excused himself after nothing more than a lingering hug. It was something of a relief, actually. As long as it had been for her, and as close to him as she felt in such a short amount of time, it would still be moving much too fast. Had they kissed, she was sure it would have been nice, but she wasn't so sure she would not have ended up regretting it. That was not something she wanted to deal with after the disaster her relationship with Dave had become.

And by showing what a gentleman he really was, Bradley made her like him even more.

All of this left her feeling rather content and satisfied once he left and the dishes were all loaded into the dishwasher. She forgot about the incidents last night for a little while and actually felt like she was living her life again. It was a welcome change from the way things had been over the course of the last year, and the first time since signing the divorce papers she hadn't felt Tommy looming over her, holding her down. Instead, she felt as though he stood at her side, encouraging her, doing exactly what she hoped for when the decision was made to try to move on in another place.

Then she noticed the house was starting to feel decidedly colder than it had been earlier in the day, colder even than it had been when she came home last night. She checked the thermostat and frowned when she saw it was still set to nearly eighty degrees. She adjusted the dial to its maximum setting of eighty-five and waited but heard no corresponding thump from the boiler kicking on downstairs.

She moaned and shook her head. The last thing she needed right now was for her heating system to go out just as the weather took a turn toward winter temperatures. True, she had been toying with the idea of having the entire system replaced and updated to a more modern central heating and air unit, but she had very nearly decided to wait a while longer and see how the older one held up through the coldest part of the year. It would be much easier to make such a time-consuming change once spring arrived, and the weather became tolerable enough to go without a furnace or an air conditioner for a while. Still, if it would happen, she supposed it was better to get it out of the way now before it really got too cold to live in without aid. If she had to, she could just run into Murfreesboro and pick up some standalone heaters for the rooms she commonly used until the replacement could be ordered and installed, but that was an added expense she had not foreseen. The repair bill on this house was starting to spin wildly out of control, and if she ended up running out of money before everything was finished, she would be in trouble. There was no way any bank would approve her for a loan without a dependable source of income, which would make matters worse.

The more she considered it, the more the solution became obvious. She wasn't anticipating using the second floor much anytime soon, so she could just have the contractor do some basic work to ensure the bathroom and a single bedroom were functional enough for use. If anyone visited with a need to stay overnight, that's all they would need to be comfortable, anyway. It would save her a good deal of money, even if she upgraded the house's heat and air situation, and could be completed once she had something more to spend on it. Besides, after her previous encounter on that floor, she had no real desire to spend any amount of time there at all, not until she could figure out what was going on and either put a stop to it or learn how to control and deal with it.

Telling Bradley about everything had been a risk, but it was one that seemed worth making. He believed her—at least from what he said to her personally—and was willing to help her look into it. He had found no success so far, but since Katherine had expected nothing this soon, it was not a real concern. She was a little surprised he had got Frank to let him handle investigating the incident with her window being broken alone, though. From what she surmised, the marshal was not one to let something like that slide so easily. Then again, Bradley had earned her trust in a relatively short time, so he obviously had a way of dealing with people that fostered that. Thankfully, the man chose to use his powers for good, not evil. If it had been the other way around, she was liable to have found herself in bed with him tonight, wondering when on earth she had become so easy.

But that was a concern for another time. Right now, she had a non-working furnace to deal with.

She sighed and collected a flashlight from the kitchen before heading down into the basement to make sure the boiler wasn't about to explode or anything. Her contractor had been nice enough to explain some of the basic maintenance procedures to her, so hopefully whatever was going on was something minor she could fix herself, rendering her entire concern moot. She would still upgrade to a newer unit, just so she would no longer have to worry about it, if for no other reason, but she could do it on her own terms, not because of dumb bad luck.

The light down here worked. It wasn't very bright, was actually only a single bare bulb hanging in the middle of the room, but it was something. It was eerie, though, how it created more shadows than it banished when it was on. She knew that was only natural, but combined with everything else, it made the house seem even creepier than it had when she first drove up and saw it.

She shivered as she crossed the room to the corner where the furnace and boiler sat and realized it was not the colder air down here that caused it. She was freaking herself out over nothing. This was only a basement, same as the ones she had seen before. More so, it was *her* basement, not the one for the local haunted house.

Of course, she *was* living in the local haunted house. Once the thought crept into her head, it wouldn't go away. She laughed bitterly. She was trying to make herself feel better, but had instead made things worse. Story of her life.

It only took a quick glance to see what the problem was. For some reason, the main control for the gas line had been shifted to the "off" position. It was strange, and Katherine could not for the life of her figure out how it had gotten to be that way without someone actively moving it, but there it was. Maybe one of the construction crew had been down here for something and turned it on accident. Maybe they had turned it off while installing the new appliances in the kitchen and didn't turn it back on all the way when they left. It made no sense, but there it was.

She reached out and turned the handle. She heard the faint hiss of gas rushing back into the boiler which suddenly ignited with a massive "whump" that caused her to jump backward, trip over her own feet, and land squarely on her ass. She couldn't help but laugh. If she kept falling like this, her bottom would end up so bruised she could not even sit down. She rolled over and got to her feet, reaching out for where she thought the flashlight landed when it slipped from her hand.

Her eyes locked on something across the basement, a shadow that seemed somehow deeper than the others around it. Once she got ahold of the light again, she turned it on and shined it at that strange shape. From here, it looked like nothing more than a blank patch of wall, but for some reason part of it was set further back than the rest, almost as though it had been a doorway at one time. If that was the case, there was a chance there was still more to this house than she had been led to believe. She crossed over to it and ran a hand across the wall, noting how it felt like something here had been bricked up. It was old, but it didn't appear to be as old as the brick around it. So not part of the original basement, but added later. More evidence to support the idea of another room being down here.

New room or not, there was no way she would get inside it right now. She lacked the tools and the strength it would require to use them to break through that wall. For all she knew, if she broke that part down, the rest of the house might just fall in on top of her. She would end up another part of the legend, the young woman who ended up buried alive when the house collapsed, so deeply entombed that her body had never been recovered. An interesting thought, but not anything she wanted to put to the test. It would be hard to appreciate the newfound celebrity if she were too dead to enjoy it.

She made her way back upstairs, reminding herself to ask the contractor about breaking down that barricade when she saw him on Monday. If he didn't want to charge her too much for it, she would just have him do it. If the price was too high, she would ask Bradley about it sometime, see if maybe he had any ideas how to get it down. That might even be better; the two of them could explore it together.

The house already felt warmer by the time she got back to the main floor. She adjusted the thermostat back down to the mid-seventies where she hoped it would do its job properly now that the gas flow was no longer restricted and returned the flashlight to its normal spot in the kitchen drawer closest to the room's entrance. She glanced at the clock on the stove and was shocked to see it was almost midnight. She supposed it made sense. Bradley left just before eleven, but she did not know she had spent an hour getting things put away and fixing the heat in the basement. She had given thought to getting the last glass of wine and heading up to her studio to work on the painting of Frank and Elizabeth for his combination anniversary and Christmas present, but it was too late for that now. The wine, maybe, but the painting would have to wait until tomorrow. She knew if she got started, she would keep telling herself she could stop once that *one last detail* was done until the sun came up. While she had been fine with skipping Black Friday shopping—as if she had anyone to buy for this year, anyway—she did want to go into Murfreesboro and take advantage of some of the good deals that would continue through the weekend. Maybe she could even find herself a Christmas gift while she was out.

When she thought of Frank and Elizabeth, she realized it would be nice if she got them something as well, something to say "thank you" for the way they had almost instantly welcomed her into their lives as they welcomed her to their town. She did not think Bradley would be buying anything for her this year, but she sort of wanted to get something for him. Something small, and not anything that might scare him off, but just something to say she was thinking about him. Something to keep the spark alive and maybe fan it a bit to make it grow.

She laughed, realizing how out of touch she was when it came to dating. Nearly ten years away from her last first date, and she already acted like it was the most foreign concept imaginable. She knew all she had to do was be herself, but like the teenager she had been years ago, she found that easier to say than to do.

She allowed her mind to wander as she went about turning off the lights downstairs before heading up to her bedroom, trying out potential gifts and either adding them to a list of possibilities or rejecting them outright. Part of the problem was in how little she knew about Bradley, despite how close to him she felt. She knew he was a former Marine who now worked in law enforcement, and that he was good with people. He told her a few minor things over the course of their conversations the last couple days, but beyond that, he was a complete mystery to her.

It was this distraction that kept her from realizing she had wandered down the second-floor hallway to the door where she had seen that strange vision before until she was opening it and stepping inside. She hadn't intended to come here, nor would she have set foot in it again given a choice, but here she was. There was nothing amiss in the room, nothing out of place she could see, only the confusion of what had drawn her here in the first place.

A whimper drew her attention to the corner just behind her. She turned and saw a figure huddled there, as though by curling up as tightly as possible they could keep from being seen at all. The figure was that of a young girl wearing a filthy white nightgown that was several generations out of fashion. Lank, blonde hair hung down her back. One pale eye watched Katherine warily over a stick-thin bare arm.

The dormant mothering instinct within her took over before she could even begin to wonder where the girl came from or why she was here. All that mattered was that a scared child was in her house and in need of comfort. Katherine took a single step forward, stopping when the girl drew more tightly into the corner she hid in. Not wanting to scare the child any more than she already had, Katherine knelt and held out a hand to her.

"Hey," she said, trying to keep her voice soft and as non-threatening as possible. "I'm not going to hurt you. Where did you come from, huh?"

The girl said nothing, only continued to watch her with that single terrified eye.

"It's okay," Katherine said. "You're safe here. It's just you and me, okay? I only want to help."

Katherine thought she saw the girl turn slightly toward her, but it might have only been a trick of the light. Still, she couldn't just let the girl sit there in the corner all night. She needed to get her to come out so she could call Bradley or Frank and have one of them come figure out where she came from and get her back to her own family. She duck-walked forward another step and settled back onto her heels again.

"I'm Kat," she said. "What's your name?"

The girl mumbled something Katherine did not catch.

"I'm sorry, honey," she said. "But you're going to have to speak up a little. I can't hear you when you're talking into your arm like that."

"Lucy," the girl repeated. Her voice sounded weak, and scared, and for some reason as though it were coming from much further away. Something in Katherine's mind leaped on that detail, but she ignored it, focusing solely on Lucy and how to get her to come out of the corner.

"What are you doing in here, Lucy?" Katherine asked, inching another half-step closer. "What are you hiding from?"

The girl shook her head but said nothing. Still, the motion allowed Katherine to see more of her face, enough to realize Lucy could be no more than twelve or thirteen years old. Something about the way she carried herself made Katherine think she should err on the younger side of her estimate. She didn't look like the same girl

Katherine saw the last time she was in this room, which was more of a relief than she would have imagined.

"It's okay, Lucy," she said. "You don't have to tell me anything you don't want to. But you can't stay there all night. You need to get back to your mommy and daddy. I'm sure they miss you."

Lucy shook her head again and mumbled something else, but as before, it was too quiet for Katherine to make out.

"Where are they?" she asked. "I'll go and call them right now, and they can come get you. What's your daddy's name? I'll look him up in the phone book and give him a call."

"Daddy ran off," Lucy said, her voice never rising above a whisper. "Mommy died."

Katherine's brow furrowed at this news. "Then who watches out for you, who takes care of you?"

"Mistress," Lucy replied. Something about the way she said the word added a touch of reverence to it Katherine found both confusing and disturbing. "Mister, too. He says I'm his favorite."

"Well, see there?" Katherine asked, forcing herself to smile despite the unease she was beginning to feel. "If you're his favorite, I'm sure he misses you a lot. Don't you want to hurry and get back to him?"

Lucy shook her head again, more violently this time, and retreated further into her corner. Katherine thought if the girl kept trying to push herself into that spot, she would end up inside the wall itself.

"He'll punish me," Lucy said. "Tonight's my turn. He'll be mad I ran from him."

Katherine frowned. "Your turn for what?"

Lucy did not respond, simply turned her head away and tried to cover it with her arm again. It was all the answer Katherine needed. Whoever this "Mister" was, she had a pretty good guess he had been abusing this girl. Her concern became tinged with fury, and she decided this was no longer something she could deal with on her own. She would go downstairs and call Frank. She knew Bradley would come, and he was liable to be upset she hadn't called him as well, but he needed his sleep. Besides, it could turn out to be nothing. It could be a case of her reading more into the girl's reaction than was really there. If so, she would feel more foolish discovering it with Bradley than if it was the marshal. He would still hear about it, but it wouldn't be the same.

She got to her feet and took a step toward the door. "Lucy, I'm going to go call a friend of mine. He's going to come and help you out, maybe even fix it so Mister won't get mad at you or... do things... to you anymore. Okay?"

The girl made no motion to indicate she even heard what Katherine said. She had returned to her original position, curled in the corner and hiding behind her hair and arm.

Katherine watched her for a moment, then turned to the door. Before she could leave the room, she decided enough was enough. Lucy was not a big girl, and she didn't need to hide from anyone any longer. She was coming downstairs with Katherine, whether or not she wanted to. She turned back, fully intending to pick the girl up and carry her downstairs, then froze in place, her body beginning to tremble all over at the sight that greeted her.

Lucy was no longer there, only a dark patch of what might be either dried blood or urine stain on the old, worn floor boards where she had been sitting.

CHAPTER NINETEEN

The last thing Katherine wanted after yet another night of no sleep was for someone to knock on her front door so early in the morning. That this was Sunday and her last chance to sleep in before the construction crew renewed their work tomorrow only made her more irritable. At first, she tried just lying in bed and ignoring the knocks and the doorbell. Whoever it was appeared to be more persistent at getting her to answer than she was at getting them to give up and go away. After five full minutes of that relentless noise, she realized her only two options were to get up and see who was there or lie here and lose what little mind she had left.

There was a window in the room that overlooked the front of the house, but with a covered porch the only thing she might see from here would be their vehicle. Ultimately, that would do her no good. She hadn't lived here long enough to recognize anyone's vehicles other than Bradley's and the marshal's official truck. She knew Frank owned a personal vehicle, and knew Elizabeth had a car of her own, too, but she did not know what they were. The only way she would figure out who her morning visitor was would be to answer the door.

She finally gave up after the doorbell chimed through her thoughts again. She kicked the covers down to her feet and got out of bed, not even bothering to grab a robe to throw on over her pajamas. Whoever was down there, they would get her as she was. If they got offended or titillated by a woman in a pair of flannel onesie pajamas, that was their problem, not hers.

She paused on her way down the stairs, glancing briefly down the second-floor hallway to the room at the end, the room where she had seen that man molesting a girl last week and then seen a different girl named Lucy last night. Her heart sped up as she remembered Lucy's frightened face, and her words indicating that maybe that same man had been at her as well. It was almost enough to cause Katherine to rush back upstairs and hide under the covers again like she had last night, but she forced herself to keep moving. As if reminding her there were things to do, the doorbell chimed again, followed by the steady beat of a hand against the door.

Whoever it was must have heard her stomping across the floor because the ringing and pounding ceased as she reached the first floor and strode toward the door. She made up her mind if they had given up and walked away just as she was about to see who it was, she would spend the rest of the day hunting them down so she could give them a piece of her mind. She threw the door open hard enough to nearly knock herself off balance, but the rude greeting died on her lips as confusion set in when she recognized her visitor as the old man that ran the grocery store.

"I woke you," Clay said, his eyes passing over her rumpled hair, puffy eyes, and thick nightclothes. "Should outghta knowed I would. Sorry about that."

"It's okay," she said, realizing once the words were out of her mouth that they sounded very much like a question instead of a statement. "I'm sorry, I know who you are, but I don't think you ever introduced yourself."

"Nope," he said. "I was right rude to you first time you saw me, no need to whitewash it. I know I can be an ass, so you ain't gonna offend me none by sayin' so. Clayton Davison. And you'd be Miss Ransom. Now we're acquainted. To the point, we need to talk, you and me."

"No offense intended, Mister Davison," she replied. "But like you said, you were downright rude to me, not only the first time we met but every time I went into your store after that, too. I can't imagine what you think we need to talk about, so if you don't mind, I had a long night and I haven't even had my coffee yet, so..."

"You've seen him, ain't ya?" Clay asked, taking a step toward her and lowering his voice despite the fact they were the only two people around. "He's the one what broke your winder, ain't he?"

Katherine froze in the act of closing the door on the old man and looked up at him sharply. "Seen who?"

Clay sighed. "That old bastard, pardon my language if'n it offends you. The one what's livin' in your house with you, only he ain't exactly what you'd call livin' no more."

"I don't know what you're talking about," she said, but even to her the words felt hollow and spoken only by rote.

"Fine," Clay said. "You ain't seen him. You ain't got nary a clue what I'm yammerin' about. But you ain't gonna stand there and tell me you ain't seen nothin' strange since you moved in this place and do it so I believe you. I might can help you figure it out, but if'n you don't want no help from the likes of me, so be it. I wash my hands of it."

He turned and started to walk away, but Katherine put out a hand and touched his shoulder before he could. She immediately regretted the way she had treated him. Even Frank, the first time they met, told her the old man was rough most times. If she treated him the same way in return, she was no better than he was. Worse, maybe, since he was old and set in his ways and she was supposed to be trying to fit in here.

"Wait," she said. "Please. You're right, I have been seeing weird things. That's why I didn't get much sleep last night, which makes me irritable. I'm sorry."

He turned back around and studied her face for a silent moment before finally offering a nod of understanding. "I reckon I can see how dealin' with livin' here would put somebody in a bad mood. It did that Blackmore fool often enough, no reason you should be any differn't."

She offered him a smile, and even though it felt fake, and even though he didn't return it, she felt like maybe it had helped to break the ice somewhat. She moved out of the doorway and motioned for him to come inside. He studied her again for a moment before nodding once more and entered the house. She led him to the kitchen and offered him a seat at the island counter.

"I wasn't kidding when I said I hadn't had my coffee yet," she said as she moved around the island and grabbed the carafe from the Mister Coffee. "Could I offer you a cup?"

"Don't suppose you got brandy to lace it with, do you?"

She turned and looked at his impassive face, trying to decide if he was joking or not. "I, um, I'm sure I can find something. No brandy, but I might have some whiskey somewhere."

He held up a hand, forestalling her. "Just splash a little milk in it and that'll be fine."

"That I can do," she said, returning to the preparations. "So, you said we needed to talk. Any topic in particular?"

"I'll make a deal with you, Miss Ransom," Clay said, his voice utterly devoid of humor. "You don't play the fool with me, and I won't go treatin' you like one. That sound reasonable to you?"

She gave him a brief look of shock over her shoulder before turning back to the coffeepot. "You don't have much in the way of social graces, do you, Mister Davison?"

"Ain't got time for niceties," he replied. "And God's truth, this country'd be a damn sight better off without 'em. I done gave up on worryin' about offendin' folk a long time ago. That bothers you any, well, ain't much I can say since I ain't all that sorry 'bout it."

"No, it's fine," she said, turning around to face him while the coffee brewed. "It's just going to take some getting used to. So, you wanted to talk about what I've been seeing here, I assume."

"Doubt we'd have all that much else in common," he agreed. "I can't tell you exactly what's happenin', but I can tell you why. You do with that whatever you feel you need to."

"You can tell me why this thing's haunting me?" she asked.

"Ain't what I said," he replied. "Said I can tell you why it's happenin'. It aint' hauntin' *you*, it's just this damned place. Tried to warn you first time I saw you. You didn't listen. Didn't expect you would."

"Okay," she said, nodding. "Then who's haunting this house?"

"My guess?" he asked. "Bunch'a folk. Leastwise there's a bunch'a folk got reason to. The old bastard what's the worst of 'em? If I'm guessin' right, that'd be old Henry Alston, too damn evil for even Hell t'take 'im."

Katherine felt a chill run down her back that had nothing to do with the temperature. "I know that name. I think I saw his grave down at the back of the property, in that little graveyard down the hill."

"That'd be him, yeah," Clay agreed. "Him and his wife was the last Alstons what owned this property. After they…died, the state took it over, then those idjits auctioned it off to that Blackmore fella, then some dumbass city real estate folk bought it, then it went to you. And here we sit."

This was not too far removed from what Katherine had been told when she bought the house, but she still had expected more owners than that in all the years it had been around. Based on what Clay was saying, she was only the second person outside the Alston family to own this house. Considering the way most houses were sold off, fixed up, flipped, then sold again, it was a little shocking.

"The Alstons didn't have any kids?" she asked. "No one to keep it in the family line?"

"Not in the way you're meanin' they didn't," Clay said. "Henry Alston had a passel of young'uns, but didn't a one of 'em want nothin' to do with that ole man, least none'a the ones what lived."

Katherine furrowed her brow. "His kids were estranged from him?"

"They wasn't all that strange," Clay said. "It was him that was the strange one."

"No," she replied, shaking her head. "I mean, his kids didn't talk to him after they grew up and moved out?"

Clay let out a snort of disdain. "You ain't gettin' it. Henry Alston's young'uns didn't grow up and move out. Those who survived the night him and his bitch wife died become wards of the state and was adopted out. A bunch nobody ever found. The rest, well, they's buried out there in the boneyard right next to him, and if that ain't a Goddamned travesty I don't know what is."

Katherine shook her head. "You're not making any sense. Maybe you better start from the beginning."

Clay sighed. "Reckon that'd make it easier. Also reckon I ought to say I'm sorry right up front, since it ain't exactly a tale needs repeatin' in mixed company, but with you livin' here and dealin' with what you prob'ly are, I reckon you better hear it all the same."

The coffeepot chose that moment to beep softly and alert them it was done. She held up a hand for him to wait while she served them, adding a dollop of milk to his before loading hers down with cream and sugar. He gave her a look of disgust while she fixed it, making her think he might wonder whether she wanted a little coffee with her cream and sugar. If so, he kept it to himself. That was fine by her. Joking around like that would probably require a level of friendship with this man Katherine didn't think they would ever have. Once they each had a steaming mug in front of them, she leaned on the counter facing him.

"Okay," she said. "No more stalling. What makes this story so bad? Why do you seem to hate a man so much that you never met, and why do you think he's haunting this house?"

Clay took a sip of his coffee, sat it down on the counter, and met her eyes. "'Cause Henry Alston and his wife raped and murdered God only knows how many young'uns 'fore they was stopped, and you're livin' in the same damn place it happened."

Katherine suddenly found her legs no longer had the strength to hold her.

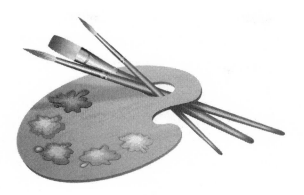

CHAPTER TWENTY

"You remember, most of what I know comes handed down mouth to ear over a lotta years," Clay said, once Katherine took a seat on one of the vacant stools near him. "So I can't promise how true some of it is. But all the evil shit Henry Alston done, them things are fact. You can have that marshal look it up, if'n you're so inclined."

Clay took a long breath, let it out slowly, then began.

"Edward Alston was some important English gov'ment man who was stationed up in Canada 'round the time they rebelled against the British. 'Stead of supportin' his country, though, Alston took advantage of the situation and started pilferin' money and valuable goods from the gov'ment, all the while makin' it look like it was the rebels what was doin' it. Don't nobody really know how much he got, but when he hightailed it to the States sometime after everything was all over and done, he had enough what to buy a good-sized parcel of land and hire men to build a right mansion smack in the middle of it. That'd be the house we're sittin' in now, case you had any wonders about it.

"Ain't much knowed about the Alstons 'til sometime 'round the start of the Civil War. Supposedly some folk tryin' to recruit for the

Confederate Army showed up askin' Alston about him or his son servin' against the damned Yankees, and the old man was supposed to've told 'em that far as he was concerned anybody didn't come from England was a damned Yankee, so they could fight their war without him or his son. That's not to say he didn't do nothin' durin' the war. Alston was always looking for a buck, so he bought him some slaves, told 'em he wanted to help free 'em, and set them recuitin' escapees from the Underground Railroad. Not that he was bein' true to his word, mind. He was turnin' around and sellin' them darkies back to their owners, collectin' a reward for their capture, anything he could do to get paid off the sufferin' of somebody else. Usually, them same slaves ended up shot on the spot, earnin' Alston a smile with his coin. Was durin' this time the whole area back here come to be knowed as Dead Hollow, and that road officially got its first name. Didn't take long for word to spread, even back in them days: you was colored and caught out here in the hollow, you was good as dead.

"Finally old man Alston took his dirt nap, and everything went to his boy, Matthew. By all accounts, Matthew was just as greedy as his old pa, but nowhere near as crooked—least not in how nobody else could see it. Fact is, you look at it an' it seems like Matthew Alston did a lot for this town, but it's all just smoke and mirrors. The man helped build us up, but he was milkin' us dry to do it, all the while makin' it seem as he was puttin' his own money up to do it. He was one what helped write the first town charter and even done a stint as one'a the first town recorders we had. Supposedly there was talk about him trying for mayor, but he never would do it. Probably never wanted to be the one officially in charge, even though 'bout everybody knew he was the one really runnin' things.

"Wasn't 'til he died the Alston family really went to shit, though. That was when his boy Henry got the house and the land and the freedom to do whatever struck his fancy. Most folk thought he might end up bein' a breath of fresh air after his pappy and grandpappy, and he sure tried to make it look true enough. He told that him and his wife couldn't have no kids of their own, so they was gonna use all that space they had to help out young'uns what didn't have nobody else to watch out for 'em. They took in whatever orphan came their way, sayin' they was gonna raise 'em up in the right with God and all sorts of other horseshit that prob'ly sounded like angels singin' to the simple folk livin' 'round here.

"For a while, seemed like he was doin' just what he claimed he was. Even got the town to give him money ever so often to take care of those young'uns. Didn't take long though 'fore things started lookin' wrong. 'Bout every boy what come here ended up disappearin' within the first month or so. Then some of the girls went missin' too. When the marshal at the time came out here checkin' things out, Alston told him he couldn't help some of the runaways what wanted to spend their lives out in the cold rather than conform to the warmth of God's love, or some other such bullshit. From my understandin', didn't nobody believe it, but since they couldn't say what *did* happen, they didn't do nothin' about it. Buncha damn idjits.

"This goes on for a while, new ones comin' in, but the old ones never comin' out. Finally, one of the townsfolk gets wise to somethin' not bein' right and heads out to see what's what. Them and the marshal come out here and tell Alston they want to see them what he's ward over. Alston lets 'em in and has the young'uns come downstairs and line up, neat as you please. Right off the bat, the marshal knows somethin' ain't right. He's lookin' at three girls and two boys, when there outghta be more'n twice that. Add to it, one of the girls looks to be in a family way, though from what I was told her dress was too loose to tell for sure.

"Now that marshal, he means well, but he ain't got the sense God gave a damn billy goat. He asks the girl who the daddy is, right there in front of Alston and his bitch wife. The wife gets offended, as you might guess, and starts ravin' at the marshal over his suggestion that her husband could do such a thing. Somehow the situation gets calmed back down, the girl says it was some drifter found her 'fore she showed up here, and that was the end of that.

"Marshal done blew his chance to get answers 'less he does it by force, which ain't how he chose to do things, so he says thankya very much, sorry to bother ya, and off he goes. That man what was with him followed along, not really havin' much other choice nor no authority to do nothin' even if he chose to stay. T'was on his way out the door the man heard another baby cryin' upstairs. That didn't sit right with him, what since Alston didn't say nothin' 'bout no other babies in the house. He tells the marshal 'bout it, but the marshal's still stingin' where Alston's wife tore into him so he says let it go.

"The man didn't though, and thank God for it. He come back to town and gets some of the older folk what suspect somthin' strange out on the Hollow already and tells them what all happened. They don't much care for it none, neither, and decide if the marshal won't do his duty and take care of it, it falls on them as good, upstandin', God-fearin' folk to deal with it their ownselves.

"Come dark, they gather up and head out the Hollow, meanin' to get the truth and put a stop to any kinda depravity Alston might be up to. Marshal somehow got wind of it and tried to stop 'em, but they told him he could either help, get out the way, or they'd just go through him. He musta had a little sense, seein' as how he let 'em go and just followed along to make sure things didn't go too far. Waste a'time, as it turns out.

"They start poundin' away at the door, but don't nobody answer. After this went on a while, they get more and more fired up over it, more sure somethin' shouldn't be happenin' is takin' place right under their noses. They come around the back and start poundin' away there, too, tryin' to either rouse somebody or break the damn door down, whichever what comes first. Don't know how with all that racket they must'a been makin', but they saw or heard somethin' down back of the property, down toward the little plot where all the other Alstons was planted after they died out. They head that way and don't take long 'fore their suspicions get confirmed.

"Alston hisself was down there, lantern in hand, watchin' as a ten-year-old boy dug up a grave so they could plant the dead baby what was lyin' next to 'em. Once they saw that, well, weren't no contest. Them folk dragged Alston out of there and headed back up the house, determined they was gonna set things right. Way I heard tell, Alston tried to fight back, but once that happened it was good as done. Soon as Alston tried to throw a punch, all thoughts of the law went to shit. Them folk rounded on him and beat him flat to death right there in the damn graveyard. Least he was in the right spot, I reckon.

"Wasn't no knocking this time around. Once they got back to the house, they busted out the back winders and climbed through. They didn't find no sign of Alston's bitch nowhere, then finally they heard whimperin' comin' from down the basement. They got down there, and what I hear was they found a sight that haunted every damn one of 'em 'til their dyin' day.

"What they's supposed to have seen was Grace Alston standin' there covered in blood like she was workin' a slaughterhouse, which I reckon in a sense she was. That other boy the marshal'd seen earlier was layin' there with his throat slit wide open, the girl what was knocked up sprawled right there next to him in the same state. The other two girls was kneelin' down in front of her, tears runnin' down their faces, waitin' their turn to die it looked like. One of 'em was clutchin' a little baby to her chest, beggin' that woman to let *her* little girl live.

"Well, Grace Alston looks up, sees all these folk crowdin' down her basement stairs, and what I heard was she started laughin' at 'em. Said they wasn't gonna take her for doin' what she felt was right, then dragged the blade a'that knife cross her own throat just like she'd done them two kids. They said she was still smilin' as she hit the floor and died once she bled enough.

"By mornin' the whole damn town was in an uproar over it. Questions got asked 'bout why nobody knew such atrocities was goin' on out the Hollow. That marshal damn near got lynched hisself for not tryin' to put a stop to it soon as they suspected somethin' wasn't right. They sent word out to the county sheriff who come out with a buncha other big-wigs and talked to them kids and the ones what did the killin' on old Alston.

"Turns out, them babies was Alston's and his wife was pickin' who he'd be puttin' it to what to try to get 'em knocked up. She was the one what couldn't have no kids, but they wasn't happy with the ones they was gettin'. Least that's what them kids was told. Ask me, I think that old bastard just enjoyed it too much to quit once he had his bastard heir.

"Case was closed after that. State buried 'em out in their family boneyard, them kids what lived was sent to proper orphanages, and the marshal got told to get his ass out of town. Frank Bradshaw's grandpappy was elected to take his place, seein' as how he'd been the one what led that group helped put an end to the Alstons, and Poplar Bend tried to forget 'bout what they'd let happen and even paid for.

"State wouldn't let nobody forget nothin', as it turned out. 'Bout fifteen years later one a'them kids tells some state cop what all went on out here. They sent some folk down to investigate. Ended up diggin' up half the back yard and found more'n two dozen bodies buried out there. Once the town realized it, they voted to have markers put up in that boneyard to memorialize them young'uns what Alston and his wife been killin' for so long. Stupid as hell, want my opinion on it. Put their markers next to those what killed 'em? That's a damn travesty right there. Then vote to change the name on that road, like it'll mean shit to change that. Damn fools, every blamed one of 'em. Didn't even do no good nohow, since from what they was told, they didn't even find all the ones supposed to be killed out here. Just about half, if that. The rest of 'em's still out here somewhere, and everybody done forgot about 'em. Just a few of us what was old enough to get the story while it was still somewhat fresh remember. Won't be long before we'll be gone too, and it'll be like them poor dead kids never even was."

When he remained silent for several moments, Katherine realized his story was finished, or as finished as he could make it. While it explained a lot of what she had seen and experienced since moving in here, there were still some gaps that needed to be filled, still some questions that needed to be answered. Clay might have those answers, but the question became whether or not he would be willing to share them. There was one she knew she could start with.

"I don't know if you'll know," she began. "But was one of the girls found here named Lucy?"

The old man jerked in his seat, his hand shooting out involuntarily to knock his coffee mug to the floor where it shattered. The sound was like a gunshot in the preceding silence.

"Where did you hear that?" he demanded. Despite her first impression, he didn't seem angry at her. Instead, he seemed shocked. "Who told you that name?"

"I..." Katherine said, not entirely sure how to respond. "Last night, I saw a girl upstairs. She was hiding in a corner, and she said her name was Lucy. When I went to call the marshal to come help her out, she disappeared."

Clay looked shaken and his hand was not entirely steady as he raised it to wipe his mouth. "She talked to you? What'd she tell you?"

"Just that her name was Lucy," Katherine replied. She was a little surprised by his vehement reaction. "She said her mother was dead, she had no idea where her father was, and that Mister was coming for her because she was his favorite."

"Sweet merciful Christ," Clay whispered. He had begun to tremble all over and raised a shaking hand to cover his eyes. He stood suddenly and started for the door "I'm sorry 'bout that coffee cup, Miss Ransom, but I need to go."

"Wait!" she cried, getting up and rushing after him. "Please, I can tell you know something. I really need to know this, it might be important. Who was Lucy?"

He paused with one hand on the knob for the front door and appeared to debate himself. Finally, he turned to face her, his expression a careful blank.

"Reason I know what I do about this place," he said, choosing his words carefully. "Is on account of it bein' told to me by my mama, God rest her soul. She learned all about it from my granny, way back 'fore I was even born. Thing is, it wasn't just some story to her. She'd lived it, even though she couldn't remember nothin' about it. But she was there when Grace Alston done herself in. She was bein' cradled in her mama's arms, while her mama begged for her life. Thanks to the Goddamned gov'ment, her last name was made Alston, seein' as how her mama didn't really have no family name, and that was her daddy's. When I was born, she gave me her daddy's name too, even though he wasn't no count, just so I wouldn't have to carry that burden 'round with me my whole life.

"Her mama, though," he said, locking eyes with her. "My granny? She had a sister was there with her, and was supposed to've been with child when she got her throat slit. Her name was Lucille, but mama said Granny called her Lucy."

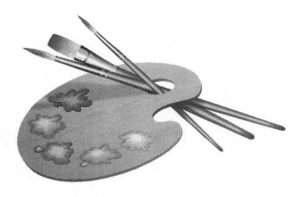

CHAPTER TWENTY-ONE

In the moments before it all came to an end, Clayton was sure it was that one last glance back at the woman standing in the doorway to the damned house that did him in. He couldn't explain why he was so sure, nor would he ever get the chance to think it through, but he knew that was the moment he doomed himself. Had he not looked back, had he not allowed himself that one moment of concern for another human being, had he not allowed himself to feel *hope* for the first time since he learned about Henry Alston and his depravity, he might well have escaped the encounter relatively unscathed.

She didn't want him to leave, but once she mentioned speaking with the ghost of his great aunt, he was beyond telling her anything more. It was irrational, he knew that, and a part of him was angry he would feel such a reaction over a woman he had never met, but something about knowing she was there, the connection back to his own life made the matter much more personal than he was comfortable with.

He intended on letting his story sink in and then telling her about that Blackmore idiot. How he went and had a cocktail spiked with drain cleaner once things got too bad for him. He was overcome with such an urge to get out of there that the story flat slipped his mind until he was pulling away. Not that it mattered. It wouldn't have been entirely true. Or then again, it might have been. He only knew he hadn't been the one present for Blackmore's final moments. Someone else might have, but no one 'fessed up, even after all these years. If she wanted that part of the story, there was plenty still around who could tell it to her. Unless the man really was as weak as he acted, one of them was even the town marshal.

It could be a test of sorts, even if the thought was just rationalizing things after the fact. If she was determined enough to put a stop to what all was happening there, the Ransom woman would ask around. If not, well, there was nothing Clayton Davison could do to force her down any particular path.

He didn't feel the tension ease itself out of his shoulders until he guided his truck around the gentle curve in the long driveway, hiding the house from view. If he didn't know any better, he would have sworn that place was watching him leave. Impossible. He was not so far gone he did not know a building had no eyes and was incapable of doing things living, breathing folk could, but the feeling was there all the same. Maybe it wasn't the house he felt, but those what was inhabiting it. He couldn't say they were *living* there. They stopped doing that back before he was even born.

The truck hit a pothole he hadn't noticed on the way in and the wheel leaped beneath his hands. He swore as he fought it for control and somehow stalled it out right in the middle of the driveway. He slammed his palms against the rebellious steering wheel in frustration. Here he was the better part of a century old, driving for damn near all of that, and he stalled out the truck like a kid behind a stick shift for the first time in his life. He took a deep breath to calm himself, pushed down on the clutch with his left foot while he held the brake with his right, dropped the truck out of gear, and turned the key.

Nothing happened.

He tried again, straining his ears to listen for the click of the starter trying to engage, but again, the blamed thing would not start. If he was hearing right, it wasn't even attempting to turn over. If he was on a hill, he could just let off the brake and pop the clutch once the thing picked up some speed, but he managed to kill the engine just as soon as the road leveled off coming away from the house. He reached for the hood release, thinking maybe he could whack the thing with a hammer and get it back to town where he could call Wally over at the filling station to come take a look at it, but the voice coming from almost directly behind him stopped him before he could bend over far enough.

"*You shouldn't have done that, you old fool,*" a man said.

Clayton jerked upright in his seat and turned, but the cab of his old pickup was empty save for him, the passenger seat still littered with old cigarette packs and scattered beer bottles. He glanced into the bed to see if someone had snuck in there while he was in the house talking, but it was empty except for a spare tire that was in desperate need of air and a couple of stray bottles that somehow ended up back there instead of in his floorboard.

"*You had no right telling her those nasty things,*" the voice said. This time, it sounded as though it were not coming from any one place in particular, but filling the air around him. He had heard it said in stories that a voice came from everywhere and nowhere at the same time and thought it one of the more ridiculous things he'd ever heard. Now, he was experiencing the sensation for himself. He was forced to admit how very apt the description was.

"And who the hell you s'posed to be?" he asked. It felt foolish to be effectively talking to himself, but a response seemed required. "I know you ain't God 'cause me and Him done come to an agreement while I was sittin' in the mud, feelin' it squeeze down into my shorts while bullets was flyin' around me over in Korea."

He heard a sound, and after a moment, recognized it as mirthful laughter.

"No," the voice said. "*I'm not God. He and I are not on what one might call 'speaking terms' at the moment.*"

"You don't say," Clayton muttered. "And just so's we're clear, I didn't tell that woman nothin' weren't true, so you can get over that tellin' me how wrong I am shit right now. Hell, I ain't even told her half the full truth, so stick your threats right up your ass!"

"*That's irrelevant,*" the voice said. "*You shouldn't have told her anything. You should have just stayed in your little hole and not come out until she was completely mine. Now you've made my work harder. That displeases me.*"

"Well don't that just chap your ass?" Clayton asked. "I got to say, if you're who I'm thinkin' you might be, I don't rightly give a rat's ass what displeases you or don't. I'm just sorry you ain't down there in Hell with the Devil's pitchfork jammed up your ass."

"*That is his failing,*" the voice said. "*Not mine. Why don't you tell him so when you see him?*"

Clayton felt his heart lurch in his chest. At first, he was confused since the voice's threat was more amusing than frightening, but as his arm began to tingle and he struggled for breath, he realized it was more than just a contrary reaction. That had been no mere threat—it had been a promise.

He clawed at the door latch, not liking the way his fingers had gone numb one little bit. It took more of an effort to get that door open than he cared to think about, but he finally managed it. When he stepped down out of the truck's cab, his legs no longer had enough strength to hold him. He crumpled to the ground, smacking his head a good lick on the open door as he went. He could tell he was bleeding, but that was not the most pressing concern he had at the moment.

Somehow, he got himself turned over onto his belly facing back up the driveway in the direction of the house. The Army hadn't done a lot for him, but it did teach him how to crawl. Thankfully, the memory was not gone like so many others from those years when he was young and full of fire. He put one hand in front of the other and started pulling as he pushed with his feet. His knee screamed in agony as the old wound there protested the strange motion, but he ignored it by focusing on the irregular heartbeat pounding in his ears.

He hadn't even made it as far as the back of the truck when he noticed someone standing in the middle of the driveway. Clayton looked up and saw a man, somewhere around middle aged, wearing a fancy suit and a hat smiling down at him. He had never seen so much as a picture to compare the man to, but he had no doubts he was staring at Henry Alston, somehow untouched by over a hundred years of being dead.

It was the last thing he saw before his heart gave one final, hammering lurch in his chest and went still. As his head drifted to the gravel beneath him in what seemed like slow motion, he wished he had spared himself that final look back at his great-grandfather's house. It probably wouldn't have saved his life. Not coming here at all would have been the only thing that would have guaranteed such a thing.

But then again, maybe he was wrong about that, too.

No one would ever know.

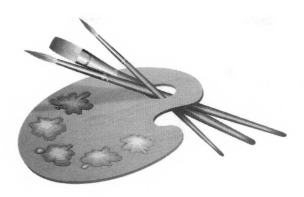

CHAPTER TWENTY-TWO

That she was upset over the fact Clayton Davison had been found dead in her driveway was to be expected. That she was nearly inconsolable and convinced it was her fault was what Bradley had a problem trying to comprehend. As far as he could tell, it looked like the old man died of a heart attack. How such a thing could be Kat's fault was something of a stretch in his mind.

From his understanding, the old man showed up on her doorstep this morning intending to educate her about the history of Alston House. On the one hand, this gave her the information she wanted. On the other, whatever motivation the old man had in doing it was lost along with him. Bradley couldn't think of any reason the town's biggest grump would feel the urge to offer anything to anybody, much less a woman who had just moved here and would be considered an outsider to pretty much everyone in Clay's age group. It was a mystery that would have to remain unsolved.

He turned and glanced over to where she now sat on her sofa, a cup of coffee in her trembling hand, tears trickling down her cheeks. It was a marked improvement from how she had been right after he told her about the old man's death. She had been so distraught that

Bradley ended up convincing one of the paramedics who arrived to tend to Clay's remains to come up and give her a sedative to calm her down. Hopefully, whatever storm had consumed her was now passed, and would not return once the medication worked its way out of her system. Bradley hoped that would be the case. As far as he was concerned, she had suffered enough these last few days.

When he turned back to the window, Frank's SUV was rounding the corner on its way to the house. The paramedics must be finished loading Clay's body up. While Bradley thought it was a waste of time, Frank had insisted on an autopsy. While he couldn't know for certain, the marshal swore Clay had never shown or mentioned any heart condition that could have been fatal. Bradley didn't think it really mattered. Clay was old, and once your body decided something wasn't working right, that was that.

After one last look at Kat, Bradley went outside to wait for his boss on the front porch. Despite how cool it had been the last few days, today was relatively warm by comparison. The warmer weather, combined with that lost, drugged out stare on Kat's face meant being out here was preferable to being inside.

Frank parked, got out, and meandered up the yard to meet him on the porch. He nodded in the direction of the door as he stood next to him.

"How's she holdin' up?"

Bradley shrugged. "Better, but that could be the meds. Once those wear off, who knows? Everything wrapped up down there?"

"For the most part," Frank said. "They got Clay loaded and on his way to cold storage, and I pulled his truck off to the side of the driveway so we can get past it. Wally ain't answerin' his phone, so if you're agreeable to it, you can drive the truck over to Wally's garage then I'll bring you back here for your car."

"Sounds good," Bradley said.

The two men stood in silence, looking out over the front yard, neither realizing it but both unconsciously staring at the place where Clay had died. Finally, Frank shook his head and ran a hand across his face. When Bradley glanced over at him, he noticed the man's eyes were a little red around the edges. He pretended not to notice. How to deal with your boss when they were in tears was not something he was prepared for.

"It's a damn shame," Frank said. "I never cared much for the old fart, but he was a fixture around here. Goin' to be strange not seein' him sittin' there in the grocery store every day."

"Going to be strange not having a grocery store," Bradley added. "It's not like he had any kids to take over for him."

Frank grunted in surprise. "Never thought about that, but you're right. Damn shame."

"Can't stop change."

"Nope, guess not."

The two lapsed into silence again. This time it was Bradley who broke it.

"So, Kat thinks it was her fault," he said. "Clay having a heart attack, I mean. She thinks she caused it."

Frank turned to him, frowning. "That why she was so upset when you told her about him? And why you got the paramedics to look at her?"

Bradley nodded. "She said Clay had come by to tell her about the Alstons, and the history of this place."

"Shit," Frank said. "That's all she needed, scares she's been havin'."

Bradley didn't understand the comment, not knowing much about the history of the house himself, but said nothing. There were other things on his mind. "What I don't understand is why the man did it in the first place."

"What do you mean?" Frank asked.

"It just doesn't seem like him," Bradley said. "Tell the truth: you ever heard of Clay Davison offering information about anything to anybody without some ulterior motive to why he was giving it? From what Kat said, she never even asked him about it, much less offered him anything in return. So, why'd he do it?"

"Just because he acted like an ass most times don't mean he always was one," Frank said.

Something in his tone said he was holding back, and at first Bradley was willing to let it go. The more he thought about Kat, sitting inside, drugged out of her mind and blaming herself for killing an old man who was probably near death anyway, the more he felt he needed to know what was going on.

"What did you do?" he asked.

Frank jumped as though Bradley had just goosed him a good one. "The hell's that supposed to mean?"

"Exactly what I asked," Bradley said. "What did you do? Come on Frank, out with it. I let you keep your secrets because I respect you, but this time there's somebody else being affected by them. So out with it."

The marshal refused to meet his eyes. He was not cowed—nowhere even close to it—but he did seem to be ashamed of himself. Bradley did not know if it was because he had done something, that he had kept it from his deputy, or because he got caught at it. Probably a combination of the three.

"I went and talked to Clay yesterday," Frank said, looking out across the yard. "You suspected some kid might've been the one messin' with Kat, I figured it might be somebody older. Somebody who was part of a group didn't like change much."

"You thought he broke her window," Bradley said. "Or knew which of his friends had."

Frank nodded. "He didn't know nothin'. If one of his buddies broke her window, they didn't tell him nothin' about it. It was strange, though. I was pushin' him some, ended up tellin' him she was havin' some issues out here. He didn't seem surprised by it, which I expected, but he did seem scared by it, which I didn't. Maybe that was it. Fear makes a man do a lot of things he wouldn't normally do."

"Maybe," Bradley agreed. "It still doesn't seem like something he'd do, but at least it's a reason."

"Well, there's your problem," Frank said, turning to look at him. "You're lookin' for reasons in a world that ain't nowhere close to bein' reasonable. Sometimes things happen don't make no sense. Sometimes people do things don't make no sense. It's just how things are, no more and no less."

Bradley nodded, feeling the need to say more but not knowing what to say. After another moment or so, Frank slapped him on the shoulder.

"You good with movin' that truck now?" he asked. "Get it done, then get back to look after your lady there."

"She's not my lady," Bradley said, rolling his eyes as he turned to the door to let Kat know he was leaving for a little while.

Frank laughed. "You keep thinkin' that."

When her paintings began taking a dark turn, Katherine didn't worry about it overmuch. At the time, she believed it was simply the product of how much her life changed in such a short period. That, and the depression she was fighting even as she told herself it didn't exist. Then, when she saw what she now understood was the spectral figure of Henry Alston raping the young girl she painted one night, she realized there might be more going on in the house than she believed. This was reinforced by what happened to her on Thanksgiving night, and after speaking with Lucy just last night. It might have frightened some people away, but it had only made her more determined.

After Clay showed up on her doorstep this morning to tell her the history of Alston House, and gave her the reasons it might be haunted. It made her think she was on the right path. She was supposed to figure out all she could and put a stop to it if that were even possible. It served to focus her task, and made her feel like she stood a chance of coming out on top.

Then Clay died almost immediately after she told him his great aunt's ghost had spoken to her. He didn't even make it to the end of the driveway, and he had been in a hurry to leave. It could have been the shock of what Kat told him that brought it on, which made it directly her fault. Part of her even thought it could have been something else that caused it, something reaching out from within her house to collect one of its own in a sense. If that were the case, she was still responsible, albeit indirectly. He wouldn't have come here and exposed himself to that potential danger had she not been living here. Either way she looked at the situation, it boiled down to the same thing: his death was *her fault*.

For the first time since everything began, she considered giving up. She had invested some serious money in renovating the house, but if it ended up costing her either her sanity or her life, it would not be worth it. Better to take the loss, get back whatever she could recoup, and go on to live a somewhat normal life somewhere else.

But a large part of her balked at that idea. She wasn't one to give up, for starters. To do so now would feel like her attempt at a new life was a failure. She survived the death of her son and the loss of the man she was positive was her soulmate with her sanity relatively intact. There was no way some child molester's ghost would be the one to send her over the edge.

She had to do something about this. She had no idea what, but there had to be a way to find the answer. Someone in this town knew more. Someone would know why the previous owner abandoned his renovation project, how he had died. And if they didn't, surely they could point her in the right direction.

There was the risk they wouldn't be willing to talk to her, would consider her an outsider unworthy of sharing in their town's secrets. She would just have to convince them otherwise. She had tried being nice, and it had gotten her nowhere. Clay was the one who seemed to resent her the most, and that probably played as much of a part in getting him killed as she had. If he had been willing to tell her what he knew the first time they met, maybe it would have kept him from coming out here. If something *had* reached out to kill him from the house, maybe being at his store would have kept him out of its reach. She was to blame for his death, she would not argue that fact. It didn't stop him from having to share some of the blame for his obstinacy. Fair was fair, after all.

Her mind was made up. She would get to the bottom of this, no matter what it took. She would do it for that old man who was as much a victim as her, even if he would have refused to admit it. She would do it for Lucy, a young, scared girl who had died through no fault of her own, all for a bad man's selfishness.

Above all, she would do it for Tommy, to make him proud, wherever he was now.

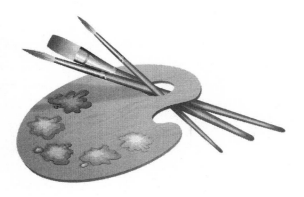

CHAPTER TWENTY-THREE

Seeing the old man tinkering beneath the car hood inside the gas station's single garage bay was enough to make Katherine's heart hurt. There was no reason it should—the man looked nothing like old Clay, other than just their comparable ages, but knowing the two men had been friends for most of their lives made her feel a touch of the loss he must be dealing with. Had Bradley not been standing next to her, she might have let this go for another day. As it was, she took strength from the deputy's presence and stepped into the open bay.

Wally Barton barely even glanced away from whatever engine part he was working on to acknowledge their entry. The way he ignored them did a fantastic job of making Katherine feel uncomfortable. Finally, before the silence could stretch into an unrecoverable awkwardness, Bradley stepped forward and leaned against the car's engine compartment next to the man.

"What broke this time?" he asked.

Wally snorted and spat a long runner of brown tobacco juice out the side of his mouth. Katherine fought the urge to wrinkle her nose in disgust as it spattered onto the concrete floor alongside several other stains that might have been motor oil, but she had a feeling were not.

"What ain't?" Wally replied. "Injectors clogged, air filter ain't been changed since Hector was a pup, oil's so damn thick you could tar a road with it, and I'm bettin' the head gasket got a crack in it somewhere from the way she's smokin'. Gonna make a pretty penny fixin' it, but gonna be a right bitch to do, too. I'll earn every cent, you can be damn sure of that."

Bradley shook his head. "I thought Randy Young had more sense than to treat this old car like that. He's had the thing for years."

"He does," Wally said, sending another line of tobacco spit to join the previous one. "He gave it to his dumbass kid for a graduation present. You might not know that little shit well enough to know, but he ain't got no respect for nothin'. That's kids nowadays, though. Mama and Daddy give 'em every little thing they ask for, and they grow up not knowin' what it means to get somethin' on the strength of your own sweat. Make him have to pay for this, maybe he'd change the damned oil once in a while."

The old man turned whatever tool he was holding one last time, letting out a massive grunt as the bolt he had been working on finally came loose. He reached in and backed it the rest of the way out with his fingers before dropping it into a plastic bowl that once held Country Crock margarine and took a step back. He put his hands into the small of his back and stretched, working the kinks out of his old muscles. Only after this ritual was complete did he cast a disparaging glance at Katherine and turn his full attention to Bradley.

"You didn't just wander in here to shoot the shit," he said. "Whatta you want, Deputy?"

Bradley motioned for Katherine to join him. "This is Katherine Ransom. She moved into the old Alston House about a month ago. You two had a chance to meet yet?"

"Nope," Wally said. "Ain't been in no rush to, neither."

"Kat, this is Wallace Barton," Bradley said, ignoring the man's comment. "Everybody around town calls him Wally. You ever need anything on that truck of yours fixed, bring it to him. He's not the cheapest around, but you can be sure it'll be fixed right the first time."

"If you're tryin' to flatter me," Wally said, scowling over at Bradley, "you're pretty shitty at it. I ain't exactly one for none of that butterin' up bullshit no how. Case you didn't notice, I got work needs to be done, so tell me why you're here so I can get you to go somewhere else."

Bradley frowned at the man and appeared to be on the verge of saying something about the way he was acting, but Katherine put a hand on his arm to stop him. She had experienced the same thing from Clay the first time she met him—albeit not as severely—and took no offense to it this time around, either.

"Mister Barton," she said. The old man turned his eyes to her. It was a start, if a small one. "I don't want to take up too much of your time, I just have a couple of quick questions for you. If you don't want to answer them, I'll understand. I know there's a lot of people around here that don't like the idea of me living out there on Dead Hollow."

His eyes narrowed slightly at her use of the original name for the road she lived on, and though his expression never changed, she thought she detected a miniscule relaxing of his posture. With luck, the things she learned the few times she dealt with Clay would help her win this man over, enough to get the information she needed.

"I ain't promisin' to answer you," he said. "But you can ask your questions."

"The day he passed," she said, choosing her words carefully. She didn't want to remind him about his friend's death, but she had to try and loosen what she knew would be a very tight pair of lips. "Clay Davison came out there and told me some of the history of the place. He told me about the Alston family, and what they did out there."

"Got a point to this?" Wally interrupted. The man's tone was brusque, but his posture hadn't tensed back up, so she felt she was relatively safe.

"What he didn't tell me was about the man who lived there before me," she said. "Paul Blackmore, I think? I know he died there, but I don't know how or why. I was hoping maybe you could fill me in on that."

"What for?" Wally asked, sending another dollop of tobacco juice to the floor as if it were additional punctuation. "It bother you knowin' somebody died in that house? If so, Blackmore's the least of your worries, if what you're sayin' Clay told you is true."

"It bothers me," she said. "But not as much as what the Alstons did. Call it another piece of a puzzle I'm trying to solve."

"Again, what for? If what Henry and Grace Alston done ain't runnin' you out of there screamin', that sumbitch's story sure won't."

Katherine sighed. The old man wasn't acting like he would *not* answer her, but he showed every indication he would make her work for it. "If you believe the same things Mister Davison did, you already know just as well as I do there's some strange things going on at that house, even now, after all these years. I've seen... well, I guess you'd call them ghosts since I moved in. Henry Alston's one, I think, and I've seen a couple of girls there, too. One of them was related to Mister Davison's grandmother, from what he said."

Wally grunted at that. "Always suspected he had some kinda ties to the place, never knew it 'til just now though. Explains why he always got so fired up about it."

"At any rate," Katherine said. "He told me about the Alstons and about his grandmother's sister Lucy, but he left before he told me about Mister Blackmore. If I know what happened to him, I can watch out for it. It might keep me from going down that same path. It also might help me figure out how to fix whatever it is that's keeping all those ghosts there."

The man watched her with a wary eye, then, amazingly, began to chuckle before finally laughing out loud.

"Fix it?" he asked between gales of laughter. "You got a time machine stashed away somewhere? 'Cause 'bout the only way I know you're fixin' anything related to that place is to go and bash Henry Alston's head against a rock right after his mama shat him out."

Katherine opened her mouth to explain that she believed if she could figure out why the ghosts were still there, maybe she could help them move on to wherever they were supposed to be, but Wally held up a hand to stop her before she could get a single word out.

"I'll give you this much," he said, once his chuckles wound down. "You got a set of brass ones on you, that's for damn sure. You ain't got much sense, but you got a pair and you made me laugh, so that's got to count for somethin'.

"I don't know much about Blackmore," he continued. "Other'n he apparently mixed up some rye and drain cleaner and sucked it down out on your front porch one night. He come in here to get some winterizin' done on his car not long after he moved in. He was all a twitter 'bout how he was gonna fix that old place up and sell it for twice, maybe three times what he bought it at auction from the state for. Said he couldn't hardly wait to get back to Florida or wherever the hell it was he said he was from. Tell the truth, I done my level best to ignore his stupid ass while he was in here. All that mattered to me was his money spent just like anybody else's did. I got his tune-up done, handed him a bill, took his cash, and the next I heard I felt worth payin' attention to was when Max Bradshaw said he found him tits up on the porch out there, empty glass layin' there next to him with the shit was in it eatin' its way through the floorboards.

"I know Clay said then that the house done got it somebody else to chew on for a while, and that it'd be quiet a bit, but I didn't pay him much mind. Always sounded so damned superstitious and a little foolish t'me. Wasn't right him thinkin' that way, bein' a veteran and all. Not that I thought Clay was crazy, mind you. Ain't a one of us don't know what's still wanderin' around out there in the Hollow. I guess for the rest of us ain't nothin' but stuff we grew up hearin' about. A few of us seen things, too, but that ain't no story I'm sharin' with you, girl. You amuse me, but that don't mean I'm about to start lookin' at you like one of us just yet."

"That's not a lot to go off of," Katherine said, her heart sinking. Bradley was sure Wally would be the most open to talking to her out of the older folks left in town, and if he knew nothing more about Blackmore than what he already told her, it would be a dead end she might never find a way around. "Is there anything else you remember about him, anything at all that might help me piece together why he killed himself?"

Wally shook his head. "Sorry, darlin'. I can't tell you what I don't know."

He scratched his chin and considered what he said. "There was one more thing, but I can't say it'll do you no good. I seem to remember him talkin' about a brother back where he was from. I don't know if they was close or not, but if he mentioned him, it stands to reason they had some kinda relationship. Maybe you could try trackin' him down, see if he knows and is willin' to talk to you about it."

She looked over to Bradley, who shrugged.

"Maybe," he said. "There's bound to be a next-of-kin listed in the police reports from Blackmore's death. I can try to track it down, or maybe get Frank to do it."

"There you go," Wally said, turning back to the car he had been working on when they came in. "And I'll tell you what, since you made me laugh, I won't even overcharge you if'n you bring your vehicle in here for me to work on like I was originally plannin' on doin'. But I wasn't kiddin' 'bout havin' work to do here, so if ya'll will excuse me, I best get back to it."

"Thank you," Katherine said, stepping up next to him and offering her hand. Wally gave her a bemused look and shook. She could feel the grime on his hand transferring to her, but found she didn't care. She knew good and well he was waiting to see her reaction to it, and was determined she would pass whatever little test this was to him. "I know it wasn't much, but you at least gave me more than I had before."

Wally offered her a slight smile. "For a city girl, you ain't so bad. I hope you do pull off whatever the hell it is you're tryin' to pull out there. You do, you might even start earnin' some points around town. 'Fore you know it, might not even be nobody thinkin' of you like you ain't a local."

Most people would think his words not much of a compliment, but to Katherine it was high praise indeed and even more proof—if any was needed—she was doing the right thing by not giving up.

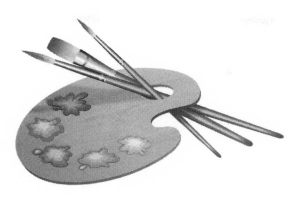

CHAPTER TWENTY-FOUR

She picked up the phone, began dialing the number, and then turned it back off again for what felt like the hundredth time. Bradley told her he didn't mind if she made this call without him, and that he trusted her to fill him in on anything important that came of it, but Katherine felt like she needed to. After all, it had been his work that found the number in the first place, not hers. Admittedly, it had not been *much* work. Bradley said Blackmore's brother was listed at the very beginning of the file he found down in the storage area in the marshal's office basement. Still, he had been the one who did the legwork, so he should be the one who got the reward, such as it was.

Maybe if she had some idea when he would be back, it would help ease her anxiousness, but she did not. The call had come in not long after he arrived, so he gave her the scrap of paper he copied everything onto. It was an accident out on the main highway leading to Murfreesboro, and from the sounds of it, a bad one at that. Frank hadn't come right out and ordered Bradley to the scene along with him, but it was implied. Katherine just hoped there were no fatalities involved. It would be a tragedy so close to Christmas, but even more than that, she was dealing with way too much death for her liking already. That she hadn't been directly involved in any of it in no way lessened the impact it had on her. Tommy's loss was still too fresh in her mind, she supposed.

A glance over at the clock told her it was not even five in the evening yet. Still plenty of time to make the call before it got too late. Chicago was in the same time zone as middle Tennessee, so as long as she made called before around nine, it should be considered a reasonable hour. Unfortunately, that meant she couldn't use the hour as a reason to justify making the call without Bradley being here, not even to herself. She would need to come up with some way of occupying her time.

She made her way upstairs, pointedly ignoring the second-floor hallway as had become her habit since seeing the things she had there. She knew it would happen whether or not she invited it to. She would just rather feel she had some kind of control over things, even if it was only imaginary.

No visions assaulted her, no specters came to pay their visits or try to terrify her. When she stepped into her bedroom and let out a sigh of relief, she finally realized how tense just that simple journey up a couple of flights of stairs made her. To feel this way in her own home was more than annoying or a mild irritation. It was a constant reminder of this place's history, and something she would be glad to put behind her.

Assuming, of course, there was a way to do such a thing.

She looked over to her bed and considered lying down for a brief nap, but decided against it. Even if she set an alarm, there was no guarantee she would get up when she wanted to. Her sleep had been broken at best for the last little while. A nap might do her some good, but ultimately it would only serve to delay the things she knew needed to be done. She could sleep once this was all over and she had the house to herself once more.

Instead, she ventured into her studio and turned on the lights. The painting of Frank and Elizabeth was right where she left it, looking forlorn on her easel next to the window. She had made considerable progress on it, but now that she saw it again after so long not working on it, her artistic eye caught every imperfection, every unfinished detail, and threw them into sharp relief against the rest of the painting. She studied it carefully, mentally noting each component still needing work and finally came to the conclusion it could be done with only a couple of uninterrupted hours. This had not been her intention when she came up here, but the longer she looked at the painting, the guiltier she felt that it was taking her this long to get it done. She had promised Frank a couple weeks. It was already overdue, and if she put it off much longer, it wouldn't be dried in time for him to give it to his wife for Christmas as he intended.

That decided for her. She started for the bedroom to change into what she thought of as her work clothes—a paint-stained t-shirt and nearly shapeless jeans that bore the remnants of finger marks and errant brush strokes as she considered what to do next on one of her previous projects—but it occurred to her if she took the time to go change, she might well lose her motivation. If that happened, there was no telling when the urge might return. Instead, she unbuttoned her shirt. The pants were old and bordering on being a size too small for her, so they could stay. The shirt was relatively new and while it wasn't expensive, it was somewhat nice and went well with several of her dressier outfits. She draped it carefully over a chair before moving to her worktable to mix up the colors she would need to finish the painting.

She wished she could send Bradley a text message or something, let him know where she was in case she was too wrapped up in her craft to hear him knock on the door downstairs. It seemed cell reception was not something she would ever get out here, though, so it was a pointless wish. Besides, if she didn't answer when he knocked, surely he would just come inside to check on her. She had told him where her emergency key was after the incident on Thanksgiving night. Her face reddened at the thought of him coming upstairs and finding her painting without her shirt, but it wasn't like she was taking her bra off. It would be no different than if he caught her in a bikini top. Better even, considering her swimsuit left considerably less to the imagination than her choice of underwire did. And honestly, would it be so bad for him to see her naked? She was in good shape, and her reduced diet that resulted from her lack of sleep had helped her lose that last five pounds she could never seem to get rid of. He was a good-looking man, too, and seemed to care about her. If he caught her up here naked, she might just have to get him to reciprocate. After all, they were both adults, and it had been a long time.

She glanced back toward her bedroom, her thoughts drifting to the little pink cylinder tucked into the back of her nightstand drawer. She couldn't remember when the last time she changed the batteries was, but even without them it could get the job done…

She shook her head, forcing the thoughts away as she turned back to the tubes of paint before her. Daydreaming was all well and good, but the thought of Bradley coming upstairs to check on her, worried because she hadn't answered the door, and catching her doing *that* was not one that titillated her, but was instead too embarrassing to even dream of. If the urge was still there after he came back and they made their phone call, she might revisit it then. Give him a proper goodnight kiss to start the engines revving, too. But for now, there was work to be done.

Once everything was mixed and ready, she picked up her palate and stepped up to the easel. She took a deep breath, dipped her brush into the paint, and got to work.

She did not know how long she worked—this was not uncommon for how her painting sessions went lately—but when she stepped back and gave the painting a final once-over, she was fairly confident it was finished. The colors were bright where they needed to pop, muted where they needed to be subtle. As perfect as she could make it. She put the palate on the table, and reminded herself to give the canvas its first layer of clear-coat before bed. She would do another tomorrow, once the paints and the first application had dried completely, and maybe a final one the next day if it still needed it, but now she could get it to Frank well ahead of his Christmas plans for it.

When she came out of the room and saw the clock on her nightstand, a frown creeped onto her face. It was now after seven-thirty, and Bradley still had not returned. That could only mean either the accident out on the highway was worse than either of them thought it would be, or he had gotten tied up with some other piece of minutia that probably went with being one of the town's dual law enforcement officials. On the plus side, it gave her a chance to clean herself up some before he got back. On the other hand, it meant if he was not here once she finished with that, she would have to make the phone call on her own.

She pulled a pair of sweats and a t-shirt out of her dresser and tossed them onto the bed along with a fresh pair of underwear. None of the garments were anything fancy, but they didn't need to be. Bradley was not coming over for a date, he was coming so they could figure out how to put an end to the ghosts that were plaguing her. Still, she couldn't help but think about how cute she would look in them. Date or not, dressed relaxed or not, she still wanted to look appealing to him. It was silly, especially considering the state he had seen her in on Thanksgiving, but it didn't change what she felt. Maybe it had been a long time for sex, but it had been an even longer time since she found herself as enamored over a man as she did Bradley.

When she turned on the bathroom light and saw herself in the mirror, it surprised her to see the smile on her own face staring back at her. She shook her head and laughed softly as she pulled a towel from the closet by the door and put it on the edge of the sink where it would be in easy reach once she got out of the shower. She really was acting like a teenager again in many ways. Had anyone told her a man would bring such behavior out of her after the way things went with Dave, she would have told that person they were crazy. That it was happening amid dealing with a house that was haunted by a child molester and his victims only made the situation that much more surreal. At least it was a bright spot in an otherwise dreary month. She supposed she should focus on that and not let the rest of it worry her so.

She balanced on one foot and tugged off her sock before repeating the dance with the other. They went into the hamper along with her pants and underclothes. The pile in there was getting fairly large. She would have to remember to take it downstairs with her so she could start a load of laundry before making the call. If things went well, she could probably get them in the dryer before heading up to bed. Of course, if things went like they usually did for her, she would forget until the next time she got ready for a shower and then try to remember again with similar results. While she waited for the water to heat up, she dragged the wicker container out into the bedroom itself and left it next to the door. If it was in her way, maybe she would stand a better chance of remembering it than if she left it tucked away, hidden inside her bathroom.

The mirror was already steamed over by the time she made it back into the room. She smiled again, impressed that for a house with heating as old as this one, the water heater always worked at peak performance. She did not know why that would be the case, maybe something about how it connected to the boiler that controlled the central heating unit, but she was glad for it.

Her smile faded as she noticed a hazy form in the clouded surface of the mirror. She spun around, arms already rising involuntarily to cover her exposed body, but there was nothing there. It was only the shower curtain moving slightly from the water striking it. The gentle motion reflected poorly in the mirror, making it appear as though someone was standing there, watching her.

Even knowing what it was, though, she felt unseen eyes upon her. Not wanting to allow herself to overreact, she quickly stepped into the shower. She knew, realistically, if the ghost of Henry Alston was watching her, that shower curtain would do nothing at all to deter him. Still, something about the water pounding against her skin and the way the curtain shielded some of the light from the fixtures over the sink made her feel like she was receiving much more privacy. A mind trick, but it worked, so she felt no need to argue with herself about it.

It didn't take long for the heat and pressure of the shower's spray beating against her shoulders to relax her muscles. She reached around and kneaded her neck with the heels of both hands, helping the water untie some of the knots that had formed there. She tilted her head back, sighing as the drops beat a staccato rhythm against her face. She heard nothing but the sound of her own breathing, her heartbeat, and the drops of water striking her body and the shower floor. It was isolating, soothing, and exactly what she needed, even if she hadn't known it until now.

She turned around, and soaped her chest, pleased there was less paint on her than she expected there to be. What was there seemed to come away easily, without the vigorous scrubbing she sometimes had to administer to her skin to get off some of the more particularly troublesome spatters. That done, she turned back around and soaped the rest of her body. She could skip her hair for tonight. It would only end up a tangled mess unless she had the time to brush it out, which if Bradley did get back soon, she would not.

Thinking of him brought back her thoughts from earlier in the night, thoughts of him walking in on her while she was painting topless. She almost wished he would come in now and catch her in the shower. She imagined his hands running across her skin, cleaning her as they explored her. She unconsciously varied her touch, applying more pressure here, a slightly lighter application there. It was similar to how she painted, her fingertips like her brushes, her skin the canvas, both coming together to create something that would be beautiful when done.

She felt heat grow in her groin, but rather than push the thoughts away this time, she let them flow forth. She imagined Bradley's hands upon her, teasing her, caressing her, learning through the way she reacted what thrilled her and what she wanted more of. When her palms ran across her breasts again, she couldn't help but notice her nipples had grown stiff, her gentle touch enough to send tingles of pleasure down to that warm center between her legs. She allowed her hand to trail lower, across her pubic hair, finally cupping that warmth as if to hold it in where it could never escape. Her finger twitched in time to her increasing pulse, begging her to insert it and speed this moment along. She forced herself to wait, her only accommodation to her body's demand a brief flick across her clit as she pulled her hand away. The sensation was nearly unbearable. She sucked in breath so hard she thought for a moment she would drown herself.

"*A little old for my tastes,*" a voice whispered into her ear. "*But exceptions can be made, just this once.*"

She spun around, barely keeping her balance on the slick floor, her heart suddenly beating faster not because of what she was doing to herself, but from sheer terror. He was there, still dressed in turn-of-the-century finery, but seemingly untouched by the shower's spray. He grinned at her, his teeth black as the grave they belonged in, and tipped his fancy top hat to her in a mockery of politeness.

"*I do not believe we've been properly introduced*," he said, settling the hat back onto his head. "*My name is Henry Alston, and you are living in my house. That, I'm afraid, makes you mine as well. So, by all means, please continue. I insist.*"

Katherine shrieked so loudly that for a moment it even drowned out the horrible sounds of his laughter within the echoes of the room.

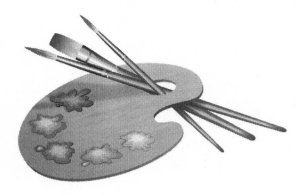

CHAPTER TWENTY-FIVE

It was bad enough to have to deal with the mess of an accident for the last several hours, but coming back to Kat's house and having no one answer the door when he pounded on it only made things worse. Under normal circumstances, Bradley wouldn't have given it a second thought. Take into consideration how shot his nerves already were and add in everything he knew she was going through? It made his adrenaline levels begin to skyrocket. When no one answered after pounding on the door, he thought he heard the wood crack, he circled around to the back of the house.

He peered in through the window, cupping his hands around his face to preserve enough of his night vision to see inside the darkened room. It was empty, not even a trace of embers in the fireplace to show she had been in there at all tonight. Stops at the dining room, kitchen, tower, and den windows yielded similar results. If she was in there, he could be relatively certain she wasn't on the first floor. More than likely she was upstairs in her studio, working on one of her paintings and had lost track of time. At least he hoped that was the case.

Kat kept a spare key tucked away beneath a loose slat in the floor of the porch for emergencies. Bradley debated for a moment whether this constituted one, then went and lifted the board to retrieve the key. It might not *technically* be an emergency, but she had told him where it was for a reason, and if she was not in some kind of trouble, he would apologize and they could laugh about his overreaction later. He might feel a little silly to break in and discover she had simply fallen asleep, but he would know she was safe. If that was the case, he would just make sure to lock the door behind himself when he left and come back to see whether she made the call to Blackmore's brother tomorrow.

The first thing he noticed when he stepped into the house was how eerily quiet it was. It was relatively warm inside, so the radiators not being on was okay. The large clock hanging on the wall in her sitting room not ticking at all was not. She had just bought it a few days ago and had made sure to put fresh batteries in it before hanging it up. He thought it was foolish, since it came with batteries already installed, but she had pointed out there was no way to know how long it sat on the shelf with those batteries running before she bought it. It made sense, and more importantly for this particular moment, it screamed trouble at him like a blaring alarm.

He had only been a deputy marshal for just over a year, but in a town this small with so many residents who were getting on in years, he had experienced his fair share of death. Someone would call in because they could not get in touch with one of those older folks, he or Frank would go out to their house to check on things, and they would be found lying on their beds, on their couches, or occasionally on their bathroom floors, stiff as a board with open eyes staring at nothing. In every one of those instances, when he had been the first on scene, the house always had a peculiar feel to it, a sensation of emptiness that let you know almost immediately there was no life contained within its walls anymore. As he stood listening for the tick of a clock that never came, he realized he was feeling that now. He forced himself to remain calm as he methodically made his way through the downstairs rooms, verifying what he had seen outside. They were all empty. Kat was not on this floor.

Bradley glanced at the door leading down to the basement, but disregarded it for the time being. There was no reason he could think of why she would have gone down there. If he could not find her anywhere else, he would of course check, but it could wait for now. He bypassed it and mounted the stairs so he could check her bedroom and studio. He ignored the second floor for now. Kat told him many times how unnerving she found that particular floor, probably due to the fact nearly everything strange she had seen had its origins there. As with the basement, he couldn't think of any reason why she would be in one of the rooms here. Then again, he could, but none of them were for reasons he was ready to face just yet.

Her bedroom was as empty as the rest of the house, but there was some indication she had been in here tonight. A wicker laundry hamper was positioned near the door, and fresh clothes were laid out on the bed. He peeked into the studio and saw more evidence of her presence, namely the sharp tang of aerosol that lingered near the painting on the easel in the corner. He was beginning to put the pieces together already. She had come upstairs to work on the painting of Frank and Elizabeth, then decided to have a shower. She laid out her clothes, pulled her dirty laundry out, probably so she could take it down to wash, and then gone into the shower. Crazily, he almost hoped she *was* injured or in some kind of trouble. It would be extremely embarrassing to open that door and have her freak out for peeping on her while she showered.

As he approached the bathroom door, he heard the water running and mentally kicked himself for not noticing it the moment he entered the room. He allowed his mind to run away with him and heard what he expected to hear. He pressed his ear against the door and listened closely for several moments, trying to determine if Kat was indeed still in there, but all he heard was the sound of water striking porcelain. If she was in there, she was being silent.

He knocked tentatively and listened again to see if there was any response from inside the room. There was not. He knocked again and called out for her, but again, there was no answer. He tested the knob and found the door unlocked. Taking a deep breath and readying himself in case he needed to make a quick retreat, he opened the door and stepped inside.

She was not in here, but that wasn't what worried him so much. That she was not in here and the shower was still on, the curtain a tangled mess on the floor where it had been ripped down *was* cause for concern. He reached in and checked the temperature of the water, wincing at the almost icy feel when it struck his hand. He turned the knobs off and turned toward the mirror, frowning. There was a towel there, still neatly folded on the vanity beside the sink. She had obviously made it as far as the shower, but then something happened that interrupted her and made her leave without even bothering to dry herself. The situation was getting stranger by the moment, and for an instant Bradley felt he might be traipsing into something well beyond his depth.

He left the bathroom and checked the bedroom again, this time paying closer attention to the floor, looking for signs of water left behind by her passage. Now that he knew what to look for, it was easy to see. There was a trail of sorts, dark spots in the wood where water had seeped in and begun to dry. He knelt and studied the pattern, not sure what he hoped to learn from it and equally unsure why he was not rushing to follow it, but feeling it was something he needed to do.

None of the spots were very large, which was expected since Kat was not a large woman. It could also mean her steps had been quick, her feet not remaining on the ground long enough to leave any residual moisture behind. He glanced behind him and gauged the distance between the spots. She hadn't been running—the stride was too narrow for that—but she had been walking at a rapid pace. From the irregular pattern, he could also assume she had not been entirely steady as she made her exit from the room. He still did not know what caused her to flee, but whatever it was could not be good.

He followed the trail out of the room and back down the hall, where it seemed to stop at the stairs. The lighting was not as good here, preventing him from knowing for sure that she had descended them, but there was nowhere else for her to have gone. She hadn't been on the main floor, which meant he shouldn't have dismissed the second floor or basement so out of hand. They were now the only two places he could think of where she might be found.

There was always the possibility she had left the house, but even dazed he could not imagine her walking outside wet and naked, not with the temperatures as cool as they were tonight. Surely the shock would have brought her out of whatever fugue state she might have been in. There was a chance, of course. After what he had already seen, he would be foolish to ignore the potential. It was more likely she was still in the house somewhere and he just had not discovered her yet.

He stopped on the second story landing, studying the floor to see if the trail resumed here, but since she hadn't been using the rooms on this floor, she hadn't bothered to replace any of the light bulbs in the hallway. There was enough residual light coming from the floor above and the one below to see where he was going, but not enough to make out the kind of details that would indicate a trail to him.

As he stood there trying to work up the nerve to check the rooms, he heard a scuttling sound from one at the end of the hallway. He frowned and held his breath, waiting to see if it came again so he could narrow down exactly where it came from. Finally, he heard it again. Last room on the right, if his ears were not deceiving him. According to Kat, it was the room where most of the paranormal activity took place. He should have guessed it from the start, but he was sure part of him had been trying in vain to deny that possibility.

He started down the hallway, wishing he'd brought his pistol in with him from the car. Then again, he wasn't sure what good a gun would be against ghoulies or ghosts or whatever it was that inhabited this place. Most likely he would just end up terrifying Kat more than she already was by pointing it at her, thinking she was a spook of some sort.

He stopped just before reaching the doorway and tilted his head, listening. The room was generally quiet, but he thought he could make out the sound of someone breathing inside occasionally mixed with the scuttling sound he heard back at the stairs. Both were encouraging sounds: breath indicated life, and that scuttling indicated weight and mass, both things he had a hard time picturing in a ghost. He took one last deep, steadying breath and stepped through the open doorway.

A figure stood at the other end of the room, the scant starlight drifting through the window rendering them nothing more than a silhouette amidst the deeper darkness of the room itself. Bradley thought the size and build were comparable to Kat, and felt a relieved breath escape his lungs at the realization he had found her, and she was alive. Whether she was otherwise all right, he could not say.

She was naked and facing away from him, her head tilted slightly upward as if bathing in that starlight coming through the window. Her arms hung at her sides loosely, her legs slightly apart with her weight evenly distributed to both feet. Her hair still appeared damp, hanging down her back with stray strands of it sticking to her shoulders. She gave no indication that she knew of his presence here, nor did she seem to even fully realize where she was. That in and of itself was enough to send chills down his spine.

He took a tentative step forward, his eyes locked on her back, fighting the sudden temptation to let his gaze trail lower across her bare bottom. He knew how to function in an emergency, knew the line where it became no longer appropriate to even entertain such thoughts, much less act on them, but the urge was so unexpected and nearly overpowering that for a moment he didn't even feel like himself.

When she moved, he froze in place, afraid of startling her out of whatever dream or trance or whatever it was she was experiencing. She took a couple of shuffling steps backward, her head dropping, her arms slowly coming up to cover her face before returning to the exact place and position she had been standing when he first came in. The sounds she made matched the scuttling he heard from the hallway. He did not know what it was, no clue whatsoever what she was doing, but he had the distinct impression she did not want to be here and simply couldn't figure out how to get away.

He remembered the panicked expression on her face when he awoke to find her in the grips of a horrifying night terror, remembering the day her son was killed, and wondered if this was something similar. He hoped it was. He managed to bring her back from that, and if it was the same, he stood a chance of bringing her back from this as well. He had to try. He couldn't very well just leave her standing here naked and staring at the moon like a lunatic.

"Kat," he said softly, afraid of raising his voice too much and startling her. "Kat, it's me, Bradley. Let's get you dried off and dressed, okay? Then we can talk about it."

Her head tilted languidly from one side to the other, pausing just above one shoulder before slowly shifting to the opposite one. When it returned to center, she turned toward him, her motions jerky and irregular. It was as if she were a puppet being controlled by someone with little experience in how the strings worked. Finally, she faced him, and even through the shadows across her face he could see she was smiling. Instead of being reassuring, it only served to add to his growing terror.

"Do you like this?" she asked. Her voice sounded strange, her accent different, her tone deeper than it normally was. In a way, it sounded like she was talking in her sleep, but Bradley was sure her eyes were open and staring directly into his own. "Does my body appeal to you?"

Bradley swallowed the lump that was forming in his throat and forced himself to continue holding her gaze. The urge to ogle her was overpowering him, and he knew if he gave in tonight would wind up heading in a direction he did not want it to go. She might be offering, but she was also not herself. If he gave in, if he succumbed to the urges he could feel bubbling beneath the surface of his restraint, it would begin a journey down a path he could never turn away from. He didn't know how he knew this, only that he did. For now, that was enough.

"This isn't the time for that, Kat," he replied. "I'm more worried about your mind than your body right now."

"Liar," she said. She giggled, and Bradley felt goosebumps rise on his arms at the sound. "Tease."

"Kat," he said, adding a touch of authority to his voice. Not too much—he wasn't trying to turn her against him—but enough to make her want to pay attention to him. "Stop this. You need to come back to me, and you need to do it now."

Her body shivered as though a draft of cold air had blown across her skin. He noticed the smile on her face vanished just before her head bowed so deeply he thought he heard her chin strike her chest. Another shiver wracked her, then her knees buckled. He was already in motion and managed to catch her just before she crumpled to the floor. Another brief insistence he was now holding her while she was naked ran through his mind and then was gone as quickly as it appeared. He eased her to the ground, then felt her trembling again and realized this time it was because she was crying. He pulled her close and held her and felt a flash of relief as her arms wound around his back and clutched him closer while she sobbed into his chest.

"It was him," she said, her voice now hoarse but decidedly her own again. "Alston. He was here. He..."

"Shh," Bradley said, stroking her hair. "You're okay now, he's gone. It's just me."

"I understand now," she said. Bradley found he had to strain to hear her, as she was barely speaking above a whisper. "I understand what he wants."

She pulled away and met his eyes again. Bradley wanted to look away, to not see the helpless terror within her eyes, but he forced himself to keep looking at her.

"He knows he's damned," she whispered. "He knows he's damned for what he's done. He just wants to take as many people with him as he can."

PART THREE

HIDDEN HEARTS

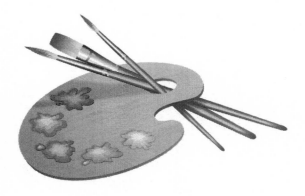

CHAPTER TWENTY-SIX

She was going home again, and while it shouldn't feel strange to her, it did. Part of it was just fear, the dread born of understanding exactly what she might end up facing while she was back in the house. Part was knowing she *needed* to go back and had been away too long already.

Another part of her, however, rather enjoyed spending the last week with Bradley at his place. She might have enjoyed it more if he were more willing to share the bed with her—it was his, after all—but she had to respect his chivalry in refusing to do so. He'd told her what happened when he found her in the second-floor bedroom, and she remembered all too well the feeling of someone else influencing her actions. She could understand his desire to keep her at arms' length for now. She only hoped it didn't continue once they got rid of Henry Alston's troublesome ghost.

Katherine sighed and watched the empty pastures pass by as the car made its way back toward Poplar Bend. She held onto the belief that somehow they *could* get rid of him, somehow clear the way for her to have the life she wanted in the house she never realized she had been dreaming about, but so far they had little to work with. She'd done a considerable amount of research in the last week, but while it made good suggestions, there was always the assumption she had more to start with than she really did. Knowing the history of the house and the ghosts who haunted it was a benefit, but only good as a starting place. Based on the many internet articles she discovered, until she knew what bound the spirits to the house, she would have no way of getting rid of them.

She had even given serious thought to having a priest come and bless the house, but she wasn't confident enough in her own faith to think it would succeed. She was a lapsed Methodist, and the only members of the clergy suggested to perform such things by the internet seemed to be of the Catholic variety. Whether this was due to their propensity toward rituals and ceremony or just playing into a stereotype, she did not know. Bradley was of the opinion that if they approached the local preacher with the problem, he would only lecture them on the dangers of playing with the occult and supernatural. She didn't know anyone else she trusted enough to ask, so the point was effectively moot. Besides, after what happened to Tommy, she was not inclined to believe God would lend his assistance to her, anyway. He had certainly not given her any Divine Providence last Halloween, so why should He start now?

"Christ," the woman in the back seat said, pulling Katherine out of her thoughts and back to the here and now. "You think you could have moved any further out into the damn sticks?"

Katherine looked back and smiled. She hadn't wanted to involve Leslie in any of this, but Bradley was adamant that she not go back to her house and stay there alone. He could not be with her all the time, so it had to be someone else. When he asked if she knew anyone she could convince to come out and stay for a week or so, Leslie had been the only person she was willing to mention. The other option would have been her mother or father, and she was not in any way ready for that particular conversation.

She was not surprised Leslie agreed to come. Katherine knew the second she mentioned she needed help, the woman would be on the next flight from Charleston to Nashville. It *did* surprise her how easily Leslie appeared to believe Katherine's story. When Katherine went through her crystals and "psychic energies" phase back in college, Leslie told her she had lost her mind. That she would fully accept not only the existence of ghosts but the fact Katherine was living in a house where one was tormenting her was unexpected, to say the least.

"This is still the main road," Bradley said. "Wait until you see the town itself. And Kat here is deeper in the wilderness than that."

"Oh, come on," Katherine replied, slapping him playfully on the arm. "You make it sound like I have bears congregating on my porch every morning or something. It's not *that* bad."

"So you think," he said, smiling. "I've got my invitation to the bear get-together tomorrow, I just haven't told them I'm coming yet."

"Get a room," Leslie said.

Katherine was also surprised how easily Leslie had taken to Bradley. Her friend was not much for men in general, and was especially critical of the ones Katherine took a liking to. When she and Dave first announced their engagement, Leslie hadn't spoken to her for a week afterward. When finally confronted about it, her friend had insisted he was worthless and nothing more than a leech who would drain her dry then move on to greener pastures. That her warning turned out to be correct was irrelevant. There was no way she could have known such a thing. Leslie just didn't like him, plain and simple, and Katherine was convinced the only reason their friendship had survived was because the woman cared more about her than she'd hated Katherine's choice for a husband.

At least she kept the "I told you so" to herself when Dave finally lived up to his presumed nature.

She glanced over at Bradley and was amused to see a slight blush had risen in his cheeks. It made him look boyish rather than manly, and it was nice to think that despite his macho exterior, he was still like a little kid when it came to her. Maybe that was why Leslie accepted him. She was one of the most perceptive people Katherine had ever met, so her approval was well worth noting.

When they turned off the main road and onto the arc of a side street that was Poplar Bend's main thoroughfare, Leslie grunted. When they began down the twisting blacktop that led to Kat's driveway, she had begun to mutter to herself. Once the gravel driveway came into view and she realized that was their destination, she laughed.

"You have got to be kidding me," she said. "Do you even have indoor plumbing out here? Electricity? *Cable?*"

"Yes to the first two, no to the last," Katherine said. "Not exactly. It's some little mom and pop company that provides phone and internet service out here. Television comes via satellite."

"Dear God," Leslie said, craning her neck to watch the trees pass by overhead. "I've gone back in time. It's the nineteenth century out here."

"Come on," Katherine said, turning in her seat to face her. "It's not that bad."

It was at that moment they rounded the corner, the house coming into view for the first time. Leslie raised one eyebrow pointedly and stared up at the sprawling Victorian atop the hill.

"You were saying?"

Katherine rolled her eyes and turned back to face the front. She had to admit, with all the lights off and the sun starting to go down behind it, one truly could believe they were in a different time. Only the sight of her Pathfinder and the hood of Bradley's Toyota broke the illusion.

"There are houses older than this one back in Charleston," she pointed out.

"And every damned one of them have a Kwik Stop within walking distance," Leslie replied. "Maybe that's what makes it feel normal. Build one next door, then talk to me."

Bradley chuckled as he turned around and backed up near the door so they wouldn't have far to carry both her and Leslie's bags. Katherine gave him a pained look.

"Thanks for the help," she said, mock-angrily.

"What?" he asked. "She has a point. Never thought about it 'til now, but nearly every classic home out there nowadays has some kind of modern building right next to it. It does make you feel grounded in the right era, that's for sure."

"I like this one," Leslie said, smiling. "He agrees with me. You can keep him."

"Like that's all it takes to please you," Katherine mumbled. She was sure Leslie hadn't heard what she said, but her intent must have come across clear enough because the woman laughed out loud.

The three of them piled out of the car and gathered around the trunk while Bradley opened it and removed suitcases. Three of them—the largest three, Katherine noted—were Leslie's. The other two were hers and were now filled with more dirty laundry for her to do. Thinking about it now, it was a good thing she'd convinced him to let her come home. Another day or two and she would have been forced to walk around his house naked because she was out of clean clothes. Of course, considering how much of a gentleman he seemed insistent on being, he would have just let her wear his instead. Eventually, though, they would both be out. He would probably be a spoilsport and go to a Laundromat or something before that happened, damn the luck.

"Are you going to come on or stand there fantasizing all night?" Leslie asked. "In case you haven't noticed, it's freaking cold out here."

Katherine jumped and looked up, suddenly embarrassed to find that she was still standing next to the trunk with her bags in her hands while the other two were already waiting for her at the front door. She was thankful it was twilight so her blush would be hidden as she quickly mounted the steps to join them.

"Flighty artists," Leslie said teasingly. "Never could keep your mind on where you were, could you?"

"Shut up," Katherine muttered, blushing even more furiously. "You sound like Yoda."

Leslie immediately began croaking in a horrible approximation of the character's voice. Katherine found herself unable to do anything but laugh at her. Bradley shook his head, smiling at their banter, then unlocked the door and opened it.

The smell hit them as soon as he pushed the door inward, a foul, bitter blast that was so potent it actually left Katherine's skin feeling soiled just from the stench of it. Her nose wrinkled, and Bradley took an involuntary step backward to escape it.

"Christ!" Leslie exclaimed, turning her head away and ducking down to blunt the force of it. "What the fuck is that? Indoor plumbing meant running water, not shitting in the damn corner somewhere."

"It didn't smell like that when we left," Bradley said. "You think maybe the septic tank's gone out? Has to be something like that."

"No, it doesn't," she said, her eyes locked on the open doorway. "And you know it doesn't."

He looked over at her, momentarily confused. After a moment she saw understanding blossom across his face. He nodded.

"I'll go check it out," he said. "You two wait out here."

"With pleasure," Leslie said, setting her bags down next to the door. "Light a match while you're at it."

He turned away from the door, took a couple deep breaths, then went inside. Katherine turned to see Leslie staring at her, a blank expression on her face.

"What?" she asked.

Leslie shook her head. "You really think some ghost is doing this instead of something reasonable like ancient plumbing finally breaking down?"

Katherine sighed and instantly regretted it when she forgot herself and inhaled through her nose.

"I don't know, Les," she said, once she could breathe properly. "At this point, I'm just willing to look at all the options, even the ones that don't make a lot of sense."

"That's fair," Leslie said. "I'll be straight with you: when you called me up and told me all that shit, I thought you'd finally lost it. I'm still not convinced, but I believe *you* are. I'm here because Prince Charming there thinks you might be in danger if you're left alone. Ghosts or crazy rednecks—which for the record is what I'm leaning toward—could both be a problem. The other thing that could be a problem is you finally hitting your breaking point."

"I'm not crazy, Les," she said. "There's something in there. Something that is not happy I'm living here."

"Like you said, I'll look at all the options," Leslie replied. "But the second I think this is all in your head, you'll be on a plane back to South Carolina faster than you can say 'involuntary commitment', capeesh?"

"Bradley's seen it too, Les."

"Has he?" her friend asked, taking a step closer to her. Leslie's face was all seriousness now, no trace of her normal humor in evidence. "Has he really? Because from what the two of you told me, he's not seen anything other than you acting weird. I'm willing to give him the benefit of the doubt, penis or not, since he seems like he was there for you when you really needed somebody, but don't go thinking that just because some hick cop from rednecksville says what you're saying is the truth that I'm going to believe him. I've known you for years, Kat, and I know what you've been through. I know how much that shit can weigh on you. And I also love you enough to be willing to slap you down before you get too far gone. I'm off work 'til New Year's. That's three weeks. If by the time that's nearly up I haven't seen anything that makes me believe you're living in a haunted house, I'm taking you home and getting you some real help. If you're unwilling to agree to that, then I'm sorry. Put me back on the plane right now, because I'm not going to sit by and watch my best friend turn into a raving loon without being able to do anything about it."

Katherine wanted to feel anger at the woman's outburst, but there was so much care and love in her eyes, despite the sternness in her voice, that she could not. She also thought it was a fair request, and one she was liable to have made herself if their roles were reversed.

"If you haven't seen anything to convince you by New Year's," she said. "Then I'll go back with you willingly. But I don't think I'll be leaving."

"Think what you want," Leslie said. "I only want what's best for you. Crazy as it sounds, I hope you're right and I'm wrong. I always thought you were stronger than that, and I'd hate for you to prove otherwise."

"That's kind of messed up, Les," Katherine said, the hint of a smile creeping onto her face. "You'd rather me have ghosts out to get me than be proven wrong?"

Leslie tried to hold on to her firm expression, but her lips twitched too much for the effect to maintain its potency. "That's not what I meant."

"Actually," Kat said, letting the smile turn a little wicked. "If you're staying with me for three weeks, I should probably be more afraid of you than of the ghosts. I'm liable to wake up one night and find you dressed in leather holding a branding iron."

"What the shit, girl?" Leslie said, giving up the pretense and laughing in return. "I'm not some deviant just because I like girls."

"Remember that night, sophomore year, after the Omega party?"

"That involved too much tequila and way too much ecstasy," Leslie replied. She pointed a finger at Katherine. "And as I remember, what little I can, you were the one egging me on. 'Ride me like a Shetland pony,' I think you said."

Katherine felt herself blush again, more furiously than before. "I don't know what you're talking about."

"Keep telling yourself that."

Bradley chose that moment to return, stopping as he exited the house, his face growing confused as he looked from Katherine to Leslie and back again. "Did I interrupt something?"

"Yes," Leslie said, sounding put out.

"No," Katherine said at the same time.

"Right," he said, wisely choosing to ignore that entire line of conversation. "I didn't see any issues with the toilets. They all flushed okay, so I opened the windows to air the place out a bit. It's already better than it was. Should be fine in a little while. You two want to chance going on in, or maybe grab something to eat then come back?"

"Yeah," Leslie said. "Like I've got anything resembling an appetite after smelling that."

She turned to Katherine. "You have alcohol in there?"

"Yes," Katherine replied. "No tequila though."

"Too bad," Leslie said as she picked her luggage back up. "Your boy here might have gotten himself one hell of a show if you did."

She pushed past Bradley, who gave Katherine a confused, helpless look that sent her off into a giggling fit. Somehow, she got both herself and her two bags inside without dropping them or falling in the process. She hadn't realized until now how long it had been since she could laugh like this and was thankful for what she knew would only be a brief diversion from her troubles.

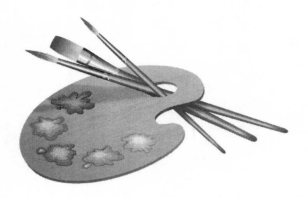

CHAPTER TWENTY-SEVEN

Frank paused inside the bar, giving his eyes a chance to adjust to the sudden change from bright daylight to shadowed darkness. There were lights in here. They just weren't doing much to illuminate the place. He supposed that was the way the patrons preferred it. For most of the group that frequented Horace's watering hole, it was better to be hidden than exposed to the light. At this particular moment, he could understand the urge. He was thankful anyone just sticking their head in wouldn't be able to tell it was him in here, either.

Once he could see a little better, he realized the only person actually in the room was Horace himself, planted in his accustomed place behind the bar, the end of a cigarette waggling as he scrubbed at an apparently troublesome spot on the countertop. He looked up as Frank approached and tipped his head in welcome.

"Get you anything, Marshal?" he asked around the butt. "It ain't happy hour yet, but I reckon I can start it up a little early."

"You kiddin' me?" Frank asked. "It's barely three in the afternoon. Who's doin' any heavy drinkin' this time of day?"

Before Horace could answer, the door opened and Wally Barton stepped inside, the dank odor of old grease preceding him. From the looks of it, he hadn't bothered cleaning his hands before heading over from the service station across the street.

"Shot of Jack and a Bud," he said, nodding as he passed Frank on his way to the bar. "And let's get on with this. I got a bitch of an engine tore apart over there, and I'd like to get done with it 'fore Christmas."

Horace shot Frank a bemused look before turning to prepare Wally's order. Frank shook his head and took the stool next to the old mechanic. The man had the shot downed before Horace could even get the beer pulled from the tap. Frank was amazed, as he always was, how someone could build up such a tolerance to hard liquor that it didn't seem to faze them at all when they drank it. Frank was not a teetotaler and had spent more than his share of time inside a bottle or two, but he still winced every time he took that first drink of the stuff. Who knew? Maybe if he kept it up, he could do it without a reaction in another fifteen or twenty years just like Wally could.

"Guess whatever we need to talk about's gonna depend on you, Marshal," Horace said, leaning on the counter. "Let's start with whether or not that bastard's the one killed Clay."

Frank sighed and ran a hand over his face. "Be a new one on me if he did. Never happened before. The medical boys haven't come back with anything yet, but if I was a bettin' man I'd say the only way he could have had anything to do with Clay dyin' is if he scared the old fart to death."

Wally downed half of his beer in two long swallows before letting out a belch loud enough to nearly rattle the glassware in front of him. "That's what I figured most likely, too. Clay wasn't exactly no young'un, and I doubt he did himself no favors gallavantin' around out there."

"You think he shouldn't have said anything?" Frank asked. "Just let her flounder on her own 'til she killed herself like Blackmore did back in the day?"

"I think Clayton Davison took whatever happened out the Hollow too personal for his own good," Wally replied. "And you can drop that other bullshit right now, Frank Bradshaw. Ain't a damn one of us sittin' here actually believes that Blackmore asshole did himself in. I know I didn't do it, and Horace didn't do it, and I believed Clayton when he said he never worked up the damn nerve to do it, and that only leaves one person could've done it."

"I was twelve when that happened," Frank said, chuckling. "You really think it was me done it?"

"Your pappy weren't twelve," Wally said, locking eyes with him.

"Just exactly what are you accusin', Wally?" Frank asked, matching his stare.

"You know damn well. Good for him if'n he did, too. A deal's a deal, and all he done was fulfil our end of it."

"This ain't solvin' shit," Horace said. "Tryin' to figure out ancient history ain't the issue here. Dealin' with what's happenin' right now is."

Wally continued trying to stare Frank down for another moment before finally looking away, finishing his beer, and motioning to Horace for another one. Horace got it for him, then returned his attention to Frank.

"She gettin' anywhere tryin' to fix it?" he asked.

"No idea," Frank said, shrugging. "I know she's dragged my deputy into it, just like I hoped she would, and I know they've made some kinda progress, but he's not bein' very open about his extracurricular investigations."

"He know how tied up in it you are?" Wally asked, not looking at him.

"No," Frank said, scowling at the man. "Despite what you and Clay might've thought, I do know how to keep my gob shut. Clay never knew how much I was involved neither, so that should tell you somethin'."

Wally shrugged, but kept any possible comments on that to himself.

Frank sighed. This next part was not something he wanted to tell them, but the promise he made to his Daddy back when the old man was on his deathbed still meant something to him, something he could not easily discard. Like it or not, he was—as Wally so crudely put it—"tied up in it".

"There is somethin', though," he said. "Bradley asked for the day off so he could take Kat into Nashville and meet some friend of hers at the airport. Way I understand it, whoever it is plans on stayin' out there, too."

"Goddamn it all," Wally said. "So much for keepin' town business inside the damn town."

"You met this friend yet?" Horace asked, shooting Wally a look that told the other man he would be better off just shutting the hell up while he was ahead.

"No," Frank replied. "I was plannin' on headin' out there tomorrow, checkin' on that paintin' Kat was workin' on for me. Bradley said he thought it was done, but since she was stayin' with him, he didn't know for sure. Looks like I still got that as an excuse for just showin' up."

"That was the stupidest plan I ever heard tell of," Wally muttered. "Too damned limitin', you ask me."

"No one did," Frank said.

The old man ignored him. "She gets done with that, you ain't got no reason to pop in and check on her. Might even resort to lettin' her in on why you been elected all these years, even though you ain't much of shit for law 'round here."

"And just maybe I damn well should," Frank said, rising from his stool and forcing his hands to not ball up into fists like they wanted to. "Let her know about the cocky old fuck who's been breakin' more cars than he fixes and thinks he knows more and better than everybody else lives in this town, too. Let her know how that same old man thought killin' her the day she moved in to keep a damn ghost happy was a better idea than lettin' her try to get rid of that same damn ghost."

"You ain't doin' that, Frank," Horace said, reaching over the bar as if that would prevent a fight if one was about to break out. "And Wally, you need to shut your damn mouth, too. The days where you had enough pull to rig a town election's long gone. Look at the mayor, for Christ's sake. He sure wasn't what we wanted in office, some outsider don't know nothin' 'bout nothin' when it comes to this town's secrets. How 'bout we solve this instead of fightin' about it?"

"Since that's worked so well all these years," Frank muttered. He looked up and saw Horace staring at him, irritation plain on his face. "Sorry. I know, I'm not helpin'."

Horace continued to stare at him until he finally forced himself to relax and sit back down.

"Ya'll both need to remember," Horace said, his voice that of a stern schoolmarm lecturing her students. Frank figured in a way that comparison was not far from true. "With Clay gone, we're all that's left to keep that old bastard contained out there."

"Should've just burnt the damn place down soon as we learned 'bout it," Wally said. "Wouldn't have to deal with this shit no more that way."

"Unless that made it worse," Horace replied. "We discussed that a long damn time ago and decided that not knowin' what would happen was reason enough to not do it."

He looked back to Frank. "You go on out there tomorrow, feel 'em out. Maybe that friend of hers is what's needed to make it happen. You think that's the case, we'll give it a little longer. It looks like she's not gonna succeed, or that it might make things go back to the way they was, we'll decide what to do, then, just like we done with Blackmore. Only thing I need to know is are you goin' to be able to deal with it if we need to contain her, too?"

"Deathbed promise still means somethin' to me, even if you two don't think it does," Frank replied. Horace gave him a considering look, and for a moment Frank thought the man had caught the hesitation in his voice. Then he nodded and looked over to Wally.

"That settled for you?" he asked.

Wally snorted, finished his second beer, and rose from his stool. "Waste of damned time comin' over here. You call me once you both grow a pair and feel like doin' what needs t'be done."

He slapped a ten-dollar bill on the bar and left without another word. Frank watched him go, frowning. His Daddy had told him a long time ago that both Clay Davison and Wally Barton would be hard to deal with, but he had no idea just how much the comment failed to capture the realities of the two old men's personalities. Talking to both of them was like talking to brick walls that were liable to collapse and bury you at any minute. Now that Clay was gone, it was as though Wally felt he had to become twice as obstinate to make up for it.

Frank turned back to the bar, shaking his head. Horace was somewhat reasonable, if irrationally committed to this same horrible deal they all maintained. He glanced up and found the old bartender was still looking at him curiously, the ten-spot ignored on the counter.

"I know you like that girl, Frank," Horace said at last. "And I know you ain't too fond of this arrangement, but like you said, you made a deathbed promise. And to your pappy, to beat all. He believed in this, so you have'ta think maybe he wasn't just doin' it for no reason."

"I'll do what I promised, it comes to that," Frank said, rising as well. "Don't mean I have to like it none, though."

"No," Horace agreed. "It don't. You let us know what you think of that girl's friend. And keep an eye on your deputy. He's brighter than I think you give him credit for. You ain't careful, he'll sniff you out. Then we're all in for it."

He considered telling Horace he was well aware of how talented Bradley was at law enforcement and investigating things that needed to be looked into, but kept it to himself. He also kept to himself how he had been secretly hoping that Bradley would dig deeper than he had into what actually happened to Blackmore all those years ago.

Maybe it would help keep him from becoming a murderer like his father had been.

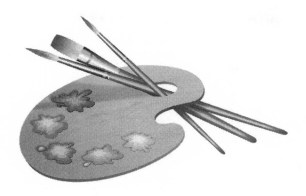

CHAPTER TWENTY-EIGHT

Katherine tried hard not to laugh at Bradley, she really did, but at the sight of yet another look of bewilderment crossing his face, she couldn't stop herself. It had been this way since they picked Leslie up at the airport this morning. The strait-laced deputy just couldn't seem to figure out how to deal with the boisterous and opinionated woman. He did not act like anything she said or did particularly offended him, which was always a possibility where Leslie was involved, but he had definitely been embarrassed more than once. Not as bad as when Leslie asked whether he had, in her words, "been sticking it to her best friend yet," but his face had been continually red since.

At least this time she had some idea why he looked so confused. She and Leslie were seated in the middle of the sitting room floor, all the furniture pushed to the sides, a Ouija board resting on the floor between them. They had saved him a space beside Leslie, across from Kat. He stared at the two of them and then at the board, his head shaking slightly as he took it all in.

"Are you sure this is such a good idea?" he asked.

"Did Blackmore's brother return our call from the other day? Or the one I made before that?" she asked in reply.

He sighed and shook his head slowly. "I left another message, but still nothing."

"Then what else do we have?" she asked. "It's either try to talk to Lucy this way, or hope she's the next one to show up around here and not...him."

Bradley made his way around the clutter of furniture slid out of the way and settled onto the floor in the spot waiting for him. "I don't think that's how it works. At least, I've never seen it work like that, not that...*specific*."

"Had a lot of experience playing with a witchboard have you?" Leslie asked, her eyes twinkling.

"Hardly," he said. "Last time I saw one of these things, my little sister was playing around with a bunch of her friends at a sleepover."

"You spy on your sister and her friends a lot, then?" Leslie retorted, the corners of her mouth twitching up.

"Actually, yes," Bradley said. He sounded pleased he finally got one over on Leslie. "Anything I could come up with to get her in trouble. Either I used it to distract our parents from something I had done, or I used it as blackmail so she wouldn't tell on me. And as for spying on her friends, I was only two years older than her, so once we were both in high school, you're damn right I spied on her cute friends."

Kat smiled and shook her head. He thought he would come out ahead here, but for someone with wit as quick as Leslie's, he had just given her miles of ammunition to use against him. She held up a hand, stopping her friend before she even got started with her comebacks.

"Let it go, Les."

"Are you kidding?" the woman asked, her face a shining ray of amusement. "This is too easy!"

"Exactly," Katherine replied. "That means there's no challenge in it for you. Just wait until a better, more subtle opportunity comes around."

Leslie glanced over at Bradley, who had lost his triumphant smile at some point during their brief conversation. He now stared at the two women, obviously trying to figure out what he said that they thought such an easy mark.

"Yeah," Leslie said. "You're right. There'll be a better one come along soon enough, and it's always more fun when they don't see it coming."

"Hell," Bradley said. "It is just like being around my sister and her friends again. Let's get on with this. How are we supposed to do it?"

Katherine spoke before Leslie could hijack the conversation with another cheap shot. "We all put our hands on the pointer thing there and clear our minds."

"Planchette," Leslie said. Katherine turned and gave her a confused look. "The pointer's called a planchette. Read it somewhere."

"Okay," Katherine said. "We all put our hands on the planchette and clear our minds."

"Fingertips," Leslie said.

Katherine rolled her eyes and looked over to her friend. "You want to explain this?"

"No, go ahead," Leslie replied. "I'll just correct when needed. Have to make sure the perv there doesn't screw it up."

It was Bradley's turn to roll his eyes.

"Fine," Katherine said, giving Leslie a look that said playtime was over, please shut the hell up now. "We put our *fingertips* on the *planchette* and try not to think about anything in particular. I'll lead and try to make contact with Lucy. If she's willing or able to answer, she'll move the *planchette* across the board and spell out words to communicate with us."

"And if it's not her?" Bradley asked. "If we get something else, then what?"

"If it's willing to answer us, I say we keep going for it," Katherine answered. "If it looks like it might be Alston or his wife, we stop. That sound reasonable?"

"What if it's Clay?" Bradley asked. "I wouldn't put it past the old man to get the last word in, even if he has to do it from beyond the grave."

"Then maybe he'll be more willing to talk to me," Katherine said. "Since he knows what the stakes are this time around."

Bradley shrugged. "I still think we're tempting fate, but it's your call, I suppose."

"Since you won't let me drink until we're done with this," Leslie said. "Let's get on with it, please."

Katherine placed the pointer in the middle of the board and nodded. "Okay then, fingers on the pointer... the *planchette*, I mean, and clear your minds."

The others did as she instructed, Bradley with a resigned look on his face, Leslie with a smirk Katherine thought was related to her disbelief in this entire process but could have meant anything. She gently rested her own fingers on the plastic pointer next to theirs and closed her eyes, forcing her surface thoughts away for the time being. She tried to remember how Lucy looked that night she saw the girl upstairs, but it wasn't easy. For one thing, it had been dark, and she had only seen the girl in deep shadow. For another, Katherine was all too aware the girl had been a spirit. There was every possibility the girl she saw looked nothing at all like the real Lucy had.

"We're looking for a girl who once lived here named Lucy," Katherine said aloud. She did not know if this was how she was supposed to do this or not, but it was the only way she could think of. "She had a grandnephew named Clayton Davison, and she was killed by the woman whose husband owned this house. You spoke to me once, upstairs, in what I think was your old bedroom. Will you speak to me again now?"

She felt the pointer move under her fingers and opened her eyes. It was trailing slow, tight circles around the center of the board. She glanced up, her gaze travelling from Bradley to Leslie and back again. Both of them wore expressions that were slightly different versions of the same amazement. Still, she felt the question needed to be asked.

"Are either of you doing that?" she whispered. "If you are, tell me, please."

"It's not me," Bradley said. His mouth turned down in a slight frown. "That's weird. I was going to pull my hands away to show you, but they won't let go."

"They're probably not supposed to," Katherine said. She was tempted to try herself, but was too afraid that as the one directing the session, she might stop it before it really began. She glanced over to Leslie instead.

"I'm not doing it," Leslie said. "In all the times I played with shit like this as a kid, it never happened like this. Usually, it *was* somebody moving the stupid thing. It's not you, is it?"

Katherine shook her head and returned her attention to the board. "Is someone here, someone other than the three of us calling to you? Hello?"

The pointer shifted then, rapidly moving across the board, the tip pausing just beneath some letters printed there.

"H," Katherine read. "E. L. L. O. Y. O. U. R. S. E. L. F."

The pointer resumed tracing those tight circles in the center of the board.

"Hello yourself," Bradley said softly. "Well, I suppose that's a response."

"Is this Lucy?" Katherine asked.

The pointer moved across the board again, stopping at the word "no" in the corner.

Katherine sighed. "Do you know her? Is she there?"

"It's not a phone call," Leslie muttered, but the pointer was already spelling out its response.

"L. U. C. Y. W. A. T. C. H. M. E. L. U. C. Y. C. A. R. E. 4. M. E."

"Weird," Bradley said. "You think maybe it's one of the other kids who lived here? One she took care of or something?"

"Maybe," Katherine said. "Mister Davison wasn't clear on anything, so I don't even know how old the kids were who died here."

A chill ran down her back as she realized the statements could have another meaning.

"Was your last name Alston?" she asked, terrified of what the answer might be.

The pointer drifted to the "no," hesitated, shifted to the "yes," then back to the "no" again.

"Is that an 'I don't know?'" Leslie asked.

"I think so," Katherine said. "If it was one of the kids who were fathered by Alston, they might be confused about it. Is that what happened?"

The pointer remained on the "no" briefly, then dropped back to the circling motion again.

"Okay," Katherine said slowly. "We don't understand. Can you explain what you mean?"

The pointer moved. "M. E. A. N. N. O. T. H. I. N. G."

"Mean nothing," Leslie said. "That clears it right up."

Katherine considered for a moment. "Names. You mean names mean nothing after you die?"

The pointer moved to the "yes" and stopped.

"Okay then," Katherine said. "So what should we call you?"

The pointer hesitated, then repeated its previous message.

"Means nothing," Katherine repeated. "So I guess we're not getting a name. Are you willing to help us, then, or are you here to harm us?"

The pointer shifted from "yes" to "no" and back again.

"That's encouraging," Bradley said. "Your call, Kat."

Katherine bit her lip and weighed her options before finally letting out a frustrated sigh and shaking her head. "What other choice do we have? We keep going. After all, could it get any worse than it's already been?"

"Why do people ask that question?" Leslie said, moaning. "You know that just means somehow it *will* get worse."

Even though she knew her friend was right, Katherine ignored her. "The man who lived here a long time ago, the one who killed all the children. Do you know who that is?"

The pointer went to the "yes" and remained.

"Why is he still here?" Katherine asked. "Why did he not pass over when he died?"

The pointer resumed those tight circles, then finally spelled out four letters.

"Pain," Bradley said. "Does that mean he won't go away because he's in pain, or something else?"

Katherine asked. The pointer hesitated, then began moving again.

"L. O. V. E. 2. G. I. V. E. G. I. V. E. F. O. R. E. V. E. R," Katherine read. "I didn't catch that."

"Love to give, give forever?" Leslie said. "I think that's what it was."

"So there's no way to get rid of him," Katherine said, feeling her heart lurch at the thought. "He'll stay here as long as he keeps getting to bring pain to someone."

The pointer lurched beneath her fingers, pointing to the "no."

She frowned. "No, there's no way to get rid of him, or no, he won't stay here so he can hurt people."

"U. C. A. N. G. E. T. R. I. D."

"Okay, we can get rid of him, then," she replied. "How?"

When it began spelling out the response, it moved so fast Katherine struggled to keep up with it. She wished they had the forethought to keep one of them out of this ritual or whatever so they could take notes. Too late for that now, apparently, and she was too afraid whatever spirit was speaking to her would leave if they broke the connection to grab a pen and some paper.

"You have to slow down," she said. "I can't understand you when you go that fast."

Strangely, the pointer hesitated, then started over. She remembered how Tommy used to get so excited about something he would talk too fast for anyone to understand him, then when she would point this out, he would say it again, much slower than before, almost mockingly but with no real ill intent behind it. She supposed it was common for all young children. The thought brought on a wave of sympathy for this sad soul. They died so young, and were trapped here, in this hellish place, with the ghost of the man who killed them.

"Set. Them. Free," she read as each word was completed. "Give. Them. Peace. They. Stop. Him. Send. Him. Away. Set who free?"

"B. E. L. O. W."

"Below what?" Katherine asked.

The planchette repeated itself again, slightly faster this time as though the spirit was growing irritated with her. That wasn't something she wanted to happen, but she still didn't understand.

"Do you mean below the ground?" she asked, hoping if she clarified what part of the message she wasn't understanding, the spirit wouldn't be as upset with her. A strange thing to consider, but it had been a strange couple of months.

"Yes."

"Where, then?" she asked. "Where should I look?"

"B. E. L. O. W."

"I get that part," Katherine said. "But where should I look below?"

The pointer hesitated, then began to rapidly spell out words again.

"Have. To. Go," she read. "He. Comes. Now. Must. Run. Must. Hide. Lucy. Calling. Me."

As soon as the final word left her mouth, it felt as though the entire house shook. If they were in California, she could say it was the starting tremor to an earthquake, but they were in rural Tennessee, not directly on top of a fault line, so there was no explanation for it. She felt the pressure beneath her fingers growing, until the planchette shot forward off the end of the board, flipped twice in mid-air, and clattered to the ground between Leslie and Bradley.

"What the hell was that?" Leslie said, her hands trembling. "Felt like something shocked me."

"Same here," Bradley said. "I tried to replace a wall outlet at home once, and the breakers were labeled wrong so there was still juice going to it when I grabbed ahold of it. This felt just like that, only a little less powerful."

"I have no idea," Katherine replied. "And what was it talking about? Who was coming? Alston?"

"Who else could it be?" Bradley replied. "I'm more worried about what 'coming' actually meant."

"That's disgusting," Leslie said. It was obvious she was trying to lighten the mood, but the fear that resonated in her voice made the attempt fail miserably.

"*Soon.*"

The voice came from everywhere and nowhere, booming through Katherine's mind rather than her ears. A voice she heard before, most recently in the shower right before she woke up in Bradley's arms. Her suspicion had been correct. It was Alston who had frightened their contact away.

"What the fuck is that?" Leslie screamed. Her voice was easily an octave higher than normal and filled with hysteria. That frightened Katherine more than the presence of the spirit. In all the time she'd known Leslie, she'd never heard her this shaken.

She reached over and took both of Leslie's hands in hers. For a moment, the woman tried to pull away, her eyes rapidly jerking from side to side as if trying to figure out the best route for escape. Finally, they settled on Katherine's, and she stopped struggling.

"It's okay," Katherine said. "We're together. He can't do anything to us while we're together."

She did not know if the statement was true or not, though she doubted its veracity. From what she could remember in her shower the other night, there was nothing at all that would indicate it couldn't have happened with someone else in the room.

"*You are mine,*" the voice said. "*You are my playthings, in my home. I cannot touch you, cannot feel you beneath my hand yet, but soon you will be wholly mine, to do with as I please.*"

The words, the very concept of what Alston suggested frightened Katherine to her soul, but she fought to keep control of herself. This was *not* Alston's home any longer. He was a filthy child molester who deserved to rot in Hell for what he had done, but he was too stubborn to go. More than that, he had underestimated one crucial thing she learned about herself in the days right after Tommy was killed: She was stronger than even she allowed herself to know. She would *not* run—she had overcome that urge long ago. No, instead, she would fight.

"No, we won't you bastard," she called out. "We're not going to let you have us. We're going to send you back to Hell where you belong!"

The sound of resonant chuckling filled her mind. The bastard was *laughing* at her. The thought made her more furious than ever. She wished he were here in some physical form so she could punch him right in his smug face.

"*You will try,*" he said. "*And you will fail. I admire your fortitude. I will enjoy breaking you.*"

Every window in the room suddenly exploded, shards of glass flying through the air like razor-sharp rain. Katherine held up her hands to protect her face and winced as several slivers worked their way into her forearms. Wind raced in from outside, chilling her bare skin, raising gooseflesh and making her wounds throb. When she was fairly certain the storm was over, she lowered her hands and peered out at her backyard, the lack of anything between it and her eyes making her crazily think of an advertisement for a high definition television she had seen a couple of years ago. *An image so clear, you'll swear you were living it,* the tagline had been.

Leslie and Bradley had sustained their own nicks from the broken windows, they were both otherwise fine. She looked back to the shattered panes of glass and let out a frustrated sigh.

"Why can't he just leave the windows alone?" she asked. "This is getting way too expensive."

She turned and saw Bradley staring at her, his mouth slightly opened, his eyes confused. She tried to give him a smile she hoped was reassuring, but before it could form completely, she began to laugh instead. His face changed, and she knew exactly what he must be thinking, for she was beginning to wonder it, too.

How much longer could she deal with this and keep her sanity intact?

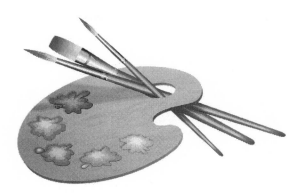

CHAPTER TWENTY-NINE

While Leslie meandered around her studio, Katherine finished getting dressed for bed, thankful to be back in her own house despite the events from earlier in the night and the possibility there might be more yet to come before the sun came up again. She hadn't intended to take a shower—the thought crossed her mind to never take one again, even knowing how implausible that would be—but Leslie had insisted if she was serious about the two of them sleeping in the same bed, there was no way she would lay there smelling her funk all night. It was a fair point. Helping Bradley put plywood over the shattered windows had not been an easy task. Katherine relented, but only after she made her friend understand the door and shower curtain would remain open, and Leslie had to sit outside the door and talk to her until she finished. She had expected more of an argument than she got, but considering the fact Leslie had experienced Alston's message to them the same as Katherine had, it was no real surprise how quickly she agreed.

Katherine pulled on a pair of socks and joined Leslie in the other room. The woman was flipping through the finished paintings propped against the table, occasionally pulling one up to get a better look at it. Katherine leaned against the door frame and watched her, unable to stop herself from smiling. Leslie had always been both her biggest critic and her staunchest fan, quick to tell her if something was a potential masterpiece or just a piece of shit. The greater benefit was that while Leslie didn't possess any creative talent of her own, she did have an eye for it, and could critique her honestly. Sometimes that criticism was a bit on the brutal side, but Katherine long ago came to understand that sometimes harshness was exactly what she needed to grow.

Leslie looked over her shoulder and caught Katherine watching her and rolled her eyes before turning back to her browsing.

"I assume you're going to want to hear the feedback," Leslie said.

"Sure," Katherine replied. "Since you're going to give it whether I want it or not."

Leslie snorted and pulled out the first painting Katherine had done when she arrived here, the one of the girl behind the house. Katherine braced herself for whatever might be coming. Especially with all that had happened to her since she set foot inside the house, that one held a particular place in her heart. She intended to hang it on the mantle, right next to the brighter version of the house. Or she would, once she painted it.

"Had you heard anything about this place when you did this one?" Leslie asked.

It was not the question Katherine expected. "Nothing. Just what the realtor said over the phone when I put my offer in on it."

"So you didn't know it was—and I can't believe I'm about to say this with a straight face—haunted."

Katherine shook her head. "I heard that a day or so later, when I met the marshal for the first time."

"Can't believe this town's so backwater it's still got a freaking marshal, either," Leslie muttered. "But that's neither here nor there."

She put the painting down and picked up the one of the girl on the second floor.

"And is this the Lucy chick you said you talked to?" she asked. "The one you were trying to contact through the Ouija board?"

"No," Katherine replied. "Or, well, I don't think it is. This looks more like the girl I saw...the one I saw Alston with a couple of days later."

Leslie nodded, put that painting down, and picked up a third. Katherine frowned. As far as she could remember, she had only done three complete works since arriving: the house, the girl, and the one of Frank and Elizabeth. Since the last of those was still sitting on her easel, she thought the canvas Leslie picked up must be blank, until she turned it around and let her see what was on it.

"And when did you do this one?"

It was a doorway filled with deep red shadows and strange streaks. Katherine assumed they were supposed to be lights, to give it a counterpoint of color and make the whole work feel eerie as opposed to balanced. The edges of the doorway were ragged, as though it wasn't something created naturally but rather something that had been constructed roughshod, without conscious effort or intent. She leaned closer and saw there was much more detail in the painting than it seemed on first glance. There were gradients within the shadows, forms that almost looked like small figures standing in the room beyond the doorway.

The painting was one of the best she had ever seen, even if the subject matter was well beyond the level of disturbing she normally found comfortable. That could be just a byproduct of the painting itself, but she thought it had more to do with the fact she couldn't remember painting it at all. There was no question she had been the one who did it. The style was distinctly hers, and the little mark she made in the lower right-hand corner of every painting she did was plain to see. Still, she had no memory of making the first stroke on the blank canvas, nor could she recall spraying the protective clear-coat over it when she was done.

Leslie apparently mistook her silence for rebuke rather than distress, because she shook her head as she put this new one back down and turned to the portrait.

"We'll start here," Leslie said. "Since I'm betting you didn't come up with this one on your own. It's not bad, a little vanilla, but you really laid on the shadowing on the guy's face. I'd have to see the original picture it was based on to say for sure, but if it looked like this, the photographer was shitty and you know better than to not fix it along the way."

"I don't know," Katherine said. None of what her friend was saying even came close to sinking in. She was still seeing that mysterious black-out painting in her mind. "I don't know when I did it."

Leslie turned back to her, confusion etched into her face. "What does that mean? I assume you did it during your final touches, isn't that when you told me you normally do light and shadow?"

"No, not the portrait," Katherine said, finally catching up to where the conversation was. "The other one. The doorway. I don't remember doing it."

Leslie frowned. "You mean it's one you did before you got here? One that's old enough you don't even remember doing it?"

"No, that's not..." Katherine shook her head, trying in vain to get her thoughts in order. "It had to have been done after I moved in here. I didn't bring any paintings with me. They're all in Dad's garage back in Charleston. I'm saying I don't remember painting it at all. The other two, I do. The portrait I just finished. That one, I didn't even know it existed until you showed it to me just now."

"You painted it and don't remember it?" Leslie asked. She moved to the side table where her glass of wine sat and drained the last little bit from it. Katherine was sure if it had been full, she would have drank it all. "That's not exactly normal, Kat."

"Kinda well aware of that, Les," Katherine said, unable to hold back the sarcasm. "And while I have absolutely no memory of doing it, I don't really remember much more about painting the other two, either."

Leslie looked at her glass as though she could refill it by willpower alone, then sat it back on the table. "Okay, you're not making a lot of sense anymore."

Katherine sighed. "I don't know how to explain it. I just... I have no memory of working on them. I remember starting them, then I'd wake up in bed or something and the painting would be finished. Hours would have gone by, and I didn't even know it."

"And you don't remember the one of the doorway at all."

Katherine shook her head.

Leslie chewed on her lip, a habit Katherine knew she had tried to break but still came out when she was very confused or trying hard not to let on how frightened she really was. This time, a good bet it was for both reasons.

"Okay," Leslie said, obviously trying to put the pieces together in her mind. "The one of the girl running from the house, I understand. Maybe your subconscious was warning you of something, maybe you were seeing yourself running away from everything back home."

"What makes you think that girl was me?" Katherine asked. "She doesn't look anything like me."

Leslie gave her a "bitch, please" look but otherwise ignored her. "The girl in the hallway, I get too, since you ended up seeing the ghost of one girl and talked to another down there."

"I painted it before either of those things happened."

"Then let's go out on a limb and say they influenced you, just like you say Alston did when you were showering last week," Leslie said, her tone clearly indicating her frustration with Katherine's constant interruptions. "Either way, both of those make sense. I assume the portrait was commission work since it doesn't match up with anything else you've done on your own before you stopped way back or now that you've started again, so we'll ignore that one. That leaves the doorway. You don't remember painting it: fine. But you must have. I know your work, Kat. And your eyes are screaming that you know it too. So forget that it was some kind of sleep-painting or whatever the hell. What does it mean?"

Katherine stepped around the table and looked at the painting again, trying to figure out what she must have been trying to tell herself. The others Leslie mentioned all fit the pattern of trying to warn herself of what lay ahead for her. The desire to run, the girls who had been abused, but what was the doorway?

She raised a hand to her mouth as she realized there was something familiar about the backdrop for that doorway. It was not in what lay beyond it, but what surrounded it. She had seen this doorway before, only it was not open then.

"Oh my God," she whispered. She grabbed the painting and took off for the bedroom stairs as quickly as she dared. The last thing she needed was to slip and fall and break something.

She could hear Leslie cursing as she chased after her, asking her where the hell she was going. Katherine ignored her. She would see soon enough.

At least she hoped she would.

She took the stairs two and three at a time, barely registering for the first time since she painted that girl near the bedroom, she did not so much as glance down the second-floor hallway. When she reached the first floor, she nearly leaped the last few steps to it, barely stopping long enough to catch her balance before racing toward the basement door.

When Leslie finally caught up with her, she was staring from the painting to the bricked-up doorway she had discovered in the basement, a smile of astonishment on her face. It was another premonition, only she had painted it without knowing and long before it would be anything she would consider. Maybe she had seen it the first time she came down here after moving in, maybe it had come from the spirit who spoke to them through the Ouija. Either way, she was nearly giddy with the excitement at solving the puzzle.

"What the shit, Kat?" Leslie asked, breathless. "You trying to give me a heart attack?"

"Look!" Katherine said, pointing from the painting to the old doorway. "It's here."

Leslie looked between the two for a moment then shrugged. "You painted the bricks busted away, so what?"

"You're missing the obvious," Katherine replied. "Think about what the spirit said. Set them free, and they'd stop Alston."

"Yeah, and he was real helpful about how we were supposed to do that," Leslie said. "He just said, they'd be…"

She stopped, her eyes going wide as she got it. Katherine nearly laughed out loud.

"He said they'd be *below*."

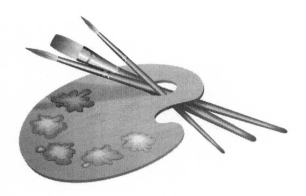

CHAPTER THIRTY

She was walking down what she knew to be Katherine's second-floor hallway, but something about it looked off. She had undergone the "grand tour" shortly after arriving and remembered this entire floor being in wild disarray, the one place in the entire house Katherine had not bothered to start renovations. Now, however, even in the scant light...

Candlelight

...coming from beneath the closed doors, she could see the floor had been recently cleaned and waxed, and the wallpaper was pristine and no longer peeling.

Much as her surroundings looked different, so did her body *feel* different. Her normally in-the-way breasts felt like two tight balls against her chest. Her hips were somehow narrower, altering her stride from wide and determined to an almost dainty one. Her mind was a jumble of angry thoughts that had no relevance to anything she had encountered in her life, all seeming to focus around *him* and *those brats* and *nosy townsfolk*.

It was beyond disorienting. The only other time she could remember feeling like this was when she was fourteen and realized she was excited looking at the other girls showering with her after gym class. It had taken nearly two years to come to grips with the fact she thought she was gay, another three beyond that before she worked up the nerve to tell her parents and began to enjoy her life again free from the lies and cover-ups. The thoughts raging in her mind were a stark reminder to how she felt back then, even though it seemed she was now holding back a secret of a much darker nature.

The last thing Leslie could remember was lying down in bed next to Katherine, reassuring her friend she was no longer alone and nothing would bother her, and then rolling over to go to sleep. She had no memory of waking, much less of getting out of bed and coming down here. She could not remember ever sleepwalking before, so she had no way to tell if what she felt was commonplace in such situations, or if this was a completely new thing.

When she reached the stairs, she assumed whatever was happening was over, and her dreaming mind was taking her back to bed so she could go back to sleep. When she stopped and turned to look back the way she had come, the first doubt crept into her mind alongside great confusion. She tried to will her body to turn, to put the first foot on the steps leading up to the third floor and the master bedroom, but she remained stock-still. It was as though her body was no longer her own, and she was just along for the ride.

Instead, her hands came up of their own accord and clapped together three times, briskly. "I said come *now*," she said, in a voice she had never before heard. It was demure but forceful, its tone conveying that whoever she was, she was used to getting her way without having to ask twice.

If this *was* a dream, it was the most vivid one she could remember having. She often found herself playing other roles, as though her subconscious mind had crafted a stage and she was merely an actress performing a part in some psychological play designed to reboot her mind. The concept was the only thing this situation had in common with those particular dreams. She could feel the constricting bulkiness of her shoes—low heels, which Leslie avoided at all costs. Her dress was rough, obviously dried on a line outside instead of in a machine with fabric softener or dryer sheets to make it feel smoother against her skin. She felt a single bead of sweat break loose from the hair at the back of her neck, running into her dress and down her back, creating a tingling sensation as it went. Leslie wanted nothing more than to reach back and scratch, hopefully to make it stop, but the woman whose body she was in simply ignored it.

Curious, Leslie allowed herself to pay more attention to the woman's thoughts. She was impatient, annoyed, and wanted to be done with this dreadful task—whatever it was. This was all *his* fault for not being careful, and now the busybody townsfolk had gone and shoved their nose in it. Sure, the marshal had left without causing trouble, but he would be back soon enough. He hadn't been alone when he came here, after all, and even if *he* could mind his business, it was only a matter of time before the rest of those nobodies started passing around vile rumors that got everyone worked up. Once that happened, they would be back, *that* could be counted on, and they would take justice into their own hands, no matter what the marshal said.

A door at the end of the hallway opened, drawing the woman's attention and Leslie's. Two girls, one younger than the other came out, heads down, and shuffled toward her. She could see one of them—the eldest—carried an infant in her emaciated arms, cooing softly to the babe to keep it quiet. The woman was pleased at that— the girl had learned her place, though it had taken many beatings to get her there.

Another thought drifted below this one, just beyond what Leslie considered conscious thought. She reached for it, snatching it from the depths and cringed at the implications of it. The woman secretly *enjoyed* administering those beatings, not to mold the girl to a certain behavior pattern, but because she had become *his* favorite. Their arrangement had been that the two of them would have no disruption to their marital congress, that these girls were nothing more than breeding stock in the attempt to find an heir, but *he* had gone to her three nights in a row last week, despite the fact that the younger one was due to begin her cycle soon and was therefore more fertile.

Leslie wanted to cry out, to beat the woman within an inch of her life for what she had allowed to take place under her roof, but she was impotent. She was nothing more than a gentle puff of air, and just as likely to affect the world around her. She could only watch as the woman stood aside, allowing the two girls to lead the way down the steps to the first floor.

Unable to do anything else, she watched as the girls reached the landing and waited on their mistress to show them where to go next. When the woman opened a door revealing another set of steps leading down, the younger girl began to shake her head and whimper.

"Get down there!" the woman ordered, but the girl's terrified eyes never left that sliver of light illuminating the top step, nor did she make any attempt to move toward it. The woman let out an exasperated breath, then reached out and closed a hand on the girl's shoulder, clamping down hard enough the girl let out a low cry of pain. "You will go down there, on your own two feet or sliding on your back, it makes no difference to me. Do you understand me?"

Tears ran from the girl's eyes as she nodded and took a tentative step forward. Leslie wanted this to end, *begged* for it to end, even prayed to a God she had decided didn't exist when her parents told her she was going to Hell because she had no sexual attraction to men. She could see what this woman intended, could feel her rage and excitement, and wanted no part of it, even as a passenger along for the ride. But nothing happened, her prayer was not answered, and she had no choice but to keep watching. She couldn't even close her eyes to block it out, since they belonged to the woman she inhabited, and not to herself.

Obviously unwilling but too afraid of the consequences to refuse, the two girls started down the steps. The woman followed, feeling smug that they had been so easily cowed. When they reached the bottom, the woman lit the overhead lamp, casting the room in an ethereal glow that did little more than make the shadows even darker than they had been without the light. Her eyes drifted to the other side of the room, to a closed door set into the wall. *He* would want her to do this in there, since that was where he had drawn the symbols he claimed would grant the two of them immortality once enough blood had been spilled to fuel them. She fully understood the foolishness of believing such a thing now. There was no immortality, there was only the life they had. His promises had been for no other purpose than to convince her, to make her amenable to letting him diddle these little girls in the name of creating an heir.

In all honesty, she couldn't care less where he put his manhood, so long as he remembered who he was wedded to, and did not bring any diseases back to their marital bed. And now see where his fancy words and promises had brought them: to the very brink of destruction. They would be arrested, tried, and thrown into prison like a pair of lowlifes. The rest of their lives would be spent among the scum of the earth. All their money, all their prestige, cast aside and wasted. The town would profit off their good fortune, and they would be left with nothing. Provided some judge did not just order their deaths for what they had done. The woman refused to allow that. No one controlled her life or death other than herself, and foolishly, her husband.

No, she would not do this in his *special room*. She would do it here, in the middle of the cellar, and if he did not approve, she would cut his throat, too, and tell the mob who came for them what she had done, and how afraid of him she had been, and beg for their forgiveness since she had already sent the real criminal to Hell.

"That's far enough," she said. "Turn around and get on your knees."

The girls stopped moving, trembling at the sight of the boy she'd already finished with lying nearby, and shared a glance before turning to face her again. The oldest did as instructed, carefully maneuvering herself onto her knees, taking great pains to not drop the infant in her arms. The younger however, was shaking wildly from the force of holding in her sobs, and reached down to the hem of her tattered nightgown before slowly lifting it up, revealing her pale, skinny legs and the light wisps of hair that had just begun to form on her pubic mound.

The woman slapped her hands away, causing the gown to drop back down. "Stop that! I have no wish to see either of you unclothed ever again. Now get on your knees or see what happens to the little one first!"

The girl dropped immediately to her knees, slamming the ground hard enough to make her hair bounce. Had she been in control of the woman's body, Leslie would have winced.

"That's good," the woman said, her voice all sweetness and niceties again. She reached over to a nearby table and picked up something...

A knife

...that felt wooden and a little heavy in her hand. She took a step closer to the girl and crouched down so she was closer to eye level with her, then cupped the girl's forehead and pushed her head up. "No need to cry, this will all be over soon. And I promise, he will never touch you again."

The girl's eyes widened slightly, her lips twitching either to smile or to speak, and then the woman jerked the knife's blade across her throat and whatever response she had been about to give became lost to the terror of her final moments in life.

Blood sprayed out in a sheet, dousing the woman's face and dress with a warm, sticky spray. Mercifully for Leslie, the woman closed her eyes and tilted her own head back, cutting off her vision of the young girl's death. Not so mercifully, she could feel what the woman felt: the exhilaration, the sheer *pleasure* of knowing that with one simple act she had sent the girl's soul to whatever life lay beyond this one.

The older girl was screaming now, hysterically, a chorus of madness with her baby's cries echoing around the room in counterpoint. Leslie thought she was screaming the younger girl's name, but it was too frantic to make out.

The woman stood, then opened her eyes, and turned to look at the older girl, a smile spreading across her face. "Oh, don't carry on so. You'll be joining her soon enough."

Before she could take the step she wanted to, a loud crash came from above and behind her. She spun, facing the stairs just as several men armed with rifles and pistols came rushing down the stairs.

"Grace Alston!" one of them yelled. "Drop that knife and get the *hell* away from those children!"

The woman—Grace Alston, Leslie supposed—felt a momentary flash of what could only be described as inevitability, then laughed.

"You don't control me!" she cried, and Leslie's terror deepened as the woman decided what to do. "Only *I* control me!"

Leslie tried her best to scream, but it was as useless as anything else she had attempted. The woman's hand came up and quickly pulled the blade of the knife across her own throat. Her laughter became garbled, a gurgling sound that had no business in a place of normalcy, and then dwindled. Leslie felt the woman growing colder, barely noticing as she fell to the ground. Just as one of the men reached her, a hand extended toward her, the world went black.

Leslie jerked awake, a scream threatening to rip forth from her throat. She held in check—just—terrified of what might happen if she let it out. Her eyes darted around, but she could see nothing but darkness and shadow. Gradually, she became aware of the packed dirt beneath her bare legs, below the shorts she wore to bed. She felt around with her hands and realized she was on the floor of what had to be the basement. She scrambled to her feet, the top of one scraping roughly against something, and stumbled to where she thought the stairs had been in her dream or whatever the *fuck* that had been.

Her hands slammed into the wall, and she felt a splinter break off from the beam and slide neatly into her palm. She shuffled around and felt her fingers land on something familiar. Without waiting for her mind to fully comprehend what she was doing, she flipped on the light switch and turned around, her back pressed against the wall.

She was in the basement, as she surmised. Her eyes scanned the ground, searching for the bodies of the boy, the young girl, and Grace Alston, but saw nothing there. The room was empty, save for her. She had apparently sleepwalked and dreamed the events she witnessed, but it felt like so much more than that. She felt as though she had lived them.

It took several deep breaths, holding it, then releasing before she restored herself to something even-keeled again. As soon as her legs would hold her, she turned and raced up the steps, not bothering to shut off the light or close the door before turning and heading for the steps back up to the bedroom. She stopped with one foot on the step, realizing she would have to pass the second-floor hallway on her way up, not yet willing to chance what she might see there.

Instead, she turned and made her way into the den, dropping onto the couch, still breathing harder than she would have liked. She shook her head, grabbed the remote, and turned on the television. An infomercial was on, but she couldn't even focus enough to see what was being sold. It didn't matter. She only wanted to hear voices that could be labeled as normal. She leaned back on the couch and wondered if she could get back to sleep tonight.

She was still wondering as the sun rose above the trees and lightened the room.

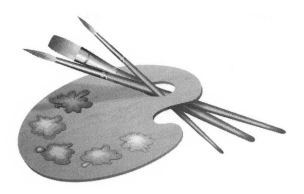

CHAPTER THIRTY-ONE

Had his father told him about the sheer amount of mindless, inane paperwork that went along with even a normal, slow day as the town's marshal, Frank thought it very likely he would have turned down the job rather than actively campaign for it. There was no chance of that happening, of course, not with people like Clay Davison, Wally Barton, and Horace Price pressuring both him and the mayor into it, but he could entertain the thought. It was a wonderful "what might have been" moment, even if it was nothing more than a pointless daydream.

He supposed he should consider himself lucky he wasn't working some place much bigger than Poplar Bend, where the list of reports awaiting his approval or perusal would be three or four times larger than the stack currently on his desk. Here, none of it was life and death—not usually. Requests for either him or Bradley to be present at some function or another, invitations to speak at the local church or school about crime prevention or the dangers of speeding or something along those lines. It wasn't an endless parade of robberies, murders, traffic accidents, rapes, and the more violent crimes that plagued even moderately larger towns nowadays. If he had to do this job, he could take comfort in how much worse it *could* be.

On the other hand, if he were in one of those larger cities it was highly unlikely he would be caught in a situation anywhere near as troublesome as the one he was in now.

Bradley did not have much to say about Kat's friend from out of town, other than to repeat many times that the woman took a great deal of getting used to. Frank had hoped he could learn all he needed to set Horace and Wally's minds at ease from his deputy, but it looked more and more like he would have to drive out there and see for himself. Considering what fate might lay in store for the woman, meeting her and running the risk of liking her was not on his list of things to look forward to.

Come to think of it, Frank was not finding much relief in the changes he saw in Bradley. He was definitely growing more attached to Kat, something Frank hoped would give her a fighting chance of getting rid of the problem out there at the house, and by extension, the one that threatened the peacefulness of the town as a whole, but instead it was only making things more confused for him. He would not be allowed to wait and see much longer. If he wanted to keep Poplar Bend safe for the people who lived here, he would have to act sooner rather than later. He knew it. He didn't much like it, but he knew it.

That Bradley had pulled the number for Blackmore's next-of-kin from the file did not bode well either. It would only be a matter of time before he realized the problem along that particular line of thought and started asking questions Frank couldn't answer without giving too much away. He had been opposed to that part of the plan all along, but was outvoted. To Frank, what Bradley was doing by looking that number up made logical sense. To everyone else, it smacked of desperation. It was hard to argue against something when it had been his own father who put it into practice to start with, no matter how ill-conceived the thought process behind it was.

He heard the front door open and shut and felt a moment of hope. Not for the bigger things going on in town, but that maybe Elizabeth was back and could help him finish up this paperwork sometime before he normally was home and changing for bed. That hope faded when Bradley ended up being the one who opened the door to his office and stuck his head in.

"Just letting you know I finished up over at the Peterson's," Bradley said. "He still hasn't got that fence yet, so those cows are probably just going to be right back out in the road again in an hour or so, but they're all back where they belong for now."

"Any of 'em get hit this time?" Frank asked.

"No, he lucked out this time around," Bradley replied. "Though that dead man's curve leading out to his farm will end up catching somebody if he doesn't get a handle on it. If I hadn't known to watch for it, I'd have ended up with ole Bessie riding shotgun with me."

Frank chuckled at that, even if he felt anything but humorous right now. "That might not've been such a bad thing. Haul her over to old man Martin once you were done and have some burgers fresh from the tap, so to speak."

Bradley barked a laugh at that. "All it would've cost me is a lecture from you for not paying attention and damaging the car."

"You mind ridin' out that way and makin' sure he took care of it?" Frank asked. "Just do it when you head out for the night."

"Actually," Bradley said, coming all the way into the room. "I was going to run out to Kat's here in a bit. She needs my help with something, said it might solve all her...problems."

"She still think that place is haunted?" Frank asked. It wasn't a lie—not quite, anyway—but he could hear his mother's voice in his head, chastising him for leading Bradley on like this.

Bradley shrugged, and Frank had to admit the man was just as good at covering this up as he was. Under ideal circumstances, he would be a great ally in the task before them, but the others would never allow it. Bradley was still too much of an outsider for their liking.

"Yeah, pretty silly isn't it?" Bradley replied. Frank's eyes immediately went to the spot on his deputy's cheek that twitched whenever he lied. "But if that's the case and doing this helps her feel better, what's the harm in trying, right?"

"I suppose," Frank agreed. "What's she got in mind? Séance, exorcism, something along those lines?"

"Nothing like that," Bradley said. "She found some room bricked up down in her basement. She thinks if we bust it open, it'll let whatever's in there out so it can cross over or whatever they call it. Asked me to help her. I figure it shouldn't be that hard to bust down a brick wall with a sledgehammer, so I'll give it a shot and see if it eases her mind some."

Frank felt a chill run down his back. If they were planning to break down that barrier, the one his Daddy and the others had been instructed to build in the first place, things were well beyond the point even reasonable old Horace would tolerate. That was playing with fire in a way Frank himself had to admit could lead to nothing but more pain and heartache. It was all he could do to not let Bradley see how unsettled he had become.

"Sounds like a buncha work for nothin'," he said, trying hard to keep his voice calm and even. "And how do you know that ain't there as a support for the floor or somethin'? Might end up bringin' the whole damn house down on your head you break that in."

"I doubt it," Bradley said. "She said they looked like normal old clay bricks to her. If somebody was using those to support the weight of the house, I'd think they'd be cracked or something by now, but since she says they're not, I doubt that's what it's for. Probably just somebody's way of blocking out coons or skunks or something like that."

"Could be," Frank said. He could feel himself trembling and didn't trust himself to say anything more than that.

"I can swing by Peterson's once I'm done with that, if you want," Bradley said.

Frank shook his head. "Naw, it's fine. I'll check it out once I'm done here."

"You sure?"

"Positive."

Bradley gave him a broad smile that nearly broke Frank's heart. "Thanks, boss. See you in the morning?"

"Same as always," Frank replied.

Once Bradley was out of the office with the door closed behind him, Frank picked up the phone and dialed Horace's bar. He didn't want to do this, didn't want to betray the young man he had mentored the last three years, but if that barrier came down, there would be much worse than a betrayal to worry about. The call was answered on the second ring.

"Horace," Frank said before the other man even had a chance to speak. "They're plannin' on bustin' down the barrier in the basement."

"Damn it all," Horace muttered. "I'll call Wally, fill him in. You fixin' to try to stop it?"

"I got any choice?" Frank shot back.

Horace sighed. "Don't look much like it. Don't you screw this up, Franklin Bradshaw. There's a lot more than just your word to your Daddy ridin' on doin' what's got to be done, you understand?"

"Yeah, I understand," Frank said. "I understand I'm fixin' to have to do a buncha shit I don't want no part of on account of a buncha old men did some stupider shit a long time ago."

"Watch yourself, *boy*," Horace said. His voice no longer held any trace of his normal easy-going nature. "Just 'cause you're the one took on the duties don't mean me and Wally ain't perfectly capable of doin' it ourselves if you won't. And you know well and damn good what happens you become a part of the problem and not one a'those handlin' it."

"That a threat?" Frank asked. "You threatenin' an officer of the law, Horace?"

"No," came the reply. "I'm speakin' truth to a smartass don't want to hear it. Now do your damn job and protect this town. Call me when it's done and I'll tell Wally. Luck with us, the bastard'll be content for longer since he's gettin' more and won't wake up again 'til we're all dead and gone and don't have to deal with it no more."

"I'm sure that'll be a relief to me while I'm down in Hell with the pair of you," Frank said and slammed the phone back into the cradle before Horace could lecture him anymore.

He sat at his desk, drumming his fingers against the surface, trying to get his anger under control. He never asked for this, and while he did understand what was at stake, he wanted no part of it, just like he said. The problem was there was no one else. Horace could threaten all he wanted, but neither him nor Wally stood a chance of doing anything and both of them knew it. They would know Frank knew it, too, which was the reason the threats got to him so badly in the first place.

What had his blood pressure near the point of explosion was that they both also knew Frank *would* do what he had to do to keep the larger part of this town safe from the threat that Alston bastard represented. As much as he liked Kat, and as much as he had come to love Bradley, if they were going to jeopardize the entire town by what they were doing, they had to be stopped. If that meant they had to die, that was exactly what would happen. He would do whatever it took to keep people safe.

That didn't mean, however, that he had to take any joy from it. It also did not mean he couldn't take a moment or two to mourn two people he now realized he thought of as friends before their passing and afterward.

His vision blurred, and he was a little surprised to find a tear standing in his eye. He hadn't cried since his Daddy died years ago, but he supposed if ever there was a time that warranted tears, it was in the moments before you became the very thing you despised.

He took a deep breath, checked his pistol to make sure it was loaded, grabbed a shotgun from the rack behind his desk, and headed for his truck. Bradley would need to go home, change, and grab a sledgehammer before they could start on their plan. Whatever happened, now that the idea was in their minds, those three would have to die. Frank only hoped he could get to the house and stop them from causing a lot more people to meet the same fate.

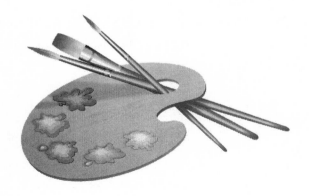

CHAPTER THIRTY-TWO

She was excited when she opened the door to let Bradley in, and while Katherine wouldn't admit it to anyone, the reason for her excitement had as much to do with seeing him again as it did the possibility of putting an end to the haunting she endured. It was something she knew Leslie would pick up on—which was why she was pointedly not turned in such a way her friend could see her face—and there was a distinct possibility Bradley himself knew it, but so long as she didn't confirm any suspicions aloud, the secret was still hers to keep. It might not make any logical sense to anyone else, but it made "Kat-Sense", and that was all that mattered to her.

He sat the massive iron head of the sledgehammer on the floor and leaned it against the wall so he could take off his coat. She looked over at it and then back to him.

"You think that's going to be big enough to do the trick?" she asked.

"It should," Bradley said as he hung up his coat. "Heavy as all get out. If that thing won't break through that brick wall, I really don't know what will."

"Fair enough," she replied. "Should we get to it?"

"Not just yet," he said, turning to face her. "I want to try to get ahold of Blackmore's brother one last time. If he was the one who put that up, he must have had a reason for it. I'd like to make sure we're not about to do more harm than good by bashing it down."

"And if he doesn't know?"

Bradley shrugged. "Then maybe we can learn something else. You have to admit, if there's a better option than knocking that wall down, we should at least listen to it."

She sighed. This was not what she wanted to do, but he had a point. Once that wall was knocked down, they would have done something they could not easily undo. It would be better in the long run to make sure it was the best course of action available to them before going through with it. She nodded and gestured to the phone near the kitchen, trying hard to hide her disappointment.

He patted his pockets and looked over to her. "Forgot my wallet when I changed. You still have that number written down somewhere?"

"It's in the kitchen," she replied, leading the way. "I'll get it. No reason you can't sit down to make the call, too."

He took the handset, followed her into the kitchen, and sat on one of the stools while she rooted around through the stack of papers that had accumulated on her island countertop. She didn't find it the first time, but did on a second pass, just beneath the final bill of services from the contractor. She tried not to look at that one. The cost of the modern heat and air system as well as the conversions needed to install it easily made up half that invoice's total, if not more. It was something she would need to pay, but it could wait until after the holidays. Or until after they got rid of the ghost that was terrorizing her.

She heard a knock at the front door just as Bradley dialed the number. She wasn't expecting anyone, but there was a chance it could be the contractor showing up to make some final adjustment on something somewhere. If so, it would be fortuitous timing: He could tell them if breaking that wall down in the basement would affect anything else in the house. It could put Bradley's mind at ease, if nothing else.

Not wanting to miss out in case Blackmore's brother answered this time, she called out for Leslie who was still watching television in the den.

"What?" came the response.

Katherine ignored the look of mild irritation that crossed Bradley's face as he plugged his free ear with a finger.

"Can you get the door?"

"What am I, your friggin' maid?" Leslie replied. The woman had been exceptionally grumpy all day, but when Katherine confronted her about it, she just waved it away and said she hadn't slept well last night. Grumbling about it or not, Katherine heard the padding of footsteps as her friend went to the door.

Bradley perked up, and Katherine could just make out the sound of the line being picked up on the other end.

"Hello, is..." Bradley trailed off, his smile becoming somewhat sheepish as he looked up at her. "Voice mail. Gets me every stinking time."

He waited for the introduction to finish, then spoke again. "Mister Blackmore, this is Deputy Marshal Bradley Morgan down in Poplar Bend, Tennessee again. I'm still trying to get in touch with you about a rather urgent matter concerning your late brother. If you could, I'd really appreciate you getting back to me so we can talk."

He left his number, ended the call, and sighed as he looked back up to Katherine.

"I just don't get it," Bradley said. "You'd think if there was something going on in the town where your brother died, you'd want to call back and see what it was. Or call back and tell the people hassling you to leave you the hell alone."

"I don't know," Katherine replied. "Maybe they were estranged or something. Either he'll call back or he won't, guess we better not hold our breath."

"Best not," said a man's voice from the kitchen doorway.

Katherine looked up and frowned, unable to comprehend exactly what she was seeing. Leslie was standing stone still, a single tear trickling its way down her cheek. The barrel of a shotgun was pressed into her chin, forcing her head to sit at a slightly cocked angle. Katherine's eyes trailed down the length of that steel barrel to the hand holding its grip, one finger resting just beside the trigger like she saw people do in the movies when they wanted to be ready to shoot at a moment's notice but didn't want to accidentally pull the trigger. She looked back up, her eyes tracing the arm, the hand attached to it, coming to rest on the face of Frank Bradshaw, still in his uniform, his face utterly devoid of expression.

"Frank?" Bradley asked, getting to his feet. "What the hell?"

"I wouldn't move much more than that," Frank said, his voice eerily calm. "'Case you didn't notice, there's a scattergun ready to take this young lady's head off if you do."

"I don't understand," Katherine said, trying not to focus on her friend's face just now. If she did, she was apt to lose it, and she had the distinct impression doing so would benefit exactly no one. "Why are you threatening to kill her?"

Frank sighed, and for a brief instant his face filled with such weariness Katherine felt a flash of compassion for the man. Then what he was doing slapped her across the face and the terror and confusion returned.

"'Cause you're about to do somethin' I can't let happen," he said. "I held out long as I could, but then you wanted to go and break that barrier down, and I can't take no chance of that happenin'. Might make *him* mad, and too many people been tryin' way too long to take the risk of that happenin' now."

"What the literal *hell* are you talking about, Frank?" Bradley asked.

Katherine looked over and saw the deputy moving away from her. She almost felt offended, as though he was abandoning her when she needed him the most, then she realized he was trying to get to an angle where he stood the best chance of knocking Frank away from Leslie without her losing her head in the process.

"As it stands, you got one chance to come out of this with your ass attached," Frank said. "But son, you take one more Goddamned step and I'm apt to make a mess in here. I was born at night, but it damn sure wasn't *last* night."

Bradley froze in place and raised his hands up beside his head, palms out.

"That's better," Frank said. "Now move back over where you was, next to your girl, there. She ain't much longer for this world, so you might as well give her what comfort you can while you can and quit tryin' to get this other'un killed."

She didn't want to show weakness in the face of this threat, not after what she had already endured while living here, but the casual way in which this man she had considered a friend stated the fact of her impending death was too much for her to bear. She let out a low moan of terror.

She didn't see Bradley move back to her, unable to peel her eyes away from Frank's hollow expression, but she felt his arms wrap around her protectively and was glad for them. They gave her some strength, though whether it would be enough was yet to be seen. She swallowed hard and forced herself to meet Frank's eyes. They were not as blank as his face, but what she saw in them was even more disturbing. He didn't like this, what he was doing, but he had absolutely no intention of stopping. Despite what he told Bradley, Katherine was sure not a one of them—him and Leslie included— would see another sunrise.

"Will you tell me *why* you're going to kill me, Frank?" she asked. She was a little surprised at how strong her voice came out, but she was thankful for it all the same.

"You ate at my table, darlin'," he said. "I invited you into my home. This here ain't nothin' personal, just doin' what I have to. I wish you could've figured it out 'fore it reached this point, but things gone too far to turn back now."

He turned his head slightly so his lips were right next to Leslie's ear, but his eyes remained locked on Katherine and Bradley. "I let you go, you gonna go over there and sit down like a good girl, or do I got to go ahead and end you now?"

Leslie trembled all over, and the sight of it hurt Katherine's heart. Her friend had always seemed so much tougher than she was, and to see her so unnerved now drove home how truly bleak the situation was.

"Good..." Leslie said, her voice hitching so badly she was barely able to force anything coherent out of her throat. She swallowed and tried again. "Good...girl."

"On three, then," Frank said. "One. Two. Three."

The instant he said the word, he moved the shotgun and Leslie darted forward. She tripped over her own feet and would have gone sprawling had Bradley not let go of Katherine and reached out to steady her. He eased her onto a stool between himself and Katherine, then turned back to his boss.

"Okay, Frank," he said. "We're no threat to you."

"You sure about that, son?" Frank said, resting the shotgun's barrel on his forearm. "'Cause you sure look like you're 'bout ready to tear me a new one I so much as blink."

"I try, and one of them dies," Bradley replied. "So yes, I'm sure."

Frank sighed again. "Suppose that'll have to do. Least you understand the seriousness. And I suppose you all deserve some answers. You want to ask questions, or should I just get to talkin'?"

"Just one, for now," Katherine said. "Why don't you think Blackmore's brother's going to call us back? Why shouldn't we hold our breath waiting for it?"

"Easy enough to answer," Frank said. "Lots of reasons, but the biggest is that he's layin' under the dirt down there in your basement."

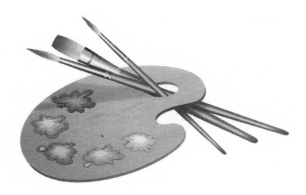

CHAPTER THIRTY-THREE

There were four ways Bradley could see that would allow him to subdue Frank, but the chance of someone getting shot was extremely high with all of them. If the man had been holding anything other than a shotgun—which Bradley knew was loaded with double-aught buckshot—he still might have tried for it. As it stood, however, if somebody got shot with that thing, it was extremely unlikely for them to survive it. The only option he had was to bide his time, let the man talk, and hope a better, safer alternative presented itself.

He glanced over to make sure Katherine and Leslie were still holding it together. They were, but it looked like Leslie was going to lose it any second. Katherine sat with her arms around her friend, who had her head leaned over on Katherine's shoulder, her breathing still ragged. Bradley could understand. Having a shotgun shoved under your chin like that would make even the bravest person feel fear.

When he turned back, he caught Frank staring at him, his face still that carefully controlled blank he used whenever he had to reprimand someone he was normally friends with after they'd done something wrong. It was a distinct "cop" look, and one Bradley himself had tried to emulate. Had he known he would be on the receiving end of that look while having done nothing to warrant it, he might not have tried so hard.

Frank nodded once. "Okay, son, most of this is goin' to be for your benefit. Like I said, you got a chance to come out of this alive, but it's gonna take you makin' some hard decisions about what you're willin' to do to keep this town safe."

"If you think I'm going to keep on like this never happened," Bradley replied. "You really have lost your damn mind."

"Yeah," Frank said. "I was about the same way when I first heard, yet here I am now. A man can change his mind, son. I'm hopin' you'll see sense enough to be one who does."

He looked over to Katherine, seeming to accept he would get nothing else he wanted to hear from Bradley until his story was done. "You said old Clay told you 'bout this house some, 'bout Henry and Grace Alston and what they done out here all them years ago. What he didn't tell you was that the story don't end with their dyin'."

"Yeah, I kind of got that already," Katherine said drily. "Just get on with it."

Frank sighed again but did as she asked. "Guess it was 'bout eighty-one or eighty-two when it started back up again. My Daddy was town marshal at the time, after bein' elected once his daddy got too old to keep on with it. He knew all about the Alstons and what they done, hearin' it from the mouth of the man who was there for it, so when some kids started turnin' up dead, he 'bout went off the deep end. Not to say dead kids wouldn't be serious in any circumstance, but knowin' the history of this town and what all kids had already endured here, it hit a little harder, if that makes sense.

"Anyhow, it started when he was out patrollin' one mornin' and come across somethin' strange out in the field where old man Richmond still grew his cotton. Bunch of the plants was all trampled down, broke off, and basically a big ole mess. Knowin' it was gettin' close to pickin' time, he figured somebody must've headed out in there and swiped some of the buds for themselves. Wantin' to make sure it wasn't no drunk out there sleepin' one off instead, he parked 'longside the road and headed into the field to make sure.

"He didn't find some drunk, but he wished it had been. Instead, he finds the Prichard twins layin' there nekkid as the day they were born, covered head to toe in blood. Didn't take a genius to know they were dead, but Daddy went ahead and made sure 'fore he called it in. His secretary in those days was a woman name of Elaine Fraser, sweetest lady you'd ever hope to meet, always had a kind word for everybody, didn't matter if they was friendly back or not. As you can imagine, hearin' a pair of eleven-year-old girls was layin' dead in a field hit her pretty hard. From what Daddy said, she was on the phone callin' the mayor before she even let go of the button on the radio.

"Knowin' it was only a matter of time 'fore the place was crawlin' with folk, Daddy went back and started lookin' around for some clue who done it. You can imagine how shocked he was to see that trail he'd followed continued right on up through the field toward Richmond's house. He puts two and two together, marks the area, radios in that he's goin' to check on somethin' might lead to who done it, and drives up to the house.

"Richmond's standin' on the porch when he pulls up, smokin' on his pipe with an irritated look on his face. Daddy asks him if he's seen anything strange in the last little while, and the man says he sure enough has. Said his fourteen-year-old grandson come in after midnight the night before, all shakin' and actin' weird, and that the boy wouldn't come out of his bedroom for nothin'. Richmond said he was plannin' on waitin' 'til about noon then try again, since he knew teenage boys got that way sometimes. Daddy asked if he could talk to him, and Richmond said to go right ahead.

"Daddy went inside and knocked on the boy's door, then told him who he was so the boy might be more inclined to open up. Daddy said all he could hear was the boy repeatin' the phrase 'I done bad' over and over again. Well, considerin' what he found out in the field definitely qualified as somethin' bad, Daddy didn't waste no more time. He knocked that door down quick as you please.

"Bobby Richmond was sittin' there nekkid in the middle of a pile of his bloody clothes, streaks of it on his face, holdin' onto some kind of rag while he rocked back and forth mutterin' to himself like a fool. He never so much as looked up when Daddy busted the door down, just kept right on mutterin', runnin' that rag through his hands. It was only when Daddy snatched him up and slapped the cuffs on him that he realized the boy'd been holdin' a pair of one of them Pritchard girl's underpants.

"He gets arrested, processed, and sent down to the county jail while arrangements was made to send him to juvenile hall. He never said a thing other than that one phrase the whole time he was there. Only time he ever *did* say anything else was on the night he got transferred to juvie. He hung himself in his cell, and the note he left only said 'I done bad, but he made me do it.' At first, everybody thinks he's talkin' about his granddad, and by the time they figured out otherwise, the old man's reputation had been damaged beyond repair. He ate the barrel of his shotgun almost a year to the day his grandson done himself in.

"'Fore any of that, though, it came out that Bobby Richmond, the Pritchard twins, and some other kids were goofin' around out here. All the other kids said it was spooky, so the girls wanted to leave. Bobby had offered to walk them home, on account of how scared they were. Had the case ever gone to court, that would've been enough to put him away for it, but it never happened. Still, it convinced Daddy, so that was that as far as he was concerned.

"Time passed, and while the town didn't really forget, they got over it. Things were gettin' back to normal 'til the night Willy King come tearin' ass though town, damn near takin' old Clay out while he was leavin' from checkin' on his wife at the store. King stops in front of the marshal's office and jumps out, screamin', cryin', and hysterical. Daddy runs out in time to stop Clay from knockin' the boy on his ass for nearly hittin' him, and while he's tryin' to make sense of what the boy's sayin' he notices the girl laid out in the back seat.

"I swear, it seemed like everybody in town knew Willy King and Frances Weathergood were a thing, and it seemed like they also knew Willy wasn't gonna get nothin' he wanted out of her 'til he put a ring on her finger and they'd stood before her preacher daddy and got right in the eyes of God. The boy's friends all said Willy'd pretty well resigned himself to it, but seein' as how he really did love her, he was willin' to wait it out. They was gonna graduate the next year and was plannin' on getting' hitched right before he headed out for basic trainin' in the Army. As it turned out, neither of 'em got to see that happen.

"Daddy was gettin' ready to leave for the night, so Elaine had gone home. Since Clay was on the town council, Daddy had him take Willy into the office and try to get him calmed down while he checked on Frances. Soon as he opened the back door, he saw two things: her skirt was hiked up to her hips with the only thing left of her underpants bein' the waistband, and from the way her neck was all bruised up and her eyes were bugged out, she was dead as could be. He shut the door, went inside, called the paramedics, the mayor, and the county sheriff, then went to get Willy to tell him what happened.

"Somehow Clay had gotten the boy to relax some, or else shock'd set in and numbed him to what was happenin', but whatever caused it, Willy talked so Daddy could understand him. He said him and Frances had come out here to park. They hadn't gone all the way, but she wasn't opposed to makin' out and lettin' Willy cop a good feel to hold him over 'til they was married. He didn't know why they'd picked this place, bein' there were a lot more romantic places they could've gone, but they'd both felt like it had to be here. They'd come out here and been goin' at each other like they always were, and then Willy'd suggested movin' to the back seat so they'd be a little more comfortable. He hadn't expected Frances to agree, but she did. He said while they was back there, he kept hearin' this voice in his head tellin' him to go further, do more, don't stop. He said he asked Frances once if she'd said anything, but it wasn't her. The voice was that of a man, anyway. He said he tried to ignore it, but what it was suggestin' was somethin' he kind of wanted to do, so he did.

"Way he told it, he'd gotten further with her that night than ever before, and even when he knew he should back off, it was like somethin' wouldn't let him. Said he remembered thinkin' she was goin' to stop him any minute, then the next thing he knew he was starin' down at her face with his pants around his ankles and his hands around her neck. He'd panicked, tried to wake her up, and when he couldn't, he come racin' out of there and went straight to the marshal's office to turn himself in for what he done.

"The sheriff come and got him, and thanks to his confession, Willy ended up gettin' sentenced to twenty-five years up at the state prison. Died of heart failure 'bout ten years later. Had he made it to the Army, they'd have picked up on it and disqualified him from enlistin', but it might've kept him alive a little longer. As it was, considerin' what happened, I suppose he was grateful when the end finally came.

"Next day, Daddy said him, Clay, Wally Barton, and Horace Price—the other two men on the town council at the time—all ended up sittin' there in his office tryin' to figure out how a boy as good as Willy had went so bad. Elaine was there, listenin' in but not sayin' nothin' yet, but Daddy said he thought she was already gettin' an idea what was happenin' only she wanted somebody more important than her to say it first. Anyway, he said it was Clay first mentioned maybe Henry Alston wasn't rottin' away like he should've been, and that they ought to be lookin' at this house a little closer. 'Fore anybody had the chance to tell him he was crazy as hell for thinkin' that, Elaine piped in and said it sounded like a good idea to her, too.

"Daddy always said there were two things about Elaine he couldn't ever get to match up in his mind. First, she was the most honest and forthright woman he'd ever met, other than my mother, and second, she was a little on the nutty side. She was always readin' weird books, and had crystals all over her desk and such, and didn't bother with horoscopes in the paper since she did her own. Still, for all that, Daddy said when she said something, he was inclined to listen to it. The others there felt that same way, so when she said coming out here was a good idea, they ended up agreein' with it, too.

"They all headed out that very night, and Daddy said the moment they got here Elaine started actin' weirder than he was used to. Didn't take long for her to suggest they hold a séance and ask Henry Alston directly what they could do to stop good folks from killin' other good folk for no reason. Somehow, she talked all of 'em around to it.

"He never would explain how things played out, but he told me the end result. They ended up talkin' to Alston through Elaine and found out he was influencin' the killins as a way to keep himself amused after death. He fed on the fear, the pain, all of it. He'd been a damn pervert in life, so he was makin' other people into one now he was dead.

"They weren't happy with that, but there wasn't much they could do to get rid of him, so they made a deal with him. He stopped killin' townsfolk, and they'd provide for him every so often. He agreed, on the understandin' the first time they didn't hold up their end of the deal, he was free to do whatever the hell he wanted.

"That barrier ya'll planning to break down? That was the first thing he told them to do. If he said why, none of 'em's bothered to tell me about it."

He stopped, looked over their faces, and then let out a chuckle. "I see how you're lookin' at me right now, like you want to tell me I'm full of shit, but you've all seen too much out here to think I'm lyin', haven't you?"

"What about Blackmore?" Katherine asked. "How does he fit into all this?"

"Should be obvious, shouldn't it?" Frank replied. "He was the first offerin'.

"Right after they made that deal, they voted to put the house back on the open market. Sell it cheap, get someone in here. Everybody knew that wasn't a soul who lived in this town goin' to even think about buyin' the place, not with the history it had, so we knew it was goin' to be an outsider. Elaine even got her real estate license and acted as the seller for it. 'Bout eighty-four or eighty-five, Blackmore shows up and asks her about it. She convinced him it was the perfect place to fix up and resell, and he bought it hook, line, and sinker. He signed the papers and moved in around a month later.

"What none of them expected was that Alston was the type liked to play with his food. I don't know what Blackmore had to endure out here, just like I got no idea what you did. All I know, all Daddy told me, was the man was fit to be tied 'fore the first month was up. It got so bad, he called his brother up in Chicago and had him come out here to prove he wasn't just losin' his mind, I suppose.

"All of them knew Blackmore had to die to fulfill the bargain, but none of them were sure how that was supposed to take place.

When his brother showed up, they knew they were the ones goin' to have to take action. None of them wanted to, but a deal was a deal and they had to keep the town safe. They drew straws, and Clay got the short one. Only thing left to figure out what how to deal with Blackmore's brother.

"Daddy didn't tell me any of this 'til he was already diagnosed with the cancer that killed him. I guess he didn't want to burden me with it until he knew I was goin' to have to step into his shoes one day. However he thought it, what he told me was somethin' not even Clay, nor Wally, nor Horace, nor Elaine—God rest her soul—ever knew.

"He realized pushin' Blackmore to kill himself wasn't goin' to happen with his brother hangin' around, so he decided to take care of both problems himself. He drove out here, caught Blackmore's brother alone, and snapped his neck for him. Then he went face to face with Blackmore. He told the man what was goin' on and told him that even if he were to leave, Alston would just follow him. For all he knew, it might've even been the truth. He gave the man a choice: go out on his own terms or be taken out right then and there. Blackmore asked about his brother, and Daddy pointed out he was already gone. Blackmore asked to bury his brother, and Daddy agreed to that, too. He stood watch with a rifle in his hands while Blackmore buried his brother in the basement, then watched while the man poured drain cleaner into a glass and topped it off with some Scotch. Daddy said he waited until he saw Blackmore drink it down, then went home and went to bed. He came back the next morning to check on the man and 'discovered' the body on the porch."

"And then he put the next-of-kin information in Blackmore's file," Bradley said. "But what for?"

"Sake of appearance is the way I understand it," Frank replied. "Daddy figured it was a matter of time 'fore someone reported the man missing, so by makin' it look like he'd already been notified about his brother's death, it would throw anybody lookin' into it off the scent."

"Let me guess," Katherine said. "I'm the next sacrifice."

"You are," Frank admitted. "And I'm sorry about that. I truly was hopin' when you was lookin' at buyin' this place that you'd be the one to figure out how to stop it. It was why I encouraged lowerin' the price on the place to tempt you."

"You didn't have anything to do with me buying this place," Katherine said.

"Not directly, maybe," Frank said. "What was your realtor's name?"

"Mary," Katherine said. "Mary Wilkens."

"That's her maiden name," Frank said. "Her married name is Mary Bradshaw. Mary Elizabeth Bradshaw, to be precise. Dispatchin' wasn't the only thing she took over from Elaine when she passed."

"How is that possible?" Katherine asked. She jerked a little as she realized where this was going. "I saw her picture. I had Thanksgiving dinner with you two!"

Frank shrugged. "That picture's ten years old, at least. Keep tellin' her she needs to update it, but she never gets around to it. Big city, that might be problematic. Small town? Who really gives a shit?"

"So now what?" Bradley asked. "You going to shoot us?"

"Not unless I have to," Frank said. "I already said, you got a choice to make, son. I know it's a hard one to make, and I know it'll hurt you some, but surely you understand why it has to be done."

"All I understand is that your daddy was a murderer," Bradley said. "Just like you're about to be."

"He wasn't proud of that," Frank said. "He only did what he had to do. Didn't mean he had to like it."

"Really?" It wasn't the least bit funny, but Bradley felt like laughing at the man's stupidity. "He couldn't just let those two live, let Alston have them? At least they could have chosen whether or not to stick it out. At least they would've had a chance."

"You don't get it, son," Frank replied. "It's all about balance. Way I understand it, Alston keeps messin' with 'em, he just gets stronger. That's trouble for everybody. Somethin' 'bout him suckin' up their 'life essence', whatever the hell that is. So, Daddy solved it. Took 'em down, first. Kinda makes him a hero, in a sad sorta way."

"He was a worthless piece of shit killer who snuffed out two lives because he was too stupid to consider fighting back when he should have."

Frank's face darkened at that. "Watch your mouth, son. I don't take kindly to insults like that."

"What're you going to do?" Bradley asked. He was well beyond caring what his former boss thought about him. He knew the man had a temper. If he could push the right buttons, maybe he could make him act rashly, drop his guard, give the opening to take him down. "Kill me? Then get on with it, you hick bastard."

Frank shook his head. "I'm sorry about this. I really am."

He raised the shotgun, but he wasn't pointing it at Bradley. Instead, the barrel was leveled at Katherine's head. Bradley turned in time to see her close her eyes, resigned.

"Leave her alone!"

The voice came from behind Frank, just outside the room; higher in pitch but not quite feminine enough to have come from a woman or a girl. Frank spun toward the sound, giving Bradley a clear view of the little boy wearing a blue and white striped shirt over a pair of dirty jeans. The clothing was modern, which was strange considering the era in which the ghosts inhabiting the house lived, but more curious was that some of the boy's features were vaguely familiar.

When he turned to look at Katherine, he knew who it was. She was staring at the apparition, tears standing in her eyes, a look of disbelief and overwhelming joy on her face. She uttered only one word, but that word was enough. That word was everything to her.

"Tommy?" she asked.

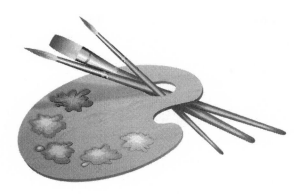

CHAPTER THIRTY-FOUR

She was dimly aware both Bradley and Leslie were moving now, the former launching himself at Frank while the man was distracted. Leslie scrambled away, apparently trying to get behind the kitchen island. Beyond that, she could not focus on anything except the face of the little boy in front of her. It wasn't possible, couldn't *be* possible, and yet there he was. He stood in the hallway outside her new kitchen, still wearing the outfit he had on the day he was so brutally murdered. She could not fathom why he would be here, even as a ghost, which some part of her deep down knew but did not want to admit. Her understanding of these things, from her limited research into Alston, indicated a ghost would stay around a place familiar to them in life, not move hundreds of miles away with one of their parents.

Then again, she didn't have to understand. Tommy was here, and he was watching her with that look of curiosity as familiar to her as the sound of her own heartbeat. She took a step toward him, expecting at any moment for him to vanish as suddenly as he'd appeared, no longer even thinking about the potential danger posed by the marshal's shotgun. Tommy watched her come, not moving from his spot until she got close enough to reach out and touch him. The moment her arm stretched toward him, he took a step away, out of range again, and shook his head.

"*I'm sorry, Mommy*," he said. "*But you can't do that. We're beyond that now.*"

She wasn't sure what was more disorienting: that his lips hadn't moved when he spoke to her, or the fact he was using words he did not know in ways that were well beyond his grasp of grammar and vocabulary when he died.

"Wait," she said, frowning as she realized what he actually said. "Who's we? It's you, it's my Tommy, isn't it?"

"*Yes,*" he replied. "*Part of us is. Your child's spirit was troubled, and held onto you after he was taken from his physical body. What you see is only a representation of that, drawn from the strength of your memories. This form was chosen because it was one we felt you would listen to above all the others. The child you knew as Tommy is gone. We are so much more now.*"

"I don't understand," she said. The sound of Frank and Bradley scuffling nearly drowned out her last word, but she was sure the spirit before her understood, regardless. "What about Lucy, or Alston and that girl I saw him...doing things with upstairs? Were they just forms you chose, too?"

"*No, their link to this world is stronger than ours, so they could retain themselves after their bodies were destroyed. We are Tommy, but we are also others who lived and died here, other victims of Mister's ministrations. His and those who serve him still.*"

"Frank," she said, wiping away the tears that came to her eyes. "Him, his Daddy, Clay, those others he mentioned. You mean them?"

"*Yes. Our intelligence is a combination of them all. We did not know your name before the one you know as Tommy joined us. That is how we know you are Mommy.*"

To hear that hurt her in ways she would never have believed possible before now. A part of her understood this was not her son, even though it looked like him. Its appearance, the voice it used, and the way it only recognized her the way Tommy would have—as Mommy? It was almost enough to break her beyond what his actual death had achieved.

"*We do not have much time,*" the spirit said, drawing her back from the brink of her emotional crevasse. "*Appearing this way is...difficult. We have aided you all we can and will fulfill the promise we made when you spoke with us through the device, but you must set us free so we can do this.*"

This dumbfounded Katherine. "You mean the Ouija board? That was...all of you?"

"*Yes. Should your friend stop Mister's servant, Mister will try to stop you himself, but there are rules even he must adhere to. He can only come to you in one of three ways: he can touch and speak to you, he can appear and speak to you, or he can influence you. He cannot do all three. However, your fear sustains him, so hold fast to what supports you. Break the wall, set us free, and we can stop him. Fail, and his evil may never end.*"

"Wait," she said. "Why didn't you tell Blackmore this? Why wasn't he able to stop him?"

"*Your connection to us allows you to see and hear us,*" it replied. "*You have felt a pain like ours, and that binds us. The one before you had no such connection. He was doomed the moment he set foot in this house.*"

"Tommy," she replied. "Because I lost Tommy, and he was with me when I came here, it connected us."

Before the spirit could respond, its head turned to the side, eyes widening. *"Our time is done. We must go. Free us, or we are lost forever!"*

She turned to see what had alarmed the spirit so much, but the explosive blast of the shotgun going off caused her to turn away quickly, her hands flying up to cover her ears. It was too late to help other than to muffle the ringing buzz that dominated her hearing. She heard a series of smaller pops like the sound of those little Black Cat firecrackers going off after someone had detonated a stick of dynamite, then the room went silent.

Fearing the worst, she opened her eyes. Bradley was sitting with his back against the doorway leading into the kitchen, blood trickling down his face from a cut just below his hairline and running in twin trails from both nostrils. His breathing was heavy, but he *was* breathing. She turned her head to see what he was looking at and felt her own breath catch in her throat.

Frank lay sprawled on the floor just outside the kitchen doorway, four ragged holes punched into his shirt across his chest. Blood was seeping from the wounds, and while he was also still breathing, it was much more labored than Bradley's. She looked around for the shotgun and found it lying on the floor near his feet, well out of his reach, the barrel still smoking where it had been fired. His service pistol also lay nearby, the barrel also smoking. Bradley must have been able to grab it during their scuffle. Realizing Frank was no longer a threat, she crawled over to him, stopping to kick the shotgun further away as she went.

His eyes were open and seemed to focus on her as she approached him. They watched her as she watched him, then finally blinked and moved away. His mouth opened, as though he were about to say something. Katherine could imagine it would be an apology, but she never got the chance to find out, for all he could manage was a low groan as his final breath left his lungs and he took in no more. After counting out a full two minutes in her head, she realized he was gone, his last words forever unknown.

She turned and looked at Bradley, shaking her head at his questioning gaze. He closed his eyes and let out a long breath, his head thumping softly against the doorframe as he leaned it back. The sound made her realize her hearing was coming back, which also made her realize there should be more sounds to hear than there were. She slowly turned around and peered into the kitchen, dreading what she would see. She let out a long, anguished wail when she saw her fears confirmed.

Frank was not the only casualty.

Katherine stood and slowly made her way back into the kitchen. Bradley looked up as she passed, then scrambled to his feet as he realized where she was going and why.

"Kat," he said. "Don't. Don't do this to yourself. She's gone."

She stopped, not because of what he said, but because she knew he was right. Mercifully, Leslie's head was turned away from them, hiding the worst of the damage, but Katherine could see enough. She could see the raw, bloody mess that used to be the side of her best friend's face. She didn't need to see anymore. She closed her eyes and fought back her tears. All she wanted was to collapse into a heap and mourn the woman who, in another life, might have been her sister. She couldn't allow herself that luxury. She had to focus. There would be time for tears later, and she intended to shed every single one Leslie had earned over the years. For now, there was still a task that needed completing. If what the spirit told her was true, it was more imperative than ever to finish it. She turned and looked to Bradley.

"Can you still do it?" she asked.

"Do what?" he replied, confused.

"Break down the wall?"

"Kat, we need to call the sheriff," he said. "We need to report this. We can break that down later, if you even want to stay here after all of this…"

"I'm not going anywhere," she said, and the fury she felt must have bled through, either in her eyes or her tone, for the man took an involuntary step away from her. "This house is *mine*. I bought it. Alston already took two of my limited number of friends away from me tonight, he's not taking my home, too. We're going to finish this. For Leslie, for Tommy and me, and even for Frank. You can either help me or stay the hell out of my way."

She turned and went into the hallway to grab the sledgehammer before making her way to the stairs that led to the basement.

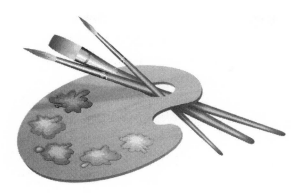

CHAPTER THIRTY-FIVE

As Katherine descended the stairs leading into the basement, she felt as though there were eyes upon her, watching her every move. She supposed there were, even if those eyes had last physically seen something nearly a hundred years ago. There was a sense of malice and foreboding surrounding her now, and that was new. Considering what she intended, she should have expected it. She was about to attempt something that would result in banishing Alston to the pits of Hell where he belonged. He was here. There was never any question of that once he made his presence known. And if he knew what she was doing, he most assuredly would not be happy about it.

She stepped onto the dirt floor of the basement and idly wondered exactly where they buried Blackmore's brother. She supposed if this worked, the cops would end up finding it. At least she hoped they would. She was about to get rid of the ghost haunting the place, and that was bad enough. To think she was basically living on top of a man's grave was disturbing on an entirely different level.

When she heard the stairs creak behind her, she spun around, somehow managing to get the sledgehammer pulled up into a striking position without tearing her own shoulders out of socket in the process. Bradley hadn't been joking about how heavy it was. Simply carrying it down the stairs had been a grueling process that had her almost dreading actually putting the thing to work.

Bradley stood three steps up, his hands raised beside his head, his eyes locked on the steel head of the hammer. "Take it easy, it's just me."

"You're not changing my mind," she said. "I'm doing this."

"I'm not trying to change your mind," he replied. "But I doubt you'll be able to break that wall down. You can barely hold that thing. I'm here to help you, so let me. Give me the hammer."

She eyed him warily. Normally she would trust him without reservation, but this had been a night for strange turns, and she could not be sure they were over yet. "You're not just trying to get me to give it to you, then go back upstairs to call the sheriff, are you?"

"Kat, stop it," he said, lowering his hands and moving one more step down. "I said I'm going to help you, and I meant it. Leslie and Frank aren't going anywhere. Yeah, it's going to take more explaining the longer we wait to call it in, but it's going to be a tough sell no matter what we do. So we do it your way. I'm on your side. Give me the hammer."

Still somewhat reluctant, she lowered the sledgehammer and allowed him to take it from her. Despite her misgivings, she was relieved to be rid of its painful weight. Her arms felt like they were made of feathers after even the short amount of time it had taken to walk down here.

"Thank you," Bradley said, balancing the handle on his shoulder. "Now, where is it?"

She pointed to the area where she thought she could remember seeing the walled-up doorway. She still hadn't changed the bulb down here to a brighter one, so it was buried in shadow. She wished she'd remembered to grab a flashlight on their way down.

Bradley, it seemed, *had* thought ahead. He pulled a flashlight from his back pocket, turned it on, and ran the beam across the wall. Finally, the dingy red bricks came into view. Katherine hadn't imagined the whole thing. She did not know what she would have done if that had been the case. He handed her the light, keeping it pointed at the wall, and moved past her toward it.

As he accidentally brushed against her arm, she realized she felt a bit light-headed. She shook her head, trying to clear it, but the feeling only intensified. It had to result from the adrenaline starting to wear off, or the shock of what had already happened tonight beginning to set in. She tried to remember the last time she had eaten anything, just in case that was at fault. It was only when she felt herself standing up a little straighter that she realized exactly what was happening.

She tried to call out, to tell Bradley something was going on, but something kept her from it. Her cry of warning instead came out as a sultry-sounding come-on.

"Hey," she was made to say. "Hold on."

Bradley stopped and turned. From the way the cords in his neck were standing out, Katherine was sure he wasn't in control either. The spirit hadn't warned her of this possibility, that Alston could control both of them, but that was exactly what appeared to be going on.

The pain threatened to wash away the world. Had shock not set in almost immediately to deaden it somewhat, it would be beyond bearable. It was bad enough, knowing she was stuck in a place somewhere between life and death, with the latter creeping ever closer. Leslie could feel oblivion just beyond her thin hold on consciousness, and a part of her welcomed it all while another part of her felt nothing but regret for the things she still wanted to accomplish in her life. Strangely, she felt nothing at the idea she wouldn't get the chance to say goodbye to Marie. Perhaps that relationship wasn't as important to her as she thought these last four years.

Her bigger concern was with Katherine, and to a lesser extent, Bradley. She'd heard their voices drifting across the daze she drifted through, and while she could not make out what they were saying, she'd gleaned enough to know they somehow survived the encounter with the insane marshal. While it would be easy to feel anger and bitterness over the fact she would not be as lucky, she could pass to whatever lay on the other side secure the woman who should've been her sister had a chance to come through this a victor and not a victim.

She took in a shallow, shuddering breath, wondering idly if it would be her last, and waited to die. When she heard a voice softly calling her name, she was sure she was crossing over to the afterlife and felt her heart beat at the thought she might be about to face Saint Peter's judgment for all the things she'd done wrong in her life. Little by little, she realized the voice was not as authoritative as what she would ascribe to Heaven's doorman, and it seemed to affect only her ears and her mind, not her soul. If this was her eternal judgment, it certainly left a lot to be desired.

"*Leslie,*" the voice said, insistent. She tried to ignore it but found it nearly impossible. It cut through the fog of her mind and forced her to awaken more. The pain was waiting for her, and she wanted nothing more than to retreat from it, but that voice would not let her.

"*Wake up, Leslie,*" the voice continued. "*We know you want to go away, let go of everything to relieve the pain, but you're needed here. We need you. Katherine needs you.*"

Leslie groaned at that, a rough and barely audible sound that sent a wave of agony from her face all the way down to her toes and back. She tried to open her eyes, to figure out who was talking to her, but one eye didn't seem to want to work at all, and the other felt as though it had been glued shut. She felt the subtle cracking as the eyelid finally broke free of whatever held it shut. Her vision remained blurred and had a red twinge to it, for reasons she didn't want to think about too deeply.

She was still in Kat's kitchen, sitting atop the stool beside the island. Blood had covered the faux marble countertop, and she was fairly certain it was hers. She didn't want to look at it anymore, didn't want the reminder that something terrible had happened to her, so she turned her head in the direction she'd heard the voice. She thought the pain from moaning and opening her eye had been bad, but what she now felt racing through her was a thousand times worse. How she wasn't dead yet was beyond her, but something was keeping her alive, and by extension keeping that pain fresh as air drifted across her shredded nerve endings.

"*Our reach extends only so far,*" the voice said. "*We can help you, but you have to help us in return.*"

She fought against the pain and tried to open her mouth to respond, and for one terrifying moment, realized she couldn't get it to work, either.

"*You are closer to us now,*" the voice said. "*Speech is not needed. All you have to do is think, and we will understand.*"

It was difficult even to make her mind focus enough to get a point across. All she seemed capable of were images, so she hoped it would be enough. She formed Kat's face in her mind and tried to get across the impression of a question.

"*She is going to confront Mister,*" came the reply. Leslie felt relief her rudimentary thoughts were enough to get her message across. "*He will not allow that to happen, not without a fight. She will need you. You need to go help her. Her and the one with her, trying to help her.*"

Leslie shuddered as she brought the image of the blood covering the kitchen into her mind, and the echoing blast from the shotgun that was the last thing she remembered coherently before the voice spoke to her.

"*We will help you,*" the voice said. "*But we are not strong enough to do it on our own, nor can you perform the task unaided. Working together, we may be able to help her.*"

Another image came to her mind, one she hadn't directed. It was a field, sunlight, and her walking side by side with Katherine through it. She wasn't sure what it meant, but whatever it was speaking to her did.

"*No, we're sorry,*" it said. "*The damage to you is too great. You will not survive this. If you find it a consolation, we will be gone by morning too. Your final moments can be spent saving your friend. But you have to do it now, or Mister will win.*"

Leslie pulled in as deep a breath as she could, and tried to get down from the stool, but again found her body unwilling to do what her mind told it to. She felt like a puppet whose strings had been cut. She let out a long, low whine, which seemed the only sound she could make at the moment.

"*It will hurt,*" the voice told her. "*But it must be done. You must begin the process, then we can help when the time comes.*"

She drew in another breath and tried again. She found if she focused hard enough, she could make one of her legs flail out, and could get her arms to move pretty much as she wanted. She prepared herself for the pain, then pushed away from the island as her leg kicked out again. The stool went over onto two legs, balanced precariously for a single heartbeat that seemed to go on forever, and then it fell over, dumping her unmercifully to the floor.

The voice's warning of pain had been an understatement. As her body slammed onto the tile floor, the sheer agony that raced through her once more grew to near-unbearable levels, and her consciousness waned as her damaged body fought to escape it. Somehow, she kept herself awake and aware—as much as she could—and rolled over onto her belly.

Just ahead of her, she saw Tommy standing there, semi-translucent, wisps of something akin to smoke drifting off of him. He smiled at her and motioned for her to come toward him. She tried her hardest and got her hands in front of her. She pushed down on them and shoved with her one good leg and felt herself slide forward a couple of feet. Tommy nodded, still smiling, and took a step backward, still urging her to follow. Little by little, she did, moving with agonizing slowness as she followed Tommy's ghost to the door leading down to the basement, and whatever fight was happening in its depths.

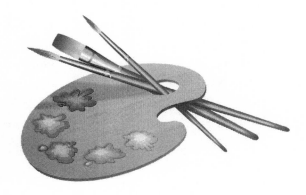

CHAPTER THIRTY-SIX

Her legs began to move, propelling Katherine toward Bradley even as she screamed inside her own mind for them to stop. His throat worked as she approached, trying to say something but was denied. She stopped before him and tilted her head up, smiling at him despite feeling the desire to do anything but.

"Since we're waiting anyway," her mouth said. "Why not make it a little longer? Clear our heads, forget about everything but us for a while." Her hand reached out and traced a path down his chest to the waistband of his pants. "See what *comes up?*"

If she could, she would have groaned at the cheesiness of the line Alston made her use. It was only a distraction, though. She knew that. The spirits had warned her Alston would do whatever he could to stop her. She just had to figure out how to turn the tables on him.

The spirits had also mentioned strength. They could not manifest themselves individually due to the amount of power it would take to do so, power they lacked because of their lost connections to this place. If Alston was controlling both her and Bradley, he must be expending a lot of power to do it. He had rules, he had limits. This had to stretch both near their breaking point.

That meant all she needed was a way to force him to spend more of it, so either she or Bradley could break free and end this.

Strangely, a memory of Tommy came to her mind, of how he always got her to let him do almost anything other than go to bed when she wanted him to. Dave told her it was because, even as a child, he knew how to turn what he wanted to do into something she wanted to do as well. Tommy never did it out of any sense of maliciousness, but because kids were natural manipulators. She had told Dave he was nuts, that kids were not cruel enough to manipulate someone into something, but the concept always stuck with her.

She concentrated, trying to think of something Alston would want her to do. When she managed to stop caressing the front of Bradley's pants and cup her hand around his burgeoning erection, she almost laughed out loud. She had thought to do that, not Alston. She was sure of it. Only one way to tell for certain, and that was to test it.

She took one step back and ran her hands down her sides, causing her shirt to stretch across her breasts, highlighting them. She felt a twinge of surprise that had not come from her own mind and fought to keep her excitement hidden. Alston would perceive it as coming from what he was having her do instead of her own discovery. She raised one arm, focusing her thoughts on the idea of removing her shirt so Bradley could get a better look at her. She smiled teasingly, reaching for her shirt, then her hand froze in place, inches from the first button.

"So foolish," Bradley said, and Katherine knew from the cadence of his voice, the strange accent it had acquired, that this was not Bradley speaking, but Alston himself. "Did you really think that would work? *I own you.* You are mine now, all but completely. I had hoped to toy with you longer, but the time for that has passed. I will simply amuse myself and be done with you."

Katherine could not help but remember Frank's story about the boy and his girlfriend who had come out here to make out, to be kids, and ended up with their lives ruined. In her head, she saw all too clearly how this would go: she and Bradley would end up on the floor, in the throes of passion, and then his hands would creep around her throat and strangle the life from her. She wondered if he would turn himself in, the way the boy in Frank's tale had done, or if he would just go upstairs, stick the barrel of his pistol in his mouth, and put an end to himself before he faced justice.

But what kind of justice could be had when it wasn't him who committed the crime, but a ghost inhabiting his body?

She trembled as her hand finished the trip to her shirt, picking at the buttons, slowly unfastening them as her eyes remained locked on Bradley. She could see the lustful desire etched onto his face, but she could also see the anguish beneath that, his true feelings. The muscles in his neck stood out as he fought to regain control of himself.

"A pity, really," Alston said through Bradley's mouth. "Your friend lies above, clinging to life by the barest thread, yet rather than save her, you chose to exercise this foolish plan. Now, because you dared imagine you could resist me, your precious friend will die, as will the both of you."

Bradley's eyes went wide, his mouth dropping open in shock. Before Katherine had a chance to wonder what he'd seen that surprised him so, a fist slammed into the side of her jaw, knocking her from her feet and sending her sprawling onto the floor. The pain was exquisite, and she touched her tongue to a back tooth and found it felt loose now. The positive was that she now had control of her body again, and a quick glance over at Bradley showed he was shaking his head, finally coming back to himself.

She looked up to see what had struck her and had to swallow the scream that threatened to tear from her throat. Leslie stood before her, the left side of her face a ruined mess. One eye hung loosely against her raw and bloody cheek, and her shirt was soaked with gore. Katherine was positive she could see some gray mass sticking out from a hole in the side of the woman's skull and knew without a doubt she was looking at her best friend's brain leaking from her head.

"'M not dead yet," the woman said. Her voice was hoarse and the words heavily slurred, but Katherine had no problem understanding her. She looked down at Katherine, swaying slightly on her feet from the simple act of lowering her head. "Finish it."

Her strength expended, Leslie crumpled to the ground and remained still. Katherine wanted to go to her, to check and see if she was still breathing, but she didn't dare. She was too afraid of what she'd discover if she did.

Bradley staggered and started toward her, but she held up a hand to stop him.

"No!" she yelled, ignoring the flash of pain along her jaw. "The wall! Before he tries again!"

He nodded and turned, renewing his grip on the sledgehammer, then froze as the air before him shimmered, revealing the wispy, translucent form of the man Katherine assumed to be Henry Alston.

"*That was intriguing,*" he said, smiling slightly. "*That torrid night the two of you spent at university so long ago must have bound you more closely than I thought. Even now she yet lives. You could save her, if you act quickly. I shall even show mercy and grant you the chance to do so. But you must decide now.*"

Katherine had no idea her heartbeat could speed up any more than it already had, but somehow it did. The odds were Alston lied to them, that Leslie was already dead before they came down here. Knowing this did nothing to stop the thought from coming immediately on its heels: *but what if she wasn't?* If she died because Katherine insisted they ignore Alston and break the wall down, she did not think she could ever live with herself afterward. She had already lost Tommy, and despite what she knew, she blamed herself for his death. Could she really accept it if her best friend died because of her, too?

Your fear sustains him, so hold to that which gives you support.

The spirits had told her as much. They knew this would happen, that she would face this choice. And they had pointed her in the right direction through the most evocative means possible. They came as Tommy. He was what gave her support. And he said this had to be done. She gave one last look to Leslie and knew Alston was lying. Even if she wasn't dead yet, there was no way she could survive. With her face ruined, Katherine doubted she would even want to.

"He's not there!" she yelled to Bradley. "He's not a physical presence! Go *through* him if you have to! Do it!"

"*No!*" Alston yelled. "*I forbid this!*"

Bradley ignored him, lifted the sledgehammer, and swung it at the brick wall so hard Katherine heard his shirt rip from halfway across the room. The hammer's steel head passed through Alston's wispy one, dissipating him like a puff of smoke the instant before it slammed against the wall.

The bricks were old and had been assembled hastily. Katherine saw this the first time she examined this wall. Still, never in a million years would she have expected a single blow would bring them all down in an explosion of dust and noise. Bradley's aim must have been immaculate, allowing the hammer to hit against the fault line at the core of that wall.

Light flooded the room, not the bright light of bulbs and electricity, but the ethereal light of a full moon on a cloudless night. As her eyes adjusted, Katherine made out shapes within that light, shapes that *caused* the light. Shapes of people. Alston's victims, all able to manifest themselves individually now.

All free.

Her eyes adjusted a little more, and she realized she could make out distinct people in that light. Lucy was there, a determined grin on her face. So was the unnamed girl she had seen Alston raping that first terrible night. Others as well, too many to even try to remember, but none of them compared to the small one standing at the head of the rest. It was Tommy, as she had seen him upstairs. This time, he wasn't a collective, but himself again, if only for a little while. His expression appeared grim, his eyes staring with determination at something to her side.

She turned and saw Alston had returned, staring back at the horde before him with a look of terror on his ghostly face. She couldn't help but smile at that. The tables were turned at last, and the predator was now the prey.

Just beyond him, she saw two men she didn't recognize, but from the similarity of their features, she knew they must be the Blackmore brothers. That was good. She was glad they were together again to see the end of the man who had caused both their deaths, albeit inadvertently.

"No," Alston said, drawing her attention back to him. His voice was no longer commanding, no longer filled with sarcasm and malevolent glee, but the whispered, terrified voice of a child. How fitting he should sound the same now as she imagined some of his victims must have sounded before he amused himself with them. *"Stay away from me. Please. I'm sorry! Please stay away!"*

"Get him!" Tommy cried, pointing at Alston. *"Get the bad man!"*

The ghosts needed no further invitation or instruction. They raced from the open doorway, the light streaking around them like small comets blazing through the basement as they sped toward the specter of the man who tortured and killed them. When the first one collided with him, Alston shrieked. The ghost who attacked him vanished, but Katherine could see a dark hole in Alston's form where it hit, as though it had taken a piece of him away when it left.

"When it crossed over," she whispered, suddenly understanding why Alston was so adamant that wall not come down. She also understood what Frank meant about his hopes she could stop it. She understood what the spirits meant about Blackmore not having the connection they needed.

They were there all along. They just needed a general.

She turned back to the wall, tears streaming down her face as she laughed. There he was, her son, her precious little boy, standing in the midst of the blue inferno, leading the charge for an army of ghosts against the evil old man who dared try to hurt his Mommy.

Alston's shrieks were constant now, so she turned back to him, not wanting to miss the end. The ghosts of his victims swirled around him, almost dancing, teasing him before they passed on, and taking chunks of him with them. They devoured his soul, and Katherine laughed all the harder at the creature's torment. It was nothing less than he deserved, even if it would be over much too quickly.

Lucy was the last of them, as only was appropriate. Lucy, his favorite. Lucy, his destroyer. She stood before the remnants of his specter, somehow still standing despite being nothing more than a vague shadow in the shape of a man. The girl turned to Katherine and smiled, then reached forward and wrapped Alston in an embrace that looked anything but loving. The longest, loudest, most anguished wail yet thundered through the air before trailing off like a battery-operated radio running out of juice. When it faded away, so had Alston, returned to whatever punishment awaited men like him in the afterlife.

Katherine looked up at the spirits of the two Blackmore brothers. They nodded at her before fading away. The room was considerably darker, but there was still a slight bluish tint to the air. Only one remained, as she knew it would. She turned back around and saw Tommy standing before her, smiling that beautiful smile that never failed to melt her heart.

"Hi, Mommy," he said. "*I missed you.*"

"I missed you, too, honey," she replied, her words barely more than a choked whisper. She knew what was coming, dreaded it, but she refused to let her sadness take away from this one last chance to speak with her baby again. "And I'm so sorry for what happened to you. I should've just bought you the costume and kept a better eye on you. I'm so sorry, baby. I never meant for you to get hurt."

"*It's okay, Mommy,*" he replied. "*That costume was kinda stupid, anyway. I was being a poopy-head. You're a good Mommy. You didn't do bad. It was the bad man. You're a good Mommy.*"

She broke then, wanting to say more but unable to find the words. He didn't blame her. He said she was a *good mommy*. It was the sweetest thing she could ever hope to hear.

"*I gotta go now, okay?*" Tommy said. She knew it wasn't really a question. "*I have a puppy now, and he's fun to play with, so I'm gonna go play with him now.*"

"You do that, sweetheart," she said, wanting to reach out and caress his cheek but knowing how futile such a gesture would be. "I'll see you later, okay? It might be a while, but I'll be there before you know it."

"*Okay.*"

He turned and started back toward the shattered remains of the brick doorway. Halfway there, he stopped and looked at her over his shoulder.

"*I love you.*"

And then he was gone.

EPILOGUE

EVER AFTER

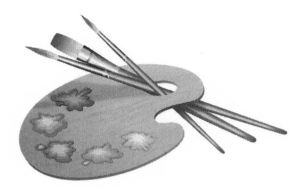

Katherine smiled as the chime sounded to let her know the front door had been opened. She knew she locked it when she came upstairs to work, so there was only one person it could be. He was the only other person besides herself who had a key to the place. She quickly added the final dash of color to the canvas in front of her, dropped the brush into a nearby glass of acetone, and grabbed the envelope off her desk before heading downstairs to greet him.

Strange to think she now had an actual, official boyfriend again. After ten years of marriage and the way *that* ended up, she would never have thought it possible. That it made her feel like a kid again was only icing on the cake. Life truly did move on, even if there was a time she didn't think it would.

Bradley rounded the corner when she stepped onto the tower's first floor landing and smiled up at him. He laughed, then leaned over and kissed her, as he knew she would expect him to. Her body tingled as their lips touched, and when he started to pull away, she draped an arm around his neck to hold him there a few glorious seconds longer. She finally let him go, knowing if she kept it up much longer things would end up in a different place than a simple "hello." They still hadn't slept together yet, and while they both knew it was on the horizon, she respected his wishes to get to know one another first. He said it would be worth the wait, and from the way she felt about him already, she would take him at his word. The kissing was enough for now, even if she would prefer a lot more of it.

"Well?" she asked.

"Well, what?" he replied.

She raised an eyebrow at him and he laughed.

"You're no fun," he teased. "It's official. I'm no longer the interim marshal but the duly elected actual one."

She laughed and clapped her hands softly like a little girl. "I told you! And you doubted me."

"I'd never do that," he said, leading her into the kitchen where he started making a pot of coffee. "I doubted myself."

"Well, stop that," she said, taking a seat on one of the stools while she waited for it to finish. "You're more than qualified, and I can't think of anybody in town who thinks otherwise."

"Yeah, you're right," he said, leaning on the counter and smiling back at her. "I should accept you always *will be* and get on with it."

"That might be the smartest thing you've ever said," she replied, smiling back. "How about the inquest?"

"Just about done," he said, sighing. "The consensus is that the pressures of the job got to be too much for Frank, which is why he snapped. I'm cleared, since they ruled my shooting him was in self-defense and to protect you. Still only the interim marshal until the inquest's done, but I'm not worried. Things are changing, and I'd bet that includes accepting 'outsiders.'"

"Poor Elizabeth," Katherine said. "How's she holding up?"

"She's struggling, but she's hanging in there," he said. "Apologized for the hundredth time over her role in all this. Still insists she didn't know everything, or she never would've done it. Also, told me to tell you thanks for the painting. She would've done it herself, but the last few months have been hard on her."

"I can imagine."

Bradley started to say something else, stopped, and studied her face. "Okay, out with it. You've got news, too, don't you?"

Katherine laughed and pulled the letter out of the envelope before handing it to him. He read over it, then looked back up at her, an amazed smile on his face.

"You got the show?"

"I got the show," she confirmed. "The gallery's in Nashville, and the curator says she thinks it will be the best of the year so far. She *raved* about the samples I sent her."

"I guess we should start listening to each other, then," he said. "Since, as I recall, I told you she'd love them."

"Uh-huh," Katherine said. She tried to be aloof and ignore him entirely, but his sincere manner made her smile despite herself. "She asked me what I wanted to call it so they can get started on the marketing. I think I'll go with 'Hidden Hearts: The Light in the Darkness.' What do you think?"

"I think if you came up with it, it will be awesome," he said. "I also think there's more, so what is it?"

She smiled. "I finished it."

"The big secret painting you were working on?" he asked, turning to fix them both a cup of coffee. "No kidding?"

"Still needs the clear coat, but it's done otherwise," she said.

"So, I can see it?"

"No, I'm going to make you wait 'til the night of the show," she said. When he gave her a confused look, she laughed. "Of course you can see it, dum-dum. Hand me my coffee and come on."

She led him upstairs, both excited and nervous. She had told him nothing about this painting, and she hoped in doing so she hadn't built it up as better than it was. To her, it was a masterpiece, but for the first time she didn't feel qualified to judge her own work objectively. As he studied it in silence for what felt like forever, her nerves grew. When she saw the look on his face as he turned to her, relief flooded through her instead.

"You're not selling this one," he said. "You finally found your mantelpiece painting."

He turned back to it, smiling. She had been hoping for that reaction. She had no intention of selling this one, in any case, but his validation told her she was not just being sentimental.

It was a variant of the original "Freedom" idea she had when she first moved into this house, only instead of one girl dancing through the fields, now there were easily a dozen children playing. To a casual admirer, they would be random faces. But she knew, and she was fairly certain Bradley did as well, that Lucy and the others were all represented. Tommy was there, running after a small dog on the left side of the wide field. What she wasn't sure about, because she didn't think he would understand it, were the three adults in the background, all smiling and laughing together while the children played.

She had thought long and hard about including them, but without them it felt incomplete. Bradley might not have seen it that night in the basement, but she had. There had been a total of *six* spirits who took no part in sending Alston where he belonged. Tommy and the two Blackmore brothers—Bradley had seen them. The others, Katherine was fairly sure only she noticed, standing in the broken bricks that once blocked the door to the interior graveyard where Alston buried some of his victims, now immortalized in this new version of "Freedom".

The man on the left was Clay Davison, who had been as much a victim of Alston as the rest of them, if not directly so. In the center was Leslie, laughing at something Katherine imagined Clay had told her. And at the far right of the group, smiling in that comforting way he did before things went so badly was Frank Bradshaw. The three Alston victims who would never be realized as such.

Leslie's presence in this picture would be easy to explain; the others were more difficult. Everyone had their secrets, and everyone had their reasons for keeping them. Clay did, and once she got past the initial anger over the situation, Katherine realized Frank did, too. She preferred to remember him the way he was before that terrible, wonderful night, the man who had welcomed her to this new town and introduced her to the man she was now falling deeply in love with.

She couldn't help it. It was just how she saw him in her own hidden heart. For her, it was better that way.

And she felt Tommy would agree.

THE BEGINNING

ABOUT THE AUTHOR

If you ask his wife, **John Quick** is compelled to tell stories because he's full of baloney. He prefers to think he simply has an affinity for things that are strange, disturbing, and terrifying. As proof, he will explain how he suffered *Consequences*, transcribed *The Journal of Jeremy Todd*, and regaled the tale of *Mudcat*. He lives in Middle Tennessee with his aforementioned long-suffering wife, two exceptionally patient kids, four dogs that couldn't care less so long as he keeps scratching that perfect spot on their noses, and a cat who barely acknowledges his existence.

When he's not hard at work on his next novel, you can find him on Facebook at johnquickbooks, Twitter @johndquick, or his website, johnquickauthor.blogspot.com.

"A stand-out book for 2019."
—Sadie Hartmann, *Nightworms*

Most kids dream about a new bike, a pair of top-dollar sneakers endorsed by their favorite athlete, or that totally awesome videogame everyone's raving about. But thirteen-year-old Jake and his little brother Matthew want nothing more than to escape from their abusive father. As soon as possible, they plan to run away to California, where they will reunite with their mother and live happily ever after.

It won't be easy, though. After a scuffle with a local bully puts Jake's arch-nemesis in the hospital, Sheriff Theresa McLelland starts poking her nose into their feud. During a trip to the family cabin for the opening weekend of deer-hunting season, Jake and Matthew kick their plan into action, leaving Dad tied to a chair as they flee into the night. Meanwhile, the bully and his father have their own plans for revenge, and the events to follow will forever change the lives of everyone involved...

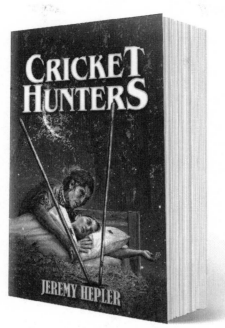